TRAIL OF CROSSES

LOST COLONY SERIES, BOOK #2

JO GRAFFORD

Sign up for my New Release Email List at www.JoGrafford.com.

No part of this book may be reproduced in any form or by any electronic or mechanical means, including information storage and retrieval systems, without written permission from the author, except for the use of brief quotations in a book review.

*To my parents, Elijah and LouElla, for their endless enthusiasm,
encouragement, and love*

ACKNOWLEDGMENTS

A very special thank you to Trudy Cordle for beta reading this story.

CONTENTS

INTRODUCTION

To escape the drudgery of London's working class, Jane Mannering joins a colonial venture for the sheer adventure of it and sails for the New World. She soon becomes embroiled in a far more dangerous game than she bargained for — one that leads to a deadly ambush. She plots the escape of her fellow colonists, never dreaming her quick trigger finger and courageous efforts will spark the heated interest of the most feared tribal leader in Virginia.

Following the rapid influx of foreign wars and diseases to his land, Chief Wanchese had decided the only good Brit is a dead one — until he's asked to rescue an enslaved English-woman. One encounter with Jane, and he decides the plucky school mistress is one foreigner he could stand having around. With his ruthless reputation preceding him, however, convincing her to court him won't be easy.

The Lost Colony Series is an epic historical romance saga, based on the Lost Colonists of Roanoke Island.

LOST COLONY SERIES

MAP

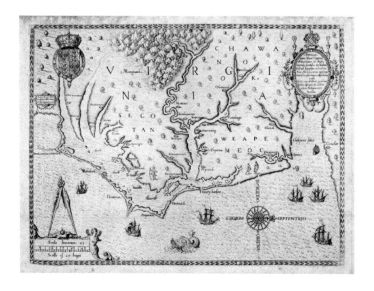

SETTING OF THE LOST COLONY SERIES

Titled "**The Carte of All the Coast of Virginia**," this map was engraved by Theodor de Bry. It is based on John White's map of the coast of Virginia and North Carolina, circa 1585-1586.

CAST OF CHARACTERS

Jane Mannering - a tall, tanned, chestnut-haired amazon of a woman, huntress, tracker, and main character in Book Two of the Lost Colony Series, TRAIL OF CROSSES

ROANOKE TRIBE

Chief Wanchese - Chief of the fearsome Roanoke tribe which is not an ally of the English, cousin to Chief Manteo of the Croatoan tribe which is an ally to the English

Riapoke - Chief Wanchese's elder half-brother and councilman, Chief Manteo's cousin

Amonsoquath - strong warrior and trusted friend of Chief Wanchese; brother of Askook

Askook - a duplicitous, distant cousin of Chief Wanchese; in line to become the next Copper Mountain chief

Nadie the Wise - Wise woman of the Roanoke tribal council

Amitola - Chief Wanchese's sister, daughter of Nadie the Wise

Dyoni - pregnant Roanoke tribeswoman, works closely with Nadie the Wise

Bly - another maiden who works closely with Nadie the Wise

Chitsa - the tribeswoman whose dead husband James is assigned to replace

Alawa - the tribeswoman whose dead husband William is assigned to replace

Kanti - Wanchese's former concubine

Keme - brave Roanoke warrior, Kitchi's brother

Kitchi - brave Roanoke warrior, Keme's brother

Noshi - Roanoke priest, romantically involved with Nadie the Wise

Mukki - young Roanoke lad whose life Jane saves

Achak - Roanoke Medicine Man

Cutto - Chief Wanchese's half-wolf hound

GREAT TRADING PATH

Kokoko - slave auctioneer

Skull Face - Jane's nickname for the hateful slave trader, leader of the headhunters

Odina - another employee at the Great Trading Path, responsible for guarding and caring for the prisoners

Chief Dasan - Chief of the Copper Mountain people, a wealthy slave owner

ENGLISH WOMEN

Agnes Wood (*pronounced ANN-es*) - a stunning china-doll beauty, gifted apothecary, and main character in Book Three of the Lost Colony Series, INTO THE MAINLAND

Eleanor Dare - daughter of the absent Governor White; wife of the interim leader of the scattered English colonists, Ananias Dare; mother of the kidnapped baby Virginia

Helen Pierce - kindhearted widow and mentor to the younger women

Emme Merrimoth - friendly colonist who is sweet on farmer Mark Bennet

Margaret Lawrence - not-so-friendly colonist who is sweet on Reverend Christopher Cooper and wildly jealous of Rose, Jane, and Agnes.

Joyce Archard - noblewoman who was widowed during the ambush; served as a slave on Copper Mountain until she was rescued by the surviving English colonists

Virginia Dare - infant daughter of the Dares

ENGLISHMEN

Ex-con James Hynde - flirtatious jack-of-all-trades; Jane's adoring and faithful follower and self-appointed guardian

Ex-con William Clement - balding, faithful sidekick to James; equally loyal to Jane

George Howe, Jr. - darkly handsome and adventurous aristocratic teen, cocky and impulsive to a fault, orphaned in BREAKING TIES when his father is bludgeoned to death by a few rogue Roanoke warriors to avenge their fallen leader Pemisapan

Blade Prat - son of Assistant Cecil Prat, the cutler; separated from his father during the ambush on the English

Anthony Cage - charming aristocratic explorer, trades in his badge as Sheriff of Huntington to become a colonist on the Roanoke venture

Reverend Christopher Cooper - white-blonde demigod of a vicar whose loyalties are divided between the English Crown, the English colonists, and the missing Roanoke tribal princess, Amitola

Mark Bennet - giant of a man, humble farmer, Emme Merrimoth's beau

Thomas Harris - retired professor and fellow of Corpus Christi College at Cambridge, skilled cartographer, employed by Anthony Cage

Richard Berry - another gentleman adventurer, missing after the ambush on the English

William Nicholes - highly skilled tailor, missing after the ambush on the English

Thomas Ellis - pious former member of the St. Petrock parish vestry, grieving father of the missing young Robert Ellis

Robert Ellis - son of Thomas Ellis, missing since the ambush on the English

Edward Powell - surviving husband of Winnifred who died in the ambush, missing since the ambush on the English

Will Withers - orphaned teen of a missing English soldier, missing since the ambush on the English

FIRST MARRIAGE ALLIANCE BETWEEN THE NATIVE AMERICANS AND THE ENGLISH

Rose, Princess of Croatoa - main character in Book One of the Lost Colony Series, BREAKING TIES; marries Chief Manteo of the Croatoan tribe

Manteo - Chief of the Croatoans, the only local tribe friendly to the English colonists on Roanoke Island, marries Rose

THE SURVIVING MEMBERS OF THE ENGLISH GOVERNING BOARD

Assistant Ananias Dare - husband of Governor White's daughter, Eleanor

Demoted Assistant Christopher Cooper - expected to be named lead pastor over the new City of Raleigh church until his role as a double agent puts his loyalties under scrutiny

Assistant Cecil Prat - culter by trade, excellent hunter and woodsman, father of Blade, missing since the ambush on the English

NAME CHANGES IN THE LOST COLONY SERIES

Jane Pierce became Helen Pierce, a delightful widow, to differentiate her from Jane Mannering, the huntress who takes center stage in Book Two of the Lost Colony Series, TRAIL OF CROSSES.

Roger Prat became Cecil Prat, a well-to-do cutler serving as Assistant to the Governor to differentiate him from Roger Bailie

John Prat (Roger's son) became Blade, a fitting name for the son of a cutler *(knife maker)*

The two Elizabeths became Beth Viccars (wife of Ambrose the cooper and mother of Brose) **and Lizzie Glane** (the slightly insane wife of the missing Darby Glane).

I named the dog **Valentine**.

COMPLETE LIST OF THE LOST COLONISTS

(Not all names are depicted in The Lost Colony Series. Name spellings and precise list of names may vary in historical records.)

MEN
John White, Governor
Roger Bailie, Assistant
Ananias Dare, Assistant
Christopher Cooper, Assistant
Thomas Stevens, Assistant
John Sampson, Assistant
Dyonis Harvie, Assistant
Roger Prat, Assistant
George Howe, Assistant

Morris Allen
Arnold Archard
Richard Arthur
Mark Bennet
William Berde
Henry Berrye
Richard Berrye
Michael Bishop
John Borden
John Bridger

John Bright
John Brooke
Henry Browne
William Browne
John Burden
Thomas Butler
Anthony Cage
John Chapman
John Cheven
William Clement
Thomas Colman
John Cotsmur
Richard Darige
Henry Dorrell
William Dutton
John Earnest
Thomas Ellis
Edmond English
John Farre
Charles Florrie
John Gibbes
Thomas Gramme
Thomas Harris
Thomas Harris
John Hemmington
Thomas Hewet
James Hynde
Henry Johnson
Nicholas Johnson
Griffen Jones
John Jones
Richard Kemme
James Lasie

Peter Little
Robert Little
William Lucas
George Martyn
Michael Myllet
Henry Mylton
Humfrey Newton
William Nicholes
Hugh Pattenson
Henry Payne
Edward Powell
Henry Rufoote
Thomas Scot
Richard Shaberdge
Thomas Smith
William Sole
John Spendlove
John Starte
Thomas Stevens
John Stilman
Martyn Sutton
Richard Taverner
Clement Tayler
Hugh Tayler
Richard Tomkins
Thomas Topan
John Tydway
Ambrose Viccars
Thomas Warner
William Waters
Cutbert White
Richard Wildye
Robert Wilkinson

William Willes
Lewes Wotton
John Wright
Brian Wyles
John Wyles

WOMEN

Joyce Archard
Alis Chapman
------ Colman
Eleanor Dare
Elizabeth Glane
Margery Harvye
Jane Jones
Margaret Lawrence
Jane Mannering
Emme Merrimoth
Rose Payne
Jane Pierce
Winnifred Powell
Audrey Tappan
Elizabeth Viccars
Joan Warren
Agnes Wood

CHILDREN

Thomas Archard
Robert Ellis
George Howe, Jr.
Thomas Humfrey
John Prat
John Sampson
Thomas Smart
Ambrose Viccars

William Wythers

BORN IN VIRGINIA
Virginia Dare
Baby Harvye

PREFACE

July 26, 1587 — Roanoke Island

If it had not been for the barking of the dogs and chattering of the lads who scampered at her side, she might have heard the shot — the low vibration of the string as the thin, wooden shaft released, the faint whistle of the arrow as it sliced an invisible yet deadly path through the air, the scattering of wildlife as the forest itself braced before the world's most fearsome predator. *Man.*

Instead, she merely felt the gentle lifting of her late father's top hat as the arrowhead sank into the aged leather and pinned it to the heart of the oak behind her.

The men assigned to guard her fired their muskets wildly into the perimeter of trees. Her ears rang with their gunfire and frenzied oaths. Then the slow burn of anger took over.

She pivoted to yank the arrow, top hat and all, from the trunk. Separating the two, she jammed the damaged hat back on her head and tapped the lone arrow against her gloved hand. The miss was deliberate, meant as a taunt. Had the shadowy creature intended to kill her, she would be dead.

She glared over her shoulder as the gunfire ceased. He remained out there, she was certain. Watching. This was simply a reminder that he was the hunter.

She was the hunted.

CHAPTER 1: UPRIVER

*H*er whole left arm was numb. She rolled to her back and drew a sharp breath to discover her hands were tied. Distant whoops and yells peppered the air.

"Jane," a man mumbled in a voice that shook. "Jane Mannering?"

She cracked open her eyelids at the sound of her name. The sun blasted across her face, bringing her to full consciousness.

A dry wind nipped at her brown workaday gown, playing across patches of bare skin. *Ugh!* The thin cotton provided blessed little cushion between her shoulder blades and the hard, smooth wood beneath her.

Blast it all! Where am I?

The rushing of water filled her ears, along with the sound of oars dipping in rapid unison. The events leading up to her capture wafted in and out of memory in hazy bits and pieces.

She craned her neck to examine her surroundings and grimaced at the pain the movement caused. The walls of a hollowed out log rose on either side of her.

Not good. The wind expelled from her chest in a single

whoosh at the gravity of her predicament. She was trussed up like a wild animal in the belly of a canoe. A canoe that was traveling at the speed of one being pursued.

The fading whoops and screams jostled the events of the previous night from the darkened recesses of her mind. Images flowed one over the other, ghostly and dreamlike.

Memories of her fellow colonists.

Ten hastily constructed rafts loaded down with their travel bags and supplies. They'd traveled in a watery caravan over the Sea of Roanoke and its treacherous sounds to the mainland, anxious to leave behind their dreary, weather-beaten fort on Roanoke Island. They wanted plenty of distance between them and the island's original inhabitants, the hostile Roanokes.

Flickering camp fires had beckoned them to the mainland, signaling the location of the first wave of English colonists who'd arrived before them.

Or so they'd thought.

Instead, a whole army of savages had erupted from the surrounding forests and overpowered them the moment they'd stepped on the beach. Men who wore garish symbols and horrifying red paint all over their faces and bodies.

The men who now held her and her comrades captive.

Stifling a groan, she forced herself to focus on the figure hunched over her. A blonde version of Goliath, Ambrose Viccars served as the cooper for their colony.

She tried to speak, but only a hoarse squeak fell from her lips.

Even though he'd just uttered her name, no recognition sharpened his features as he studied her.

She coughed and gave his boot a light kick, but his brown gaze drifted beyond her, vacant and unfocused.

By all that is holy! Had the ambush turned the man daft?

He cradled one arm within the other. She neither cared

for the lump rising on his wrist nor the pinkish cast to the swollen skin. It was broken.

Her own limbs felt like they'd been trampled by a herd of cattle, but she recalled no beasts of burden on the beach front. Only the stampede of red-painted warriors.

They'd pulled her from her raft as she'd pushed away from the coast in a desperate bid to escape their massacre. No doubt her arms sported a rainbow of bruises. *The ham-fisted brutes!*

She wriggled her bone-weary frame, inch by painful inch, until she managed to prop herself on her elbows. She peered over the side of the boat at the narrow river they sailed on. The banks rose like a prison, higher than normal. The prolonged drought had taken its toll. Jagged rocks jutted out where lush and flowering shrubs should have been. Thirsty trees stretched their gnarled roots toward the ever-retreating gush of water beneath them.

She committed the shallow stream to memory, noting each bend and each pebbled sandbar that thrust itself through the water's surface.

A premature autumn was settling over the surrounding forests, robbing them of their green. Short bursts of scorching wind did little more than kick up dust. She would remember this place, and her memories would help her retrace their path if the opportunity to escape manifested itself. *Nay!* Not if. *When.*

Three canoes travelled in front of them. Other than their copper-skinned rowers, the rest of their occupants were bound like herself. Their garments stretched across too-thin frames, torn and blowing in the wind. Some of them wept. Their tears streaked down dusty cheeks. Others fixed their gazes beyond her in varying shades of hopelessness and supplication. Although more than one set of eyes skittered over her person, none of her fellow colonists acknowledged her with so much as a nod.

Odd. Dread settled more heavily over her chest.

How long had she been unconscious, and what had happened to her English comrades during that time to leave them so desperate? Far too few of them remained. Including Ambrose and herself, she counted only thirty-one. Fewer than half their original number. Fifteen or so captors were rowing the canoes.

Anxious to know if her missing fellow colonists had perished or escaped, she scanned the canoes a second time, searching in particular for her dearest friends. Her heart thudded in consternation as she inclined her neck for a closer view of the farthest canoe. Neither Rose nor Agnes were present. Were they still alive? If so, where were they?

The muscles in her chest and stomach tightened painfully.

An arrow whizzed past her ear and found purchase with a sickening thud, eliciting a huff of air from its recipient.

She swiveled to face their attackers, but the sun blasted her line of vision. All she could see were the silhouettes of darkened figures swarming the river's edge behind them. A pair of men ran alongside the shore in their direction, but the canoes quickly outpaced them. Their shouts grew fainter.

A foot slammed her shoulders to the floor of the canoe.

Her breath came out in a wheeze of pain. She tipped her head back to glare at the owner of the foot and stiffened. *May the good Lord have mercy on us all!* He was the man who'd yanked her from her raft in the middle of the ambush.

He'd been hideous to behold in the moonlight and was even more fearsome in the light of day. His face was painted to resemble a skull. The whites of his eyes fairly popped from their blackened sockets.

Her gaze locked with his. She suppressed the urge to shudder.

Not a spark of human compassion stirred in him. He appeared as cold and detached as the farmers back home who drove their herds to the London slaughter houses. An unspeakable hardness oozed from his pores. Massive arms crossed a chest painted like the rib cage of a skeleton. Unlike the smudged, red paint his companions wore, the sooty outline of bones and sinew were permanently etched on his skin. The maze of bones continued with unwavering precision down his torso and disappeared beneath a rectangular strip of leather. Tied by a rope around his waist, the fringed scrap did little more than cover his nether region. His legs and feet were also marked with skeletal bones.

Jane swallowed hard to tamp down on the terror rising in her throat. He might be painted like a veritable demon from hell, but he was only a man.

A second arrow thudded home somewhere in the canoe, and Skull Face lunged forward and squatted over her on all fours. The arrow was followed by a third and a fourth in rapid succession. With a guttural expletive, he flattened himself atop her.

She silently begged the shooters on shore to embed one of their arrows in a vital part of her captor. His crushing weight and foul stench robbed her of her breath. *Faugh!* Since her hands were bound and trapped between them, she pushed with the heels of her feet and arched her entire midsection upward in an attempt to roll him off.

To her immense disappointment, he grunted in response. Alas, he still lived. When the shooting around them ceased, he raised himself up to crouch over her again on all fours.

A hot breeze swirled into the narrow gap between their bodies. She choked at the ensuing scent that swept past her nostrils. The man smelled like a mixture of raw innards and feces.

Her fighting instincts took over. She swung her bound hands upward and chopped at him with all her might.

This time her captor emitted the low growl of a wounded animal and shifted his bulk away from her.

Gagging, she flung her face to the side and scrubbed her hands up and down the front of her gown.

He rocked back on his heels to a squatting position and surveyed her from narrowed, black pupils encircled by far too much eerie white.

She tensed and braced for the next strike, but he merely stood and stepped over her. He returned to his seat behind her head. Moments later, a filthy foot connected with her shoulder. He pressed harder than before, as if he would not mind separating her arm from its socket this time.

She closed her eyes and drew in quick shallow breaths, willing her arm to relax. It would reduce the risk of injury. She refused to give him the satisfaction of crying out. Perhaps she should not have shoved at him so hard while he lay atop her. Better to let him presume she was injured, beaten for now.

Her mind raced to assess the details of their situation. They'd been ambushed en-route to the mainland, where they had planned to build the first permanent English colony. She did not recognize any of their short, muscular captors. They certainly did not resemble the tall, proud Roanokes from the island she'd just departed.

A wave of unexpected regret hit her. Perhaps, now, she might never learn the name of the cunning Roanoke warrior who'd shadowed her for weeks in the forest. The man who'd shot at her on purpose, pinning her late father's top hat to the tree behind her.

It was sad not to know who would have reigned victor in their game of cat and mouse.

She'd caught a glimpse of him only once. Unless his height had been enhanced by the shadows, he was the tallest man she'd ever laid eyes on. Taller than her own impressive five feet ten inches. Clad only in the leather breechcloth of the local males, he'd boasted the upper body of a boxer while his lower half moved with the speed and lightness of a wildcat.

Nay, her current captors did not share the tribal blood of the colonists' dreaded Roanoke neighbors. This was some new and even more brutal enemy. They'd lost only two of their colonists to the angry Roanokes, whereas this new group had slain every colonist who'd raised a weapon to fight, only preserving the lives of those who'd waved a shirt in surrender.

She frowned, unable to recall her own surrender. Strange, because she could easily recall her attempt to escape on her raft. After her attackers pulled her into the water, however, she could remember nothing.

For what purpose did their enemies keep them alive, and where were they taking them? She tried not to let the possibilities shake her. It was not the first time she'd fallen on hard times. She'd survived before. With a little luck, perhaps she would survive again.

She squinted at Ambrose. Still no sign of recognition lit his large, round face. Nevertheless, she detected a certain awareness she'd missed before. Eyes nearly swollen shut flickered with concern over her before he dropped his head.

Bless him! At least the man has enough of his wits left to shield his emotions.

She wondered how his wife, Beth, fared in the canoe ahead of them. And where were their eight-year-old son, Ambrose, or Brose, as the rest of the youngsters in their colony liked to call him? Her last glimpse of him had been on the beachhead, where the Englishmen had formed a protective line in front of the Englishwomen and lads. It had not been enough to stop the arrows of their enemies from pelting down from high overhead, igniting their piles of baggage and crates resting on their beached rafts. Had the lad perished in the ensuing melee? She shuddered at the thought.

Guilt flooded her over her actions during the ambush. She still felt like a traitor at the way she'd pushed away from shore with her long wooden paddle — the lone person remaining on her raft. But Rose had screamed at her to go for help. She'd meant it, too. She'd speared Jane with her striking green eyes full of desperation, as if Jane was her last hope. Then she'd fallen beneath the hands of their attackers with Margery Harvye's babe still cradled in her arms.

Jane's few moments of hesitation had cost her own freedom. *Forgive me, Rose! Forgive me, my friend, for I could not bear to leave you even when I knew you were lost.*

Instead of sailing for help, she was captured only seconds later.

Shaking off the horror of her memories, she willed Ambrose to look at her again. Perhaps there would be answers in his kind, gray-blue eyes. She was skilled at reading expressions.

However, he kept his head lowered.

The foot on her shoulder relaxed. She took advantage of the lapse in pressure to sit up again and swivel around, knowing she would not be afforded much time to spectate. Three canoes sailed in a diamond-shaped formation in front of them. The canoe she was in brought up the rear point of the diamond.

Ahead of her on the left, the sallow-cheeked Audrey Tappan clutched her sniveling babe, Tomas. Her canoe sat a little lower in the water than the others, because she shared it with the obese Joyce Archard who, for the first time she could recall, was not staring down her nose in contempt at the rest of the colonists. She looked genuinely scared.

Jane's attention snapped to the next canoe. Beth Viccars. No doubt Ambrose had already noted the presence of his wife. *What in the—?* She clutched Virginia Dare, but neither of the infant's parents were in sight. *Not good. Not good at all.*

Her gaze fell on the swarthy features of James Hynde next and the shiny bald pate of his over-sized friend, William Clement. Two ex-convicts, they'd been falsely accused of theft and imprisoned in Colchester Castle before they'd sailed from Portsmouth. Though rough in appearance and old enough to be her father, they were her most faithful friends besides Rose and Agnes — assuming the latter two women still lived.

She swallowed hard and scanned the faces of her fellow colonists again, desperate to discover a face she had overlooked.

So intent was she on searching for her two missing friends, she was unprepared for the foot that slammed between her shoulder blades again. This time, the impact sent her toppling over the side of their narrow boat, but strong hands snatched her hair at the last second and pulled her back inside.

She muffled a yelp of pain.

Lips curling in a snarl of protest, she detected the merest shake of Ambrose's head before her captor yanked her around to face him. Thankful for the timely reminder, she schooled her expression to one of indifference.

Black eyes raked her face, as Skull Face tightened his grip on her hair with a sharp twist.

She felt the blood drain from her cheeks, but she refused to beg for mercy. *The cur!* Apparently his kind fancied the idea of tormenting unarmed women. Well, perhaps not

9

entirely unarmed. Though her pistols had been confiscated after the raid, she still possessed three blades on her person — one in her hair disguised as an ornamental pin and the other two in her work boots.

She stared straight through Skull Face, fingers itching to reach for them.

A trickle of red caught her attention. The man sitting beside Skull Face hunched over in the act of rowing. Nay, he no longer rowed. Two arrows protruded from the left side of his back about a hand's width below his coppery shoulder blades. Fresh blood flowed from his wounds.

Skull Face barked something in his guttural tongue. Then with eyes fixed on hers in sinful glee, he slowly raised a hand and shoved his dead companion from the boat. His complete lack of compassion made her want to vomit, but she fought to keep her expression neutral.

She presumed the danger was past, since no further arrows pounded down on them from the shoreline. *Pity.* She would have enjoyed witnessing more of her captors absorb them like pin cushions.

They maintained their rapid pace in the canoes until the sun settled directly overhead, marking high noon. Her tongue felt as dry as goose down. She tried not to think of the river water churning past them. What she would not give for a single gulp of its murky depths!

Skull Face administered another vicious nudge with his foot, but she feigned indifference. She focused instead on the remaining two red-painted warriors rowing the canoe, trying to learn their faces and study their moves.

The whole group of them were shorter, more squat in stature than the only other native Virginian she'd met. Manteo. He was chief of the Croatoans, the sole tribe in the area who'd welcomed the English to the New World. The rest of their neighbors had been hostile, especially the

Roanokes who were led by Manteo's cousin, Wanchese. His braves had filled one of their city officials with arrows shortly after they'd arrived. Manteo swore his cousin had nothing to do with the murder, but she had her doubts.

She forced her attention back to her captors and found herself almost admiring their efforts. She knew no other men — certainly not any of the Englishmen of her acquaintance — who could maintain such a rigorous pace in rowing. Massive amounts of muscle banded their bare backs and arms and rippled across an interesting pattern of body paint as they rowed. Snakes of black ink appeared to slither through the red paint around their upper arms. Skeleton bones stretched and bent beneath the red on their backs as they dipped their oars.

Good gracious! Skulls and snakes. What strange people! Their appearance was clearly intended to inspire fear in the viewer. Whoever they were, they drew their four canoes to a halt at a wee bit past noon, according to the position of the sun overhead. They pulled into a shaded inlet along the river's edge.

They urged the colonists from their crafts with much prodding of cudgels and ushered them into shallower waters. As he had before, their youngest captor bent to drink from his cupped hands and indicated they should follow suit.

The lad appeared to be about the age of our teen colonists, Blade and George. Though more slender and less scarred than his companions, his chest was corded with muscle and wickedly painted like theirs. And his eyes glittered as black and emotionless as his elder companions. He made her think of a dark angel.

As the youngest and least experienced among them, Angel — as she dubbed him on the spot — would surely be the weakest link in their chain. She would locate his soft underbelly and use it against him if she could.

She drank until sated but continued to cup the water in

her hands and pretend to drink while she took the opportunity to identify each surviving colonist. Besides Audrey and her babe, Madam Archard, Elizabeth and baby Virginia, Ambrose, James, and William, she also spotted Cecil Prat and his son, Blade, Edward Powell who'd lost his wife Winifred in the ambush, one of their gentleman colonists, Richard Berry, the rather quacky Dr. John Jones, and George Howe — son of their slain crab fisherman.

Something was amiss with George. The fifteen-year-old was sprawled against an aging oak instead of drinking like the others. Long, dark lashes lay in repose on his once-fair cheeks, and his chin rested on his chest. His aristocratic brow, darkly tanned with a hint of pink from overexposure to the sun, lay blandly smooth.

He would have been the rage back in London with the young ladies. Should have been, that is. Good, solid family name. Plenty of coin in the purse. An oversized sense of adventure, though, and a bit too cocky at times for his fine linen shirts and silk trousers. Alas, his fancy wardrobe was history. One shirt sleeve was missing, and the knees were shredded from his pants. His once lordly sideburns now stretched to a stubbly beard, but the growth was not thick enough to hide the pursing of lips in concentration.

She stiffened and looked away so as not to draw attention to him.

Not so with William. Bless the daft man, but his heart was many sizes bigger than his intellect. He scooped up more of the river water and squatted next to the youth, letting it trickle against the boy's mouth.

George's eyelids shot open in surprise, far too keen for one so recently immersed in the world of dreams, far too angry.

She edged closer, prepared to make a scene if necessary to distract their captors. His slain father had served as one of the governor's Assistants in their failed colony. Aye, young George carried a grudge the size of a mountain on his shoulder for the loss of his sire, and who could blame him? If only he'd sprout an ounce of patience, he might actually prove helpful in their escape from their current captivity. Jane deplored his impetuous nature but took some responsibility upon herself for his faults. As the school mistress of their colony, she'd failed to train those less desirable traits out of him.

She gave a delicate cough, hoping George would glance up at her. She shook her head in the event he did but dared not turn in his direction to ensure he'd seen the gesture.

Out of the corner of her eye, she watched Angel's head pop up. His dark eyes narrowed on George. Quick as a panther, he leaped on George and yanked him away from the tree by his shoulders. The lad went crashing to his back in a cloud of dust.

The colonists uttered a collective gasp. She shot a furtive glance at the place he had vacated. *Whatever was the lad up to?*

William, who had been squatting before George, lost his balance and tumbled against the base of the tree but not before she detected what George had been doing.

Scratched into the lowest few inches of the trunk was a Maltese Cross. It was the colony's secret signal of distress. They'd promised Governor John White, who'd returned to England in the attempt to acquire resupply ships, that they would carve such a sign into the trees if they found themselves in any danger during his absence. He would use them to find and rescue the colonists, if need be, upon his return.

Ah, George! She'd underestimated the slick workings of his mind, after all. It was too bad that William, in his infinite kindness, had mistakenly interrupted the lad's effort to leave a message for Governor White.

Shamefaced, William sought to right his ample figure and

succeeded only in tumbling to his backside. There he lay, panting against the tree. Thank the good Lord for the smallest of miracles, because William's large frame now covered George's rough etchings, which were more beautiful to Jane at the moment than the most glorious works of art back in London.

She closed her eyes, relieved, even as Angel proceeded to pound George with his cudgel all the way to the water's edge. She could not fathom how their captors had missed the carving of the Maltese Cross. *Careless*. She wasn't exactly the religious sort like the rest of her comrades, but it was proof enough to her that Providence was on their side.

Her lips moved in a rare and silent prayer of thanksgiving. She hadn't intended to go down without a fight. For the first time since their capture, however, something akin to real hope burgeoned in her chest.

Allowing the captives to drink water was significant. Their captors were keeping them alive. For now, at least. But why? And for how long? Her thoughts raced one over the other, but she failed to conjure up even one good reason.

"Rassunnemum! Rassunnemum!"

Her eyes flew open at the raucous cries of their captors.

They prodded the colonists to their feet. A dozen or more new red-painted warriors materialized at the edge of the clearing and formed a semi-circle, waiting. Three women stood among them. Bare-chested and unsmiling, they were heavily etched and painted in the same manner as their male counterparts. The only difference in their appearance was the fringed leather skirts that fell to their knees.

The cedars at the perimeter seemed to close in on the captives. The tallest trees she'd ever laid eyes on towered over her like giant sentinels. They would be the only witnesses to whatever their enemies planned next.

Skull Face stepped up to Audrey Tappan, knife point

outstretched. She shrank from him with a whimper. One of the Englishmen attempted to run to her aid and was pummeled to the ground.

Jane waited, horrified, for Skull Face to begin his abuse, but he merely slashed apart the bonds that held her wrists together.

Audrey screamed and grabbed his arm as he yanked Tomas from her and thrust him at one of the native women. Dark squares and triangles dotted her forehead and cheeks. The woman promptly lifted him to suckle. *A wet nurse?*

With a nod from Skull Face, the other two women rushed forward and wrestled Audrey out of her dress. She stood before the colonists in her shift, eyes glassy with fear. In a vain attempt to cover herself, she tugged together the torn pieces of her underclothing but not before Jane caught a glimpse of her rib cage. Each bone rose in stark relief.

It was a far worse sight to her than Skull Face's skeletal torso. At least the narrow strands of sinew hanging to his bones were painted on. Born of endless weeks of the scantest food rations, Audrey's emaciation was quite real. They'd been betrayed by their own countrymen in a brawl over land grants. They'd been brought to the point of starvation before being marooned on Roanoke Island, a place inhabited by one of England's gravest enemies.

Their captors fell on the tiny, birdlike Beth Viccars next. Her large eyes brimmed with tears.

When Angel relieved her of baby Virginia Dare, Jane detected no remorse in him. The infant gurgled with surprise and latched on to the same wet nurse who held Tomas. *Poor little poppet!* Hunger and thirst must be clawing at her insides.

Skull Face ordered the same pair of women to remove Beth's tattered gown of worsted brown wool, along with her filthy cotton shift. She put up no fight but raised her head in silent indignation. Skull Face grabbed her chin, turning it this way and that. She held his gaze as he reached behind her, flicked the pins from her hair, and sent them flying into the dirt. The frazzled bun at her nape uncoiled itself like a dusty rope and slid down her back.

All of this he did with a cool and detached poise, which Jane found alarming. She would have preferred anger — anything but the hard, unblinking assessment he bestowed on each colonist.

Fresh tears trickled down Beth's cheeks at his prolonged perusal. She wrapped her arms tightly over her chest and hunched forward to cover more of herself. Skull Face gave her coil of hair one last experimental yank and turned his dark gaze to the next captive.

Joyce Archard towered over him, but it rendered her no advantage. Like the proverbial elephant trembling over a mouse, she stood with head bowed and bulbous jowls quivering. Unlike the other women, she made no attempt to cover her sagging figure after the pitiless removal of her garments. Vast rolls of pale skin lay exposed to the sun, a stranger to its rays.

Our men, several of whom had been beaten to the ground in their attempt to fight their way to Audrey and Beth's aid, averted their faces.

Vacant of all emotion, Madam Archard stood with her arms hanging at her sides. Gone was the pompous tilt to her head, the haughty cast to her expression. Muddy hues of exhaustion smudged the valleys beneath her eyes.

Jane wanted to howl with frustration at how easily her comrades had accepted their defeat. She'd expected far more from these gutsy pioneers. They were clever, hardworking men and women who'd evaded arrest in London to come worship freely as Puritans in the New World.

Once upon a time, they'd been the ones to speak life back

into her existence, to offer her hope after weeks spent wandering the streets of Cheapside in search of employment. Where was their bravery now? Their faith? They acted like God, Himself, was dead.

Skull Face crouched before Jane. As if savoring a particularly succulent morsel, he sauntered around her in a full circle.

She felt a spark of unholy glee when he had to tilt his head up a few degrees due to her superior height.

She lowered her chin a notch and stared back each time he passed in front of her. His rude assessment continued down the flare of her hips and ended with a grunt of derision at the sight of her dirt-caked boots.

Without taking his eyes from her, he snapped out a hand, palm up. Angel offered him a coiled length of leather. He curled his fingers around it and slapped it against his other palm. It resembled a whip cord, though it was several inches longer than the flanges the bo'sun had employed aboard ship during his frequent floggings of the crewmen.

Her blood chilled. So this was what Skull Face intended for her. Complete humiliation, a breaking of both body and spirit.

She glanced over her shoulder at Audrey and Beth. They clung to either side of Madam Archard and wept in silence, their faces a study of horror and pity as they registered what Skull Face held in his hands. Their distress washed over her like a flood, penetrating, choking, and filling her until the air around her pulsed with the hum and cadence of their collective grief.

Then, like a bubble, it burst. Jane's anger rekindled. It sputtered to life inside her chest and spread to her belly. Her fingers tensed with the power of it.

When Skull Face swung the whip in her direction, she was ready. Teeth bared, she danced from its path and wrenched her wrists from their bonds with a single twist. She'd loosened the ropes hours before and left them in place, waiting for the right moment to reveal her freedom. It was not the opportunity she'd hoped for, but it might be their best chance of escape. Their only chance.

She bent and whipped a dagger from her left boot and faced her opponent, panting with anticipation.

With a whoop of anger, he snapped the whip at her forehead. She ducked and slashed as it screamed past her. Her blade sliced clean through it, and a circle of cord dropped into the dust between them.

She stared at it. *What in the blazes?* It was not a whip but a noose.

She reached for the shorter dagger hidden in her hair and danced in front of Skull Face on the balls of her feet. Though she'd hunted every creature indigenous to England, she'd never killed a person before. Oh, but she desperately wanted to do so now!

With a cry of anguish, she flung both daggers at Skull Face. Perhaps she could slow him down long enough for some of her comrades to make a run for it.

A second coil of leather snaked out from Skull Face's other hand, capturing one of her daggers in midair. Her second dagger embedded itself to the hilt in the dirt between his feet. He danced aside and nearly lost his footing, which might have been comical under different circumstances. Alas, the man was fresh out of humor. With a roar, he turned and lunged for her.

She spared a rapid glance at her fellow colonists before he threw her to the ground. New fury surged in her chest at their gaping stares.

"Run, blast you!" she shouted.

No one moved.

"Nay, Jane," Beth cried brokenly. "For we are well and truly trapped. There is no way out."

Then Jane could no longer see the sun for the number of warriors who swarmed atop her. She allowed her mind to drift in a detached manner as they relieved her first of her gown and then her boots. Too much was happening too quickly for her emotions to catch up. The anticipated sense of shame evaded her altogether.

Hands yanked the pins from her hair and searched the length of her tresses for additional weapons. They yanked it by the roots with such ferocity, she was certain she would have no hair left when they were finished. They dragged her to her feet and dumped her in the river. Despite their rough handling, however, she suffered no real injuries.

When Jane dared meet the dark, searching eyes of one of the women, she administered a stinging slap to her cheek and drew back her arm to repeat the action.

Skull Face barked a terse command.

The woman snarled and lowered her arm to resume her abrasive washing. Several times she dunked Jane beneath the water and kept her there long enough to have her gasping for air when she finally surfaced.

After she was scraped from head to toe of what must be the entire top layer of her skin, they retied her hands in front of her. This time, they bound her feet also, so she could only take half a step at a time. They tugged her thus into the tree line.

The three women waited with none-too-pleased expressions. They dumped something slick and oily on her bare arms, legs, and torso and rubbed it in. The scent of herbs and berries wafted upward. Next they lathered the oil in her hair.

Ugh! Although grateful to have her life breath still in her lungs, Jane's alarm escalated to a new level as they greased her down like a pig. Was this the deadly marinade of some breed of head hunters? Did they intend to roast her over a spit and consume her when they finished?

Her captors attacked the male colonists next, disrobing and scrubbing them down.

Afterwards, they painted strange multi-colored designs out of squares and circles on everyone's foreheads, forearms, and chests. Then they forced the colonists to their knees at the river's edge once more and allowed them to drink but not talk. There they waited another two hours in the whipping breezes.

At long last, they ordered the Englishmen and women to their feet. Miracle of miracles, they even returned their clothing, still torn but freshly washed. *Egad.* They must have been waiting all this time for the colonists' clothes to dry. Many accessories were missing, of course. Jane's father's top hat was gone along with her knives and boots. Her heart squeezed at the thought of never again seeing these precious items.

After donning their sparse, still-damp apparel, the colonists marched bare of feet another few miles through the woods. Here the trees grew so closely together, nothing but shoots of thin, greenish beams lit their way. They marched in silence, wincing as the ground cover tore at their feet and sneaking glances at one another.

Time was of little consequence, considering how each hour might be their last, but Jane kept meticulous track of every passing hour and day. According to her calculations, it was mid-September. The fifteenth to be exact. Out of habit, she mentally reviewed the distance they'd traveled during the time they'd been held captive, while Beth Viccars whispered a prayer next to her. Audrey wept in deep, gasping sobs and craned her thin neck to keep the wet nurse in sight.

Faint at first, a cacophony of sounds murmured to life and grew louder. A quarter mile later, they emerged from the woods into another world from the one where they had immigrated. Instead of the gilded manor homes and merchants' rooftops of every sort imaginable that had crammed the streets of London, before them stretched row after row of leather and canvas tents.

Their conical shapes rose skyward. Their outer walls displayed a full rainbow of colors and designs. Mud-hued deer raced across some of the canvases, while fascinating shapes and figures decorated others.

Coppery men and women entered and exited the tents from narrow flaps of animal skin that served as doors. Swirls of smoke rose from another set of flaps at the tops of the cones and appeared to serve as chimneys.

All in all, it was like stepping into a brightly colored dream. Except the long, narrow platform rising at the end of the tent city was anything but a dream. Five copper-skinned women, with their hands tied in front of them, paraded across the platform in nothing but short fringed skirts. Their captors prodded them to a halt. One of the red-painted warriors squatted in front of them and began to bellow at the audience. At times he sprang towards the young women and lifted their chins or turned their bodies to give the onlookers a better view.

A man in the audience raised his hand and yelled something in a guttural tongue. The man on stage answered him gleefully and shoved one of the young women towards the stairs. Another native led her from the stage and delivered her to the one who'd raised his hand. In exchange, he produced a pouch of miniature shells that were poured out and exclaimed over. Like a farmer with his livestock, the new owner examined his purchase carefully and led her back to one of the conical tents.

With no further ado, the tiny burst of hope Jane felt at being allowed to live shriveled. It didn't mattered how she'd memorized every stream they had sailed and every trail they had marched since their capture. They had arrived at the Great Trading Path that Chief Manteo had warned them about.

Their captors intended to sell them as slaves.

CHAPTER 2: GREAT TRADING PATH

*S*toic-faced natives bartered loudly for the young women until the auctioneer accepted their prices. Fresh horror burgeoned in Jane's throat as the second young woman sold for a pouch of the delicate white seashells. A third went for a collection of copper vessels and yet another for a litter of pups. One by one, their new owners led them away. None raised any resistance. Their lack of emotion cut through her own fears and inspired a morbid fascination. The captives offered no tears, no pleas for mercy. Rather, their expressions mirrored the stoicism of their captors. Was it stubborn pride or something else? Either way, it was utterly barbaric to be so accepting of slavery.

Slender as a reed with delicate wrists and ankles, the fifth captive could not be more than fifteen. Her inky-black hair lay in thick braids over the front of her shoulders and fell past her waist. In a proper gown, she would be deemed lovely by London standards — for a foreigner, that is. Her dark, exotic coloring and fine-boned features would present a stunning contrast to the droves of fair-skinned, blushing debutants of the season.

Higher cheekbones, a few shades lighter skin tone, and greater height set her apart from the other young women. She must be from a different tribe, because she also bore none of the ink etchings that adorned their faces and arms. One last difference manifested itself.

Unlike the previous slaves who'd been sold, her owner did not lead her to his tent. Instead, he led her away from the tent city altogether and into the forest. As she exited the crowd, Jane glimpsed a trail of bear claws inked across her upper back. *Ah.* She was not completely unmarred with ink as Jane had previously supposed.

She frowned at the young woman's departing figure. Didn't Chief Manteo of the Croatoans possess the same bear claws etched on his upper arms? Did that mean a tribal or familial connection existed between the two? She tucked away the bit of information for future reference.

Regardless of her origins, the lovely young slave's people clearly associated themselves with the brazen strength of the bear. Too bad it had failed to prevent her capture. Had she wandered away from her group as Assistant George Howe had done during his crab fishing expedition? Or had the red painted warriors lay in silent ambush until her people stepped into their snare as Skull Face and his cronies had done to the English colonists on the beach? Was she the only survivor, or had the rest of her tribe also been captured? Jane wondered what lay in store for her, what lay in store for all of them.

Jostling her from her silent pondering, Skull Face and his cronies began to march along their line, barking commands in a language the colonists did not understand. They prodded them to the base of an uneven staircase, whose stony steps tumbled from one end of the massive platform to the hard-packed ground beneath it. Built of rough-hewn planks graying with age, the platform rose a good ten feet above their heads, bringing to mind a scaffold. Jane blinked and squinted, but thankfully no executioner awaited them.

The noise of the crowd quieted as they half-hopped, half-stumbled their shackled feet up the stairs, all thirty-one of them. Their captors fanned the colonists out across the long platform and stood guard over them. To Jane's surprise, the bartering and bidding did not immediately begin. The auctioneer beckoned to Skull Face in the same superior manner as a lord summoning his lackey. *Interesting.* There appeared to be some sort of class system here.

After hearing it spoken several times, she perceived Skull Face was calling the auctioneer by the name of Kokoko. She wondered what it meant. Skull Face responded to the man's questions with much gesturing. Even if he had not pointed in her direction, she would have deduced they were discussing her.

Kokoko turned and examined the English captives. Taller than Skull Face and finer dressed, his straight black hair fell in an inky curtain around his shoulders. Nonetheless, his eyes were equally cold. Draped over his left arm, he wore a cloak adorned in a complex design of porcupine quills, beads, and seashells. The deerskin folds pulled back to leave his right arm bare. Odd, for he wore no quiver of arrows like so many of the men. Manteo had explained to the colonists back on the island how the native men kept their right arms unencumbered so as not to hamper their shooting.

With one sharp, upward movement of his arm, Kokoko dismissed Skull Face and issued a command to the men in the tents stretching below the slave trading platform. It was a call to action. In response, several young men darted up and down the rows of conical structures. A few disappeared inside the door flaps. An aged man emerged from the largest tent, which was graced with elaborate murals.

Jane did not need to understand the language of the

natives to recognize the deference bestowed upon him by the crowd. Stiff bearing and highly decorated garments underscored his elevated social status. His lined face held no expression, but he carried his tall frame with dignity and with only the slightest of limps. He also wore more attire than the other men milling about in little more than loincloths. A full headdress of eagle feathers draped over greying plaits and fell down either side of his face to rest against his chest. Multiple strands of copper beads graced his neck. He boasted a pair of embroidered buckskins and just as richly embroidered leather moccasins.

He raised his head to stare straight at Jane. Her heartbeat quickened. His sharp eyes continued down the line to take in the rest of her comrades. Audrey Tappan emitted a muffled sob at his perusal. After a moment, the dark eyes returned to Jane. Did he intend to enter a bid for one or more of the colonists?

She stared over his head and raised her chin a notch. Let him gawk. There was nothing for him to see but a tall, overly-thin woman well past the age of marriage at four and twenty. Back in London, no one would have ever taken such keen notice of a spinster.

The aged man did not seem to object to his view of her, however. He ogled her with undeniable masculine appreciation.

She lifted her chin higher. No stranger to being stared at, she was accustomed to overhearing the muttering behind hands about all the various and sundry things wrong with her appearance, every objectionable attribute that drove away any would-be suitors. Her mouth was too wide. Her skin was not fair enough with its golden tan and ghastly sprinkling of freckles across the bridge of her nose, both of which were entirely her fault. She rarely carried a parasol when she was out walking, because she was too busy toting her weapons and traps.

She did not hate men or deplore the thought of marrying one of them someday. They just seemed to prefer all the features she did not possess. Buxom blondes always seemed to draw more attention from the eligible bachelors than her tall, lean frame and chestnut locks. As if that particular crowd had any room to judge! Why, those same London dandies danced around like popinjays in their striped pants and silken hose. *Bah!* She found some of their styles to be downright unmanly, to say the least.

Her most objectionable trait to them, however, had always been her height. Few stood eye level with her, which tended to dim the romantic fantasies of most young men of her acquaintance. When a man had to crane his neck up at a woman of five feet ten…

The warrior shouted something at Kokoko who rushed to her side to pivot her this way and that for a better view.

Though tempted, she did not stoop or cower like her companions in the attempt to cover the skin exposed by her torn and tattered gown. Let their enemies see by her stance that they could do as they pleased with her person, but they would never rob her of the dignity that only comes from within. Nonetheless, the heat of a traitorous blush stung her cheeks at the thought of her dishabille. She could only hope the onlookers credited her heightened color to the sun blasting down on her.

A flicker of movement caught her eye from the edge of the tent community. A tall warrior clad in buckskins stepped from the forest. Several leather pouches with straps of varying lengths draped crosswise across his chest from shoulder to waist.

He looked startlingly familiar. Was he their native ally, Chief Manteo? Hope vibrated through her. The man had much wealth at his disposal. She imagined he could afford to purchase the entire row of colonists, if he desired.

As the warrior drew closer, however, her hope plummeted. He was not Rose's beau, after all. Nay, this man was two or three inches taller. Though he resembled Manteo, his cheek bones were more pronounced, his chin squarer, his eyes a lighter brown that glowed with a reddish hue in the sun.

Like Manteo, his blue-black hair was shaved on one side and spiked straight up from forehead to nape in the center. The other side flowed freely like a lion's mane over his bare chest. He strode towards the platform with a predatory grace.

The arms hanging at his sides bulged with strength. Bear claws, identical to those of the striking young woman sold earlier, were etched in his upper arms in the same manner as Manteo's. They rippled and flexed with his movements. Surely, they indicated a connection among the three. But the resemblance to the colonists' kind-hearted ally, Manteo, ended there.

Jane did not care for the cold challenge in this warrior's expression as he glanced straight up at her.

Here stood a man to be reckoned with. She made no pretense of staring through him or beyond him. Caught in the cobra spell of his mahogany gaze, she was powerless to look away. His movements contained a suppressed violence. This warrior had killed before. More than once. Many times, in fact, and he would kill again if provoked. Black anger simmered just beneath the surface as he beheld her. She fought the effort to squirm with discomfort. Then her ire sputtered to life.

She was unarmed and her clothing in shreds, *burn it!* She had done nothing to deserve such seething disdain from this man or any other person present, nor had the colonists standing with her. It was not their fault that another group of Englishmen had clashed with the local indigenous tribes two years earlier. She'd been horrified to learn how the previous group of English explorers and soldiers had invaded their towns, stolen their food, and burnt their homes in retaliation to a series of petty arguments.

To their credit, the most recent governing board had attempted to mend their poor relations with the locals. In the end, however, Governor White had bumbled those efforts. The English were further than ever from establishing a peace treaty with their native neighbors.

Before God and men, however, the thirty-one Englishmen and Englishwomen standing on the slave trading block today were innocent of all the ill will stirred before their arrival. There were no soldiers in their ranks, just ordinary colonists. Brick masons, homebuilders, tailors, weavers, farmers, cooks, explorers, educators, men of the cloth, and politicians. Though Jane was unmarried, many of her fellow colonists journeyed with children, siblings, or friends, and two traveled with their entire families. Three carried babes in their arms.

Alas, if these local tribes were the unforgiving heathens they were reputed to be, then Jane and her comrades could expect no mercy. They would be held accountable for the sins of their countrymen.

She continued to meet the probing gaze of the newest arrival. May he gawk and examine, ridicule and hate. She and her companions had Providence on their side, and that had to count for something. They might die as martyrs today, but they would triumph in the end when he and his cohorts burned in an everlasting hell.

The warrior in question took a running leap and grasped the front of the platform with both hands. He swung himself up and approached. Only once did he look away from Jane, long enough to take in the shuddering ranks of her comrades. His expression spared them no pity.

More prospective buyers ascended the stairs, making a far less dramatic entrance than he did. They circled the English, murmuring and exclaiming, prodding and touching. With their dignity already violated to levels they'd never known before, the examinations came as somewhat of a surprise, because the biggest emotion exhibited by the natives was curiosity.

They brushed fingers across the skin of their arms and legs, as if expecting their fair coloring to rub off. The stoicism in their faces was transformed to sheer fascination. In the end, however, they turned cool and calculating. *Prices.* She'd seen money changers carry those same expressions back in London. Their thoughts centered on the forthcoming auction.

Skull Face marched up and down his prized collection of captives, raising an arm of a colonist here, tilting a head there, and shouting unintelligible phrases. He stood before James and William and mimed the swinging of a hammer. *Egad! How did he know they were home builders?*

Jane tightened her lips in anger. *They've been watching us, that's how.* Many times during the past several weeks, she had sensed they were being watched but had chalked it up to her imagination when more than a month passed without seeing any action.

Their attackers had been patient. They had waited until the English colonists crossed the channel to the mainland. Aye, it was a most disturbing display of patience. It had given them the cover of night and the luxury of ambushing after the English had divided themselves into three smaller groups. By then, they were far from the protection of their coastal fort with its mounted cannons.

The tall newcomer stepped in front of Jane once more,

blocking her vision and claiming her full attention. It wasn't every day a man could see eye to eye with her at her excessive height, but this one towered over her by at least half a hand's width.

Four black lines slashed the sides of his face from brow to temple. Around his eyes swirled an intricate pattern of black and red lines and zigzags, like a sinister masquerade mask.

She sucked in a slow breath of unease.

A quiver of arrows hung from one of his shoulders. Startled, she recognized the intricate design carved on the upper shafts, a series of jagged blood-red lines encased within two thicker black lines.

"You," she breathed, addressing him directly. "It was you who shot at me on Roanoke Island." She expected no response. He could not possibly understand her.

Yet he inclined his tall frame towards her. "Aye." The word was spoken in the merest whisper, for her ears alone.

She froze at his perfect English. Her back tensed as he remained bent, his breath stirring her hair.

"Who are you?" she hissed. Apprehension tightened her throat.

"Wanchese." Again, the word was spoken against her ear. He straightened and observed her with a masked expression and cunning eyes.

Wanchese was Manteo's cousin. For a fraction of a second, she entertained the hope that Manteo had sent him to rescue them all, but she knew such a thing was unlikely. To their grave misfortune, Wanchese served as chief of the Roanokes, their sworn enemies.

He'd relocated his people to the neighboring town of Dasamonquepeuc after the first fleet of English ships had landed on his island. Then he'd halted his plans to return to the island when their second set of ships arrived and dropped anchor, including the one she'd sailed on.

The truth was, Jane and her friends had been marooned there at gunpoint by their ex-pirate navigator who preferred to chase Spanish treasure ships instead of delivering them farther north to their intended destination in the Chesapeake Bay area. But none of that mattered to Wanchese. To him, the English were intruders, every last one of them.

Returning on her ship after a diplomatic tour in London, his cousin Manteo had endured the mutiny alongside the colonists. Shortly afterwards, he had secured a promise from his cousin to do the English newcomers no harm. The promise had hinged upon their rapid removal from Roanoke Island, which was why they'd constructed rafts to carry them to the mainland.

The agreement did not keep Chief Wanchese's renegade braves from tracking their every move, however. They'd shadowed the colonists from dawn 'til dusk. It was like being surrounded by ghosts. The promise hadn't kept Wanchese away, either. His shot at Jane, and his deliberate miss, still rankled.

She hated how her comrades had fired back. English firearms are not so accurate as bows and arrows, and she did not wish to harm any of these local men and women like their countrymen had done two years earlier. Alas, the previous group of Englishmen had slain the island king, Pemisapan, in a military skirmish, which was how Wanchese had risen to power. According to rumor, he now bore a grudge against the English the size of the ocean stretching between their two motherlands.

"Chief Wanchese," she murmured and stifled a shudder at the sound of their dreaded enemy's name on her lips, but he was already striding away. She stared after him, shaken by her discovery of his identity.

Why bother to reveal himself? Had he come to witness their shame? To gloat? Manteo had refused him the enjoyment of slaughtering the English. But here at the Great Trading Path, Wanchese could revel in their suffering as a spectator while keeping his promise to his cousin.

Angry at the unfairness of their circumstances, Jane scanned the faces of her fellow colonists. Short and petite with dark hair waving over her shoulders, Beth Viccars' lips trembled in unceasing prayer. Young Robert Ellis's hand was tucked in hers. He stood beside her, eyes saucer-wide with shock. He'd been separated from his father during last night's skirmish. It amazed her how the sweet poppet remained on his feet after their forced march inland.

Ambrose Viccars hobbled up the uneven stairs, no longer cradling his broken arm. A sling now secured it. He took his place next to the cowering John and Alis Chapman, a brother and sister-in-law who'd traveled all the way across the ocean to be reunited with Alis's husband, Robert. Alas, Sergeant Chapman had been slain months before their arrival. His bleaching skeleton in the clearing outside the fort had served as their welcoming party to the New World.

Alis muttered to herself, fear leaping from her hazel eyes. Jane didn't know if she was praying or if her senses were wandering. Her brother-in-law's kind features were shuttered with resignation and despair. He made no move to defend his sister-in-law during the curious prodding of the prospective buyers.

The teen colonists — all students of hers during their trans-Atlantic journey — tried to appear brave, though Blade's knees shook and Will's hands trembled within his bonds. Only George seemed unafraid. His upper lip curled in undeniable disdain for their audience. Hot-tempered to the core, he was given to quick bursts of rage at some of the most inappropriate times. She willed the handsome lad to keep his composure. They had enough trouble on their hands.

The eccentric Dr. Jones sweated profusely on the other side of George. Large droplets rolled from his sideburns and splattered to his chest. Jane wondered if the shaking was from fear or his abrupt withdrawal from the bottle. The man adored his wine. Next to the doctor stood the long-faced Cecil Prat. He remained hunched in pain from an injury sustained during the ambush, but the arrow was gone at last from his shoulder. In its place rested a muddy poultice. She eyed it with caution. It was a far cry from the careful stitches and clean white linen bandages their English apothecary, Agnes, normally applied; but it seemed to be doing the trick. His pale chest displayed no red streaks of infection so far.

Other colonists prayed and wept softly. She caught James's eye. His overgrown brown hair, speckled with gray, lifted in the hot breeze. He gave her a solemn nod, the rugged lines of his face a study of fatherly concern. She swallowed hard and nodded back. His coffee-colored eyes were void of their usual sauce and wit. William stood by his side, completing the long line of colonists. His plump cheeks waxed pale, and his eyes bulged with distress, but his lips were moving. She craned her neck closer to take in his words.

> Your vows you've broken, like my heart
> Oh, why did you so enrapture me?
> Now I remain in a world apart
> But my heart remains in captivity

James's bushy eyebrows rose as he recognized the tune. He joined in the chorus, adding his warbling tenor in perfect harmony.

> Greensleeves was all my joy
> Greensleeves was my delight

> Greensleeves was my heart of gold
> And who but my Lady Greensleeves.

George uncurled his lip and filled his chest with air. When the two men launched into the next verse, he blended his rich baritone with their voices.

> Well, I will pray to God on high
> That thou my constancy mayst see
> And that yet once before I die
> Thou wilt vouchsafe to love me.

The colonists lifted their heads. Damp lashes fluttered open. The women joined on the next round of the chorus, their soprano and alto voices adding a new layer of richness to the song. Jane's throat tightened as her fellow colonists paid their last respects to England. She joined the final chorus.

> Ah, Greensleeves, now farewell, adieu
> To God I pray to prosper thee
> For I am still thy lover true,
> Come once again and love me.

The natives made no attempt to interrupt, nor did their cudgels rain blows upon the singers. They stared in wonder until the last strains of the haunting melody died on the colonists' lips.

Only then did the air erupt into a frenzy of chatter. Men pointed and shouted at the English from the city of tents below. Jane could not understand their words, but she perceived the negotiations for their sale had begun at last.

Rubbing his hands in satisfaction, their auctioneer rapidly

ushered the prospective buyers from the platform and gestured for Audrey Tappan to step forward.

When she ignored his summons, Kokoko slung his dark locks over one shoulder and snatched her from the line. She wept piteously through the entire ordeal and sold for a pouch of the same white shells they'd witnessed exchanging hands earlier. She fell bonelessly into the arms of the scarred warrior who purchased her. Without breaking stride, he swept her over his shoulder and disappeared into the crowd.

The remaining colonists gazed at each other in numb disbelief. The unthinkable had just happened. One of them had been sold. Already the auctioneer reached for the trembling arm of Madam Archard. It appeared there would be no miracles coming their way today.

Why, then, was Jane unable to share in the utter despair of her comrades? Why wouldn't the tears come? Unlike them, all she felt was grim acceptance of their lot, along with a strange elation over the fact they would live to see another day. For weeks, death had teased and taunted them from every shadowy corner of the forest. Most of them had not expected to live this long.

Aye, slavery was far from the life they'd planned for themselves. But so long as they still lived and breathed, there remained the hope of escape.

It wasn't as if her life leading up to this point had been easy. She'd spent the past six years in London trying to cram small bits of knowledge down the throats of unruly, spoiled children. In a fit of temper last spring, she had dared to suggest to her noble employers that she might better be able to teach their sweet darlings French if she could first brandish a switch across their backsides. Naturally, the family had turned her out on her ear without a reference for her insubordination. If one of the underground Separatist churches had not taken her into their fold — the same men

and women who stood with her on the auction block now —
she might very well have starved on the streets of Cheapside.

Maybe this was her chance to return their favor. It
seemed unfair for these virtuous pilgrims to journey so far
from their homes and families in search of religious freedom
only to be thrust into a life of hard labor for their efforts. She
had no intention of standing by and shedding useless tears
about it, though. She would escape and spend the rest of her
days, if need be, rescuing her comrades from whatever parts
of the world they would soon be scattered to.

Perhaps she had been raised by trappers for such a time
as this. Her impoverished genteel mother had married for
love and taken to the hills of England with her father, *God
rest their souls*. There they'd taught her how to love, respect,
and live off the land. At their death, however, a distant and
aging cousin in London had continued Jane's education.
Deploring her uncommon upbringing, she had trained Jane
to serve as a lady's companion and eventually a
schoolmistress.

Alas, the aging cousin had not counted on how much of
her father and mother remained in her. She'd longed for the
hills her entire stint in London and leaped at the opportunity
to join her Puritan friends on their pilgrimage to the New
World. The challenge of building the City of Raleigh and
colonizing this wild, untamed land had appealed to her on
every level.

What a castle in the clouds that had turned out to be!

Kokoko resumed the auction and ended her musing. He
bartered off Madam Archard next. He forced her to step into
the direct glare of the sun to display her bountiful attributes.
Jane winced at the piercing light and ducked her head. It
took the entire bidding session for the sunspots to stop
clouding her vision. By then, Madam Archard was sold.

She spotted Wanchese and was drawn again by the

sorcery of his eyes. Hard. Piercing. Observant. Suppressing a sliver of premonition, she doubted they missed anything.

He stood on the far side of the tent city, away from the teaming crowd. It was hard to tell from his expression if he was gloating, though she suspected he was.

Like a fly caught in a spider's web, she was once again powerless to avert her gaze from his. She shook her head in self-disgust and wracked her brain to remember all Rose had shared with her about Wanchese. Her thoughts drifted to the evening her friend had confided her worst fears.

---

*T*he night stole upon them, lengthening the shadows cast by the canopy of trees around the tiny earthen fort. White moonlight spilled across the protective palisade wall, glancing over the loaded cannons mounted to the bulwarks and illuminating the fearful vigil of her fellow colonists. They were spread along the mud walls of the fort, facing inland, armed and ready for the red-painted warriors to attack. Cecil and Blade Prat had spotted them closing in on their location with hatchets and knives in hand during an earlier patrol.

Hours passed with no action. Had Cecil and Blade imagined the strangely painted natives? It was understandable after the recent and brutal murder of Assistant George Howe. The poor man had taken sixteen arrows and endured a bashing that left his head unrecognizable. His untimely death had them all jumping at shadows and more determined than ever to leave the island. They'd have already launched their rafts for the mainland if their men hadn't spotted the hostiles.

Rose sighed and edged nearer to Jane. The pistol relaxed in her hands. "My gut says they are not coming tonight."

Jane raised a brow. Her body language indicated she wanted to talk. "Spill it, clerk," she whispered.

She flashed a quick smile and tucked a stray lock of bright-red hair behind one ear. "It's about Wanchese. He promised Manteo he would not attack us. They are cousins, you know. As much as he may wish to declare war on us, his hands are tied."

Jane was no longer listening merely to be polite. Rose possessed her full attention now. Chief Manteo was smitten with Rose, an unexpected complication as the English sought to establish an alliance with his tribe. Alas, he was already married to the daughter of a neighboring tribe — more of a political alliance than a love match, or so she'd been told. Still, he had dared propose to take Rose as his second wife. Egad! What a storm in a teapot that whole affair had stirred amongst the pious colonists. Rose was still recovering from the scandal. Although an epidemic had since swept through Manteo's tribe and rendered him a widower, he had not yet renewed his courtship with her. Jane figured it was only a matter of time. She'd never seen two people more in love.

"Did Manteo confide this in you directly?" With danger looming like a specter behind every tree on the island, Jane sought assurance.

She nodded. "Still, I worry how long it will hold him off. Wanchese utterly despises us."

"He certainly has his reasons," Jane muttered, considering all her countrymen had done to raise his ire against them.

"Aye, and there is more to it. I just found out." Rose sidled closer. "Do you recall the governor relating to us how Wanchese traveled to England several years ago as a diplomat?"

Jane nodded. It had been Chief Manteo's first trip to London, as well.

"Well, some questioned whether the two of them arrived at the Queen's Court of their own volition, saying they were persuaded by...ah...the barrel of a rifle."

"Indeed? That would be enough to persuade me." Sarcasm laced Jane's words, even as alarm gathered in her chest.

"Aye. Me, too. As it turns out, the English explorers thought it would be a great lark to display the two of them at Court alongside the bushels of corn, copper trinkets, and felled trees they'd carted from the New World. Figured their presence might help inspire the investments needed to fund the next colonial venture."

Jane listened in growing horror to the rest of the story. Apparently, the English explorers had paraded the two native Virginians before their Queen and her Court to gawk at, except Wanchese had been uncooperative. He'd refused to participate in their parties or adhere to their customs. Fortunately for him, he and his cousin were sorely needed as guides on the next colonial venture and were allowed to return to their homeland a year later. Instead of remaining at the English fort to serve as a guide, however, Wanchese escaped shortly after the ships dropped anchor.

Jane grimaced when her friend finished speaking. "What you're trying to say is, we are truly doomed."

She shrugged, green eyes wide. "According to Manteo, his cousin will not fight us so long as we leave the island with haste. Wanchese gave his word."

Jane sniffed. "And if his braves somehow manage to prevent us from leaving the island by keeping us barricaded here? He won't exactly be breaking his word, then, will he?" She hunched over her rifle and squinted to ensure her barrel was aimed for the tree line.

War was coming. They might as well accept that fact and be ready for it.

*anchese and his men never attacked, though. The strange, red-painted warriors had. So why had Wanchese pursued the colonists to the Great Trading Path? What was he planning?

He remained at the edge of the tent city with his arms folded, taking in the flurry of activity. Abruptly he ceased studying the English and began to circulate the camp. He paused on occasion to speak with the braves who hustled around like a bevy of page boys. Each time Wanchese pointed in the direction of the English colonists, the young men gestured to the important man at the front of the crowd.

Jane had all but forgotten about him. When her gaze flickered in his direction once more, his unwavering stare alarmed her. By all that was holy, the man was at least twice her age, old enough to be her father. Yet his dark eyes glittered with an emotion that made her heart sink. Lust.

The filthy lecher. "Please, God!" she muttered. "Let it not come to that for me." She much preferred to endure hard labor, to live on meager rations, and to bide her time for the right opportunity to escape. She would just as soon not suffer her time in captivity while lying on her back.

Young Robert Ellis sold next. Jane wanted to press her hands to her ears to shut out his frantic cries for his absent father as he was separated from their group. Her tied hands prevented her. Instead, she tried to memorize every detail of the sordid transaction. Like Rose, who had served as the clerk for their colony on the ship ride over, Jane possessed an impeccable memory.

Instead of numbers, however, she was skilled at remembering faces, emotions, and details others often overlooked. Like the slightly paler skin of the men who purchased James, William, and George. These men were unaccustomed to the sun. Her gaze fell on the matching copper pendants they wore. Those were details that might prove useful.

Baby Virginia sold for a wild-eyed, snarling hound. Under different circumstances, Jane would have been appalled. Before God and man, a healthy human babe was worth so much more than a dog. Then again, nothing made sense anymore.

Between the sale of Edward Powell and Richard Berry,

Wanchese recaptured Jane's attention. Something in his keen, dark gaze cut through the horror of the hour and steadied her. Perhaps it was no more than the distraction of wondering what the man was up to, for surely their greatest enemy in the New World had not journeyed all the way to the Great Trading Path without cause. Despite his familial connection to Manteo, however, Jane harbored no hope of rescue — certainly not with how quickly her comrades were being sold.

Come to think of it, it was awfully strange for a man of Wanchese's stature to travel alone. She recalled the number of *cockarooses* who traveled with Chief Manteo. As best as she could tell, they served as both council members and body-guards to their beloved leader. Wanchese, too, served as the chief of his tribe. Where were his *cockarooses?*

The passage of time blurred and slowed. Rays of sun licked at her skin until it stung. Her eyes danced with spots from its unforgiving glare. She spiraled towards thirst and delirium, and her legs trembled from the effort to remain standing. Soon, she remained alone on the platform.

In slow, dreamlike movements, the native elder drew abreast of the stage and signaled his bid to the auctioneer. Kokoko walked to the furthermost edge of the platform and held up his arms for silence. He spoke loudly, gesturing first at Jane and then towards the aged warrior. She saw a few shrugs in the audience, a handful of hurried words exchanged amongst neighbors, but no one else approached the stage. Kokoko stepped back and reached for her hand.

In that same moment, Wanchese emerged from the throng to stand before the platform next to her would-be purchaser. He raised an arm and shouted something at the auctioneer.

A collective gasp rose from the audience.

Jane was stunned as she watched him join the bidding. She fought a wave of dizziness.

It appeared that Wanchese, Chief of the Roanokes, king of their greatest enemies, was attempting to acquire her as his slave.

CHAPTER 3: SOLD

The aged warrior stepped closer to Wanchese, spewing words. His hands were a blur of abrupt signals. Wanchese gave him a slight bow of acknowledgement and otherwise appeared unmoved. When the elder man waved his arms again, his cloak slipped to one side, revealing a set of bear claws etched to his upper arm.

Well, dash my buttons! It had to be more than a coincidence. If they possessed a family or tribal connection, why then did they argue like competitors over the ownership of a mere slave?

Jane's strength continued to wane as the two men clashed over her price, but she remained very much aware each time Wanchese raised his hand and kept the bidding alive. When her knees began to shake, she gritted her teeth and focused on his copper visage. She did not want to miss a single gesture or expression.

Perhaps delirium seized her, because she found herself utterly mesmerized by the stunning creatures who fought to purchase her. Standing no more than a few strides from the platform, Wanchese was a complex study of hard lines and angles behind his painted mask. Tall, broad of shoulders, and arms banded with muscle, he moved with the careless assurance of a Greek god. His opponent's shoulders, on the other hand, stooped a bit and his skin creased with age, yet he carried himself with the same pride bordering on arrogance.

Wanchese tipped his face up to address Kokoko. The richness of his wine-colored eyes made Jane suck in a breath. Keen calculation. Pure cunning. He knew what he wanted, and he was confident in receiving it. It was not the lazy, over-confidence born of conceit, but a bone-deep sort of persistence that would settle for nothing less than his goal.

Not unlike herself. *Egad! Where did that thought come from?*

Despite the heightened color of his opponent's visage indicating his growing anger, Wanchese remained in firm control of his emotions. She sensed he was taking pleasure in needling the older man. Oddly, she found humor in this.

How she would have enjoyed completing their match of wits back on Roanoke Island. It would have been fascinating to pursue him through the wilderness and be pursued by him, to engage him as huntress to hunter, woman to man, to receive the full heat of his gaze on her when she reigned victorious.

She shook herself and blinked to clear the haze from her eyes. Such nonsense could only be the result of her growing delirium.

Throughout the bidding, Wanchese was all business. He ceased looking at her. After a while, it almost seemed as if he was losing interest in the exchange, altogether.

The elder man paused to confer with one of his lackeys. He nodded and shot a hand in the air with another bid. Wanchese shook his head, his stoic expression breaking into disbelief. At last, his gaze flickered to Jane. Perhaps she imagined it, but she caught a note of satisfaction in him before he turned and stormed into the throng.

Did this signify an end to his bidding? Several moments passed, and Wanchese did not return. Had he given up his negotiations?

Jane frowned in unaccountable disappointment before growing angry with herself. *What is wrong with me?* The fact she would not become the personal property of her greatest enemy should have pleased her.

Brooding, she paid no mind to whatever price traded hands between Kokoko and her new owner. It no longer mattered. She stared straight ahead and tried not to flinch when two lanky braves drew abreast of her to clap a heavy copper choker around her neck. A sharp tug on the adornment set her stumbling toward the stairs.

Mercy! One of them was actually leading her by a chain, as if she was a dog. The neck piece settled thick and heavy on her collar bone.

Her new captors pulled her into the crowd which, to her amazement, parted for them. Hands reached out to brush her arms and legs. Dark eyes peered at her with curiosity and interest.

They approached the group of short, red-painted warriors who had captured her and delivered her to the slave trading block. She tilted her head high, refusing to cower before them. Just as she started to pass by Skull Face, he reached out and yanked her hair none too gently. It swiveled her in his direction, forcing them to stand face to face.

A small cry of anguish escaped her — not because of the physical discomfort he'd caused her but because of her personal collection of knives which were strapped across his chest. All three had been gifts from her father. She lunged for them with her bound hands, but he tossed her aside as if she weighed no more than a sack of turnips. She tumbled to the ground, gagging at the pull of the choker and furious with how easily he had dispatched her in her weakened state.

When Skull Face drew a meaty fist back to strike, one of her new owner's lackeys protested and stepped between the two of them. Wanchese reappeared in the same instant.

He gaze settled on Skull Face with deadly intent. Skull Face took a step back, pivoted away from the group, and bounded for the tree line. Without hesitation, Wanchese followed.

Jane tasted despair as the men disappeared into the forest.

Her escorts led her to the tallest conical tent in the center of the community. Fat buffalos were painted in full gallop across its exterior walls. Smoke seeped from a vent at the topmost peak. Fresh thick swirls puffed to the sky in rapid unison. Someone inside must have stoked the fire.

It was not until her captors brushed aside the deerskin door flap that the events of the day fully sank into her bones. She had been sold. In her twenty and four years on this earth, she had known poverty and hunger, tragedy and loss, hard work and sacrifice, but she had always been her own person. Free to hunt and trap and run and explore. Until now.

She did not know what lay in store for her inside the crude structure and was suddenly opposed to finding out. The choker tightened around her neck like a noose, making it difficult to breathe. She sagged to her knees, unable to take another step.

"Water," she gasped and slumped forward.

Men shouted and hands raised her by her elbows, but she was powerless to do more than watch them through sluggish lids that refused to open all the way.

Something rough and leathery pressed against her lips. A berry flavored substance trickled into her mouth and down her chin. She gulped and swallowed, reaching for more. Her bonds loosened and fell away. Hands travelled up and down the length of her, rubbing the circulation back into her wrists and ankles, tapping and probing for injuries. More water trickled into her mouth.

Then someone lifted her. The scalding sunlight faded, and the scent of smoke intensified. She perceived she was inside the tent, at last. It took a moment for her vision to adjust. When it did, she could not have received a greater shock.

A lone woman of uncertain years tended the fire with a fierce-looking knife strapped to her waist. Crouched beyond her bent figure in a semi-circle against the far wall were James, William, George, and Blade. They stared up at her, jaws dropping in a shock that mirrored her own.

A surge of wild delight shook Jane as her captor set her down in front of them.

Bound at the wrists and ankles, they perused her anxiously.

She nodded to ensure them she was unharmed and offered a tremulous smile, which turned into a gasping shudder as emotion overcame her. She blinked, horrified to have them witness her in such an undone state. Fortunately, not enough water was left inside her to form the salty requirement for tears.

George sprang to his feet and hobbled toward her. "Mistress Jane. Are you—"

In one fluid motion, the woman at the fire straightened and leaped behind him, her knife at his neck. Three lackeys burst into the tent. They converged on the lad with their cudgels, and George fell senseless to the floor.

Jane studied him, agonized until she noted his chest rise and fall. He was breathing, which meant he was alive. *Thank the good Lord!* Bending her head, she fought to tamp down on the hysteria rising in her throat. Blast the lad's impulsive nature!

When she raised her head, she realized her mistake in

assuming all three of the native lackeys were male. The smallest one was a very young female whom the others addressed as Odina. Boasting no more than thirteen or fourteen years, she boasted a boyishly slender figure, which accounted for the original error concerning her gender. Strands of copper beads adorned her neck, and her straight black hair fell past her shoulders in two thick plaits. A deerskin skirt grazed her knees with a beaded fringe.

Resentment pooled in her sooty eyes as they skittered over Jane. In addition to her bitterness and anger, her skin was a ruddier shade of copper than her comrades, indicating some sort of variance in tribal backgrounds. Jane began to wonder if she and her fellow colonists were the only ones being held against their will.

Odina grudgingly poured a pasty porridge-like substance inside of a series of gourd halves and thrust them at the English slaves. She ladled the porridge from a wooden pot, which rested next to the fire. The contents were heated by hot rocks she drew from the fire with tongs and plopped into it.

The porridge smelled foul and tasted as bitter as tree roots. Initially, Jane wondered if they were being poisoned, but she was too hungry to refuse the sustenance.

Odina slapped George's face and shoulders to rouse him. He sat up, groggy at first, then consumed the meager fare as if starved.

Jane ducked her head, angry and ashamed. Despite all her efforts to hunt and trap, the English colonists continued to go hungry. Too few had been willing to help her gather food, accustomed to relying on servants back in London to tend their needs. In the end, most of her comrades had proven ill-prepared to eke out a living in this strange new world.

Once they emptied the gourds, Odina passed around another skin of water.

James cleared his throat to get Jane's attention, but she shook her head. Speaking would only earn him the kiss of a cudgel. Now was not the time. They were too well guarded and too weak in their current state. There would be no escaping today.

Best to spend their time learning everything they could about their new captors. She studied the interior of the tent from beneath her lashes as she ate and was taken aback at its size. It was larger than it appeared from the outside and furnished in an odd but lavish manner. A low platform covered in a wealth of glossy black furs skirted the outer wall. Thin reed mats lined the floor. Baskets of all shapes and sizes, brightly painted earthenware pots, and long wooden spoons hung from the frame poles. Like the exterior, deerskin canvases draped the interior walls and depicted more hunting scenes.

As she took in her surroundings, the horror of the day pressed down like a sodden blanket. She tried and failed to block out the image of the wailing infant Tomas being separated from Audrey. The agonized faces of Beth and Ambrose Viccars also haunted her. It had been almost unbearable to witness them pulled ruthlessly apart and sold to different owners.

It was a dark day for the would-be colonists of the City of Raleigh, but a good number of them still lived. That had to count for something. Their betrayers who had sailed with them from Portsmouth intended for them to be dead by now, yet here they were, eating and drinking and drawing breath. A few days ago, they'd been running out of food and would have buried their first victims of starvation soon. Perhaps the God of her Puritan friends did, indeed, move in mysterious ways, as they liked to claim.

"Ireh! Ireh!"

After the long march to the Great Trading Path, Jane

recognized this dreaded command all too well. It meant it was time to get up and start moving again. So much for her attempt to cajole herself into a happier frame of mind. She expelled a huff of sheer exhaustion as the sharp command was repeated. Their short-lived rest was over.

It was impossible not to stare at the intricate pattern of circles painted across the speaker's chest and torso or the long zig-zagging lines etched down the entire length of his legs. Odina addressed him as Hassun.

He pitched his free-flowing dark hair over one shoulder and raised a sinewy arm for emphasis as he continued to bellow at the captives. "Ireh! Ireh!"

She jerked to her feet and swallowed a gasp of pain. Longing for her well-worn leather boots, she tried not to think of the blisters tearing through the soles of her bare feet. *Tarnation!* A body could only go so far in this condition. If she incurred enough cuts and bruises, infection would soon set in. She shot a scowl at the backs of Hassun and Odina. *Fools! A farmer takes better care of his cattle.*

She and her comrades hobbled into the unforgiving sunlight where temporary blindness struck them. Their new captors urged them over a stretch of rocky terrain, through the woods, and to the river's edge. She searched out each landmark she could recall from their trek here. To her left, a narrow brook gurgled and fed into the river.

She glanced around, expecting to be herded into a bevy of canoes. Instead, their captors led them knee-deep into the river, itself. They expelled a collective breath of relief as the cool water lapped over their raw, scraped feet. At Hassun's order, several of the lackeys shed their moccasins and hopped in the water with them. They motioned for the colonists to sit on the river bank with their feet dangling. They proceeded to rub a white greasy substance over their soles. It was easy to forgive the foul scent of the grease due to the rapid easing of their discomfort.

The back of Jane's neck prickled. Her pa, God rest his soul, used to say she possessed an extra sense. It had come in handy during their hunts, because she nearly always detected the presence of others — be it man or animal — before they made themselves known. Once, it had given them just enough advance warning to protect themselves from the attack of a cougar.

She tossed a wary glance over her shoulder. A single shivering tree branch confirmed her suspicions. Someone was watching them. What was it with these natives? They forever stalked and lay in wait to ambush each other. She offered up a silent prayerful plea that no more Englishmen would die today.

Next, their captives distributed unadorned moccasins. Jane pulled on the soft leather shoes, surprised at how well they fit, even though their feet had not been measured in advance. They were so much lighter weight than her work boots. She fervently hoped they would offer some modicum of protection from the rocks and snarl of exposed tree roots festering atop the parched ground.

"Ireh! Ireh!" Hassun commanded again.

Jane took her time rising in order to finish drawing a Maltese Cross in the dust at the river bank. It would not last long in the hot breeze, but it was the best she could do for now. Not wishing to draw attention to her hasty plea for help, she kept her face forward as they trudged away from the river. Most unfortunately, Hassun ordered their hands and ankles retied as soon as they entered the forest.

Dreary green shoots of light filtered down, and raucous birds called overhead. One barked out a mocking laugh. Jane was grateful for the moccasins as the crackling brown leaves shifted and rattled around them in the breeze. At least she hoped it was only the breeze that sent them dancing. No doubt the forest was teaming with snakes.

The familiar itch of awareness crawled along the back of her neck and down her shoulder blades. She tensed in dreaded anticipation for their followers to reveal themselves. The terrain grew steeper and rockier as they ascended into the foothills of a mountain range. The oaks and pines of the lower lying forests merged into stately evergreens bearing holly, razor-sharp firs that stabbed the sky, and enormous red spruces.

Then the trees grew scarce, and they entered a hillside clearing where the evidence of a previous settlement remained. No structures stood, but the earth contained several flat circles where the bottom side of the hill had been built up to match the level of the top side. She imagined teepees had once rested on these circles.

They cut across the clearing to an even steeper path. Here they were forced to march single file around massive, jutting boulders. Jane heaved in the effort to fill her lungs but could not seem to get enough air. Thin air, her father had called it on the days they ventured high in the mountains of northern England.

Her legs ached from the effort of pressing onward and upward, but it grew blessedly cooler as they ascended. Minutes bled into hours before they arrived, at last, to a bustling village set deep in the mountainside. It was a spectacular sight with multi-storied dwellings carved into ridges that stretched and disappeared into low hanging clouds. What natural beauty! What keen craftsmanship!

Guilt flooded Jane. In London, these structures would have been deemed masterpieces. In her conceit, she had presumed their slave owners had purchased them for their skills in masonry and construction. One thing was very apparent now. The English would not be building this tribe new homes, because they already dwelt in castles.

Man-made plateaus protruded and held a series of domed structures extending thirty feet or more. According to Rose's husband, Chief Manteo, they were called longhouses and contained several families apiece. Smoke curled from vents in their roofs.

Long, straight rows of corn, beans, and other vegetation streaked down the mountain on either side of the village in tiny flattened tiers that resembled gigantic stairs. It was astonishing how this tribe had managed to carve out a luxurious existence for themselves here. And the view! It was like standing on the edge of the world and looking out.

Jane's heart thudded with dread. It was a defensible location, too. Most defensible, indeed. She and her fellow captives would not easily escape this place.

The village vibrated with activity. Cooking fires dotted the village, and wide vats of stew simmered inside hollowed-out logs. The scent of venison wafted her way. Women used long-handled ladles to draw red, glowing rocks from the fire and plunged them into the vats. Bubbles rose where the stones sank.

Odina stalked up to her. "*Cumear.*" She beckoned for her to follow.

Jane glanced at James, who eyed the teen with distrust.

"*Cumear!*" Odina repeated sharply.

When Jane continued to feign misunderstanding, Hassun shoved her in Odina's direction. *Aha. She was following his orders.* She trudged after the young woman reluctantly. Her hostility was thick enough to cut with a dagger and growing by the second.

She led Jane away from the village, around the vast steep gardens, and up to a stream that gurgled down the ridge. *So this is how they irrigate their crops.* A grove of white ash trees rose in the distance. The tips of them disappeared into the clouds.

Dressed in the same manner as Odina, two other young maidens awaited them. Strands of beads graced their necks, and fringed skirts fell to their knees. Their black eyes snapped with an ire that matched Odina's. What were they so incensed about? Jane would have better understood a dismissive or condescending manner, which seemed more fitting for a slave.

Her extra sense of perception flared to life, when one of the young women pulled out a knife and sliced the bonds holding her wrists together. Then she bent and severed the ropes at her ankles. Odina immediately grabbed her hair and swung her around. She delivered the first punch, straight to the face.

On raw instinct, Jane twisted away and whirled to send a bruising slice to Odina's upper arm. It loosened her hold on her hair, but a fist from behind slammed into Jane's rib cage, making it painful to breath. She kicked at Odina to put space between them and whirled again.

Fists and feet flew as the women attacked in unison. Alas, Jane's defense held less than its normal ferocity. Fueled by nothing more than a rapid burst of righteous anger, her strength quickly waned. She panted for air and blocked one blow after another. One hit finally sank home against her cheek, driving her backward.

She staggered to one side, in the effort to remain on her feet. Waves of dizziness shook her. The three women circled for a moment, ugly intent written on their features as they closed in.

A male voice shouted. Hassun and his braves ran down the mountainside. The women dropped their fighting stance, bristling at the newcomers.

Jane dazedly perceived she'd been saved from a disfiguring beating and ran her hand over her face to assess her injuries. A sizable lump on her cheekbone rose beneath her fingers.

An older woman followed close behind the men. She chastised Jane's attackers until two dropped their heads in shame. Not so with Odina. She tossed a final hateful glance in Jane's direction and flounced off.

She stared after the young women. *Faith! I will have to watch my back with this trio.*

The elder woman plunged her into the cool stream. Too spent from the fight, Jane did not resist her ministrations. She proceeded to scrub her hair, muttering to herself as she massaged oil into her scalp. By the time she finished, Jane was shivering from the cool temperature of the water.

She motioned for Jane to stand and dry in the sun. Then she bade her don a fringed skirt and kneel in it. She drew a comb of bone through her long, chestnut hair and tossed aside the remaining cockleburs she had failed to dislodge during her bath. Weaving two sleek braids, she secured them with strands of brown cord. Next she tucked a flower behind Jane's ear and adjusted it carefully, still muttering to herself. Jane suspected she was attempting to hide the massive bruise on her cheek, which was strange. Who would care if a slave sported a bruise or two?

When the woman led her back to camp, James, William, George, and Blade were nowhere in sight. Odina and her cronies were absent, as well. The mountain people watched Jane curiously. She met their questioning gazes, searching for answers of her own. What did they intend to do with her and her comrades?

"Dasan." The word whispered its way through the crowd. Men and women, alike, snapped to attention as the aged warrior from the slave-trading block appeared. Hassun stood by his side. Several more braves fanned out behind the pair like a royal guard.

Maidens and braves scrambled to their knees and bent their faces to the dirt, but he did not acknowledge their lauding. He had eyes only for Jane.

She shivered at the lust in his gaze. *Tarnation!* Whatever he was thinking, she wanted nothing to do with it. She tried to take a step back, but the woman who'd bathed her maintained a firm grasp on her elbow. She propelled her toward the vast stone structure carved into the mountainside.

Two men stood guard, one on either side of the entrance. At the woman's sharp bidding, they drew aside the door covering. She shoved Jane inside but did not follow.

She scooted to the far end of the long room and faced the door. She was alone. No fire crackled here, but plenty of sunlight poured through several small, square openings overhead. Unfortunately, they were too high for her to reach and too small to climb through. Deerskin canvases graced the interior stone walls. In the center of the room, a long platform boasted a thick pile of furs. It was a bed.

Cold acceptance filled her. This was the end, for she knew she would rather die than play the role Dasan intended for her. He was old enough to be her father and perhaps her grandfather. She scanned the meagerly furnished room for something that might serve as a weapon.

The door covering swept aside once more, and Chief Dasan entered. She trembled as dark eyes set in a leathery face roved over her person. He whispered something in his guttural tongue and raised and lowered his hand slowly. Eyes never leaving her, he removed his headdress of many feathers and hung it on a peg next to the entrance. Then he stepped from his moccasins. His hands went to the rope at his waist, and he loosened the ties of his buckskins.

His movements confirmed her worst fears. Her knees

trembled. She felt soiled already by the mere thought of him trying to bed her.

There must be a way out! There always is. Or was in the past. Then her mind emptied of all thoughts save one — the safety of her English comrades. She wondered where in this hellish city they were being held.

Dasan lowered the first leg of his buckskins.

She met the determined gaze of her owner, somehow summoning the resolve to endure her plight. However, he would have to wrestle her into submission first. *No way will I lie meekly on that blasted platform without a fight!* Her fingers flexed in anticipation.

Dasan's eyes dropped to her hands. Resignation flickered in his weathered features. He withdrew a coil of hemp cord from the band at his waist. She had missed it, because it had been tucked behind him when he entered.

Still, he would need to tie her. She braced for a struggle.

"Hassun." He did not raise his voice, but Hassun and three other braves slipped inside the dwelling. They quickly subdued her by securing her limbs to the corners of the sleeping platform.

Dasan motioned them away, and the men vanished as silently as they had appeared. He surveyed her in satisfaction. The light of passion rekindled in his gaze as he loosened the ties of his second legging.

She averted her face. *This cannot possibly be happening to me.*

Though there was no fire in the room, the scent of smoke settled over them. Dasan knelt beside her and reached for her with a sigh of longing.

The smoke thickened. She coughed to clear her lungs and blinked as her eyes began to sting.

A scream split the silence. "*Bocuttaw!*"

"Fire!" James cried from somewhere nearby. "Jane! Where are you?"

Chief Dasan shot her a frustrated look and rose. Slinging a cape around his shoulders, he ducked from the room.

Moments later, a wicked blade sliced through the canvas door covering. Wanchese appeared, a reckless glint in his red-gold eyes.

"You?" she stared, dumbfounded. "What—"

"Come," he said simply.

He intends to rescue me? The chief of our most hostile neighbors? Instantly suspicious, she wheezed between fits of coughing, "As you can see, I am detained. Perhaps you might lend me a blade."

Instead of handing over his knife, he sprang to her side and slashed the bonds away.

Shaken, she sat up, babbling, "A few seconds more and it would have been too late." She slapped at her wrists and stomped at the floor to ease the tingling in her ankles, but her legs refused to hold her when she tried to stand.

Wanchese grunted in disgust and half-dragged, half-carried her from the room. Outside, the air billowed with smoke and frantic shouts. The sentries who guarded the door lay crumpled on their sides, eyes closed. Dogs barked in the distance.

"Ungrateful wench!" her rescuer declared in perfect English as he swung her over his shoulder and broke into a run. "I was not late. I arrived just in time."

"Pray pardon," she gasped. "Of course you did. I did not mean to—" but her words were cut off as he increased his pace. She clung to him. *Drat the man for assuming I am ungrateful!* She was grateful. More grateful than words could express, apparently, for she could not seem to form any intelligent phrases at the moment.

Feet pounded behind them as they fled the village and

plunged down the mountain into a mass of spruces. They grew so close together, Wanchese had to slow his pace to maneuver around some of the clusters. Needles and branches raked her arms and stung the backs of her knees.

"They follow us." The words gasped out of her. It was difficult to speak with her mid-section grinding against his massive shoulder.

"Aye," he retorted, not the least bit winded for the pace he was keeping.

"Pray set me down," she groaned as he ran. Carrying her would only slow his progress, and she was about to be sick from the constant jab of his shoulder against her stomach. With the tingling gone from her feet, she should be able to run on her own now.

Wanchese merely tightened his hold and continued to run. As they neared the base of the mountain, a river drew into view. It snaked its way between the ridges, frothing and swirling a path through the foothills.

Alas, they did not make it to the water before she began to gag.

Wanchese muttered something and set her on her feet at the river's edge. He tore furiously through the side of a thicket and uncovered a canoe.

With a cry of excitement, she rushed to grab one end of the craft.

Wanchese shot her a look of irritation and bore most of the weight. However, she maintained her token hold on the craft and ran with him to the water's edge. He stepped inside and motioned for her to do likewise.

She complied and reached for one of the oars, but he snatched them up.

The footsteps behind them thundered nearer.

"Give me an oar lest we perish at the hands of our

pursuers," she snapped and beckoned wildly. She swiped the air, but he moved the oar out of reach.

Nay." He tossed it behind her.

She whirled, incredulous. James hurtled their way at a full gallop, his rugged features alight with concern and exhilaration. He caught the oar in mid-air as he leaped into the canoe. Directly behind him were George and his lanky younger friend, Blade. William trailed slightly after the teens. *Bless him*! His wide legs pumped against the ground faster than she thought him capable of moving, his bald head glistening with sweat.

The lads bade William climb in first, shoved off from the coastline, then catapulted into the canoe behind him.

CHAPTER 4: NEW MASTER

Jane leaned over the side of the boat and splashed water on her face, reveling in their restored freedom. She searched for the right words to thank Wanchese, but nothing simple sprang to mind. The younger lads trailed their hands in the water with wonder. William glanced anxiously at the shoreline from whence they'd set sail, but Wanchese and James stared straight ahead and paddled with all their might.

The only sound that met their ears was the rushing current. The water was deeper here, the terrain greener and less affected by the drought that had plagued the islands and coastal areas throughout the summer months.

She hunched forward, clenching her arms over her mangled bodice. Wanchese in the bow and James in the stern skillfully maneuvered the canoe around jutting rocks and fallen trees. The rest of them huddled in the center of the craft.

It seemed strange they were not being pursued. No figures emerged from the trees behind them. No arrows arched in their direction. Nothing but smoke gushed from the mountainside. It formed a seething gray canopy over Chief Dasan's village, blotting it from view.

"Did you set the mountain, itself, on fire?" Jane was horrified on behalf of all the wild critters who called it home.

Wanchese shot a glance at the tree line but continued to row.

"Look again, lass," admonished James with a shake of his graying head. "'Tis a clever trick, an' we owe him our lives for the knowing of it."

She squinted at the scene behind them. Truth be told, she could see nothing but vast billows of smoke. If a fire existed, it was masterfully set, else the acres of dry foliage would be shooting up in flames, by now. Somehow Wanchese had created a frothing smoke screen.

The rescue still made no sense. "Why did you come for us?" she persisted. "I thought all you wanted was to remove us from your island."

Wanchese gave a grunt of disgust.

She scowled at James. "And you. How did you know to follow Wanchese? That he intended to rescue us?"

James snorted. "When a man pulls out a knife and cuts away yer bonds instead of sticking it into yer gullet—"

"He kept saying your name," Blade offered, his freckled face alight with boyish adulation. "Jane. Jane. Jane. So we jes' chased after 'em until we reached the boat."

"I say, Mistress Jane." William glanced up shyly, his round face still pink from exertion. "Why ever were you summoned to the mountain chief's chambers?"

Heat flooded her cheeks. The poor man was endearingly obtuse, but he meant no harm. He was genuinely curious.

"I, er, well, I suppose we shall never know, shall we? Chief Wanchese most fortunately arrived before…" Her voice dwindled at the memory of Dasan removing his buckskins. She brushed the hair from her forehead with a shaky hand.

A tap on her bare shoulder had her tensing.

"Pray pardon," George said tersely and tossed a cloak on her lap. "I found this in the belly of the boat."

She nodded gratefully. He was far too world-wise for a fifteen-year-old in certain matters. Far too perceptive.

Not wishing to lower her arm, which was holding the pieces of her bodice together, she glanced around to discover all the eyes of her comrades were averted. Exhaling slowly, she shrugged into the surprisingly delicate garment and peeked at Wanchese from beneath her lashes. The cloak fit perfectly over her narrow shoulders, which meant it was not intended for a man to wear. Had he tucked it into his canoe with her in mind? If so, a rather keen amount of forethought had gone into the planning of their rescue. The notion left her breathless.

He spared her a brief, probing look after she donned the cloak. Approval glinted from the depths of his mahogany gaze as his eyes dipped lower to take in her bare calves. For the second time that day, she was the recipient of a blatant display of male admiration. In this part of the world, apparently spinsters were not looked upon with the dispassion to which she was accustomed. *At least not the half-naked ones.*

Her breathing hitched in discomfort. "I thank you," she muttered, trying to tuck her long limbs beneath her.

"Remove your eyes from her at once!" George demanded, with a fierce look at Wanchese.

Taken aback, Jane rested her hand on the lad's shoulder. "He means no harm, George. Their ways differ from ours, is all."

George scrubbed at the dark stubble on his chin. "Some gestures are the same in any language," he grumbled, but his shoulder relaxed beneath her grip. "Rescuing us gives him no right to take liberties with you."

She rolled her eyes. *Heavens!* What would the lad do if he

knew how close she'd come to warming Chief Dasan's blankets?

Fourteen-year-old Blade inclined his upper body in her direction. His lean face was smudged and his blue-gray eyes bright with anxiety. His sandy hair could sorely use a trim. It swept his shoulders in tangled ringlets. "Where are we heading, Mistress Jane?"

It was a good question. Even William raised his flushed face to hear her response. Thus far, he'd done little more than huddle in his section of the canoe. A painfully shy man of middling years, he was likely mortified over the wretched repair of his garments. His shirt gaped open across his belly, and one leg of his pants was torn off at the knee.

As far as she could tell, Wanchese had not yet revealed his command of their language to her English comrades. She wondered how long he planned to continue his charade. "Chief Wanchese," she said cautiously. "Pray enlighten us on our intended destination."

His head swiveled at the mention of his name, but he otherwise showed no understanding of her question. She tried again, more bluntly this time. "Where are you taking us, my lord?"

James raised a set of bushy brows. "Mayhap you could try sign language? I don't believe his understandin' of our English is, er..."

She sniffed, having little use for such shenanigans. *Tarnation!* The man had spent an entire year serving as a diplomat in Queen Elizabeth's Court. He could likely speak more eloquent English than James and William.

"Chief Wanchese, will you take us..." She fought to control the sarcasm in her voice as she gestured to include each colonist. Then she mimed the act of rowing a boat. "To our people at Roanoke Island?"

He shrugged noncommittally, though she knew he understood her question. Perhaps, though, he did not know the status of the English colonists who still resided there.

She pictured Reverend Christopher Cooper and the third wave of colonists he was supposed to lead to the mainland. None of them had been present at the slave trading block. Had Agnes, Margaret, and Emme made it back on their raft to warn him, then? Had the third and last group managed to evade their attackers, altogether? She prayed it was so, because she did not care to think of the alternative explanations for their absence.

"If not Roanoke, are you taking us to the Isle of Croatoa, then?" she asked hopefully. It was where Manteo lived.

This time Wanchese gave a definitive negative shake of his head.

Alarmed, she searched for another name. "Dasamonquepeuc?" It was the village on the mainland where Wanchese had relocated his people after the arrival of the English, though she had no interest whatsoever in traveling to Dasamonquepeuc and dealing directly with their hostile neighbors. They'd been through enough already.

This time, he gave a vague shrug, but the knowing glint in his eyes told her she'd struck the heart of his intentions.

"'Tis alright, Jane," James said as he paddled. "He does not understand, but I recognize this river from one o' Governor White's maps. Ne'er fear, lass. We be heading th' right way. An' when we git there, we'll find our people. Jes' see if we don't."

Ah, James. Bless your optimism. She studied the river. She, too, recognized their location, and it most certainly would take them to Roanoke. It would also take them to Dasamonquepeuc, which was en route to Roanoke.

Two things were suddenly and fearfully clear to her. The Roanoke tribe had not yet returned to their home on Roanoke Island — not good — and Wanchese did not intend to deliver them there — not good at all. Something or someone still prohibited his people from returning there. Exhaustion seeped through her limbs. She needed to get Wanchese away from her comrades, and soon, so they could speak freely.

*A*s the mountain and its foothills faded into distant smoke, the dusty lowlands sucked them back into their cauldron of dry heat. Gaunt trees bare of leaves stretched over the edges of the river, as if by some miracle their exposed roots might find relief in the ever-receding waters below. Now and then, a brittle branch snapped like a gunshot in the scorching wind and crashed into the water.

The sun fell beneath the horizon in a blood red streak of protest, and still they paddled on ward. James, William, and the two lads took turns with one paddle to draw out the last of their collective strength, while Wanchese kept a brutal pace with the other. To Jane's intense irritation, her comrades decided to resort to their starchy English ways, treating her like a dratted lady and refusing to let her take a turn. As the evening lengthened into night, white moonlight poured over their boat, accentuating the lines of exhaustion on everyone's faces.

"The men need rest," Jane declared.

Wanchese shot a scathing glance over his shoulder without slowing his pace. Two identical scars about a hand's width apart rippled and flexed on his upper back as he rowed.

Anger curdled in her gut at his curt dismissal of her words. *Egad!* What was it about the man that seemed to bring out the worst in her? She fought to gentle her tone. "I understand the risks of stopping, but look at them," she pleaded. "The men are spent."

At his continued silence, she snapped, "I would they survive this latest venture, else your efforts to rescue us will be rendered futile."

Wanchese dug in his paddle.

"You thick-headed brute!" she panted and lurched into a standing position on unsteady feet. She intended only to move closer to him so they could continue their conversation with some modicum of privacy.

"Mistress Jane," William groaned as the heavy canoe pitched wildly from side to side. "You should not stand."

"What sort of boat is this?" she spluttered, flapping her arms like a bird to regain her balance. "Burn it all!" She swiped the air in the effort to reach James' outstretched arm, missed, and toppled over the side.

Her first thought was a silent plea they would stop the boat and not leave her behind. Her second thought was that the water was much cooler than expected for such a sultry night.

Her limbs were blessedly unencumbered by the thick, worsted wool skirts she normally wore. She had no trouble scissor kicking to propel herself upward. Instead of returning to the surface, however, she plunked her head into something solid. Lightning flashed behind her eyelids, and the world went black.

---

*T*he scent of smoke awakened her. Jane sniffed in appreciation. "Hickory," she murmured and rolled to her side. It was her father's secret ingredient for his finest venison stew. It had taken her months to dig it out of him. "Pa?"

Her words were greeted with a male sound of derision.

The guttural voice made her eyelids fly open. A dark visage hovered inches away from her face. Bourbon eyes illuminated by flickering firelight peered at her through a grotesquely painted mask.

"Chief Wanchese!" She sat up with a squeak. Pain speared her temple. Fingering the lump rising in her hairline, she flushed at the memory of her tumble into the river. He must think her a useless damsel, not worth half the trouble he had put into the rescuing of her and her comrades.

They were in some sort of cavern. Boulders rose on either side, forming a rocky enclosure. The ceiling dripped with a waxy substance that tapered to form upside down fingers.

"Praise be ta God, ye're awake a' last." James' head whipped around from where he sat guarding the tiny entrance of their sanctuary. When he stood beneath the low ceiling, he was forced to bend his head so his thick, dark beard brushed against his chest. He ambled her way as fast as his stooped posture allowed and offered her a skin of water. "Are you well, lass?"

"Well enough. I thank you." She snatched the skin to her lips. A berry-tasting fluid trickled down her throat. "So good," she murmured between gulps.

"Iffen 'tis all the same ta you, Mistress Jane, seein' as ye survived the bump ta yer noggin' an' all, methinks I'll be a-catchin' some winks now. I can beerly put one foot afore th'..." His voice slurred as he ventured farther into the cavern and stretched out his rangy frame alongside William. The lads were fast asleep on William's other side.

Grateful the men were resting at last, Jane squinted at the entrance. Trying to determine how long she'd slept, she noted the moon suspended in full bloom.

"Foolish woman," Wanchese said. His back was to her as he crouched before a fire. "You nearly capsized the canoe."

They were wildly fortunate she had not, for neither James nor William could swim.

"Pray pardon me," she said, but her words fell short of genuine remorse. Her fall into the river had purchased the rest her comrades so badly needed, and for that she wasn't the least bit sorry. Taking in Wanchese's scowl, she wondered how he'd managed to start and maintain a fire in such a dank environment. She was grateful for the heat and a place for her comrades to sleep.

"You were equally foolish to mistake me for your father. No doubt he is a pale-face like yourself."

She gaped at the vicious bite to his tone. "He is dead, God rest his soul." *A little respect for the deceased would not be amiss.*

"Dead is what you and the men will be if you do not lower your voice," he growled with a quick glance at the cavern opening.

She jerked her gaze to the entrance.

"The slavers passed by here on their way to ambush your people and mine."

"Is that what brought you to the Great Trading Path?" she mused. "How many of yours did they take?"

Wanchese swooped on her in the dim light. "One," he rasped.

She tensed at his sudden nearness and fought to maintain a neutral expression. It would do no good to show fear.

Nose to nose with her, he emitted a sound of disgust. "You will not disobey me again."

"Disobey you!" Did he have any idea how barbaric he sounded?

"You know I intended to travel the entire night." His hard expression brooked no argument.

"Or else?" she taunted, incensed at his high-handedness.

"I will cut out your tongue." But his voice held no venom as he leaned forward and flicked a lock of hair from her eyes.

When his fingertips brushed against the side of her face, her senses leaped to life. She should have reprimanded him for taking such liberties. Instead, she reveled in the heightened awareness of each sight, sound, and scent in the cave.

Holding her gaze, Wanchese stood and stretched leisurely as if to work out the kinks in his neck and back.

Her eyes drank in his massive arms and broad chest that tapered down to a narrow torso. He was nothing like the slender dandies in London who paraded about in excessive amounts of clothing. Nay, this man required no starched shirts and ruffs or padded doublets to enhance his frame. Silk hosiery and buckled shoes would have made a mockery of such unfettered male strength. His sun-bleached buckskins and well-worn moccasins were the only adornments a man of his ilk would ever require.

"You take pleasure in what you see, huh?" He leaned her way again. She rose to her feet and backed up until the wall of the cavern pressed against her shoulder blades.

Of course she liked what she saw, but it would be unladylike in the extreme to admit it. Besides, it was grossly conceited of him to question her in such a manner. She straightened her spine and returned stare for stare. The intensity of his gaze unsettled her.

Though unsmiling, a wealth of emotions radiated from him. Curiosity, interest, desire, and ironclad determination.

"You mean to take me for yourself," she stated in a dull voice. That was the reason he wasn't returning them to Roanoke. They'd merely traded one set of captors for another.

Wanchese placed his hands against the wall on either side of her. "When I am ready, aye."

She sniffed. "Then you are no better than the rest of those savages who—"

"Heathen *and* savage," he corrected tersely. "A phrase I've heard oft enough in your own Queen's Court."

She scowled at the reference to his stint as a diplomat in her homeland. A fine time it was to rub her nose in his superior social status. She had been born into servitude, and her lot had not changed one whit on the other side of the world.

Her chest heaved with the effort to control her alarm. Too tired to fight him off, she searched his face for any sign of human compassion beneath his hard outer shell.

Humor deepened the color of his eyes as he backed away from her and settled himself on the cave floor in one swift movement. Lying back, he cradled his head in clasped hands. "You will come to me."

"Indeed, I will not!" she gasped, both relieved at the distance between them and puzzled by the game he played, a game for which she knew not the rules. "It would be unseemly."

"Aye, you will," he retorted, clearly enjoying himself. "Beneath your finery," he nodded at the remnants of her gown, "is a passionate woman who is accustomed to taking what she wants. It is I, methinks, who will be taken by you and not the other way around."

"You mock me," she accused in a voice barely above a whisper, "for you perceive I am naught but a maid, untrained in the ways of—" She clamped her lips together, furious at how much information the scoundrel had provoked from her.

His gaze narrowed in satisfaction. "Indeed? With so many bruises on your person, it was difficult to determine the extent of your injuries."

It was difficult to determine if he was concerned about

her wellbeing, or merely assessing the condition of his latest acquisition. She nodded warily.

"My cousin will be pleased."

"You speak of Chief Manteo?"

"Aye."

Her shoulders relaxed a fraction. "So he knew of your journey to the Great Trading Path?"

"He is the one who sent me to fetch you."

"Oh," she breathed. "Bless him a thousand times for sending you to rescue us."

"Nay, he only sent me after you."

"Just me?"

"Aye."

"Then why did you retrieve the men and lads as well?"

He shrugged. "Strong backs have their uses."

"What do you intend to do with us?" she demanded.

"I mean for you to earn your keep."

She frowned at his vagueness. "How did Chief Manteo convince you to travel such a distance to rescue a woman you never met?"

"His sole intent, I believe," he said dryly, "was to calm his bride before their wedding night."

Her brows shot up. "He finally married her? Rose Payne, our ship's clerk? With green eyes and red hair nearly down to her knees?"

"Aye."

Her dear friend lived. Delicious relief flooded her chest. "H-how many others?" she choked. She yearned to know the fate of her friends. At the same time, she was terrified of discovering which ones may not have survived and which ones were still missing.

When Wanchese shrugged, she fell atop him, hands slapping against his chest. "Tell me more, blast you! What about the tiny woman with hair so white it looks like spun gold?"

His gaze clashed with hers and held, but all he gave was a curt nod.

Her heart pounded in exhilaration to learn her other closest friend had survived. She leaned closer. "Who else?" She hated how her voice shook.

She described each colonist. To her delight, Wanchese confirmed that Anthony Cage, Lord of Huntington, had also survived. Agnes was sweet on him. Eleanor Dare, daughter of our governor, lived as did her husband, Ananias. Unfortunately, Jane had witnessed their daughter sold on the slave-trading block. It was heartbreaking to know they were missing their newborn tonight.

Reverend Christopher Cooper, the prune-faced spinster Margaret Lawrence, Emme Merrimouth and Mark Bennett who were every bit as sweet on each other as Agnes and Anthony, all lived on the Island of Croatoa with Manteo's people. So did the widow Helen Pierce, young Brose Viccars, and the Harvye babe whose parents Wanchese confirmed were slain in the ambush. There were others, too. Not enough. Nay, not nearly enough, but nigh on thirty names received an affirmative nod from Wanchese.

Even more remarkable, all thirty had found temporary refuge with the Croatoans until they could rebuild the decimated Fort Raleigh on Roanoke Island.

"So Rose and Manteo are married." By now, Jane was grinning like a loon. "By all that is great and good, 'tis the best news I've heard in days, nay months."

"You approve?" He sounded curious.

"Good gracious! They do not need my approval or anyone else's. I've never seen a pair more smitten. Aye, they are in love, and that's all that matters." She clasped his upper arms. "Tell me. How soon can we visit them?" He'd shaken his head earlier when she asked if he would deliver them to Chief Manteo, but surely he would not deny them a visit.

Wanchese sat up, his expression clearing of all emotion. "Hear me well, Jane. I did not promise to deliver you to Manteo or anyone else."

Her smile faltered. "I do not understand."

"I promised only to fetch you from the Great Trading Path. Nothing more."

"You play with words."

"You are alive and no longer enslaved by the mountain people," he retorted. "My word is good."

Fine. He wanted to play with words. For the sake of her sleeping comrades, she would oblige him long enough to uncover the plans he had for them. "You mentioned we would have to earn our keep. How?"

"I have not yet decided. Manteo has enough mouths to feed for the winter already. Plus, there is the matter of properly compensating me for your rescue." He leered down at her hands resting on his arms. "Behold. I said you would come to me, did I not?"

She started to snatch them away, but he caught them and turned her palms upright to examine her bruised wrists.

"Aye, you will come." His voice was low, the glint in his eyes dangerous as he bent to gaze into her eyes. "And when you do, we will take our fill of each other until our lust is sated."

A strangled sound emerged from her throat. This time Wanchese did not stop her when she pulled away.

He stretched his long frame on the ground once more and closed his eyes.

That is all? Blast the man for closing me out when I am still bursting with questions! She crouched beside him a few minutes longer, hoping he would rouse and continue their conversation. When he did not, she huffed in frustration and walked stooped over to James and William. Blade muttered in his sleep and curled into a ball. They looked utterly spent and defenseless. She prayed each of them would wake rested, for she knew not why lay in store for them on the morrow.

Returning to the fire, she lowered herself gingerly to the ground and winced. Every inch of her body hurt. With a breathy sigh, she stretched out as close to the flames as she dared.

"I thank you for stopping," she whispered into the darkness. "The men would not have lasted much longer."

Wanchese's response startled her. "We should have continued on."

He was right, yet the callousness behind his words rankled. The men sleeping just a few yards from them might only amount to a set of strong backs to him, but they were all she had left in the world.

"How much further until we reach Dasamonquepeuc?" She saw no point in keeping up pretenses. She already knew where they were heading.

He shrugged. "A day. Shorter if we had kept moving. Longer if Dasan picks up our trail."

She shivered at the mention of the mountain king's name.

"Are you cold, Jane? Come to me. I will warm you better than the fire."

"You had best hope none of my countrymen overhears you speak to me thus," she snapped. "You will pay dearly if they do."

"Whatever for?" He sounded astonished. "James watches you like a father and knows you are safe. Only George dislikes me, and he is too young to count."

She bit her lip in the darkness at his keen perception.

He continued in a colder tone. "Make certain the young lord understands he is no longer in London. He is rash and foolish, not unlike yourself."

She scowled. George might be impulsive, but he'd begun to understand they were no longer in London the moment his father was so brutally slain by the Roanokes. Wanchese's people. The whole affair was going to be a problem for them upon their arrival to Dasamonquepeuc. She could sense it deep in her bones.

"He should never have sailed with us," she murmured.

"On that we agree. 'Tis a pity all of you did not remain on the other side of the ocean where you belong."

She sighed, thinking of those who had perished and others who were missing. Much as she hated to admit it, even to herself, he was right.

Wanchese grunted and rolled to his side, bringing him much closer than she preferred.

She turned her back to him and tried to find a comfortable position with her aching head resting on her arms. Alas, she'd dropped so much weight since her arrival in the New World, her arms felt like twin bony sticks.

She doubted Wanchese slept, though his breathing evened.

As for herself, she knew it would be impossible to find sleep in such proximity to one of their greatest enemies, so she did not bother to close her eyes. Gazing at the tendrils of their dying fire, she pondered how to extricate the small band of survivors in the cave from their newest dilemma.

"*M*istress Jane." George shook her shoulder. He squatted beside her in the shadows. "The savage has gone and left us. Now is our chance to escape him."

She squinted and rubbed her eyes. "What? Who has abandoned us?"

"I awoke to, er, visit the jakes and discovered Wanchese missing."

Nay, he would not abandon us! Or would he? For a moment, her heartbeat faltered. Then the details of her conversation with Wanchese flooded back.

"Now George," she soothed. "Fear not. He is close by, probably running patrol."

He shook his head. "You mistake my concern, for I do not fear his defection. Quite the opposite. I beseeched the good Lord for such a happy event."

"Why, George!"

"I do not trust his intentions towards us. Now that we are well on our way back to the City of Raleigh, I'd just as soon travel without him."

"Despise him if you must, George, but we require a scout of his caliber, and you know it. We've not exactly done well on our own. Way too many of us have been captured, missing, or… or worse."

He ran a hand through his hair. "We are bound to catch a break sooner or later, Mistress Jane, after a run of such poor luck so far."

She smiled. "Indeed, we are. I say we caught that break when Wanchese came to our rescue."

His mouth settled into a bitter line. "He watches you in the same manner as the mountain king. I do not trust him."

"As Manteo's cousin, he is our best hope of finding our way back to our colony."

"He is also chief over those who killed my father."

"I understand how you feel, George. I truly do." She reached over and squeezed his hand. Pain lanced through her as she conjured up the face of her own father. It was never easy losing a loved one and certainly not in the brutal way George had lost his.

"Nay, you cannot possibly understand, unless…" He paused, searching her face. "Say, Mistress Jane! Did you, er, that is, was your pa killed, too?"

"Aye, and my mother right alongside him in a hunting accident." They'd been mauled by a bear.

He looked aghast. "I had no idea. You've never spoken of them."

"Listen, George. What happened to your father was the worst way imaginable to lose someone you love." She touched his arm. "I reckon we can blame our English soldiers for starting the unfortunate chain of events leading up to it."

Alas, George was in no mood to listen to reason. His grief was too fresh. "My father was innocent. They had no right to exact their revenge on him." He dashed a hand over his eyes.

"It was little more than happenstance," she murmured. "A classic case of being in the wrong place at the wrong time." Assistant Howe had wandered two miles away from his comrades during a crab fishing expedition. He'd been easy pickings for the Roanokes who'd lain in wait for more than a year to avenge their fallen leader.

"Every time I lay eyes on him," George admitted in a tight voice, "I am reminded how he killed my father."

"Nay, he did not. According to Manteo, he was not even present. A handful of angry braves on a hunting trip did the deed."

"I hold him responsible for the actions of his people. You cannot expect otherwise of me, Mistress Jane. He promised Chief Manteo we would be allowed to leave the island, unharmed, and he failed to keep his word."

The first blush of dawn crept past the entrance and stole into the cavern.

She squeezed his hand. "You've a right to be hurt and angry. Just promise me one thing, George. Promise me you understand we are no longer in England. A different set of rules governs this place."

At his stubborn silence, she pressed, "Come now. I've seen

you suffer enough to last me a lifetime. I've no wish to watch you suffer one whit more."

He turned his face away, but not before she witnessed his handsome features twist with anguish. "Aye, Mistress Jane," he said as a shadow fell across the opening of the cave, "I'll not soon forget we dwell in a land rife with godless savages." His voice rose and carried across the cave as he crouched beneath the low ceiling to face the man who entered.

"Ireh!" Wanchese greeted us.

It was a phrase that evoked all too many unpleasant emotions.

Wanchese tossed a sack at George's feet. "Ireh!" His tone was condescending, as if he addressed the lowest of servants.

George scowled when it slapped the ground, but he snatched it up and peered inside. With an incredulous look, he hurried to wake the others. They muttered in delight as they passed around the dry strips of meat from the bag.

Jane nodded at Wanchese as he held out one of the strips to her. He had come prepared. "Again, I thank you."

He inclined his head, unsmiling. No doubt he intended to collect in labor an amount equal to all the trouble he'd taken to rescue them. Regardless, she believed in giving every man the credit due him.

James Hynde was in a jovial mood after a good night's sleep and a bit of food in his belly.

"Mistress Jane," he chortled. "I declare yer the purtiest thing I ever laid eyes on. Fair 'nough to grace e'en the Queen's Court."

"If you're thinking to distract me from your debts, you can think again," she retorted with energy. "You and William still owe me the construction of a dozen animal traps. I've a mind to collect them before the week is out."

William grinned and shook his head. "You allus did track

us down and put us ta work, no matter how 'ard we tried to hide from yer all-seein' eyes on th' ship."

Blade's lips twitched. It was a welcome expression on a lad who had so recently been separated from his father at the slave trading block. Soon, she intended to pull him aside to discuss everything he could remember about the man who'd stepped forward to claim Cecil Prat as his property. Perhaps Wanchese could identify the slaver and thereby help them determine the whereabouts of Blade's sire.

In the meantime, she shared the good news about the surviving colonists. She also gingerly announced the fact that they would be staying at Dasamonquepeuc for the time being, since Chief Manteo already had his winter supplies stretched to the limit with his English guests. She didn't mention the fact that Chief Wanchese intended for them to earn their keep through labor, since she still wasn't clear what all he had planned, exactly.

George frowned. "How did you discover this? Did you actually converse with the savage?"

"George!" she chided with a warning shake of her head. "He speaks a bit of English after a year of service to our Crown, and I am fortunate that Manteo taught me a few words of their language, as well."

"Did he?" Blade's eyes danced with curiosity. "Say something for us, Mistress Jane."

"Well, ah, let me see. Corn is *rokohamin*. Coconut is *mutsun*. Oh, and grapes are *marrakummins*."

"*Mutsun*," William mused. "I remember the night Rose found a whole grove of *mutsun* for us in Santa Cruz."

Jane didn't care for the suspicions that continued to cloud George's face.

*W*anchese led them back to the river's edge. Because Jane had been unconscious during their trek to the cave, she did not know the path. Her fingers crept over her scalp to the knot still swelling. *Tarnation, but I am sore this morning from my tumble into the river.*

George took the rear of their small line, walking backwards most of the way to keep an eye on the thick forest of oak, redwood, and cedar behind them. He dropped out of view just as they reached the river and did not return until James and William had brushed off the entire screen of foliage from the canoe.

He sauntered in Wanchese's direction.

Without warning, Wanchese sprang on him and slapped him to the ground, burying his face in the dirt. He pressed a wicked blade to the back of George's neck.

"What is this madness?" Jane cried, running to crouch next to them.

Wanchese snarled something in his native tongue and rolled George over. The lad's arm shot out, but Wanchese was faster. He kicked away the lad's makeshift weapon, and it skidded into the dust at her feet.

It was a stick, ten inches or so in length and two fingers wide, with the end sharpened to a deadly point. Jane gazed at it in dismay. *Oh, George! I tried to warn you.*

"There is no harm in carrying a weapon," she protested. A thread of desperation wove its way into her voice. "But you should not have concealed it from Chief Wanchese, George." *Or attempted to stab him with it, you blasted numbskull!*

When Wanchese continued to glare menacingly down at George, she stood and stomped a foot. "Enough! We might as well get this out in the open now. Nay, George," she cautioned when he shot her a look of censure. "'Tis high time." She trained beseeching eyes upon his captor, willing him to understand. "As it happens, the Englishman slain at the hands of the Roanokes was this lad's father."

Wanchese glanced from her to George.

Ah. He had not made the connection.

George peered up at her from the ground, squinting as the first rays of sun splintered through their midst. The thirst for blood in his eyes was dimmed somewhat by the sheen of hurt. He presumed she had betrayed him.

"Oh, George," she murmured with regret. "I just…" *Wanted you to live another day.*

Despite his curt nod at her words, Wanchese produced a swirl of cord and tied the lad's hands in front of him in the same manner as the colonists had been bound while marching to the Great Trading Path.

"Is that entirely necessary?" she fumed while he secured the knot. "A person has a right to defend themselves. We would be of little use to you in an attack, unarmed as we are."

Wanchese snarled something under his breath and rolled to his feet. He withdrew a second knife and stalked over to James, offering the weapon to him.

James darted a wary glance around the group.

Wanchese grabbed his hand and slapped the blade into it.

Amazed, James examined the etching on the hilt.

"What about me?" Hands on her hips, Jane scowled at Wanchese. "I am unarmed, too."

His hot gaze raked her and came to rest on her bosom where her own makeshift weapon was secreted. He took a purposeful step towards her.

She raised her chin. "What? You do not trust me, either?"

He stopped with no more than a hand's breadth between them.

Her fingers itched to pluck out the stone blade. She'd always felt naked without a knife in hand and generally traveled with several stashed on her person. Life had taught her it was wise to have a contingency plan or two.

Unlike George, however, she had no intention of using her weapon against her rescuer.

"Ireh!" Wanchese snarled at last and wheeled away. He yanked George to his feet and tossed him in the canoe.

CHAPTER 5: DASAMONQUEPEUC

"*P*ray keep an eye on George," Jane muttered to James before stepping into the canoe. He nodded and maneuvered himself into the stern so that George hunkered as far as possible from Wanchese in the bow. She took a seat behind Wanchese. Blade and William perched in the center and took turns passing the paddle between themselves and James.

"It would be my pleasure to take a turn at the oars, Chief Wanchese," she offered as she stepped into the canoe, but her words earned her nothing more than a fierce glare. *Men and their blasted chivalry.* She blew the hair out of her eyes and settled in for a long, boring haul. Trailing her fingers in the water, she longed for a rifle to clean or a few scraps of wood to pound into a trap. Surely, Wanchese did not expect her to sit on her haunches all day? *Burn it, we have hours of sailing ahead of us.*

The rising sun illuminated the puckered skin on his back as he dug in his oar. *Egad.* Accustomed to the extensive body paint of the natives, both temporary and permanent, she'd not paid much attention to the ridges on his shoulders the evening before. However, she had enough daylight and all the time in the world to ponder them now.

On closer inspection, Wanchese's scars resembled the rungs of a ladder. She wondered at their significance. His cousin, Manteo, did not have them. Alas, Wanchese's closed off demeanor suggested he possessed no interest in exchanging chitchat.

By mid-morning, they reached the delta where the Chowan and Roanoke Rivers flowed into the Sea of Roanoke. Beyond it, the wide expanse rippled into layers of blue and green as far as the eye could see. During the colonists' stay on Roanoke Island, they'd fished in these sounds and hunted for crabs along its shores.

The elder George Howe had perished there.

They traveled another couple of hours before Wanchese held up an arm. James held his paddle wide and steady in the water to slow the canoe, while Wanchese drew a bundle from one of the pouches hanging at his side. The bundle turned out to be a fish net made of fine silken cord. When he tossed it over the side of the canoe, it unfurled and stretched a good fifteen feet before disappearing beneath the surface. It was pulled under by a series of shells that served as weights.

They drifted along the current for less than a minute before the net jerked. Wanchese dragged up the largest striped bass she'd ever seen. *Well, blow me down!* The thing was longer than his arm span and flopping within the confines of its silken cage.

With much appreciative male commentary, James, William, and Blade hauled the distressed creature into the canoe. George looked on with undisguised interest. *Good.*

The men finally allowed Jane to employ herself. While she helped them gut the enormous fish and scrape away its scales, Wanchese maneuvered their craft nearer the shore. He and Blade broke off an armload of low hanging dead branches. Bless him if he didn't set the lad to building a small fire right in the middle of the canoe on a bed of sand they scooped up at the river's edge.

It was a feast. They devoured the fresh baked fish, and nothing had ever tasted so good. Jane peeked at Wanchese over the filet she held with both hands. He was the man their colony had feared most during their brief stay on his island in the late summer months. It was remarkable how safe she felt in his presence now. James, William, and Blade were eyeing him with something akin to worship.

She fought the urge to fidget when his sharp gaze passed over her. To her, he was no god. Far from it. He was very much a man. Disturbingly so.

She glanced around the canoe and caught George scowling at her and Wanchese again. *Oh, bother!*

It took more than ten hours to traverse the fifty miles of sound waters. Along the way, they plucked branches and took turns holding them over their English comrades while they rowed. Otherwise, they might very well have collapsed in full broil beneath the unforgiving sun. Although Wanchese waved the branches away, Jane attempted to shield him from the sun, as well. After a while, she gave up. So much for trying to show her appreciation for all he had done for them.

It was early evening when they rounded the final stretch of the mainland to Dasamonquepeuc. The rugged shores of Roanoke Island emerged as a thin line on the distant horizon. Jane shaded her eyes, hoping to catch sight of a curl of smoke, anything to indicate the presence of colonists in the process of rebuilding Fort Raleigh. But she saw nothing more than a bevy of water fowls taking flight.

"Mistress Jane, how do you reckon Christopher and the other colonists fare?" William's round face glistened with sweat and anxiety.

"They are alive and well in Croatoa," she said firmly, not

caring if Wanchese heeded her words. "Either they will visit us, or we will visit them. Soon." She wished she was as sure as she sounded. "But for now, Chief Wanchese has agreed to give us sanctuary in Dasamonquepeuc, and for that we are grateful."

---

*D*asamonquepeuc was the closest town to Roanoke Island, located on the mainland directly across from the island. It stretched before them, an unbroken line of sand strewn with seashells and driftwood. Just beyond the beach, smoke wafted through the top-heavy trees and formed a light haze. This village was inhabited.

A scant few weeks before, it had lain abandoned. Jane knew this, because Governor White had escorted a war party here to avenge the murder of Assistant George Howe. Somehow the Roanokes had learned they were coming and temporarily vacated their community. She could not help but admire their ability to disperse themselves like magic into the surrounding forests.

It became harder for her to breathe as their canoe scraped its way onto the beach. A mere week ago, though it seemed much longer, they had crossed over these same sounds from Roanoke Island in the hopes of leaving behind the rapidly deteriorating relations with the neighboring tribes. It was on this ground the slave hunters had attacked her countrymen and upon this beach that so many of them had perished.

In an unspoken tribute to their sacrifice, she and her four English comrades disembarked in silence.

Jane rushed to the spot where Rose had fallen. *Thank God she is alive!* It was a miracle she lived through the volley of fiery arrows plunging into the sand around the doomed colonists.

Sliding to her knees, she re-played the scene in her mind, trying to picture where she'd last seen Margery and Dyonis Harvye. Wanchese had been vague on the details, but both had perished here in the sand. Their poor babe, born only a handful of days before the ambush, still did not even have a name. At least he was in Agnes and Rose's capable hands.

James knelt next to her. "Mayhap you can try signin' to him again. It would be best, methinks, if he carries us on to Croatoa now instead of later."

She straightened her shoulders, not quite meeting his gaze. "I tried, my friend. Last night while you slept. The chief made it very clear he wished to stop here first." James would hear what she left unsaid. "Indefinitely." She was already speculating that their stay would resemble something along the lines of indentured servitude.

"I see." He rubbed a hand over his shaggy brown beard. "Then I suppose there's naught for us to do but follow his wishes, lass."

She nodded glumly. Like James, she feared their first confrontation with the Roanokes. Perhaps the fact they were accompanied by the Roanoke chief would provide them with some measure of protection, but she had her doubts.

"God be with us," she murmured. Her thoughts drifted to George who stood fuming at the water's edge, gazing towards Roanoke Island in the distance. His grudge against the Roanokes would continue to pose a problem for them.

"Ireh," Wanchese said. The command was spoken in quieter tones this time. They did not have much farther to go. He cupped her elbow and drew her to her feet.

Her gaze jerked to his. His gesture reminded her of an English gentleman and seemed out of place on this barren stretch of sand.

"Ireh!" he commanded in a sharper tone and dropped his hand.

She sniffed at his impatient demeanor. They trudged over rolls of tumbleweed and bits of driftwood and set their course up the beach in the direction of Dasamonquepeuc.

Evening shadows gathered beneath the stalwart red cedars guarding the edge of the forest. Despite their hushed conversations, or maybe because of them, none came to greet them. Other than the occasional call of waterfowl, it was quiet. Too quiet. A frightfully familiar sensation prickled at the base of Jane's neck.

"Halt and surrender," she snarled between gritted teeth to her countrymen. "Burn it all, but we are surrounded." *Again.*

"What? Are you certain?" James exclaimed, though his hands were already going up in the air.

"I tried to warn you," George growled. "His kind can't be trusted."

"Hush, George." Dread spiraled in her gut. They had walked into the same trap as before on the exact same beach, except this time it was still daylight.

Copper-skinned natives stepped out from behind boulders, thickets, and piles of wood scattered across the beach. Others sidled into view from the tree line, arrows notched and bows drawn. Most of them wore loincloths. A few were clad in buckskins. All of them bore painted masks similar to the one covering the top half of Wanchese's face. They circled the English colonists and closed in.

"Now would be an excellent time to explain we are with you," she muttered to Wanchese.

In response, he held up one arm and barked out a command that sounded like a warning.

The warriors converging on them froze, their weapons suspended in mid-air. Straight ahead, a thicket shivered with movement. The breeze riffling the treetops was not strong enough to cause such an anomaly.

Jane inhaled the scents of sweet dried grasses and stale

fish and jolted when a figure burst through the briars. *A bear!* The white creature rose on its hind legs like a man and peered at them through bloodshot eyes. No more than twenty paces separated man and beast.

"I've ne'er seen anything like it," Blade breathed. "'Tis like a ghost."

"Wanchese!" Jane hissed, holding out a hand. "One of your blades, please. I am begging you."

But he remained unmoving at her side, his hand raised for silence.

A man whooped from the interior of the wood line. She tensed at the bloodcurdling sound. It was way too reminiscent of the last slaughter that had taken place here. Startled, the bear dropped to all fours. He swung his head from side to side and ambled down the beach away from the humans.

Several of the natives lowered their weapons, stunned, and watched until the bear trotted out of sight.

"*Waba makwa.*" An elder Roanoke, whom Jane recognized as their medicine man due to his odd garb, dashed towards them and dropped to his knees. He wore an entire stuffed blackbird with its wings spread plastered to the side of his head in lieu of a hat. Long, straight locks of unbound hair framed his face. A deerskin cloak swung against his shoulders as he rocked back and forth chanting.

"*Waba makwa. Waba makwa.*" His sing-song voice struck a melancholy note and held. He raised his staff and addressed the warriors gathered. She understood none of what he said but watched the expressions of his listeners.

In the next moment, the air erupted with the whoops and cries of battle. James was overpowered first and dragged into the woods before he could pull out the knife Wanchese had given him. William offered no resistance, his face chalky as he was led away next by a second group of natives. Bows were put away and replaced with knives that they brandished menacingly over their heads.

"Run, Mistress Jane!" Blade cried, wrestling with his captors. He broke free and scrabbled towards her on all fours, his face a piteous mixture of confusion and terror, only to be recaptured and hustled away from her.

"It's a trap. I told you the savage could not be trusted." George spat at the feet of the next broad-shouldered young brave who approached them.

At closer range, Jane gauged him to be of similar age to George but a good two inches taller. Cut in the same manner as Wanchese, his dark locks were shaved on one side and spiked down the center while the other side swung freely. His frame was not yet filled to the full maturity of manhood, but his biceps were already twice the size of George's and bore the same bear claws as Wanchese, Manteo, and Dasan.

"Amonsoquath," Wanchese greeted him and jerked his head meaningfully at George.

The fragile thread of trust Jane had placed in the Roanoke chief snapped. *Why, the cad played us all for fools! Feeding us and giving us false hope these past twenty-four hours simply to buy our compliance.*

Amonsoquath unsheathed a long dagger. She caught her breath as he approached. To his credit, George did not flinch as the lad raised the blade and made a vicious downward slice.

A jagged cry of horror tore itself from Jane. She lunged with the intention of coming betwixt the two, but another jerk of Wanchese's head had her surrounded. A firm push between her shoulder blades accompanied by a whack to the back of her knees had her tumbling to the ground. She craned her neck for a better view of George. Amazingly, he still stood. There was no crimson staining his chest. His hands were freed of their bonds, though.

A warrior with black face paint leaped atop to straddle her, whooping at the top of his lungs. She could no longer see George. Her attacker's face was a maze of blood red paint and inky black streaks. She watched him through a thickening haze as he produced an ugly hatchet. With a shrill scream, he brought it whistling down against her temple again and again.

She never dreamt one could slip into death so easily, for she did not feel the fatal blows. Perhaps, her mind had already detached itself from her body, because everything seemed to be happening from a great distance. Even after the air was thick with the coppery scent of blood, she felt no pain. Part of her wanted to laugh at the ninny who continued to whoop and holler in her face. Didn't he realize she was long gone? Dead as dead could be.

Strangely enough, she *did* feel the men tug her lifeless frame to her feet. It was particularly odd that she could still stand. So much blood covered her hands and arms there could be precious little left in her. She blinked the droplets from her lashes. They splashed down her cheeks, warm and wet. Improbable as it was, the sensations almost made her feel alive again.

Her attackers prodded and dragged her up the beach into the forest. They passed beneath giant top-heavy trees. The setting sun cast a rich red glow through their branches that made the tree trunks and hard packed earth appear as bathed in blood as she was.

They burst into a clearing where a ring of men and women writhed and leaped in a grotesque, slow-moving dance. Each of the dancers was painted with the same red and black mask that Wanchese boasted. They crouched forward from their waists in a swaying series of steps.

Five female dancers flew into the center of the ring. They locked their elbows in a tight circle facing inward and swayed back and forth, tossing their heads and wailing as if in agony. After several minutes of morbid wailing, they unclasped their arms and fell back a few steps, shrieking and clasping their middles. Then they linked their arms once more and resumed their weeping.

Her captors led her through the strange collection of dancers. The women in the center of the ring broke apart again and joined the outer ring of dancers, revealing a circle of flat-faced boulders in the center of the ring. They had been shielded until now by the throng of moving bodies.

Through a bloody haze, she counted them. Five boulders. One for each colonist. It was no real surprise when her captors draped her over the nearest boulder. Her shoulders pressed against the rock, and her face was tipped to the sky.

The world above her seemed to spin. Then it winked away altogether.

When she awoke, her hands and feet were tied. She swiveled her head slowly to the right and squinted through the dull ache in her temples. Blade was sprawled on the next boulder. He was limp and bloody, tied in the same manner as her. She shuddered when he turned his head to gaze blankly at her.

"Blade!" she shouted but could not hear her own voice above the shrieking and wailing of the dancers. "Blade!" she cried a second time. Surely he could see her mouth forming his name, but no recognition lit his gray-blue eyes. *Poor lad.* It was just as well he was beyond hearing and seeing at this point.

She turned her head in the other direction. George's bloody frame kicked and writhed. It took four braves, including Amonsoquath, to bind him. George thrashed against the cords and would have unseated himself from his boulder had the natives not held him down.

The wailing of the native dancers abated at last. In its

place, a heavy drum pounded. It mingled with the voices of the singers in a slow, menacing rhythm. A second drum joined in, and the sound crescendoed to a thunderous cadence.

Their medicine man stood in the midst of the pounding ensemble and held up his staff. He shook it and raised his voice in a mournful chant. The drums subsided to a muted cadence in the background.

He held both arms out, as if in supplication. Two warriors appeared, faces painted a solid black. They joined the dance, twirling a pair of wicked double-edged daggers. The medicine man intoned a few more words and fisted his staff towards the heavens. The drum beat accelerated, and the black-painted warriors approached George and drew back their blades.

"Nay! Let him go! I beg you. Nay!" Jane shouted, struggling against her bonds, but she failed to make herself heard above the din.

Suddenly, one of the five women in the outer ring broke free. She ran shrieking towards George and threw her body over him like a shield. The men holding the daggers fell back, astonished expressions on their faces. They turned to kneel before their medicine man, heads bowed.

Their leader followed the same sequence as before, chanting his mournful dirge and thrusting his staff skyward. This time, the armed warriors approached James with a wooden bludgeon in each hand. They pounded the air in a sinister manner that brought to mind a tortuous beating. Another woman ran to throw herself betwixt the warriors and their captive. This continued around the circle until the black-painted men approached Jane.

Three, four, five, then six daggers appeared and spun in an arc through the air before whirling back into the hands of the warriors. They juggled for several long moments. Then the blades descended in slow motion towards her neck, chest, and belly. She heard the shriek of the last woman but was uncertain she would make it in time to save her.

For a second time, darkness enveloped her.

---

a feminine humming penetrated Jane's sleep. Strange to hear only one singer instead of the choirs she expected. The woman's voice had a soothing quality, albeit she was a bit off-key. How had such an imperfect voice ever ascended to the heavens?

Jane stretched her limbs and groaned at their soreness. *Tarnation! Death was supposed to be free of pain.* Had she failed to arrive at the pearly gates and plummeted to the other place instead?

The humming stopped. "Jane?" a soft guttural voice inquired.

She opened a wary eye.

A woman of middling years squatted before her fire in a dim, smoky room. The flickering flames revealed her fine chiseled features and lent her copper skin an otherworldly glow. If she was an angel, she was nothing like the winged and haloed creatures Jane had been taught about as a child at her mother's knee.

She was missing her heavenly robes, as well. Her chest was covered by dozens of strands of shells. A deerskin skirt hugged her hips and knees. Though her lips were unsmiling, her black eyes snapped with an energy that belied the maze of tiny wrinkles at the edges of her mouth. High cheekbones ended in another maze of tiny lines at the corners of her eyes. Masses of coal black hair interwoven with gray were plaited into two of the longest, thickest braids Jane had ever seen. They hung past her waist and dangled against slender hips.

"Am I alive?" Jane inquired, not expecting her to understand.

"Aye."

Well, blow me down! Even the natives speak English in heaven. She raised a dubious brow. "And the Englishmen I was traveling with?"

"Aye."

Truly? Alackaday, there was so much blood spilt last night. Jane ran her hands over her cheeks and neck, down her arms, and across her belly. Dumbfounded, she discovered she was uninjured. Gone was the sticky feel of blood on any of her appendages. *How is this possible?*

"Who are you?" she demanded.

"Nadie," the woman answered in the same gentle voice and continued to poke at the fire with her stick.

Jane blinked and wriggled painfully to prop herself on her elbows. "You speak excellent English," she accused. *For a savage.*

The older woman raised her shoulders and let them fall. "Wanchese taught me a little of your tongue."

"Amazing!" she exclaimed. "Well, then, I am pleased to meet you, Nadie." *Only time will prove if evading death yet again was a good thing or not.*

Nadie grunted and pulled two glistening stones from the fire with a pair of wooden tongs. She plopped them into a brownish mixture that bubbled and popped. The scent of venison and spices filled the tent.

Jane gazed at the simple reed walls rising around them, undecorated by paint or any other ornaments. *Am I still in Dasamonquepeuc?* Questions peppered her thoughts, while the scent of venison made her mouth water.

Nadie ladled some of the stew in a wooden bowl and held it out.

She sat up and sniffed in appreciation at the rising steam. "I thank you." Perhaps she had not made it all the way to the glory land, but the contents of the bowl were close enough to manna for her. The meat was so tender it crumbled on her tongue. She tasted beans, pumpkin, and wild onions. A spectacular medley of flavors.

"Mmm. Pray assure me that my friends are enjoying a similar feast. Blazes!" She sat the bowl down on the earthen floor. "Where are they, Nadie?"

"Pale faces. Here," she assured and picked up the discarded bowl.

"There was so much blood." Jane pressed her temples where the hatchet had struck.

She placed the bowl of stew back in her hands. "Eat."

"Where—"

"Die," she spat. "Pale faces die."

The last bite of stew turned to ashes in Jane's mouth. "B-but you just stated the men are here."

"Aye. Pale faces die. New life." She clasped her hands to her chest. "Here. With us."

Jane's gaze fastened on the bear claws painted on her upper arms and realization slowly dawned. "It was all fake, wasn't it? Some sort of ceremony." A strange and savage ceremony. Like the pieces of a puzzle, the shocking events of the night before slid into their rightful places in her brain. "There was so much blood. It could not have been ours, or we'd be truly dead. Was it animal blood?"

Nadie nodded.

"The dance. It was symbolic, wasn't it? You put an end to our old lives as pale faces." She recalled the wailing women clawing at their bellies. "And I suppose the women — the ones who leaped on top of us — they gave birth to us, so to speak. One of them was…you!"

Her mind raced to make sense of the bizarre ritual. If the English colonists had been reborn into the Roanoke tribe, it did not bode well for their chances of being returned to their countrymen — ever.

"Uh." It was an affirmative sound.

"Why?" She did not expect an answer, certainly not the one she received.

"*Amosens,*" she muttered. "*Amosens* gone." She withdrew a small length of cord from a pouch at her side and mimed the tying of her hands together and pretended to be yanked to her feet by it. Her dark eyes glistened with emotion. She pointed to me. "New *amosens*. New daughter."

Daughter. *Amosens* meant daughter. Her daughter must have been captured and taken from her; and, for some odd reason, Jane been chosen to take her place. Her thoughts drifted to the attractive young woman on the slave trading block, the one with the bear claws painted on her upper arms. Perhaps a similar fate had befallen Nadie's daughter?

She tipped the bowl up to consume the rest of her stew. Who would the English men and lads replace? Fathers? Husbands? Sons?

The implications were mind-boggling. It was going to be a most difficult task to explain this newest form of bondage to her countrymen. George would never accept it. Not so long as he still breathed, *burn him*! He was an Englishman through and through. He would probably rather have perished last night than to wake and discover he'd been "birthed" into the tribe of heathens and savages he hated so much. The ones who'd slain his father.

Her sober thoughts were erased by lighter ones. The fact remained that they were survivors — James, William, Blade, George, and herself. No longer slaves, not even indentured servants, but full-fledged members of the Roanoke tribe. A reluctant chuckle escape her. What else could she do but smile and thumb her nose at fate? They'd lived through the impossible. There must be some reason they were still here.

At Nadie's sharp look, Jane attempted to cover her laugh with a cough, but a grin tugged at her lips. The Roanokes were in for a pleasant surprise, for they'd chosen to adopt some of the most skilled laborers from London. She and her comrades could demonstrate feats of masonry and construction far beyond anything they had ever witnessed here in the coastal forests. Why, they would be able to fold and pack away their humble tents for good when her countrymen were finished.

Having food in her stomach not only restored her spirits but her energy. Jane stood and smoothed her hands over the deerskin skirt clinging to her thighs, reveling in the freedom of movement it provided. A simple, unadorned tunic covered her upper half. She was extremely grateful for it and could not imagine ever gadding about bare of chest like many of the local women. The very thought made her blush.

The moccasins given to her by Dasan's people still graced her feet, but they were brushed clean. Ah, but she did not miss her former floor-length English skirts one whit. Nor all the collars, ruffs, pins, and other accoutrements dictated by the dragons of London fashion.

"Well," she announced briskly. "I'm of a mind to check on my friends. Am I free to go?"

Nadie placed herself betwixt Jane and the exit. "*Cumear.*" She brushed aside a curtain of animal skins and motioned for her to follow.

She frowned. As her adoptive daughter, Nadie probably expected her to obey her wishes.

To her surprise, they were not in a tent, after all, but a domed building. They exited the smoky chamber and entered a long hallway. It ran the length of what appeared to be a rectangular structure. The walls were lined with reed mats. Some were rolled up and tied with cords, allowing the sunlight to pour in. The sun was rising to a golden dawn. In her exhaustion, she must have slept the night away.

On either side of them, low platforms, each about six feet in length, lined the outer walls. Jane counted her steps. Every ten to twelve feet, an inner wall separated the next adjoining compartment. Beneath the platforms rested an assortment of baskets, bowls, and other containers. On the walls hung tools and braids of onions and herbs. Atop the platforms were scattered furs — raccoon, fox, rabbit, deer, and bear. The last animal skin made her shiver. The entire structure was thirty-five to forty feet in length and boasted three fire pits, counting the one Nadie had tended in the rear.

Two young women stoked the next fire. One had a babe strapped behind her shoulders in a most curious manner. Jane frowned at the hard board pressed between mother and infant. A snug cord crisscrossed the wee mite from neck to feet, securing him to the board. A harness of sorts fastened the contraption to the mother. It looked uncomfortable. Nevertheless, the babe sucked noisily on its fingers, eyelids drooping, and seemed content.

Dressed in the same manner as Nadie, neither woman acknowledged Jane's presence as they passed. However, both ceased stirring their vats to bow to Nadie. They pressed their hands together beneath their chins, palms to palms and fingertips to fingertips.

Eying Nadie, Jane was amazed at their show of respect to her and wondered what sort of elevated status she held within the Roanoke tribe.

The interior of the entire lodge was smoky, but not near so much as it should have been with the number of fires burning within.

She glanced up. *Of course.* That explained it. Sections of the reed mats opened to allow for ventilation. A long pole rested against the wall near one of the smoke holes, most likely to open and close the vents.

"*Cumear!*" Nadie's voice interrupted her perusal.

She led her through a doorway at the far end of the structure. They stepped onto what appeared to be the main street of a sprawling village. Before her, more long, domed structures rose on both sides of the road. Beyond them stretched acres of farmland bursting with corn, beans, gourds, and other plants. Straight ahead was the now-vacant circle where their birthing ceremony had taken place.

Cool morning air nipped at Jane's cheeks as they walked. Autumn was ripening and creeping ever closer to winter.

The village teamed with natives at work, play, and repose. Just beyond the reed longhouses on one side of the road were a series of targets where a crowd of warriors practiced archery. Nay, not all of them were natives. Blade's fair-skinned gangly figure stood out among them, as well as George's more darkly tanned features. They both held bows. Amonsoquath instructed them. Even from this distance, Jane could read the eagerness in Blade's stance and the sullenness in George's. James and William were not in sight.

Nadie increased her pace and ducked with her into the forest. She led Jane through dense patches of trees until the forest thinned and gave way to a frothing spring. A pair of unsmiling maidens awaited them with a basket held between them. One was tall and rather gaunt in her fringed skirt. The other was several inches shorter, round-faced, and a wee bit on the plump side.

Sadness wrenched Jane's chest. Aside from their copper skin and strange apparel, the tall, thin one reminded her of Margaret from their failed English colony, and the shorter one reminded her of Emme. Both had shared her cabin on the ship ride from Portsmouth. She wondered how they fared at Croatoa with Manteo's people and if she would ever see them again. According to Wanchese, if he could be believed after all his duplicity, they were alive.

The two maidens set down their basket and hurried to Jane's side, tugging at her garments and nudging her to the water's edge.

"Whoa, there!" Jane swatted at their hands. "Pray allow me do certain things for myself." She had no intention of turning her back on these women, not after the beating she'd endured at the site of her last bath.

Training a watchful eye on them, she disrobed and draped her deerskin garments across a boulder beside the spring. A sigh escaped her when she stepped into the knee-deep waters and found them blessedly tolerable. A cleft in the ridge above them fed the warm, bubbling stream.

Such an unbelievable luxury. She dunked her head and came up laughing and tossing the hair from her eyes.

The round-faced woman reached into her basket and produced a handful of yucca leaves. Wading towards Jane, she crushed the leaves and dipped them in the water. Rubbing the mixture between her hands, she worked a soapy lather into her hair. It smelled strong and sweet like daffodils.

When Jane attempted to step away and take over the washing, however, the young woman stubbornly dug her hands into her hair. Unaccustomed to having a lady's maid attend her, Jane endured her ministrations in fuming silence.

When she was bathed to everyone's apparent satisfaction, Nadie beckoned her to leave the water and kneel before her. She drug the boney tines of a comb through her hair for more than an hour until it was dry — no small feat for her waist-length locks. Her knees ached from holding the position for so long.

Parting her hair down the center, Nadie proceed to plait one side into a thick, sleek braid. Jane brushed her nimble fingers aside and plaited the other side. Nodding in approval, Nadie handed her a bit of cord to secure the end. A surprisingly strong hand on her shoulder kept her from rising as Nadie drew the comb down her forehead next, straightening the loosened strands and tugging a few more from the plaits. She severed them just above her eyebrows to form a straight fringe.

Jane ruffled the shorn strands with her fingers. *An interesting style.* It would keep her hair out of her eyes, though. She sprang to her feet and donned her garments once more.

"Jane." She stabbed a finger at her chest and pointed to the woman who resembled Margaret.

She looked startled and raised a long thin hand to her chest. "Bly."

Before Jane could ask the question again, Nadie barked an order.

Looking abashed, the other woman pressed her fingertips to her collarbone. "Dyoni."

"Pleased to meet you, Bly." Jane held out her hand. At Nadie's bidding, the young woman clasped it with reluctance. Jane gave it a hearty shake and stepped to the next woman. "Pleased to meet you, Dyoni." Without hesitation, she pressed her hand to Jane's. Neither woman smiled, but warmth radiated from Dyoni's features. Jane glanced down at her rounded figure. *Ah.* She was in the family way.

She swiveled to Nadie. "Where are the Englishmen I traveled here with?"

She shrugged and beckoned Jane to follow her back to the village.

They re-entered the town near the ceremonial circle. A two-story structure stood next to it. Jane had not noticed it during the frenzied dance the night before. A closer glance at the structure gave her a start. Two straight rows of men in embroidered garments lay sleeping on a raised platform. Guarding them was a wizened figure draped in a long robe, sitting with his legs crossed before him. A tall man even while sitting, he passively observed her and Nadie.

She pressed a hand to her mouth and swallowed hard when she noted the figure lying at the furthermost end of the row was missing his head. The two rows of men were not sleeping at all as she had originally presumed. They were dead.

She glanced again at the headless one. Was this man their former leader, Pemisapan, who had perished at the hands of the English?

Mercy! She hurried to catch up with Nadie, Bly, and Dyoni who were several strides ahead of her. "Who was that man?" she asked breathlessly.

"Noshi," Nadie answered tersely. "Priest."

A picture started to form in her head about how the tribe was organized. She imagined her friend, Agnes, would be delighted to make the acquaintance of their medicine man, because she had served as the colonists' apothecary and midwife. No doubt they would have stories and potions galore to swap with the aid of an interpreter. She also wondered what Reverend Christopher Cooper would make of the foreign priest. It was unlikely he worshipped the one, true God of the English.

Nadie led her to the hubbub of the main part of the village. Children chased each other, chattering. A few employed long-handled sticks to bat at a wooden ball rolling along the ground. Jane noted with delight that one slip of a girl with tangled dark locks held a wee cornhusk doll.

George might never agree, but the natives were not so terribly different from the English, after all. Except maybe when it came to smiling. None of them smiled, not even the children. Ever. Were they unhappy with the presence of the English? Most tended to stare to the point of rudeness.

Some of the chatter died. Women paused in their basket weaving and scraping of animal skins to incline their bodies forward from their waists, their hands pressed together beneath their chins. Men laid down their bows and quivers and stood with heads bowed. This time, however, they did not bow to Nadie.

Jane followed their gazes. Wanchese towered in the doorway of a longhouse at the center of the village. He raised a hand and barked out a few guttural phrases. The children cheered, tossing and twirling their sticks, and resumed playing. The men and women relaxed their stance and returned to their tasks.

"Chief Wanchese." She sprinted his way, with Nadie protesting at her heels, to dip in a hasty bow. She clasped her hands below her chin as the natives had done. "Pray enlighten me of your plans for us."

"Uh?" His mahogany gaze raked over her clean hair and garments and rested a bit longer than she thought necessary on her bare calves.

"What have you done with James and William?"

"What pleases me," he growled, meeting her gaze at last.

"Fine!" she snapped. "What pleases you?"

His eyes took on a mocking glint. "Lie with me, Jane. That would please me."

"Wh-what?" Such crudity was uncalled for. At his amused look, she bit off the rest of what she was about to say. He needled her a-purpose.

"I am skilled with my hands." She wriggled her fingers at him. "Pray give me some tools, and I will construct as many animals traps as you desire."

"My men have enough traps."

"Then I will hunt. I can shoot a bow."

"Nay," he answered, his tone rude. "You shall farm, cook, and weave."

Women's work. She stared at him aghast. "Blast you! I know precious little about farming and weaving. I am a trapper. At least allow me to—"

"Today you will cook. For me." He pointed to the fire crackling a few feet away from them and gave a sharp command. The young woman tending it tossed aside her stick and ran to him. She slid her hands over his chest and pressed herself against him.

He muttered something huskily in her ear and drew her inside the longhouse, leaving little doubt as to what activity they intended to engage in.

Jane gaped after them. *Was the man completely out of his mind?* Why else could he suggest she lie with him one moment and walk away with another female in the next moment? *The rutting cad!*

She stomped to the fire.

Nadie grumbled beneath her breath as the door flap fell into place behind Wanchese. Moments later, she trotted away. *Marvelous. She intends to abandon me.*

Jane picked up the stick the chief's concubine had discarded and gave the coals in the cooking fire a vicious poke. Where to even start? No doubt Wanchese had all his kitchen utensils and spices stored within his longhouse. There was no way she was stepping inside to retrieve them, not while there was any chance of interrupting his amorous activities with that light-skirt. Maybe the young woman in question was not exactly in a position to refuse the advances of her chief, but Jane cared not for the way the hussy had plastered herself all over him like cream on berries.

She peered at the murky vat of stew simmering beside the fire. A spoon rested in its bubbling depths. Ladling a sample, she bent to blow on it and gave it a tentative sip.

Ugh! She spat the contents on the ground. No wonder Wanchese desired a new cook! Clearly he'd not recruited the last one for her skill at the hearth.

She glanced away from the longhouse and intercepted a good number of curious gazes turned her way. She nodded in what she hoped was a friendly manner and bent to heft the bubbling vat of vileness. Standing upright with a puff of exertion, she carried it into the woods. Twenty-one paces inside the tree line, she dumped it in a shallow ditch and kicked clods of dirt over it.

A snapping twig made her whirl.

"Still following me, are you?" she called. Unless she was mistaken, a figure had been shadowing her ever since she stepped from Nadie's longhouse earlier. "Maybe I should give you something more worthwhile to watch."

She returned the empty vat to Wanchese's outdoor hearth and strode to the line of targets where Blade and George awkwardly practiced shooting a set of bows and arrows.

"Morning, gentlemen." She breezed into their midst and plucked up a bow from a pile propped around the base of a tree.

"M-mistress Jane," Blade stuttered and crossed his arms to cover his bare chest. Instead of his tattered English shirt and knee pants, he now wore a pair of buckskins.

"Morning, Blade. I am mighty glad to see you." She was thankful to see him alive. "Picking up archery, are we?"

He grinned. "Tis hard work but not so bad when you learn the trick of it. Sometime, I was, er, thinking..." He glanced anxiously at George who glowered at the pair of them. "Well, maybe I can show them a thing or two about knives." His father was a skilled cutler.

"What for?" George's glare deepened. "So they can more skillfully gut us in our sleep?"

Blade snorted. "They would 'ave already done so, milord, if they wished to."

Jane pulled back the string of her bow to gauge the tension. It was a heavy draw but not more than she could handle. Her arms were strong from years of outdoor labor. Hunting, trapping, chopping and hauling wood. "I say 'tis a fine idea to share your skill with the knife in exchange for your archery lessons."

A man shouted something and stalked over to them.

Was this her skulking follower? She smirked as he approached. Before he spoke, she reached around him with the intent to pluck an arrow from his quiver.

The brave caught her wrist without lowering his gaze. They stood nose-to-nose, the arrow spearing the air between them, while he searched her face. She bit her lip at the ugly gashes running from beneath his left eye to his chin. They were claw marks, puckered to a marbled pink and silver where they'd healed. He was most fortunate to still have his eyesight.

She studied his rigid jawline and the rich brandy tint of his eyes and decided they were too familiar to their chief to be a coincidence. *Brother, nephew, or cousin?*

She raised a brow at him. "Surely you don't fear a little competition?"

He may not have understood her words, but she was certain he registered the taunt in her voice. A range of emotions flashed across his features. Surprise. Suspicion. Curiosity won. His gaze narrowed a fraction, and he stepped back far enough for her to draw her bow.

She winked her appreciation. "I thank you. 'Tis the most enjoyment I've had in weeks." She turned and plugged the arrow into the nearest target. Not dead center but close.

The man's gaze grew colder, more calculating. He

reached in his quiver, drew out a second arrow, and offered it to her.

"Much obliged." She notched it and squinted down the shaft at the next target. It was about ten feet farther away than the first and had several arrows already embedded in it. She drew back and let the string fly. Her arrow whistled home, splitting clean down the center of one of the others.

She was rewarded with the sounds of male appreciation when the broken pieces fell to the ground.

Blade cheered lustily. "You're a jolly good shot, Mistress Jane. Aye, you are."

Others paused their shooting and gathered closer to watch.

The warrior with the scarred face handed her a third arrow.

A chattering in the tree above the target range distracted her as she notched it. Two fat squirrels huddled on a branch, screeching. "Turf wars," she chuckled and raised her bow. Nay, it was more that. She tensed and pulled back her arrow.

The shadow of a cobra's head moved around the trunk about a man's height from the ground. Alas, his attention was not trained on the trembling squirrels. A forked tongue darted out once, twice as he scented and moved toward the luscious heat of the lad standing next to the tree. The poor little poppet held a ball and stick in hand.

Her blood chilled. "Move, blast you!" she spat at the man who hovered near her elbow, partially blocking her aim.

Something in her expression had him leaping aside in the same moment the arrow loosed from her string. It sailed over the lad's head and sank into the cobra, pinning its expanded hood to the trunk. The body jerked and writhed, but braves converged upon the serpent before he could loose himself from her arrow.

For a moment, she could not breathe. Blade pounded her back. She coughed and sucked in air, holding out the bow.

The scarred warrior accepted it with an inclined head. He spoke something in his guttural tongue and clasped her shoulder.

"Thank you for moving," she muttered, agonized at what might have happened if she'd missed her aim.

"Riapoke." He held out his hand in an English manner.

"Jane." A trifle out of breath, she gave his hand a cordial shake.

Together they turned to observe the slaughtering of the cobra.

A dark circle formed beneath the lad on the ground. He had not yet moved from his position next to the tree. His head was lowered so that his black braids hung down either side of his dusty cheeks.

She recognized the classic signs of youthful shame. He was mortified over wetting himself.

"Pray pardon me." She moved swiftly to the boy's side. "*Cumear.*" She nodded in the direction of the spring. "I know a place you can wash."

Dark eyes, unfocused with shock, roved over her face. She might never again have her students from the ship gathered around her, but this young child could surely use some attention.

"*Cumear,*" she said again, more gently this time.

This time, he stumbled into motion.

CHAPTER 6: THE TRIBE

a half hour or so later, Jane re-entered the village with the lad, whose name she'd managed to discover after much signing. It was Mukki. He ran ahead of her, clean and ready to boast of his terrifying experience. A bevy of wide-eyed children converged on him and clamored out questions in high-pitched voices. They acted out the whistling, snapping cobra and chased each other around the trees in a reptilian version of tag.

Bemused, Jane set her course for the chief's longhouse. The embers of his outdoor pit were dying down. She crouched before them, blowing to redden them, and added small twigs to coax the flames back to life. Chasing away a spider who had dipped into the vat for a sample of residual droplets, she expelled her breath. Perhaps she would venture into the chief's abode, after all, for a few ears of corn and a handful of onions. It would not be difficult to convince Blade or George to fetch her a squirrel or two. She'd cook their chief a much finer stew than the disgusting mess she'd disposed of earlier.

Before she reached the doorway of the longhouse,

Wanchese emerged with a heavy-lidded expression. It sharpened when he took in the sight of the empty food vat.

"Where is my dinner?"

"As you can see, I am preparing it," she retorted.

"Indeed?" He eyed the vat. "Where is the stew Kanti made?"

So, Kanti is the name of the light-skirt trying to poison her chief? Her lip curled. "I emptied it in the nearest privy. It tasted like horse dung. Back home, we feed our dogs better."

Wanchese's face hardened. He snaked an arm around her waist and drew her against his hard body. "You *are* home, *cucheneppo*." His voice reverberated on a low and dangerous note in her ear.

Her breath caught. Something about his absolute possessiveness combined with the steely strength of his arm stirred her. No man had ever looked at her — Jane Mannering, the too-tall and overly-thin spinster — this way. Nay, the London dandies had downright turned up their haughty noses at her leather top hat and scuffed hunting boots.

From the interest leaping in Wanchese's mahogany eyes, he must not find her mouth too wide, her complexion too tanned, or her freckles too objectionable. Instead, his attentions made her feel utterly female. He desired her and made no effort to hide the fact. A person could appreciate such honesty, no matter how shocking and inappropriate it was.

Then she shook herself. *Faith! What is wrong with me?* Why did it matter if this savage found her comely? He was fresh from the arms of another woman, *burn him!* She wriggled to disengage herself, but his arm might as well have been reinforced with steel.

"Riapoke tells me you trained with my braves," he noted curtly.

Her gaze flew to his. "Tis not what you think, my lord."

"Indeed it is. You prefer to hunt. You do not wish to cook for me."

"True, but—"

He tightened his arm, pulling her so close that she had to tip her head back to maintain his gaze. At her height, she wasn't accustomed to looking up at anyone. She found the position uncomfortable and not to her liking.

"You *will* cook for me, Jane, and perform every duty I assign. To my satisfaction," he added grimly.

Well! So that is how you want things between us? Master and servant. "Aye, sir," she snarled. "If you would give me a single blessed moment to explain, I fully planned to gather food-stuffs for your stew but waited a spell, not wishing to disturb you and that-that..."

"Mistress Jane?"

Wanchese loosened his grip on her at the youthful inter-ruption.

She stumbled away from him, resisting the urge to press a trembling hand to her chest to settle her breathing. *Drat you for continuing to crawl under my skin with your unsettling ways!*

A grinning Blade stood next to Mukki. He ducked his head and held out two stout jackrabbits. They dangled by their ears.

"Mukki!" She clapped her hands in delight and reached for his treasure. "I am most pleased to serve our chief such marvelous fare."

Blade dropped to one knee before the lad and signed something that made his face light up. He bounced on the balls of his feet, pressed the rabbits into Jane's hands, and raced off to rejoin his friends.

"I thank you, Blade. It was a very good deed to include Mukki in your hunt."

Abashed beneath Wanchese's piercing regard, he bowed low and stuttered, "M-my Lord. M-mistress Jane."

"Nay, lad." Wanchese's voice was stern. "I am no lord. I am your *weroance*." At Blade's worried expression, he explained, "Your chief."

Blade gulped and bowed again. "Chief Wanchese, sir. I bid your leave."

By all that is holy! Was that humor in Wanchese's gaze as he beheld the bowing lad?

"You may go."

As Blade bounded off, a shadowy figure ducked behind a longhouse no more than ten paces down from where they stood. Riapoke? He moved so quickly, Jane was unsure of his identity.

Thoughtful, she laid the rabbits out flat on a boulder and sat on the ground to skin them with her rather dull, makeshift, stone blade. She longed for her old, familiar daggers and had to blink to clear the mist in her eyes. It was unlikely she would ever see Pa's knives again, and this task was going to take a good bit longer without them.

A knife clattered to the dirt beside her, making her jump.

"I wish to eat before nightfall, *cucheneppo*." Wanchese sauntered closer and studied her choppy work with a critical eye.

Cucheneppo did not sound like a term of endearment. She pursed her lips, lifted the borrowed knife with an expert twirl, and plunged it into the rabbit. Perhaps she did it a trifle more viciously than necessary.

Wanchese grunted and strode away.

Less than an hour passed before the vat was steaming with fresh rabbit stew. When Jane attempted to dispose of the innards in the fire, Nadie appeared and clucked in admonition. She fussed over the entrails and scooped them into a smaller vat with three hot stones to set them broiling.

She whistled, and a small pack of dogs came running. She tossed them the rabbit heads, which they caught before they hit the ground. The feet she wrapped in a leather pouch and trotted down the road with them cradled in her hands. Apparently, every part of the animal had its use here. Jane approved of Nadie's economizing, but she hoped the woman did not expect her to partake of the bubbling entrails.

---

*N*adie was determined, it seemed, to turn Jane into a proper Roanoke maiden. Most of her lessons centered around thrift in housekeeping. She continuously requested Jane to translate the English words for each task they performed and insisted she recite the Roanoke words she provided in return. Bit by bit, they began to master each other's languages.

The rest of their time they labored in the fields. Jane's skin baked to a burnished gold beneath the sun's rays as she worked. She no longer stood out from her Roanoke companions with the pasty whiteness most English lasses went to excessive lengths to protect with voluminous hats and parasols.

She also had plenty of time to think. With her hands engaged in the tedium of crop-tending, her mind was free to ponder and fret over the plight of her and her countrymen.

Only a few short weeks ago, she had been a member of the floundering English colony called the City of Raleigh. Alas, they had arrived too late in the season to plant any crops. Then their supplies had dwindled so quickly, they'd been forced to start consuming the grain stores they'd hoped to reserve for planting come spring. It was ironic two weeks later to find herself stooped over endless rows of crops just a few miles away from the place where she'd battled hunger pains. Starvation was quite low on her list of worries these days.

Under Nadie's direction, Jane helped her maidens pick beans, pumpkin, and squash for an entire week. Each evening, they enjoyed a myriad of spicy autumn stews. Most of the produce, however, they did not consume. They dried it, wrapped it in leaves, and buried it in long rectangular storage pits lined with gravel. The inhabitants of Dasamonquepeuc would have plenty to eat during the coming winter months.

She was grateful for the abundant harvest, but she could not help longing for the shade of the forest and the thrill of a hunt at daybreak. Try as she might to concentrate on her tasks, she often found herself yearning to trade in her hoe for a dagger or bow.

On the first day of their second week at Dasamonquepeuc, a parade of natives led by Riapoke and Amonsoquath caught her attention. In their ranks, James and William marched with fishnets in hand. Yesterday, they had gone hunting for fowl with bows and quivers of arrows. Jane sighed. What she would not give to join them.

Nadie emitted an impatient exclamation.

"Pray, pardon my woolgathering," Jane muttered and returned to picking beans.

Nadie straightened her back. "*Cumear.*"

"But we have only just begun."

Nadie gave a sharp command that had Bly and Dyoni scurrying up their rows to join them.

She led the trio of young women to her longhouse where she armed them with a set of large wooden bowls and long-handled spoons. They accompanied her farther inland to the bathing spring. This time, she skirted the narrow spring and led them along the base of the ridge until they reached a low-lying marsh. Here the stream splintered into a series of more shallow channels. She motioned them to deposit their bowls at the water's edge.

Though the channel she selected did not appear deep enough to bear watercraft, Bly and Dyoni pulled aside a leaf netting to uncover two short, narrow canoes. Jane hurried to grab the end of one. Nadie took the other end. Bly and Dyoni hefted the second canoe between them.

They plopped the two canoes into the nearest stream and climbed in. Nadie shared a canoe with Jane and pushed them off with a tall, narrow pole. She propelled them no more than a dozen yards and stopped them with her pole. She motioned for Jane to take it from her while she leaned over the side of the boat to clasp a handful of stalks.

The stalks were bound together with hemp cord. She raised one of the long wooden spoons and tapped the bundle with it. Tiny grains of rice pelted into the belly of their canoe. She continued to whack the stalks until no more rice fell from the bundle. Then she retrieved her sailing pole from Jane and steered them on.

A quick study, Jane needed no further instruction. Clearly, they were harvesting rice today. She alternated between steering and brushing the rice stalks, trying to take longer turns at harvesting with respect to Nadie's more advanced years. After her second attempt, however, Nadie looked offended and interrupted her harvesting before she was finished with her bundle.

"*Tah!*" she spat. "My back is good."

Hard put to deny her claim, Jane pressed her hands together beneath her chin, fingers pointed up, and bowed.

Nadie had to be nigh on fifty years or more. Jane was not accustomed to finding women her age with such a hardy constitution. If she lived in London, more than likely her teeth would have been black and rotting, her shoulders stooped, and her head given to megrims.

Looking mollified at Jane's acquiescence, Nadie resumed harvesting the wild rice. Her bare arms rippled with strength. Though long past the blush of youth, there was no extra flesh on her. Nothing but finely honed muscle.

When their canoe was full, Nadie poled them to their starting point and motioned for Jane to transfer the contents of the canoe into a series of wide-mouthed wooden bowls. Instead of lugging the bowls back to camp in their arms, however, Bly demonstrated a better way. She folded a strip of animal skin into several layers and set it atop her head. Then she bent at the knees, spine straight, to lift the bowl onto her head.

In this position, Bly only needed one arm to carry her burden. *How fascinating!* Wait. Nay. She removed her second arm and walked gracefully before them with the bowl balanced perfectly on her head.

Jane clapped in delight and hastened to fold her strip of leather and raise her own bowl. Alas, the maneuver was not so easy as Bly made it appear. After several attempts, Jane still required an arm to stabilize it.

"What?" she asked when the women traded amused glances. "You've had years of practice." Even Dyoni, with her blossoming belly, carried her burden with a steady grace. All the way back to the village, Jane practiced removing her arm. However, she could take no more than a few steps without having to catch the slipping bowl.

They marched into camp with their precious burdens.

Wanchese exited his lodge and folded his arms to watch them. The door flap parted, and Kanti joined him. She stood half-concealed behind one of his broad shoulders, her hand resting with propriety on his upper arm.

Unaccountably irritated, Jane straightened her back as they passed by the pair of them. Hardly daring to breathe, she lowered her arms. *Aha.* She was getting into the rhythm of the maneuver at last.

One of the camp dogs picked this moment to take up

howling. The mournful sound split her ears so unmercifully, she was sure the creature must be crouched beneath her very elbow. Her steps faltered, and the bowl tipped forward.

Devil take the dog for his untimely yammering! Her arms shot up to right the slipping vessel. Alas, a bit of rice sprinkled over the side and rained on the ground.

Kanti rushed forward with a cry of alarm and motioned her to lower her bowl.

"I am fine, thank you," she snapped, but Nadie had other ideas.

"*Tah*, Jane. Give it to Kanti."

Mortified, she lowered the vessel of rice from her head.

Kanti snatched it from her and swiftly bore it away atop her head. Her arms, it seemed to Jane, swung unnecessarily carelessly at her sides. *Burn her! Nobody admires a show-off.*

It took Jane a moment to register Nadie's next words. "No waste." She lowered her own bowl to the ground and removed a tiny bundle from a pouch at her side. Unfolding the bundle, she handed it to Jane and pointed. "Pick up rice."

She stared at the contraption in her hand. It was a finely woven net with wooden handles that opened into a palm-sized tool. A sifter of some sort? Groaning inwardly, she slid to her knees before her new master and sifted each kernel of rice from the dusty path. She did not disagree with Nadie's insistence on retrieving the fallen rice; food was too precious to waste. She only wished she had stumbled in front of any other villagers besides Wanchese and Kanti.

Less of the rice had fallen than she feared, so it took only a few minutes to correct her error. Wanchese observed her the entire time.

"Are you enjoying the view?" she muttered.

"Aye."

"Back in my country, excessive staring is considered rude."

"This is your country, now." He squatted next to her, eyes glittering with controlled anger. "Your home, Jane." He handed her a pouch. "Put the rice in this."

"My home?" Returning scowl for scowl, she tried to snatch the pouch from him, but he retained his hold on it.

He didn't budge, until she met his searing gaze. "Aye. Your home," he said again, more coldly this time.

"Well, it does not feel like home. I possess nothing that I can call my own here. No place of abode, no weapons. Not so much as a trinket. Even my garments are borrowed. Everything I ever owned or-or cared about," her voice shook, "has been taken from me." Angry at her unexpected surge of emotion, she rose and pivoted on her heel.

Wanchese caught her arm and spun her around before she could take her first step.

"You will not depart my presence until I give you leave."

Her trembling evaporated beneath a fresh burst of anger. "Very well," she said icily. "Pray pardon me, my lord chief. I have work to attend." Nadie probably had a thousand chores waiting for her.

"Nay, I have need of you here."

She raised a brow. "How may I serve you?"

He tipped her chin up with one finger. "I feared you would never ask."

"Oh for pity's sake!" She wrenched her chin away, but her skin continued to hum with awareness after she broke contact.

"Kanti is gone to finish your task of storing rice. Thus, I find myself in need of a—"

She cringed. "Do not say it!"

"Forsooth! Would you deny me a bowl of your stew?"

All he wanted was to eat? She was certain he had intended to suggest another activity altogether. She drew a cleansing breath and let it out slowly. "Nay, of course not." She set the pouch of rice aside and positioned herself before the fire pit.

"Good. It would be unwise to deny me, at any rate. I've punished men for less."

She snorted and stooped to ladle him a bowl of rabbit stew.

A low groan from Wanchese caused her to shoot an exasperated look over her shoulder. "Now what?"

His eyes were fixed on her hips. "You insist there is naught you may claim for your own." There was a hoarse edge to his voice. His gaze glittered with lust and humor as their gazes clashed. "How wrong you are, Jane. A vast many things are yours for the taking."

"Is that so?" She muttered sarcastically as she handed him the bowl.

"Aye. My blankets. My bed."

"Perhaps your memory is at fault, my lord chief, for I am fairly certain another woman already has a claim on your bed."

"Good. We make progress. Already your thoughts are occupied with my needs."

Her cheeks burned with discomfort. "Surely, a man of your position has more important things to attend to than observing me work."

"Then you underestimate the pleasure it gives me."

"Oh, give way," she spluttered. "You waste your time on me."

"Do I?"

She had not realized he was standing so close until his breath stirred the hair at her temple.

"Aye," she snapped. "There is much I admire about your people. Their hard work, thrift, and skill at building weirs to catch enough fish to feed a village. Then there's the courage you exhibited in rescuing me and my comrades." Her voice softened.

"Admiration is a good start, methinks, for a more intimate liaison."

She scowled. "You should not jest about such things. 'Tis with all sincerity I proclaim my regard for you…and for your people," she added hastily. "Nadie, for instance. She is wise and wonderful. A worthy replacement for the ma I lost so many years ago."

"And?" he prodded, turning her to face him.

Egad, but he is persistent.

She steeled her shoulders. "There is no point in sniffing at my skirts. I am not one to spread my affections lightly."

"Nor do I," he said evenly.

"Indeed!" She snorted. "Why, then, do you pretend interest in me while your affections are clearly engaged with another?"

"Huh?" He did not sound the least contrite. "Are you certain you hail from London, Jane? Nearly every nobleman there kept a mistress or two to attend to his baser needs. Surely you did not travel across the world to criticize me for doing the same?"

"I…" *Oh, give way!* His year in London should have been long enough to learn that more respectable families frowned on such practices.

"Unlike many of your noblemen," he continued, "I have no wife to dodge. Nay, I am free of all encumbrances. That makes me better than your English lords."

She studied him, growing troubled. "I did not intend to criticize you or your people, only to deploy any misconceived expectations you may harbor in my direction."

"I see." His voice was cold again. "You do not wish to ally yourself with a savage, eh?"

He still wishes to play that tired old tune? Well, he isn't the only one skilled at twisting words. "On the contrary, I am most grateful for our current alliance. I am happy to be alive and a member of your tribe." And she was.

He was not to be deterred. "I meant, of course, that you will not stoop to lie with one of us. Am I so repugnant to you, Jane?"

She stared at the warrior towering over her, cheeks turning as hot as the flames of their dinner fire. She'd never experienced such a powerful combination of admiration and attraction in all her days. It was most unfortunate his affections were engaged elsewhere.

He studied her for a moment. Then his shoulders relaxed. "Come with me, Jane. There is something I want to show you."

She eyed him warily, but he was already striding across the main village path.

Egad! What now? She scurried with reluctance after her chief.

Wanchese led her away from the village where the trees clustered so thickly they had to skirt around large clusters of them. He bade her halt in the heart of the forest. "Close your eyes, Jane."

"Why?"

"Just do it."

"Very well." She squeezed them shut, puzzled.

"Give me a moment to take my leave. Then you will identify my location while your eyes remain closed. I shall be within calling distance."

What? He wished to play a child's game with her, hiding and seeking one another? She rolled her eyes before closing her lids and counted softly for half a minute. When she finished counting, she heard nothing. However, she immediately discerned his location.

"You stand behind me."

"Aye." Wanchese's whisper stirred the tendrils of hair at the back of her neck. "Count again, Jane."

She cocked her head to one side and counted louder this time to better muffle any sounds he might make. It was no different than before. "You stand to my left. Ten paces away, perhaps?"

"Count a bit longer this time. Then, come find me."

"May I open my eyes to do so?"

"Aye."

She was annoyed at his request. Was there any point to this exercise? Inwardly groaning, she counted then opened her eyes again. She gazed first in the direction he'd departed. Nay, that was too easy. Too predictable. He would pick another path. Rolling her eyes, she twirled in a full circle.

Without thinking, she closed her eyes again, drinking in the sounds of the woodlands. Tree frogs chirped. Water gushed over rocks nearby. A distant feline cried. Minutes passed as the wind gusted against her skin. A twig snapped.

Stiffening, she turned to the sound and opened her eyes. Staring at her, wide-eyed with fear, was a doe and her fawn. Between her utter silence and the wind blowing her scent in the opposite direction, she'd managed to startle them into approaching.

"Pray pardon," she whispered. The pair bounded away, their hooves churning the underbrush. Watching them disappear, she re-engaged the full power of her senses. Pa had trained her well. To listen, observe, smell, taste, and feel.

After a few moments, awareness prickled along her neck and shoulders. She opened her eyes. "You are behind the cedar tree," she called and was rewarded when Wanchese stepped away from its thick trunk.

"Again!" he commanded.

This time the breeze came to her aid. It swirled down from the ridge above, bearing the faint yet tantalizing, scent that was uniquely Wanchese. She tipped her head back and centered her attention on the pile of boulders edging the precipice. He emerged from behind them and sprang over the ten foot drop to land in a crouch before her.

"Wherever I am, you sense my presence. It matters not if I am standing next to you or more than twenty paces away."

"I am skilled at tracking."

"It is the same with me when you are present."

"We are both trained to hunt."

"True, but it is more than that, methinks," he muttered, sounding angry. "I fought it at first, ordering my braves to shadow your people and frighten them into leaving our island. No one was supposed to get hurt. The incident with Askook's hunting party was a terrible error."

"He is the one who killed Lord Howe?"

"Aye. A distant cousin who refuses to settle down. His wanderlust brought him to my village that day. He claimed afterwards to misunderstand my orders, knowing he could easily obtain the counsel's pardon. They considered the killing vengeance for our fallen Chief Pemisapan."

Warmth flooded Jane to learn Wanchese had no part in the slaying of their unarmed colonist, but she still had questions. "You shot at me a-purpose," she accused. "It was a dangerous thing to do and might have ended badly."

"My aim was true." His lip curled. "Did you ever doubt it was a deliberate miss?"

"Nay, it was quite obvious."

"Only to you. Your men assumed they were under attack and started shooting."

"You took an unnecessary risk. One of them might have shot you."

"That bothered you?" His eyes lit.

"Of course! There was no reason to draw blood over the encounter."

"Agreed. And I sensed the challenge you issued me, *before* you demanded I show myself."

"How so?" she said cautiously.

"We are connected, you and I." He advanced on her with purpose.

She took a step back and then another until her shoulders pressed against a tree.

Wanchese reached for her hands and spun her around until he lounged against the tree instead. With their hands still clasped, he drew her towards him.

"It's a powerful connection. One even you cannot deny."

Her gaze dropped to his chest, sun-kissed and rippling with strength. She wanted to reach out and run her hands over its contours, to trace her fingertips over the bear claws painted on his upper arms. She'd always scoffed at the young ladies who preened and sighed over their latest beaus, all the while thinking them silly and weak. Strange, how so far from England, she'd finally met a man who made her sigh.

His lips brushed hers, and her eyelids drifted closed.

She shivered at the rush of awareness that assailed her well-honed senses. The velvety smoothness of his mouth, the musky scent of male and spices and smoke, the warmth of his fingers intertwined with hers, the thud of his heartbeat as it quickened to match her own.

"Nay," she choked, breaking off the kiss and taking a step back. "It is too much."

"On the contrary, it's not near enough." He tightened his hold on her hands and drew her close again.

"Please, Wanchese," she whispered. "I am not—" Her words were lost as his lips claimed hers once more.

His mouth caressed and plundered, gave and took pleasure. He did naught but clasp her hands and woo her with kisses, but she might as well have fallen through the center of a volcano for the eruption of emotion he elicited.

When he raised his head, a breathy moan escaped her. She was startled to discover her arms entwined around his neck.

"*Kear socaquinchenimum*," he murmured. "A fire rages between us. Lie with me. Now, Jane."

The command served as a dash of icy water across her throbbing senses. She stumbled back. "Insensitive boar," she muttered. "You take me to the edge of ecstasy, then offer me nothing but a cheap tumble in the underbrush. It is—" She bit her lip in horror, not intending to lash out at him so cruelly.

His jaw tightened, and his hands clenched almost painfully on hers. "Go ahead and say it. Heathen? Uncivilized?"

"Nay. 'Tis just that I-I did not mean for this to happen."

He whirled with her until her back was against the wide tree trunk once more. He slapped his hands on either side of her. "What? You are remorseful for kissing a savage?"

She shook her head, not knowing what to say or do next. Spinsters did not generally find themselves in these predicaments.

"You felt something, blast you! I was not the only one." This time he spared no gentleness. He bent his head over hers and ravaged her mouth.

Only when dampness rolled down her cheeks and pelted his chest did he draw back.

He brushed at her tears with a callused thumb and swore fiercely. Resting his forehead against hers, he muttered. "You endure ambush and capture and the gods only know what else, but only I have succeeded in making you weep." He drew a ragged breath and cradled her face against his shoulder. "Tell me, Jane. Where did I go wrong?"

The genuine regret in his voice shook her. He sounded more English than native now. She fought to bring her shattered senses under control. Their worlds were so close and yet so far apart. They stood in each other's arms, yet a vast sea of differences separated them.

"Back in London, I was deemed unmarriagable. A spinster." Hating the ugliness of the word, she swiped at the dampness on her face.

"Fools," he said in disdain.

"Naturally, I am unprepared for, well, a good number of things. Your command to lie with you made me, er..." Her voice faded to a whisper.

"If it pleases you more, I will beg."

A wry chuckle escaped her. Then she sobered. "I know you did not intend to shame me."

"Shame you!" He drew back far enough to tip her face up to his. "By the gods, how? I am your chief."

She lowered her eyes. "Perhaps your women would consider it an honor to lie with their chief. But for me, it would be a sin and a shame to lie with a man. Any man. My God and my countrymen would frown on such a thing, since we are not married."

"Your god, eh?" Wanchese stepped away from her and dropped his arms. "Is this the one you call the Christ?"

"Your service as a diplomat serves you well."

Wanchese's face hardened. "Nay, I did not meet this Christ in England. Rather on the coast of Dasamonquepeuc."

She tensed. He referred to the so-called native peace talks with the English that had taken place more than a year ago. The ensuing skirmish had resulted in the slaughter of his chief. It was what had turned his heart against the English.

"Your soldiers invited my chief to attend a peace talk." Venom dripped from his tone. "*Peace* they said, Jane! As soon as Chief Pemisapan and his council approached your countrymen, a command was given. 'Christ our victory,' they shouted. It was their pre-agreed upon signal to attack us.

Thus, in the name of *your* Christ was my leader slaughtered like a wild beast."

He had witnessed Pemisapan's death? She pressed a fist to her mouth, speechless. *Oh, Wanchese! A world of damage was birthed on that battlefield, and the weight of it landed on your shoulders.* He had risen to chief in the wake of the storm. "I am so sorry," she whispered.

"Your apology will not bring back my chief."

His chief. A man he'd revered. Unthinking, she reached for Wanchese's hands. "I know." It was his right to demand consequences for such a cruel deception. The way of the natives.

She grimaced in sympathy. "What will you do?"

Some of the ferocity ebbed from his features. "Unlike Askook, I do not seek my vengeance from the dead but from the living. You and your men will repay us for the lives we lost that day."

She drew a steadying breath. It was his first solid declaration of his intentions towards her and her English comrades. "When we first arrived, I feared you meant to execute us." The birthing ceremony had been horrifically confusing, in that regard.

He tugged impatiently on their joined hands. "What use are you to me in the grave? Nay. You shall live. I have great need of you." Passion roughened his voice as he reached up to give one of her braids a light yank.

"What about James?" she asked, a trifle breathless. "Who does he replace?"

"Chitsa lost her mate."

"Her mate," she repeated, astonished. "You mean they will marry?"

"Aye, if she wants him. If not, he will hunt, fish, and provide for her as long as she has need of him."

"And William?"

"Alawa's mate. Blade and George will serve Riapoke."

"Your brother lost two sons?"

"Nay, he lost two lives. His wife and their unborn babe. She was strolling the beach when the English attacked."

The air left Jane's chest. She wanted to howl her grief to the heavens. It was tragic to learn how much the Roanokes had suffered at the hands of her countrymen. She would have to find a way to impress on Blade and George the sacred significance of their new roles in Riapoke's household.

She laid her head on Wanchese's shoulder. He did not move. They simply stood together beneath the oak, two souls giving and seeking solace.

"Nadie calls me *amosens*," she murmured after a while. "Was her daughter caught in the crossfire as well?"

"Nay, she was taken by the slave traders. The same ones who attacked the English."

"I saw her!" Jane raised her head and pushed at his chest, excited. "At the Great Trading Path. I knew something about her looked familiar. She was so lovely and never lost her courage. Not even after she was sold. Oh, and she bore the same bear claw markings as you."

"The ferocity and strength of the bear dwells deep in the spirit of my people."

"You think she is the same young woman?"

"Aye. Her name is Amitola."

"Wait a blessed minute!" Jane exclaimed. "Did you witness her sale, then?" He'd been there the whole time. She was sure of it.

"Aye."

She took a step back. "You watched that lovely, fragile creature get led away by the man who purchased her and did nothing to save her?" She pressed a hand to her heart. "Why?"

"I was sent to rescue you."

"That is all you have to say on the poor woman's behalf?"

His lip curled. "My sister is not fragile. She is far more cunning and resourceful than you."

His sister? The revelation, coupled with his lack of concern, was staggering. She took another step away from her chief, wanting nothing to do with such callousness.

"While you ponder the blackness of my heart, I'll give you something else to think on," he said coldly. "If you mention the name of your God within a hundred miles of Dasamon-quepeuc, I will be powerless to save you or your men from the consequences. Do we understand one another?"

"Indeed, we do." She bit out the words. *Devil spawn! Heartless fiend!* Her fingers itched for her dagger. She could understand his abhorrence for Christianity based on his brief and horrendous brush with it, but she was furious with him for not lifting a finger in his own sister's defense.

"Come," he said abruptly. "I will escort you back to camp where chiefly matters await me."

A strained silence stretched between them on the walk back to the village. Wanchese paused just before they exited the tree line and turned her to face him. "You refused to mate with me, but you did not precisely object to this." He captured her lips once more in a ravenous kiss.

"Ah, Jane!" he groaned against her mouth. "Pray do not deny me the rest of you for too long."

She pressed her hands to his chest, intending to push him away and found herself sliding them higher to encircle his neck. *Burn me,* but she seemed to possess no will to resist him.

Dazzled by the fire leaping between them, she reveled in the scent and taste and feel of Wanchese. *Egad!* She was a spinster who had never been kissed before, yet here she was. Kissing her *chief!*

Emotions she'd never felt before coursed through her,

inside and out, licking like flames along the surface of her skin and shaking her to her very soul.

She sensed wants and needs in Wanchese that matched her own, so powerful it bordered on desperation. What a quagmire! If they were not careful, they would drown themselves in all those wants and needs.

Then again, if this was what drowning felt like, maybe she liked drowning after all.

*W*anchese deposited her before the fire pit at the entrance to his longhouse. She prayed none would notice her heightened color and swollen lips as she coaxed the smoldering embers back to flame.

She soon discovered she would no longer have to worry about scavenging through his lodge to gather provisions for his meals. Following the cobra incident, her stew pot remained stocked. Sometimes it was one of the Englishmen who brought her meat. Other times it was Riapoke, whom she'd learned from Nadie was Wanchese's elder half-brother. On occasion, it was another one of his braves, though she suspected Riapoke was behind the efforts.

The variety of fare was unbeatable. A set of plump squirrels one afternoon, a half dozen pigeons the next, and a leg of venison the following day. It was a blessing to have so much food to eat again. Her hungry days were slipping further and further into the past.

Raised by trappers in the uplands of England, she still preferred to hunt her own game instead of depending on others to supply it, though. So she watched and waited for the perfect moment to steal away from her work. Eventually, she would find a wee bit of time for her favorite pastime — trapping.

Plans for a newly designed trap had been spinning in her head for days. She did not like the springing nooses and loosely covered holes favored by so many of the local hunters. Way too often, the captured game merely served as a mid-day snack for another animal passing by.

She'd experimented with a good number of variations in construction methods during their ship ride to the New World. The basic concept involved building a box the size of the creature she wanted to capture and then springing a trapdoor shut to contain it.

She rushed through dinner preparations for Wanchese, but only Kanti showed up to eat. Leaving her in charge of the simmering stew, Jane hurried back to Nadie's longhouse. Instead of settling down for the night, she remained outside by the fire and tinkered by the rays of dying sun to assemble the first pieces of her newest trap design.

Alas, her progress was slow. Without her English hammers and saws, she was forced to chisel and carve each piece of raw wood down to its correct size with the use of an assortment of handmade tools. Mostly bits and pieces of sharpened rocks.

When the sun slipped behind the horizon, she moved closer to the fire, tossed on a handful of dry twigs, and stirred the coals. They leaped and crackled with flames. By the firelight, she resumed the painstaking task of whittling down the outer edges of her trapdoor. She needed it smooth enough to slide along a set of wooden tracks when it slammed shut.

As she tapped away at the wood, her hand slipped and came in at the wrong angle. She narrowly missed gouging her own finger.

Groaning in frustration, she tossed the mangled piece of trapdoor into the fire. She would have to start over on that piece.

A man squatted next to her and held out a small ax.

She glanced up in delight. It was Riapoke.

She gave him an appreciative grin and accepted the handle. "This is exactly what I need. I thank you!" Running her fingers along the bone handle of the ax, she admired its intricate design of stripes and zigzags. Why it was the same pattern as—

"Gift from weroance." Riapoke spoke the words slowly, careful to enunciate each syllable.

She was amazed to learn he knew a bit of English but flustered to realize who'd sent him to her.

"Ah," she murmured. *Of course, Wanchese is behind this.* The same design was etched on the shaft of his arrows. She peeked over the fire towards the longhouse where their chief lived.

He was standing in the doorway with Kanti. She stepped closer and stood on tiptoe in the moonlight to caress his face. He glanced over her head and held Jane's gaze for a moment. Then he wheeled abruptly and entered the longhouse. After a short pause, she followed. The skin fell into place behind them.

Her chest wrenched. *Devil take the man!* Even after the kisses they'd shared, he was making no effort to end his dalliance with Kanti. Swallowing her disappointment, she schooled her expression and turned to Riapoke. "This may look like an ordinary pile of sticks, but I assure you they will be trapping an animal a few days from now."

"Huh?" He settled down beside her and crossed his legs beneath him. To her relief, he said little and allowed her to work. He was a quick study, though. Occasionally, he lent a hand or finger to help her assemble the pieces. He also kept the fire leaping until her lids became too heavy to continue working.

Tomorrow was going to be another long, hot day of

harvesting corn and beans with Nadie and her maidens. Jane knew she'd best get some rest before it arrived.

She stretched and yawned. "I thank you for tending the fire and keeping me company, my friend." She bit her lip at the endearment the moment it slipped out. Strange. She had just met the man and exchanged only a handful of words, yet already she thought of him as a friend.

"Here." Her voice hardened a notch as she handed him the ax. "Please return this to your weroance with my thanks for the use of it."

Riapoke returned the ax to her. "Gift. Wanchese." He rose to his feet and swung away from her in the direction of his longhouse.

Unaccountably pleased by the gift, she stared after him and stiffened in surprise. His build and gait were frightfully familiar. They were a perfect match to the shadowy figure she occasionally glimpsed following her around camp.

"Why did you order your brother to follow me?" Hands on her hips, she faced Wanchese. It had taken a full forty-eight hours to catch him alone.

Wanchese finished tying the cord around his waist to secure his buckskins. Twirling his daggers, he plunged them into their sheaths.

"Did you come to watch me bathe, Jane?" He shook his damp hair like a dog and smirked when the flying droplets glistened on her arms.

She felt the start of a blush stain her cheeks. Under the guise of answering the call of nature, she had gone searching for him during her dinner break and found him submerged to his waist, washing. What a glorious sight it was to view the rivulets of water running down his massive shoulders and coppery chest.

A thick wall of water cascaded behind him, forcing her to step closer to catch his words. It crashed against the rocks and spewed into the stream below. They were deep in the woods on the opposite side of camp from the spring. Apparently, this was where the men bathed. The mid-day sun spilled over the clearing, turning the overspray from the waterfall into tiny gems.

She squared her shoulders, because she had no intention of letting Wanchese unnerve her with his outrageous speech again. "Am I your prisoner? Are you having me followed to prevent my escape?"

He glared. "You are a member of my tribe, not a prisoner. Riapoke guards you to keep you safe." He started to rise from the water, apparently not the least bit concerned about displaying his nakedness to her.

She hastily squeezed her eyes shut and spun around to give him his privacy while he dressed.

"Safe!" She bit out the word. "I reckon that safety just happens to possess the added benefit of reporting back to you my every move?" She peeked over her shoulder to gauge his progress in dressing.

He'd already donned his buckskins, so she turned to confront him again.

He shrugged. "What do you want, Jane?"

Blast him, but she liked his directness. "I wish to send word to my friends, Rose and Agnes. They need to know I am alive and well. And Chief Manteo, of course, since he was the one who sent you to fetch me."

Wanchese's expression was lazy and indulgent.

The truth sank in. "He already knows, doesn't he?"

"Aye." He slipped two leather pouches over his head and adjusted them to rest against his side.

"Well? Did he share the news with Rose?"

"Huh? I do not involve myself in Manteo's affairs." His tone was dismissive.

"Well, I *do* wish to involve myself, at least enough to deliver word to my friends. I cannot understand why you harbor such qualms against allowing me to visit the island."

"It is not safe."

"I will return to Dasamonquepeuc if that is your fear. I will swear it, if you wish."

He closed the short distance between them. "Nay. I have not the time to fetch you from another ambush. You do remember what happened the last time you attempted to cross the sounds?"

She met his steely gaze and fumed. Their capture had mostly been the fault of the squabbling, pampered noblemen who had bumbled the caravan of colonists straight into harm's way. Wanchese knew she was capable of maneuvering through the surrounding forests and waterways with far more stealth and caution.

She straightened to her full height. "I can take care of myself. All I require is a canoe to sail to Croatoa and back."

"Nay, you are not ready. Nadie will train you."

"Nadie?" *She is an old woman, not a huntress like myself.* "She is a truly amazing lady," she conceded, "but she is more intent on honing my skills as a housekeeper and farmer than a scout."

"Winter will soon be on us. Nadie is wise to spend her days running the harvest."

Jane felt a stab of guilt. He was right, of course. Nadie worked tirelessly to ensure the survival of the entire village in the coming months. It had been a lean summer. The drought had taken its toll, and the rescue of her and her English comrades gave the Roanokes five more mouths to feed.

She pinched the bridge of her nose. "Pray forgive me for intruding on your bathing, Chief Wanchese." She would simply have to find a way around him and Riapoke. She had no intention of letting an entire winter pass without getting word to her friends.

"By your leave, I will return to work." She bobbed a quick bow. Nadie would scold her mercilessly for her prolonged absence from the fields.

"Jane?"

She paused in her hasty departure and spun around. "Aye, my lord chief?"

"There is no need to seek my forgiveness. You may join me in my bath any time you wish."

CHAPTER 7: FESTIVAL OF CORN

*H*eat enveloped Jane's face. Unaccustomed to such intimate banter, she bobbed another awkward bow. "Pray allow me to return to my duties," she muttered and spun away without awaiting Wanchese's reply.

She nearly skidded into James as she flew through the entrance to Dasamonquepeuc.

"Mistress Jane!" he exclaimed with a joyful catch to his voice. He grabbed her elbows and held her at arms' length. "Be there a fire, lass?"

She snorted, trying not to blush. "You have no idea, my friend. You have no idea."

He guffawed and twirled her around and around despite her extra few inches of height. It was remarkable how their acquaintance had evolved on the ship ride over. She'd often deplored his crude jests and flirtatious manner. Somewhere along the way, however, they'd become friends.

"Why, James Hynde," she teased when he let her go. "Nay do not remove your hat," she admonished when he started to lift his brim. It was the only thing that kept his pale skin from baking in the sun.

"You resemble the cat who caught the canary. I don't suppose it has anything to do with the woman who wove that hideous contraption posing as a hat on your head? Or is it a laundry basket you're wearing? I cannot be certain."

"Now that you mention it," he chortled, looking so abashed her suspicions were confirmed. He'd always possessed an eye for a bonny maid. "Their womenfolk are downright comely. An' famously skilled at weaving an' painting an' making jewelry and such. You have to admire that in a body."

She snorted, harboring no doubts he was admiring every female body in camp. "Tribal life agrees with you, my friend. Now, tell me how the others fare before I return to my duties."

He chuckled. "Ye'll no' hardly recognize William next time you see him. He's dropping weight. In a good way," he assured when she frowned. "With no bakeries in sight, he cannot indulge in his usual pasties and sweet sauces. 'Tis all good an' well, for it ain't easy to hide the extra pounds in these here togs."

He meant the native loincloths they wore, of course. They both chuckled and flushed.

Oddly enough, the sight of so much skin no longer shocked her as it had on her first encounter with the locals. Although she would never be comfortable gadding about with so little on as the other women did — that was taking things a wee too far for her — she enjoyed the freedom of running and moving around in her knee-length skirt. She did not miss her former floor-length gowns of worsted wool with their scratchy ruffs and suffocating corsets and stays. Nor did she long to totter around once more in high-heeled slippers, pretending to enjoy herself at endless teas, luncheons, and balls while keeping a watchful eye on her spoiled pupils.

Ah, but there was something to be said for the simpler life of the Roanokes!

"I worry a bit about the lads, though." James ran a hand over his beard. "Blade frets over the whereabouts of his pa. An' George? Well, you know George. He's bent on leaving this place."

She nodded, pursing her lips. Indeed she knew George. Too well. They needed to get word back to their fellow colonists, and soon, before he stirred up a pile of trouble attempting to do so on his own. Her gaze rested on a woman hurrying towards them with a hoe in hand. She was past the first bloom of youth and bore a determined expression. "Are you going to introduce me to your admirer?"

"Who?" James's gaze followed where she pointed and his brows flew up. "Oh, ah, her name is Chitsa. More an' likely, she's coming for you and no' me, lass. To fetch you back to the fields."

She grinned at his flustered demeanor. "Perhaps someone has already explained things to you, but the whole bloody ceremony we endured on our arrival was an adoption of sorts. We are now members of the Roanoke tribe. Nadie claimed me as her daughter. What is Chitsa's claim on you?"

According to Wanchese, she could take James as her mate, if she chose.

James shifted uncomfortably. "I don't rightly know, Jane. She han't said much that I can understand, tho' I'm fair to certain she's a widow."

Indeed, she was. Jane's grin widened. It was apparent James had some idea of what was in store for him.

He eyed Chitsa with a healthy amount of male interest as she halted before them.

And he's not opposed to the idea.

She jabbered something unintelligible and thrust the hoe

at Jane, while her sultry gaze roved over James. Neither seemed aware she was still present.

"Alright, then." She fought to contain her amusement. "Keep an eye on the lads for me, James." She did not expect a response.

"I allus do, Mistress Jane." His voice was distant, distracted.

"Don't want George venturing off on a fool's errand."

James was listening closer than she supposed. "The same goes fer you," he called after her. "You fetch me first, iffen you be gettin' any ideas, you hear?"

His words were drowned out by Nadie's sharp cry. "Ireh!"

Faith, how she hated that word. She broke into a jog and spent the next several hours hoeing weeds and plucking beans and squash.

Something in the air felt different about today. Chitsa returned from her rendezvous with James and chattered excitedly with Nadie. Catching Jane's curious gaze, she paused and rested her hands atop her hoe.

"*Vunamun.*" She gestured to the neighboring field.

The platform overlooking the corn was empty. Normally, a pair of lads pulled guard beneath its protective roof. When blackbirds and other scavengers ventured into the field, the boys flew down their ladder and ran among the rows, shrieking and waving sticks. Today there was no need for their vigil, because the rows of corn were full of maidens.

The precious corn harvest had begun.

Nadie, Chitsa, and Jane remained where they were, working until dusk to fill basket after basket with the ever-ripening vines of beans, pumpkin, and squash. Under Nadie's direction, the elder women of the tribe shelled the beans and laid them out to dry. The younger girls guarded them while they dried, using leafy branches to wave away birds and other marauders. This would preserve them throughout the winter months.

The sound of drums greeted them when they trudged back to the center of the village with their final baskets for the day. A handful of dancers weaved in and out of the ceremonial circle in a series of slow undulating steps.

"Go." Nadie nudged her. "Wash."

Puzzled, Jane deposited her basket and hoe and made for the spring. A half dozen other maidens splashed, bathed, and chattered. A basket of fresh yucca leaves rested by the water's edge.

The maidens quieted at the sight of her.

Careful to keep them in front of her so she could observe their movements, Jane stripped off her sweaty clothing, grabbed a handful of the soap leaves, and stepped cautiously into the spring. She chose the furthermost edge of the stream, as far away from the rest of the women as possible.

As before, the water soothed her tired back and appendages. She loathed the thought of ever leaving its frothing depths. The women around her completed their toilettes and moved toward camp in pairs and small groups, but she lingered.

She drank in the stony ridge serving as a backdrop to the spring, noting each ledge, each crevice, each small cavern entrance. She intended to come back and explore the caverns when she had more time.

Sinking farther into the water, she closed her eyes and allowed herself to drift. It was an unheard of luxury to bathe so often. Back in London, her countrymen were a superstitious lot. They believed too frequent bathing upset the balance of the bodies' humours, and they were wrong. She'd never been cleaner or in better health her entire life.

The lack of voices returned her to the present. She opened her eyes to discover she was alone at last. Sighing, she crushed the leaves she still held, lathered them in her hair, and ducked beneath the falls to rinse. It was with great reluctance she finally waded to the edge of the stream to make her exit.

She stopped short. Her garments were missing.

A reluctant chuckle escaped her at the age-old prank. Alas, she would have to return to camp as naked as the day she was born. Either that, or she could scuttle betwixt a pair of spruce branches and create an even greater stir for the prankster.

Her chuckle died. *A pox on all the maidens who shared my bath!* She should have never closed her eyes while they were near.

She pondered her options. Perhaps she would wait for nightfall and tiptoe her way into the village. Unfortunately, that would give the mosquitoes a few hours to feast on her person. She chewed on her lower lip. How she wished for the smoky interior of the longhouse where she lived with Nadie. The swirling haze went a blessed long way to keeping down the swarms of insects who rode the night breezes.

She froze at the sound of whistling and sank back in the water, submerging herself up to her neck. *Egad! Is the prankster returning to gloat?*

To her surprise, Wanchese appeared, carrying a bundle in one arm.

"Ah." He stopped short. "Pray pardon me for interrupting your bath." He did not sound the least repentant.

She rolled her eyes and answered dryly, "Think nothing of it. I suppose this evens the score, since I accosted you during your own bath not so long ago. Why do you seek me?"

"I do not seek." He stabbed a finger in her direction as he advanced on her. "You are the one who seeks. These, I believe?"

He unrolled his bundle and deposited a set of fresh

garments on the boulder where her previous ones had rested.

Bless him for bringing her clothes! But how had he known? *Ah, right. Riapoke.* Perhaps being constantly spied on had its benefits, after all.

Wanchese straightened and propped a foot on the boulder. "Is this your idea of taking care of yourself?"

The blasted man actually rubbed his hands together in glee. He was enjoying her discomfort all too much.

She borrowed one of his favorite gestures and shrugged, hating that he had the upper hand in the matter. She could only pray he would take his leave soon.

"Wise is your silence." He crossed his arms. "Riapoke noted the departure of your garments ahead of your person. He reported the incident to me with haste."

"I shall be sure to thank him." She was unable to hide the snipe in her voice.

"Huh? No need. It is his duty to watch over you," Wanchese reminded. "Though I hear you can well take care of yourself." His sarcasm was thick enough to cut with a knife. If only she possessed one at the moment!

It took all her strength to resist the urge to splash the smirk from his face. "I thank you, Chief Wanchese, for troubling yourself over my affairs. There is no need, of course, for you to linger and play the part of lady's maid."

"You offer mere words, whereas I am more a man of action." Mahogany eyes glinting with challenge, Wanchese unclasped his arms and leaned forward. "There are so many better ways to thank a man for his service."

"Is that not Kanti's duty?" she snapped. "To make you feel appreciated in ways that do not require conversation?"

"Why, Jane," he mocked, abandoning the boulder and walking to the water's edge. Your concern for my needs is touching."

"Cad!" Blushing hotly, she ducked beneath the water to cool her cheeks. The evening breeze nipped at the waters and chilled her when she surfaced. She shivered and longed to dry off so she might don the garments he'd brought her.

Wanchese squatted and held out a hand. "Come out before you freeze."

"Turn around."

"Not a chance."

"At least close your eyes."

"I have seen you before, Jane."

"It was under an entirely different and most deplorable set of circumstances," she fumed. How dare he throw in her face her tattered state on the slave trading block? "Tonight, I desire a bit of privacy. Pray indulge me for once," she added with a touch of desperation.

To her surprise, Wanchese inclined his head and turned around, though he did not leave. "Very well. There is a matter I wish to discuss with you."

She groaned inwardly. Why couldn't he just deposit her clothing and take his leave like a proper gentleman?

"The Festival of Corn begins tonight. There will be feasting, dancing, and games. Pray do not partake in the games."

What? Her interest was piqued. "What sort of games?"

"All manner of weaponry and sports."

"Aha. I reckon this is your way of eliminating the competition?" she taunted. He had watched her hunt and trap for weeks at Roanoke Island. He knew she was highly skilled with knives and guns.

"You will not compete, Jane. That is an order."

She scowled at his back. "Why?"

"Askook has returned from his latest hunt."

"I see." He was the hated cousin who'd killed George's father.

147

"He is a dangerous man and keeps many unsavory alliances. Do nothing to draw his attention tonight."

Jane's heartbeat sped at the notion he was actually concerned for her wellbeing. "Why do you allow such a detestable creature to remain in your village?"

"He is family. So far, I have no proof for the many reasons I wish to toss him out."

"So far," she murmured. It sounded as if he was working to gather such proof. She clenched her teeth to keep them from chattering. The wind had nearly finished drying her. She shook out the garments lying on the boulder and fingered their ornate trim.

"These are lovely." She beheld a deerskin dress and a pair of fringed leggings. They were trimmed with dyed beads and shells. Wanchese's signature double black stripes and red zigzags adorned the outer sides of the leggings. A design of bear claws was stitched in the neckline of the dress.

Wanchese ignored her female delight with the new outfit when he turned around, though his gaze reflected appreciation for how she looked in it. "When Askook learns of your proficiency with the bow, he will want to challenge you."

"Then my proficiency will have to be our little secret, my lord chief." *For now.*

"Good. Keep in mind Askook is deft at provoking fights."

"Fear not, Chief Wanchese." She smoothed her hands down the soft deerskin dress. In truth, she was weary from her work in the fields. She could use one night of rest. "I will not shoot, throw knives, or engage in any other feats of weaponry tonight." His concern about her safety pleased her to no end. Perhaps there was a wee bit of heart inside him somewhere.

"And no running in the races."

There will be racing, too? How fascinating! "Is there anything

I *am* allowed to do, your worship?" She batted her eyes at him.

Humor flickered in his gaze as it roved lazily over her. "Aye. You may dine at the feast."

"Very well, Chief Wanchese." She bowed from the waist and clasped her hands beneath her chin in exaggerated obeisance. "I am hungry as a bear and will be pleased to restrict myself to gluttony at your Festival of Corn."

"Our festival," he corrected. "You are a Roanoke maiden now, Jane."

She smothered a grin, enjoying the rush of warmth at his persistence in including her in his world. Trading in her life as an orphan for that of a Roanoke maiden was hardly turning out to be the poorest bargain she'd ever made. Far from it.

Bemused, she followed the progress of her chief as he left her alone at last and strode back to camp.

———

*J*ames and William lounged in front of the large community fire at the center of the village. With their faces and chests painted and their legs crossed beneath them, they blended well with the natives. If not for their fairer skin, Jane might have missed their presence altogether.

Chitsa sat conspicuously close to James. Her hand movements and expression claimed him as her own. In turn, he appeared rested and content. A smile tugged at his lips.

William's partner was a slip of a woman with a round, kindly face. She ladled stew in a hollowed-out gourd and knelt before him with it outstretched. She must be Alawa.

He grinned his appreciation, face flushing with pleasure. They passed the gourd between them, sharing the stew.

"Already, they forget they are Englishmen."

Jane frowned at the bitterness in George's voice and turned to find him standing at her elbow.

"A part of us will always remain English," she assured gently.

"Nay, not a part. *All* of me is English," he returned fiercely. "I am George Howe, the Baron of Nattershorne and a gentleman through and through. No amount of time with these savages will diminish who I am."

Mercy! Didn't he realize his lordly titles and airs meant nothing in Dasamonquepeuc? She wanted to shake him for being so stubborn. "Of course not. Our hardships do not diminish us but rather make us stronger."

"One of us needs to have a word with James and William," he responded, undeterred from his narrow-minded strain of thinking. "We cannot afford the luxury of growing too comfortable here."

Her ire sparked at his tone. Gone was the lad who'd learned Latin and geography during her lessons on the ship. In his place stood a much harder, more callused soul. And who could blame him? At fifteen, he'd witnessed more brutality and endured more suffering than most men did in a lifetime.

She swallowed the words of chastisement bubbling to her lips and instead tried to appeal to his logic. "Methinks, our men are merely grateful to have a roof over their heads and food in their bellies again."

"Call it what you will," he growled. "We idle away precious time that would best be spent planning a rescue for our missing colonists. They serve as slaves tonight wherever they are, while we sit here filling our bellies, Mistress Jane."

She drew a sharp breath. On this matter, George was entirely correct. "You have my word. I will not stop searching for them so long as I still breathe."

"Indeed? I was not aware you had even begun your search."

His barely concealed sarcasm chafed her backside. She had begged Wanchese to allow them to visit the surviving colonists at Croatoa, had she not? She had worked from dawn until dusk in the fields at Dasamonquepeuc to ensure they would have plenty to eat in the coming winter.

Faith, if we starve to death, there will be no rescue missions! Now that George was harping on it, however, her actions seemed paltry stacked against the list of things the missing colonists might be suffering. She could not bear to even speculate about the plight of the women — the indignities they were likely being forced to bear.

She jolted as the drums began to beat, a slow steady cadence at first. The rhythm surged and built. Dancers twirled around the fire. Women carrying baskets on their heads joined the leaping men in the ring. Their hips swayed gently as they wove in between the other dancers, making the motions of threshing. It was a re-enactment of the harvest.

The Festival of Corn was beginning.

Jane scanned the gathering crowd of maidens and braves for Chief Wanchese and found him standing on the temple balcony next to Noshi, the priest. Arms folded and faces solemn, they presided over the festivities in the presence of their forefathers' spirits. It was a joining of the past and the present, the old and the new, the planting and the harvest.

She sensed the exact moment Wanchese glanced her way. A tremor of excitement ran through her limbs as his heavy-lidded gaze locked with hers. Searching. Wanting. Waiting.

Guilt fisted in her gut beneath his intense regard. He claimed they were connected. Could he discern her very thoughts?

After all he had done for her and her English comrades,

she didn't care to be caught standing next to George while embroiled in a discussion about leaving Dasamonquepeuc. Her only consolation was that Wanchese stood too far away to overhear them.

"What have you in mind?" she whispered without lowering her gaze from Wanchese's face.

He leaned closer. "A plan to get us out of here. Maybe in time to commence building the City of Raleigh before winter sets in, like we originally planned."

"Pray assure me your plan does not include anything foolhardy."

"Ah, methinks you will quite approve of my plan, Mistress Jane."

She both welcomed and deplored hearing the old, familiar George creep back into his voice. The adventurer. The lover of a good lark.

The dangers around them were real and imminent. It was not the time to be adding any unnecessary risks to the mix. "I am listening."

"Nay. Another time," he answered. "Too many eyes rest upon us now. Amonsoquath sticks closer to me than a cockle burr; and when he is not around, two brothers named Kimi and Kitchi take turns watching me."

Egad! He had three spies? She only had one.

"This is news to you, eh?" George's lip curled. "Though I do not see him at the moment, the one they call Riapoke guards you just as closely as the others guard me."

She shot him a curious look. "According to Nadie the Wise, Riapoke became your adoptive father during our arrival ceremony."

"Faugh!" George shook his head in disgust. "It was a violent and vulgar ordeal. I regret you had to endure such frightful indignities. No Englishwoman should ever—"

She laid a hand on his arm. "All's well that ends well, my

friend. We are safe, well fed, and have a roof over our heads. For these things, I am most grateful."

Sadly, George was not the least bit ready to discuss his new role with the Roanokes. *Perhaps with more time...*

"I will continue to negotiate with Wanchese," she promised.

He rounded angrily on her. "Why does he keep us here? He should have reunited us with the other colonists on Croatoa weeks ago."

Well, burn it! Her first attempt to explain the concept of their adopted families had fallen on deaf ears.

"I am hoping to arrange us a visit with them soon," she offered cautiously. "As it happens, we arrived to Dasamon-quepeuc in the middle of their harvest. Helping them gather it is the least we can do to repay Chief Wanchese for our rescue." It would only be a visit, though. Chief Manteo of the Croatoans already had enough mouths to feed for the winter. She thought she'd explained that multiple times already.

He nodded, somewhat mollified. "Perhaps. I suppose the delay also allows more time to flesh out the details of my plan. In the meantime, we need to carve as many Maltese Crosses as possible on the trees in the vicinity."

"Why, George! The crosses are a sign of distress," she protested. "We are not in distress."

"Maybe. Maybe not, Mistress Jane." His voice hardened. "I see how the heathen men ogle you. As if you are available for the taking."

Well, blow me down! She stared at him in astonishment. As an unwed woman, she *was* available for courtship, whether he liked it or not. Overly tall spinsters who'd reached the advanced age of four and twenty without securing a beau might not be a premium commodity back in England, but things were different here. In that regard, they were different in a good way.

George grimaced. "One in particular watches you more closely than the others."

She scowled, sorely tempted to box the ears of the young jack-a-napes and be done with it.

"But fear not, Mistress Jane," the pompous lad continued. "I have every intention of extricating you from the clutches of this heathen and his band of rogues soon."

Soon. The word rang ominously in her ears, giving her the start of a headache.

"Aha. Well, you know where to find me when you are ready to discuss your plan." She moved toward the community fire. George was beyond reasoning with in his current frame of mind. Let him waste the night away, plotting and fuming. She would consult with James about the urgency of talking some sense into him.

Every now and then, the hunger pains suffered during their recent captivity still dug their phantom claws into her sides. While there was food a-plenty flowing, she intended to eat.

She waved at James and William on the other side of the campfire and hurried to join the feast.

One of the swaying maidens swung the basket from her head and laid a steaming ear of corn at the feet of Achak, the medicine man. She bowed low to him and rejoined the dancers. Achak lifted the ear in a grand, sweeping gesture and drew back its outer husks and silken strands to reveal bright golden kernels. He brandished it in the air like a trophy. It was still steaming from its sojourn through the hollowed-out log resting beside the community fire. An enormous pile of corn rested there beneath a layer of glowing embers.

Achak chanted over the corn. His voice soared in a singsong quality and grew louder until his volume rivaled the power of the drums. His chanting ceased suddenly, and he plunged the ear of corn into the fire.

It was a sacrifice, Jane presumed, of the first fruits.

Afterwards, the dancing women lowered the rest of their baskets and began to toss steaming ears of corn into the crowd. Jane waited until the majority of the crowd gnawed at their cobs before snatching one out of the air for herself. She'd only eaten this marvelous vegetable on one other occasion.

Chief Manteo had delivered a generous supply of it to Fort Raleigh during their initial rendezvous on Roanoke Island. The colonists had devoured it, all the while worrying what they would do for their next meal.

Tonight, she bit into the sweet and succulent kernels with no such fear. Every member of the Roanoke tribe feasted from overflowing vats of corn and herb-laced meats, and tomorrow there would be more. The long days of harvest were paying off. Already their storage bins boasted vast quantities of beans and corn, rice and dried meat, salted fish and grain. The harvest would continue until the plants withered, and the temperatures turned to frost.

Jane gazed with pride over the faces gathered around the fire. Their tribe was remarkably well prepared for the coming winter.

---

*T*rue to her word, Jane stood on the sidelines among the spectators when the games began. The races were first. Twelve braves assembled at the starting line.

She caught her breath when Chief Wanchese strode to the line to join his men. Stripped down to nothing but his loincloth, he was a magnificent creature with bulging arms, narrow hips, and well-corded thighs. The bear claws on his upper arms flexed as he crouched low to the ground and tensed to spring. Long black hair splayed against his shoulders and swung in the evening breeze.

Silence settled over the crowd as Achak approached. He raised his staff and issued a piercing cry. It was the signal everyone waited for.

The runners launched themselves into the race. Torches marked a path along the outer perimeter of the village. Maidens, braves, and children crowded on either side and encouraged their favorite contestants with much whooping and calling. Some ran alongside their favored runner for a short distance before falling back to rejoin the spectators.

Jane remained at the starting line and leaned into the race course, craning for a glimpse of whoever took the lead. The figures of the runners flashed between the torches. Not one but two men appeared around the final bend. Wanchese and his elder half-brother, Riapoke, sprinted towards the finish line.

She drank in the sight of them. They were, by far, the most beautiful men she'd ever beheld. Their legs blurred beneath the torches and moonlight. Never before had she witnessed anyone run at such a glorious speed. As sleek and graceful as stallions, they flew across the finish line in a dead tie. Their contenders shot across the same line seconds later.

The frenzy of the crowd was deafening. It was impossible to remain still. She jumped and cheered from the sheer joy of the moment.

The runners walked around with their hands on their heads while maidens splashed them with skins of water to cool them.

Jane's mouth tightened as Kanti appeared and ministered to Wanchese. Above her head, his eyes sought Jane out, smoldering and exultant. Far from tired after his exertions, he vibrated with suppressed energy and impatience.

The light in his eyes beckoned her as surely as if he had called her name aloud. She took a step toward him but stopped when Kanti stood on tiptoe to whisper something in his ear.

In the end, Jane nodded at Wanchese and turned away. It would do no good to make a spectacle of herself. He already had Kanti to share in his celebrations.

Next came the target shooting. The crowd shifted across the main village road and re-assembled on the practice field. Wide circle targets rose from the ground at increasing heights and varying intervals. They were aligned in torchlit lanes. Men strapped with quivers took their places at the head of the lanes and notched their bows.

Soon, only four of the original ten contestants remained standing. Alas, Riapoke narrowly missed the center of the farthest target. Not so with Wanchese. He received a perfect score, along with a pair of men who looked enough alike to pass as brothers. An announcer raised their arms and shouted their names, Kimi and Kitchi.

Lads swarmed the practice field, removing the arrows from the targets and depositing them behind the starting line. Two elder men examined each arrow with care and placed them in piles. Some would require sharpening and others repair on the morrow.

As soon as the field was clear of arrows, the targets were repositioned, much closer to the contestants this time. Knives with richly decorated handles appeared in all shapes and sizes. This was the throwing contest.

Fascinated, Jane pressed closer, longing for the hilt of a double-edged hunting blade in her hand.

The crowd quieted as the throwing commenced. She closed her eyes and imagined the air peeling away on both sides of the blade as it whistled its way across the field and sank home in one of the wooden targets. She envisioned the target and knew how far to draw back her arm, exactly how much pressure to exert on the handle, and the precise angle from which it would fly free of her fingers.

"Mistress Jane!"

Her eyelids flew open. Blade knelt before her on one knee, a dagger outstretched. "My warrior friend bids you join the competition."

She reached greedily for the knife, then caught herself and pulled back. "Nay, Blade. I cannot." *I promised Wanchese.* She bit her lip. "'Tis not proper for a maiden to engage in such sports."

"You are the best, Mistress Jane. I told him so."

"Who did you tell, Blade?"

"His name is Askook." The lad's eyes snapped with excitement. "An' he speaks a good deal of English."

Her chest thudded with dread.

"These are real warriors and admire such things, Mistress Jane," he pleaded. "Pray demonstrate your skill with the dagger as you did with the bow."

"'Tis not so simple, Blade. I gave my word that I would not—"

A shout interrupted them. A man whom she'd never seen before leaped atop a boulder and addressed the crowd. His face was painted in an eerie pattern of black and white vertical stripes that made her think of an animal peering between the slats of a cage.

She didn't understood his words but could glean the gist of his meaning. He was issuing some sort of challenge. To her.

Oh Blade! What have you done?

The crowd turned to face her. In the flickering torchlight,

their faces displayed a myriad of emotions — surprise, curiosity, and doubt.

She searched for Wanchese's face among them. He stood to one side, watching Askook, his expression dark. Nevertheless, he did not interrupt the warrior's presentation.

The faces in the crowd turned eager. A few voices began to chant, "Jane. Jane. Jane."

She raised and dropped her hands helplessly at Wanchese, hoping to receive some indication of how he wished her to proceed.

Fire and fury swirled in his eyes, but he jerked his head toward the targets.

She could not suppress a grin as she snatched up the dagger Blade offered and jogged onto the practice field.

Blade gave a whoop of excitement as she took her place beside Wanchese. It appeared she would be competing with him alone.

Why doesn't Askook join in the game, and what is his purpose in pitting me against my chief? She turned to find the man in question in the crowd.

He regarded them with a dark sort of glee.

Resisting the urge to shiver, she nodded coolly and returned her attention to the targets.

Lads swarmed the field, removing the knives thrown in the previous round. Wanchese turned to her and held his blade out, tip pointing upwards, and motioned for her to do the same. His gaze swept over her hotly as he tapped his fist against his chest. It was the salute of one warrior to another. She'd witnessed his braves greet each other in the same manner. His gesture was met with a good deal of murmuring.

"My chief," she whispered and bowed low to him, hands clasping the blade to her chest. She remained bowed for several seconds. The murmuring dwindled.

Wanchese faced the target. Achak approached and stood between them, his staff upraised. More lads entered the field to set up two new lines of staggered targets.

There were five in each line, spaced at increasingly distant intervals. A rainbow of painted rings graced the surface of the targets.

Jane squinted at the bear claw in the center of each. She hadn't noticed such details from the distance of a spectator.

"I can throw the match in your favor, if you wish, chief." She tried and failed to keep the taunt out of her voice.

He spared her a sideways glance. "Nay, Jane. Do not disappoint our people. Throw your finest."

"If it pleases you, my lord." Throw her finest she would. She had been taught by the best. Thrills of excitement shot through her chest and spread to her fingertips. For a moment, her thoughts drifted.

*I*t was a typical mountain morning. A crisp wind sent a scattering of gravel rolling down the steep incline, and the sun glinted off a cluster of fool's gold straight ahead. She skipped along the familiar trail.

"I ha' somethin' special fer you ta see. Here." Pa removed his leather top-hat and clapped it on her head. "Now you look like a real huntress." The wind lifted his dark wavy hair.

She chortled and pushed his enormous hat farther back on her head. They lived in the uplands, so they did not socialize with other folks often. She believed Mum, however, when she told her Pa was the handsomest man in all of England, with the laugh lines around his eyes and graying sideburns that tapered to a short, triangular beard.

The trail steepened, but Pa did not slow his stride. She had to jog to keep him in sight, slipping at times on the rocky terrain. He never once looked back to ensure if she was keeping up, because he'd trained her to stick closer to him than his own shadow.

"Ah. Here we be."

They crested a hill. Below them stretched a valley teaming with deer and oh my! Wild horses.

"Pa!" she breathed. "Maybe we could try and catch us one?"

"Aye, lass. I was thinkin' to capture and train one of 'em as yer reward." He paused to grin at the joy leaping across her face.

"For what, Pa?"

"For perfectin' yer aim with this."

He held out his best hunting blade.

It was all the encouragement she needed to master the art of throwing a knife.

---

*C*hak shook his staff and emitted a horrific cry.

Jane fisted the handle of her weapon and leaned forward. Though she heard the whistle and thunk of Wanchese's first dagger sink home, she did not glance into his lane. Instead, she narrowed her eyes on her own set of targets, forcing herself to take a few slow deep breaths. She pushed all thoughts out of her head, save the blade in her right hand.

Closing her eyes, she fingered the course engravings on the handle and allowed its weight to settle in her palm. Cracking one eye open, she squinted down the hilt and made a swift assessment of the slight bend in the blade. She would compensate for the imperfection by adjusting her aim. All of this she did in a matter of seconds.

With no thought for anything but the blade in her hand, she squeezed the hilt between fingers and thumb, drew back her arm, and threw it with a faint huff of exertion. It hit the closest target dead center.

Their audience murmured in appreciation.

Without pause, she swept up the second blade from the pile at her feet and examined the hilt. It was constructed in the same manner as the other, but the tip was straighter. *Less adjustment needed.* She swung her arm back and sent it whizzing past the first target. It landed home with a satisfying thud. Frowning at it, she fretted over the accuracy of the throw, for the bear claw itself seemed slightly elongated. *Ah, well. Close enough.*

Just as she was about to let the third knife fly, a series of piercing barks and howls caused her gaze to flicker to the spectators. *Tarnation! The natives' dogs had a penchant for kicking up a ruckus at the most inopportune times.* She wasn't falling for that routine again.

She closed her eyes and dug deeper. Opening them a crack, she swung. It was another center hit.

Blade cheered wildly, and the crowd broke into frenzied chatter. She wondered if they were admiring or criticizing her performance. *Ah, forget them.* She needed to listen to her head and not the crowd.

The fourth target she estimated to be sitting the farthest distance she had ever thrown a knife. She could do it, but she would need to add at least another ten feet to her aim to reach the fifth and final target. By the impatience in the air, she perceived Wanchese was finished with his throwing.

She selected a fourth blade with a hand that trembled. *Focus, Jane. Focus.* She drew another deep breath and willed her limbs to relax. *Be the blade,* her father had said. *Soar with it.*

This time she soared with the knife when it left her hand. She rode the wind and curved the merest fraction to the left to compensate for the slight bend in the blade.

A flurry of chatter broke out amongst the bystanders.

She opened her eyes. The tip was so close to the red ring, she could not determine from this distance if it rested inside the black bear claw or just outside. *So be it.* She had done her best.

One more. She selected the fifth knife and cradled it in her palm to gauge its qualities. With as close as she had come to missing the center of the fourth target, she knew the odds were not good for nailing the fifth one.

Remember what is at stake. Pa's words echoed in her mind. Once upon a time, the stakes rested on a horse named Shadow. She would have done anything to earn the ownership of such a glorious creature. This time, however, she did not throw as her father's daughter for a wild filly to train as her own. This time the stakes were much higher. Respect. Acceptance. Honor.

She was Nadie's daughter now. Tasked with filling the shoes of the lovely young maiden who'd been lost on the slave trading block. She was throwing today for her new family. A thrill of inspiration vibrated through her. She would throw her final blade for the sister she'd never met.

"For Amitola-a-a!" she cried and slung the last blade with everything she had in her.

A collective gasp rose from the crowd as she bent forward to follow the angle of the blade. With her arm outstretched, she closed her eyes and willed it to sail farther and truer than any knife she'd ever loosed. She was rewarded with a distant thud.

She opened her eyes. At least she'd hit the target.

Boisterous cheering erupted. Wanchese and Jane strode together down the two lanes of targets to examine their throws. All ten knives protruded from the bear claws, albeit they both had one close call apiece. Hers was on the fourth target; his was on the fifth.

Achak joined them in the field and held up one of each of their arms. He shouted something in Roanoke.

She quirked a brow at Wanchese.

"A tie," he explained, eyes gleaming.

"Are we under attack?" She had to shout at him to be heard above the deafening whoops.

"Nay," he yelled back. "My people pay you tribute. None has ever come this close to besting me."

"No one is smiling."

"Of course not. Only imbeciles smile."

Egad! Surely the man jested. But nay. He was not smiling, either. Come to think of it, she'd never seen him smile before. Not once.

When Achak lowered their arms, Wanchese clasped her hand and raised their arms one last time, eliciting another round of tribute. He did not seem the least bit disturbed by her success. Quite the contrary. He was proud. She detected a rush of something more in him, too — an emotion so exhilarating she could not translate it into words. It bore a possessive edge.

She closed her eyes and allowed the glory of the moment to wash over her.

Kanti ran towards them, shrieking with delight. The moment Wanchese released Jane's hand, she tossed herself into his arms.

Jane turned away, not wishing to intrude on the reunion of lovers. She may have matched skills with him this hour, but Kanti would match passions with him in the next. She found herself struggling to extinguish a burst of anger. *Things are as they should be between us. No way am I going to be jealous of any man's light-skirt.*

"Mistress Jane!" Blade crowed. He, James, William, Chitsa, Alawa, and Nadie crowded around her.

"*Amosens,*" Nadie cried and threw her arms around Jane. "*Kenah! Kenah!*"

Greatly moved, she allowed her adoptive mother to rock her from side to side.

"*Amosens* means daughter," James supplied. "*Kenah* means thank you."

"You are most welcome, Mum." Jane gave her shoulders an awkward pat. "When Amitola returns, you shall have..." She held up two fingers behind her back and arched her brows at the men.

"I believe *ninge* means two." William flushed crimson across his balding head. He cast a shy, questioning glance at Alawa for affirmation.

Thanks to their new mates, the Englishmen were learning the language of the natives at a rapid pace. "Aye, Nadie, you have *ninge amonsens*, two daughters."

"*Kenah*," she whispered damply into her shoulder and let her go. She turned to congratulate Wanchese next.

"Let's return to the fire," Blade begged. "The jugglers are about to begin."

The lads, my countrymen, and their squaws found a spot within the throng that was large enough for their group to sit cross-legged together. It was also close enough to feel the heat from the community fire without becoming too warm.

Three men with red and black painted masks leaped straight through the flames, lighting the torches they bore in each hand as they exited the flames, facing their audience.

'Tis like a circus, ain't it?" Blade exclaimed. "An' Amonso-quath says it's gonna last two whole days and nights."

"This Amonsoquath," Jane said quickly. "He seems to spend a lot of time with you lads. Is he a relation of our chief?"

"I dunno." Blade shrugged. "I do know he is a brother to Askook."

Askook's brother? Did that mean he was part of the hunting party who had slain George's father? *Egad!* She certainly hoped not for George's sake, since Amonsoquath had been ordered to shadow him like Riapoke shadowed her.

The first of the three jugglers tossed his pair of flaming torches into the air and began to twirl them. Higher and faster they spun with each sequence. The man to his left added a third torch and then a fourth into the mix. The last man joined in a few seconds later. Their hands and the torches moved so rapidly Jane could not keep track of which men were throwing and which ones were catching. They somersaulted backwards, took turns rolling between each other's legs, and even formed a quick pyramid with one man standing atop the backs of the other two who knelt on all fours. Not once did they fail to catch their fiery burdens. It was an astounding feat of speed, agility, and coordination.

The English colonists clapped, while the natives whooped and hollered.

"These men would be the rage back in London!" she exclaimed, turning to James. "Have you ever seen anything like..." Her voice trailed away as she noted how engrossed he was in his conversation with Chitsa.

He spoke a few Powhatan words and signed the rest of his sentence. She repeated his signals, leaning closer to him. He shot her a lopsided grin and bussed her cheek. She pressed her fingertips to the place he'd kissed, looking stunned.

Jane turned to William on her other side. Alawa's head rested against his shoulder. Clearly, she was no longer needed here.

She rocked forward to her knees and rose, not wishing to disturb either couple. One of the youths beckoned to Blade, who eagerly dashed off to join in some sort of game. She watched as they tossed a long-handled racket to him that bore a net on one end. The youngsters appeared to be divided into two teams. The object was to catch and pass a buckskin ball and launch it between two poles at the end of a field marked with stones.

George accompanied her, uninvited, to the edge of the

crowd.

"You are more quiet than usual this evening." She followed the progress of the buckskin ball, as it flew between the poles. *Huzzah! Blade's team scores.* "Have you no wish to join the game?"

"Nay, I've no heart for festivities." He ran a hand through his freshly clipped dark hair. It waved back fashionably from his high forehead.

"Nice trim," she murmured. "Careful, else you'll catch the eye of one of these bonny maids." As she spoke, one of them shot him a coquettish glance from beneath her lashes.

He snorted in derision, sparing no more attention to those lounging and strolling throughout the village than if they were moths fluttering around a candle. "Tell me something. Who or what is Amitola?"

She cocked her head at him. "She is Nadie's daughter, captured about the same time we were. The Roanokes believe she was sold at the Great Trading Path."

"Why did you shout her name during the competition?"

"Why, indeed! I wished to comfort Nadie. She suffered a great loss when her daughter was taken. She is so different and yet so like the mother I lost at the age of twelve." She shook her head wistfully.

George's brows shot up in concern. "Tis best, methinks, not to grow too attached. It will only make our leaving all the more difficult."

"Too late," she returned and cuffed his shoulder affectionately. "I already adore Nadie. While we search for our missing colonists, I think we should search for Amitola, as well."

"Hmm." He sounded doubtful. "Speaking of the missing, I carved three more Maltese Crosses today."

"Where?" And why? It seemed dishonest. She'd already pointed out they were not in any true distress.

"Hither and thither, Mistress Jane. Away from the village, of course."

"What do you think will happen if you are caught?"

"Nothing. These savages know not what the cross means to us. At best, they will think I whittle for pleasure."

At worst, they would apprehend and interrogate him. *Foolish lad!* She frowned. "Are you ready to reveal your plan for escaping this city?"

His face turned sullen.

"What troubles you, my friend?"

"You, Mistress Jane," he burst out. "I worry that you may not be of much assistance in our mission, after all."

"Why, George!"

"Well, you stand here with me and fret over the fate of a young woman you've never met as if she were your blood relation." He splayed his hands. The crackling campfire illuminated his ominous expression. "'Pon my honor, it's as if you've already forgotten the suffering of our own people!"

Her patience was waning with his endless grumbling. "While you analyze and question my loyalties," she said dryly, "I begin to wonder whether you have a plan at all."

George drew back, sorely offended. She had never spoken to his lordship in such a manner before. His mouth tightened in anger, but her accusation failed to provoke him into confiding anything more about his plan to her.

Drat! "Maybe I will share my own plan with you, in the event you do not ever get around to sharing yours."

"*You?* You have a plan?" He eyed her warily.

"Aye. The Roanokes admire courage and endurance. They respect honesty and hard work. Thus, I've labored diligently at their harvest and contributed everything I can to the well-being of their community. I've cooked, built traps, and sewn garments. All the while I've negotiated with Chief Wanchese. The harder we work, the more he listens."

"To what end?" George exploded. "We've been here for weeks, and still their bloody chief refuses to release us."

"Where exactly would you go, George, if you left Dasamonquepeuc tonight?"

"Why to Croatoa, of course, where our colonists await us."

"On foot?"

He frowned. "Of course not. We are separated by miles of water."

"You intend to swim, then?"

He bristled in indignation.

"You begin to see the problem, eh? All I am trying to impress on you is that we are at the mercy of the Roanokes. We possess no money. Nothing of value to offer them in return for the food, weapons, and canoes we will require to launch a rescue mission, except," she paused for effect, "ourselves. We can offer them our skills and our labor. We can offer our loyalty to the families who were so willing to take us into their lodges."

"Nay." She held up a hand when he started to protest. "Pray let me finish. Every minute you spend deploring our situation here is a wasted opportunity to earn the regard of our hosts. Back in Portsmouth, you neither marched up the gangway of the nearest ship and demanded passage to the New World nor did you commandeer the ship and abscond with its precious cargo. Nay, you invested in a ticket. You put forth coin. Here in this country, we put forth labor."

George shook his head, incredulous. "That is your plan? To work and wait." His mouth twisted in distaste. "For how long, Mistress Jane? Months? Years?"

She grinned. "I thought you'd never ask. Today, I began cultivating the Amitola angle. Picture this, George. Instead of skulking about behind the Roanokes' backs and waiting for the perfect opportunity to escape them, why not negotiate a joint rescue effort? One led by the Roanoke scouts with enough weapons, food, and supplies to get us safely there and back."

Nadie glanced their way from the circle of dancers. Her arms waved and her body swung in a slow undulating dance. She beckoned Jane to join her.

George whistled long and low at her words. Gone was the sullen twist to his mouth. "Now *that* is a plan indeed, Mistress Jane."

"Aye, George, and a good one. One that requires every one of us to put forth a genuine effort to win the hearts of the Roanokes."

He nodded, frowning. "We need to work quickly, Mistress Jane, for our fellow colonists suffer every moment we delay."

Alackaday! Had the lad not heard one word she spoke the past quarter hour? "We must exercise patience, George. We know not the extent of their suffering or if they even suffer at all."

"What?" he cried. "Did you not witness them with your own eyes as they were sold into slavery?"

"Aye. We were likewise sold, and look at us now. Have a little faith. That is all I ask of you, lad." She nodded her good-bye. "Pray excuse me."

"Where are you going?"

"On a diplomatic mission." She chuckled at the puzzled look on his face. "You should do the same."

"What do you propose?"

"Throw a few balls with the lads. Strike up a conversation with Amonsoquath. Bow to Riapoke before the night is through, and thank him for his hospitality."

He shot her an incredulous look. "Wait. Where are you going?"

Glee bubbled in her throat as she spun on her heel and took her leave of him. "Me?" she called over her shoulder. "I intend to dance."

CHAPTER 8: NEW ROLE

a distant cousin on Jane's mother's side named Constance Warde grudgingly took her into her impoverished London home after her parents' deaths. To economize on dance lessons, she borrowed the services of a balding widower from down the street. Jane spent endless hours towering over the grinning fool while they stumbled their way around the parlor. Each time he asked permission to call on her the next day, she purposefully trod on his toes to end the conversation.

The Festival of Corn dance was nothing like the forced waltz lessons in Constance Warde's home.

For one thing, partners were not required. On the other hand, all the leaping and twirling gave it the feel of an athletic event. The dancers repeated each sequence of steps a good half dozen times before switching to the next sequence. Jane easily memorized the steps while watching.

By the time Nadie drew her in the ring, she was more than ready to give it a try. Nadie crouched forward and sprang into the air. When she landed on her toes, she twirled twice with arms spread as if she were flying. Then she returned to a crouch to start the sequence anew and beckoned Jane to do likewise.

Eleven other men and women danced with them around the ceremonial circle. It was as large as a ballroom. Their number grew as the hour wore on. James led Chitsa into the ring.

Bless him if the sly fox didn't kick one of the logs farther into the fire, creating a shower of gold and orange sparks. The result was a mini fireworks display. His partner's ebony eyes lit with humor at his antics.

Alawa tugged an abashed William forward. If not for his bald pate, she might not have recognized him. His skin was baked to a light honey-gold and he'd dropped a good number of pounds since their arrival.

Neither men were shoddy dancers. Coupled with the barrel full of charm both possessed, they lent a note of frivolity to the dance. They nodded and winked at each other over their partner's heads. Every so often, one of them broke into a folk jig, masterfully twirled their partner, or dipped her nearly to the ground. Alawa clung to William when he arched her beneath him. She came up flushed and dazzled.

"You charmer you," Jane teased when James broke away from Chitsa to whirl her once around the circle.

"Jes wantin' the young men to see you don' bite, after all that knife throwin'."

"Oh get on with you," she retorted.

He broke into a frenzied jig before her.

She gave up, threw back her head, and laughed. *Drat him for making me smile like an imbecile.* He must not know the Roanokes viewed such expressions as a sign of weakness. The man could have made a living for himself as an entertainer.

A trio of braves produced a tiny set of wooden horns, and the music changed to a sweet wail. They blew a heartrending melody into the night, punctuated by sobbing minor and dissonant notes while the drums faded to a mellow off-beat in the background.

"*Cumear, amosens.*" Nadic reached for Jane's hand and drew her out of the ring.

Jane strolled at her adoptive mother's side, admiring the spritely grace with which she moved. She did not appear winded despite her past hour of intense dancing. Tonight, she wore no tunic above her embroidered skirt, only the infinite strands of beads so favored by the natives. She was old enough to be Jane's mother, yet her skin was marvelously smooth, other than the wrinkles around her eyes and mouth.

"Gift for *amonsens.*" She withdrew one of the strands of beads from her vast collection. A copper pendant shaped like a dagger winked in the firelight.

She beckoned Jane to duck her head so she could drape it around her neck. "*Damisac Wironausqua.* It means Queen of blades."

Struck by the beauty of the simple ornament, Jane held it up to view it carefully.

"*Kenah.* I thank you." She fisted the lovely dagger in her palm. "I'll go change my tunic to better display your gift."

She flew to their longhouse, stripped off the deerskin sheath and leggings Wanchese had provided her, and replaced them with the unadorned cloak and fringed skirt she'd worn upon her arrival. There. Instead of being lost in all the beads and embroidery, the dagger rested in uncontested prominence against her chest.

When she sprinted back to the festival, Nadie waved at her from the ring of dancers. She studied the older woman as she swayed to the lilting notes of the wooden horns. Her eyes drifted closed, and she gave herself over to the aching beauty of the music.

It happened so fast, Jane had no chance to put up a fight.

Hands whisked her from the main village path. At first, she wondered if Wanchese had decided to steal some time alone with her, but nay. The man's scent was all wrong. He held her wrists behind her and pushed her into the tree line. Alarm thudded in her chest.

"Unhand me, knave!" She attempted to wrench free, but it was like pulling against manacles of iron.

With a brutal strength she could not possibly hope to overpower, he shoved her to the ground beside a copse of trees and crouched over her on all fours. She tensed and waited for the right moment to lash out, knowing one well-placed blow could counter the advantage of his greater size and strength.

Wind parted the top-heavy trees, allowing a narrow shaft of moonlight to illuminate her captor's features. Cold dark eyes peered at her above a bony, jutting chin. Thick vertical streaks of black and white paint shuttered the rest of his face from view.

She'd thought Wanchese hard and insensitive at times, but Askook possessed no sign of humanity at all. He pinned her thighs with his knees and yanked at the ties of her wrap.

Askook," she rasped, fighting to swallow the lump of terror rising in her throat.

He blinked. *Aha.* He was surprised she knew his name.

His hand relaxed its grip. "*Damisac Wironausqua.*" He leered down at her and lifted the pendant from her neck. "Queen of blades."

She suppressed a shiver. He knew a bit of English. His words also meant he had been eavesdropping on her and Nadie. Wanchese had warned her Askook would view her skill with weapons as a challenge. Was he trying to provoke her into fighting him?

As Askook tugged up the fringe of her skirt, her fingers inched toward the knife secreted beneath her tunic.

One moment he was caressing her kneecap. The next instant, he was skidding sideways in the dust. His silhouette rolled to the balls of his feet and sprang upright with remarkable agility.

Wanchese stepped into the moonlight. He positioned himself between Askook and Jane. The two men crouched in a fighting stance, and a heated argument ensued. She understood nothing but the occasional reference to Nadie and the term of endearment she had given her. *Damisac Wironausqua.* Queen of blades.

She scrambled to her knees and refastened her wrap, which had come loose during her struggle with Askook. Fingering the tiny dagger pendant, she sucked in short shallow breaths, not wanting to fill her lungs with the animosity poisoning the air.

For the first time since her birthing ceremony into the Roanoke tribe, Jane was truly afraid. Her instincts told her she wasn't Askook's real target. He had merely used her as bait to lure Wanchese away from the main part of camp.

But to what end? They were family. Distant cousins, at least. And why was Askook's brother, Amonsoquath, so loyal to Wanchese while Askook remained at such odds with him?

She burned to know more about the rift between them and could only pray it would not end in bloodshed tonight.

The men turned swiftly in her direction. She froze in the act of rising to her feet. Askook's cold eyes slithered over her. It was like being branded with ice.

He raised a hand. "*Chamah.*"

"*Chamah* is a greeting," Wanchese explained tersely, his face hard. "My cousin is welcoming you to our tribe. Answer him as you would a nobleman."

She stood. Not bothering to brush the dirt from her garments, she pressed her hands together beneath her chin and bowed low. "*Chamah*, Askook."

He inclined his head a fraction to Wanchese. Without acknowledging her or her words, he glided away.

Faith! The brute acted not the least apologetic for his earlier mauling.

Drawing a deep breath, Jane smoothed her skirt and brushed the twigs and leaves from her braids.

Wanchese stretched out a hand.

She grasped it to steady her trembling knees, overwhelmed at his timely intervention. His *second* timely intervention. First Dasan and now Askook.

He tugged her closer. "Jane?" His voice was husky with concern, as he cupped her cheek.

"I am unhurt," she whispered.

He rubbed a thumb across her chin, frowning. "I will move you from Nadie's longhouse and claim you as my concubine tonight."

What! She caught her breath sharply and took a step back. "Nay. Do not ask this of me."

Wanchese's hand tightened on hers. "It is the only way I can protect you from Askook. He wants you, and he means to have you."

"Well, he cannot," she snapped, shaking off his hold.

"He is slotted for chiefdom over the Copper Mountain tribe. Most maidens would be honored to warm his bed."

"I would sooner die!" She swiped angrily at the air. "Askook is a brute and a coward."

"As a newborn member of my tribe, you cannot refuse him. You bear the status of little more than a slave for the next twelve moons," he explained impatiently. "Nor can you refuse the claim I now place on you."

Her brain was still processing his first revelation. "A slave for twelve moons." She glanced away from him, her thoughts racing. "The same is true for the others, I presume? James and William, Blade and George?"

"Aye."

Ah, burn it all! She wanted to howl at the moon at the thought of George's reaction when he found out. "Pray tell me all I need to know about our role as newborns."

"You may not leave the village unescorted, you must perform every task assigned by your adoptive family, and you may not marry until the twelve moons have passed."

Tarnation! She needed to warn George right away to cease the plans he was spinning for leaving Dasamonquepeuc. It looked like they would be settling in for the next twelve months.

She drew a deep breath. It was time to address the whole claiming issue. "Might I serve you in some capacity other than your concubine?"

"Nay. Nadie is not strong enough to protect you on her own, and Riapoke cannot watch you every hour of the day. As my concubine, it is a crime punishable by death for anyone but me to touch you."

Her mouth went dry. "Pray assure me you do not plan to take me by force as Askook did."

"By the gods, Jane! I have already stated you will come to me when you are ready. And come you will, unless you cannot bear the thought of lying with a savage."

"I do not give a fig about such things," she snapped. Relief flooded her chest at the knowledge he did not intend to force his will on her. "Pray give me a moment to think."

"Nay. You will do as I command in this matter." Wanchese bent to ensnare her waist with one steely arm and hefted her over his shoulder.

"What are you doing? Put me down!" She pounded his back with her fists.

"Perhaps you prefer Askook's company over mine?" he snarled. "I can release my claim on you, if you wish."

"Oh all the blasted, harebrained—" she choked. "This

undignified display will not convince anyone of your ardor towards me."

"This will." He shifted her from his shoulder and tumbled her into his arms. Her cry of surprise he caught with his mouth.

His kiss was heated and demanding.

Her heartbeat quickened to match the distant drums. She clutched his shoulders beneath the dizzying onslaught of emotions, intending to push him away and end this madness. But all she could do was hold on as she slid beneath the delicious thrill of passion.

When he raised his head a fraction, she gasped, "Someone might see us."

He grunted something unintelligible and hitched her closer. This time his lips caressed hers with an aching gentleness. It was as if he strove to draw her out of herself and sample the very essence of her.

She fisted a hand in his hair and let him in, wanting to give what he sought and needing to take something in return.

The moon shimmered between her half closed lids, and warmth sparked through every part of her. She was acutely aware of each silken strand of his wild mane of hair brushing her cheek, the unbelievable smoothness of his jaw sliding against hers, and the heated glide of his mouth.

She rested her forehead against his. "Burn you, Wanchese. You do not play fair."

He only grunted in response. He stalked with her past the enormous community fire where the festivities remained in full swing. Askook was nowhere in sight, but James caught her eye and grinned knowingly. William stared openmouthed at her.

Egad! I am never going to live this down.

"I say, are you well, Mistress Jane?" William started to rise.

James and Alawa reached up and pulled him back down between them.

Nadie flew in their direction. Worry glinted in her eyes, and she brushed furiously at the dirt stains on Jane's garments. She snapped out a question to Wanchese in the tongue of the Roanokes.

Apparently, she didn't like his response. "Tah!" she protested.

He shook his head, unyielding, and her shoulders drooped. She lifted the dagger pendant from Jane's neck and let it fall. "*Amonsens*," she murmured brokenly and turned away.

"Nadie will collect your things." Wanchese carried her onward to his lodge.

A shadow rounded the corner of the temple where Noshi sat guard and communed with the spirits of the dead. It was George. He stopped in the nick of time to avoid colliding with them. Jane's heart sank, and she braced for a confrontation.

Alarm wrinkled his brow. He reached behind him.

"Blast it, George, do not draw your weapon," she ordered sharply.

He paused, hand suspended above his waist.

"Let me speak with him alone," she pleaded.

"Nay." Wanchese's arms tightened around her. "Askook watches us."

She shot a furtive glance at the surrounding shadows but could detect nothing out of the ordinary.

"This is an outrage!" George bit out, advancing upon them. "If he thinks to have his way with you merely because he is chief—"

"Things are not as they appear, George." Her forehead was beginning to feel feverish. "If you care one whit for our collective safety, you will stand down immediately."

"Why?" George's brow grew thunderous. "Does he threaten you? By thunder, I'll—"

"Nay," she snapped. "We merely act out a role. I have not the time to explain now, but I will seek you out as soon as I am able."

"When?" he demanded.

She glanced around them again. "Soon. You have my word."

Discerning at last that her fear was directed elsewhere than their chief, he took a reluctant step back. "How may I help?"

"Stick close to Amonsoquath." Her mind raced for a way to discourage his covert activities without revealing them to Wanchese. "Promise me, George, you will not venture off alone under any circumstances. 'Tis far too dangerous for us as *newborns* to our tribe."

He blinked, startled. Then his eyes narrowed as he registered the warning in her inflection.

"George?" she asked breathlessly, sensing Wanchese's impatience. She waited, silently begging the lad for a sign of affirmation.

"As you will, Mistress Jane. I will return to Amonsoquath." He bowed to Wanchese and stepped aside so they could enter the chief's lodge.

"Go with haste," she insisted. "Do not let Amonsoquath out of your sight."

But he held his ground, eyes boring into hers until the animal skin covering the doorway closed behind her and Wanchese.

A low fire crackled at the center of the elongated chamber. Unlike the other longhouses, this one was not divided by partitions and platforms into smaller compartments but stretched as one wide open space. Woven tapestries and canvases painted with intricate detail adorned the walls.

Most featured black bears running, fishing, or locked in combat. An array of mats formed a circle around the fire with a trail of bear claws emblazoned on them. At the farthest end of the lodge hung an enormous skin depicting the white spirit bear.

"This is where your council meets," she noted, awed to be inside Wanchese's inner sanctum. She pictured his *cockarooses* gathered with him around the fire.

"Aye." He set her on her feet beside the fire, keeping one arm around her waist. Passion simmered in his mahogany gaze as he slowly bent her back until she was arched beneath him.

"What are you—" she asked, but his other arm cupped her neck and his mouth closed over hers, cutting off her words.

The room spun beyond her half-closed lids. Smoky shadows danced in cadence with the distant pipes and drums. Wanchese increased the intensity of his kiss.

A moan escaped her as delicious warmth and awareness washed over every part of her. *So this is the ardor that fueled the pens of poets.* At last she understood Chaucer, Cervantes, and Shakespeare. Dazed, she brushed a finger over one of the copper disks hanging from Wanchese's earlobe, reveling in the molten steel of his embrace.

A startled female exclamation brought her crashing back to the council room. Wanchese straightened but continued to hold her against him.

Kanti stood in the doorway of his lodge, the edge of his deerskin curtain clasped in her hand. A mixture of bafflement and fury chased across her high-boned cheeks. Black eyes full of accusation fastened on the face of the man who held Jane.

"Kanti." Wanchese's voice held no more emotion than a casual encounter on the main village path. He spoke something in their native tongue. The only word Jane understood was her own name.

Eyes glazed with pain, Kanti allowed the curtain to swing back into place and took a tentative step into the room. A beaded dress, similar to the one Wanchese had delivered Jane at the spring, flowed over her ample curves.

Bowing low before her chief, Kanti clasped her hands beneath her chin. Then she straightened abruptly. "*Chamah*, Jane." Her flat, controlled tone was at odds with the storm brewing in her features.

Like Askook had earlier, Kanti was extending a formal welcome to her at the behest of her chief.

"*Chamah*, Kanti," Jane rejoined. This had to be the most awkward encounter in her life.

The native woman backed away from them, disbelief clouding her oval face, and exited the tent in a rustle of leather and fringe.

"Pray assure me," Jane pressed a hand to her eyes, "you did not just introduce your concubines one to another as if we are part of one big joyous family."

"Would you rather I invite her to stay the night with us?"

She sniffed. "Mock me if you will. It was cruel to inform her of my new role in such a manner."

"Kanti knows her place," he stated mildly, setting her aside and striding to the back of the lodge. He propped the giant spirit bear canvas open by tucking it behind a copper hook.

Her place? His words served as a reminder of her own humble position, which — strictly speaking — was lower than Kanti's.

She wracked her brain for a reason to excuse herself. "I will return to Nadie's lodge and assist in the delivery of my things." Her few armloads of belongings would take little time to transport across camp.

"Stay. You are not to leave my lodge without my consent."

Surely he jested. "Pray excuse me," she said stiffly. "I will need to leave daily if you wish me to continue my training with Nadie the Wise."

"Nay, she will administer your lessons here." He untied one of the legs of his buckskins.

"What are you doing?"

"Undressing."

She feared as much. "I was, ah...just wondering when Nadie might return with my things?" Besides the ceremonial dress and leggings, she had accumulated an odd assortment of cooking utensils and farm tools. Some she had constructed herself and others Nadie had given her. Then there were her animal traps in various stages of construction.

He shrugged. "Soon. It matters not. Do you have need of something?"

"Nay." She reckoned not. "Gracious! Must you disrobe so early? The Festival of Corn remains in full swing."

"Indeed. I carried you through the heart of the festival for a reason. Many eyes followed us. They will expect me to remain occupied here for some time."

Ah, that. He did sometimes retire early with Kanti. No wonder she was so staggered by his curt dismissal. Her ill-concealed distress would go far to solidify Jane's new role if anyone accosted her tonight.

"Well, now that I am here," she scanned the room in growing discomfort, "would it be too much to ask for a corner in which to build my traps?"

Wanchese paused his disrobing and returned to the council room. "Your only task is to please me. You have no more need to farm, weave, or build traps."

"Oh, but I must! Nadie, the maidens, and my countrymen depend on me. I cannot abandon them in the midst of the harvest." And George — *dear me!* — he most certainly needed looking after on a regular basis.

"Fear not, Jane." Wanchese reached for her and drew her to him. He cuddled her against his chest and kissed the top of her head in a playful manner, walking her backwards towards the fire. "I will keep you occupied. You will not miss your other tasks."

She blushed. "You forget yourself. We merely act out roles for the sake of those who watch us."

"Why pretend when we both know a real fire rages between us?" He nuzzled her throat.

Because I want more than a meaningless tumble betwixt your blankets. She drew back to stare up at him, troubled. It was true something real raged between them, but she wanted more than a turn at serving as his latest light-skirt.

Kanti knows her place, he'd said. Well, Jane never intended to be in Kanti's place. Just another toy to discard when the novelty wore off. When she came to him, she wanted it to matter. To mean something. She wanted a much more permanent arrangement.

Wanchese's expression grew resigned as he watched her. He expelled a heavy breath and dropped his arms. "As I have said before, I will wait for you to come to me, *cucheneppo.*"

She rubbed her arms, chilled despite the fire. "Er, where will I sleep?"

He jerked his head at the back chamber. "There is an extra bunk across from mine. For guests."

"In the same room?" She was aghast.

"Aye."

She shook her head. It would never do. "I prefer to sleep out here. I'll curl up on a few of these mats by the fire."

"Nay, you will not. My councilmen come and go often from this chamber. If they witness you slumbering alone, our game of deceit will be over." At which point she would be at Askook's mercy.

That wouldn't do, either. "I suppose you have the right of

it," she muttered at last. "I, ah..." She drummed two fingers against her lips, wondering what to do while her chief completed his evening toilette. She certainly wasn't joining him in the back chamber while he undressed.

"I bid you goodnight, chief. Pray allow me to tarry by the fire a bit longer. I wish to, er, meditate."

"Meditate away, *Damisac Wironasquaw*. Noshi swears it keeps the mind as sharp as one's blade." Wanchese strode into his bedchamber. *Our bedchamber.* The deerskin curtain fell into place behind him.

*S*eating herself cross-legged on one of the mats by the fire, Jane listened to the muted sounds of festivities outside. It was far enough into autumn that the nights were quite a bit cooler than the days. Someone had built the fire in Wanchese's tent around three thick logs that would burn steadily throughout the night. More than likely, Kanti had prepared it for the leisurely evening she anticipated with her chief.

She emitted a sigh and leaned forward to stoke the flames.

There was so much to think about, so much to accomplish, and so little time to make it all happen. She puzzled her way through the difficult task of how she was going to remain loyal to Wanchese while commencing her search for the lost English colonists. And how was she going to explain her new role as Wanchese's concubine, in name only, to George and win his compliance?

Her eyelids eventually started to close. Best to find her new bunk before she fell over in a dead sleep where she sat. Having no wish to be discovered this far from Wanchese by a passing councilman, she yawned and eyed the canvas hanging between her and his sleeping chamber. With a little luck, he would be asleep by now.

She tiptoed to the curtain and brushed it aside. In the dim firelight, she sought out the guest bunk. The sleeping chamber was set up more like the other longhouses in the village, with a low platform running along each of the outer walls.

She drew a tremulous breath. To her left, Wanchese lay on his belly facing the center of the room. A dark fur covered him from the waist down. Flickering firelight played over his scarred back. It was like catching a lion in a nap. Harnessed power. Virility in repose.

She crept farther into the chamber and let go of the curtain. It took a moment for her eyes to adjust to the darkness. Embers from a banked fire glowed in the center of the room. It provided just enough light to guide her to the sleeping platform across from Wanchese.

There was no way she was undressing, not with him in the room. She knelt on the bed and felt around for a fur blanket. *Ah. There.* She curled her fingers in the fur and tried to tug it over her. Her breath caught when it moved. Dash her buttons if the thing wasn't warm and pulsing with life!

"Glory be!" She leaped from the bed, preferring to discover the identity of the creature from a greater distance.

"'Tis my mongrel." Wanchese's voice rose from his platform, not the least bit slurred with sleep.

Why, the cur was wide awake!

"His name is *Cutto*. It is short for *bark*. He is fond of snapping and growling at newcomers."

How pleasant. She remained standing next to the fire. "Are you quite certain that thing on my bed is a dog? He's enormous."

"He is part wolf. Some creatures do it without shame, you know. Mix their blood with that of another breed."

A choking sound worked its way up her throat at his double meaning. She tried to cover it with a cough.

"Cutto is both wild and tame. And fast, with killer instincts. Protective of those he trusts."

"Indeed." She was not overly enamored with the thought of climbing back into bed with a dog that was part wolf.

"Win his trust, Jane. You have need of his protection."

When she hesitated, Wanchese's voice turned caressing. "If you prefer to sleep with me, I, too, can protect you."

She shuffled her way reluctantly back to the guest platform. Her gaze adjusted to the darkness, enough to make out the silhouette of the enormous dog stretched nearly end to end on the bed.

She softly called his name, "Cutto?"

He raised his head and growled deep in his throat.

"Tah, Cutto!" Wanchese commanded and rattled off a string of words she did not understand. "I informed him he is to guard you. Now, go to sleep."

That was it? He tossed a few words at the mutt and expected him to comply? Jane bit her lip and sat on the outermost edge of the platform, gauging the animal's reaction. He growled again.

"Cutto," she whispered, "do as your master commands, and I promise to trap you a juicy rabbit on the morrow."

He gave a snuffling bark.

An acknowledgement of her words, she hoped?

Grimacing, she crawled the rest of the way on the platform. Pressing herself as close to the edge as possible, she lay on her side and faced him with her head resting on her arm. They assessed each other in the dim light. His eyes glowed back at her, a startling blue.

His pointed ears twitched at the rustling of the fur blanket she pulled over her knees. Then his growl grew muffled and could almost be mistaken for a purr as he settled his muzzle between his paws.

With visions of being mauled in her sleep, Jane closed her eyes.

---

*H*er moccasins flew over the dew-tipped blades of grass as she ran. She threw out her arms to soak up the untouched beauty of the rolling foothills. With the mountains rising in the distance, it was not unlike the uplands of England where she used to hunt with Pa.

Except it wasn't Pa's rangy frame running a few strides ahead of her. This man wore no leather top hat. When he glanced over his shoulder, his jaw did not bear the familiar brown and gray beard tapered to a point. This jaw was smooth and square, the shade of rich burnished gold.

He signed to her, urging her to increase her speed. It was a race he wanted, did he?

She grinned and broke into a sprint, easily catching up. Try as she might, however, she failed to pass him. He matched her pace perfectly.

She wondered where he was taking her as they flew over the low-lying hills. They did not stop to enjoy the colorful bursts of flora or the breathtaking views. Perhaps they would come back another time to do so.

They pressed through the thickening line of trees and ran straight up a mountain. Eventually, the trees grew so thickly together they were forced to slow their pace to a brisk walk.

It was then she saw the first one. Etched into a thick cedar at the edge of the path for any passerby to see was a set of English letters.

Jane halted to examine them more closely. The top letters were illegible, as if some wild creature had brushed against the trunk and nearly erased them. The bottom two, however, were clear — an A and a V.

A chill snaked its way through her chest. Having been raised in the uplands of Northern England as an only child, she did not possess a great number of acquaintances. In her short list of friends, however, only one bore such initials. A man who just happened to reside on this side of the world. Ambrose Viccars, cooper for the City of Raleigh.

Something else caught her eye. She bent to examine the strange carving beneath the letters. It was as if the artist had been inter-rupted, because only the top of the image was clear. It was the upper half of a Maltesse cross.

It meant Ambrose Viccars was in trouble.

She straightened, alarmed by her discovery, and continued to search her surroundings. As she suspected, more trees bore the rough carvings. Dozens upon dozens of Maltesse crosses dotted the mountainside.

"Jane?" Her companion was standing closer than she realized. Much closer.

She backed into the solid warmth of his chest. "My missing friends. They were here," she choked.

"Aye."

She turned to face him. "You knew," she accused. "Why did you keep it from me so long?"

His eyes bored into hers. "You were not ready to hear the truth."

"And now I am?" Her mind raced over Nadie's endless lessons. Why didn't she feel ready?

"Aye. Now is the time." The light in his gaze chilled.

"For what?" She suspected she was not going to like what he had to say next.

a ferocious bark roused Jane. She jolted upright in the darkness, startled to find herself in Wanchese's lodge. The dream had been so real.

An enormous creature stood next to her, growling and nudging her with his snout.

"Burn you, Cutto," she whispered, pushing away his damp nose. "You brought me back too soon."

"Nay, it is time to rise."

She squinted at the speaker.

Wanchese stood next to his bunk dressed in buckskins. He strapped on a quiver of arrows. "Come with me."

She rubbed her eyes. "Where are we going? Isn't it the second day of the Festival of Corn?"

"Aye. Today, we play the hunting games."

Anticipation coursed through her. Surprised at how rested she felt, she swung her legs over the side of the platform and scrambled to find her moccasins. "You are taking me with you?"

"Aye."

"You changed your mind then? About me participating?"

He tightened the straps at his shoulder. "I hoped to keep you from Askook's notice, but it is too late for that."

"Tell me about the hunt," she begged.

He held out an extra quiver.

She slung it over her left shoulder and reached for the bow he extended.

"There will be four teams. Riapoke, Amonsoquath, and George will hunt with us. Other teams will pursue us. The object is to avoid capture while navigating a trail riddled with obstacles. Once we master the trail, a final test awaits."

"What sort of test?"

"A wild beast will charge us. We must capture or kill it to complete the game."

"A game, you say? It sounds real enough to me." Real enough for someone to get hurt.

"Child's play," he scoffed. "Stay close."

Bah! She had no intention of trotting at his heels like a faithful hound. "Aye, master," she said dryly. He would soon discover she was more at home on the trail than anywhere else in the world.

Cutto leaped from the platform in a blur of white fur. He trotted at her side as they entered the council room.

Jane scratched his ears. He growled and rubbed his head against her leg.

Bending until her lips rested above his pointed ears, she whispered, "You and I will go on a hunt of our own soon. Together we will seek out the trail of crosses in my dream."

CHAPTER 9: THE HUNT

$\mathcal{D}$awn glowed on the horizon as they jogged down the main village path. Those participating in the hunting games assembled at the ceremonial circle. The crowd quieted as each contestant approached, bowed to their chief, and settled their curious gazes on his new concubine.

Jane fiddled with the bow in her hands and tried to choke down her misery over being the center of so much scrutiny.

Menacing red paint drenched the bodies of one team, which brought on a wash of unpleasant memories. Images of slavers and ambushes tightened her chest and sickened her belly.

Another team displayed muddy gold paint, and a third boasted blue. James and William were members of the blue team. Blade strutted between them, his face painted the color of ripe blueberries. The warrior brothers, Kimi and Kitchi, completed their team.

Jane's teammates wore no dyes. Nothing but all-natural camouflage.

"Jane," Riapoke greeted her with an upraised hand. Mud smudged every exposed inch of his skin, hiding his scars.

Tiny tree branches protruded from his hair, pouch straps, and buckskins. He reached out to tighten the strap of her quiver.

George was the only member of their team not bearing weapons. It looked as if he'd been tasked with playing the part of pack mule. He shouldered a coil of hemp cord and a sack tied with provisions. He fixed brooding eyes on Jane but said nothing.

Amonsoquath deposited an armload of small branches and twigs in a pile at their feet. Wanchese proceeded to tuck them in her hair and tunic, until she waved him away. She knew how to prepare for a hunt.

Not wishing to stare openly, she eyed Amonsoquath from beneath her lashes. About the same age as George, he was enormous for his years. More than six feet tall, broad of shoulder, and corded with muscle, he looked nothing like the shorter and wirier Askook. In truth, he resembled Chief Wanchese more than his own brother.

When the others weren't looking, George nudged her foot with the toe of his moccasin. His face was full of questions.

She sought to assure him. "I slept with Cutto last night on the guest platform." Probably best she didn't volunteer the fact it was located in the chief's bedchamber. "I pray you rested well?"

He raised one brow. "Who is Cutto?"

She nodded at the dog who sat on his haunches next to her. Already he played the part of a faithful hound.

"You slept with that beast?" George's eyes warmed. He petted the top of the dog's head. At Cutto's growl, he snatched his hand back.

"Perhaps you should keep your distance." She chuckled. "Our chief commissioned him to serve as my watchdog. He seems to be taking his job very seriously."

"From what does he guard you, Mistress Jane?"

"A new threat," she disclosed in undertones, but there was no time to elaborate.

The warriors in charge of the games hushed the crowd into silence. They issued the rules with much gesturing. Then the pursuing teams were introduced.

The team assigned to shadow Jane's was painted with white and black stripes traversing their faces from forehead to chin. Askook's team. She recognized Kanti behind one of the hideous masks of paint. She was the only other woman besides Jane who attended the hunt. *Just my luck.* Meaning her team would be pursued by her two least favorite members of the tribe. Her instincts screamed they had somehow manipulated the arrangement.

"We have but a few minutes head start," Wanchese explained as those who would be tracking their team circled near. She imagined they were assessing weapons and supplies, searching for weaknesses, anything that would give them an advantage in the hunt.

"Let us not waste a single one of those minutes," he continued. "Ireh!"

They pushed past those who would soon pursue them. Kanti's dark eyes caressed Wanchese's broad frame and settled on Jane, snapping with venom.

She blinked. It was a novel experience to inspire jealousy. She planned to proceed with caution around the woman.

Taking off at a jog, they paraded down the main village path with the other competing teams, past the temple and the ceremonial circle. Noshi nodded solemnly at them from the open-sided second floor where he held vigil. The contestants exited the palisade entrance to the village beneath the unblinking gaze of a pair of guards and plunged into the forest. Just inside the tree line, the teams separated to locate their individual courses.

As it was on the first day of her arrival to the New World, Jane was struck by the vast uninterrupted coniferous forests. She skirted tight clusters of deep green pine, fir, hemlock, and spruce. Slippery layers of needles and cones littered the ground, requiring just the right amount of poise and sure-footedness to keep her balance.

The festival pipes and drums were replaced by the dim, quiet world of the woodlands. Above her, the trees inter-locked their branches, blotting out all but occasional snatches of sun. It was just enough light to pick her way over fallen logs and a scattering of roots, vines, and rocks.

Wanchese motioned for their team to stop and gather around him. He spoke first to Riapoke and Amonsoquath in their native tongue. Then he turned to George and Jane and bent to dig in the dirt. He indicated they would navigate their assigned trail in reverse.

She grinned her approval. With a little luck, it would throw off their pursuers. They would be forced to split up and search for their team or dig in and wait.

Wanchese indicated they would travel in silence. The only break in the quiet was the occasional call of a bird and the rustling of animals as they dove out of the path of their team. Jane spotted a pair of deer, countless squirrels, three wild turkeys, a vulture, and a family of porcupines.

They travelled close enough to the sea to hear the waves on the beach, though they did not exit the forest. She counted paces to measure their distance. If her calculations were correct, they jogged a mile north then cut due east for another five miles.

As the second hour of the hunt rolled around, the trees grew thicker. Though still in Dasamonquepeuc territory, Jane and her team pressed inland to areas less frequented by the Roanoke patrols. A sense of unease filled her. The forest was vacant of men other than themselves, but it possessed the evidence of recent guests. She noted more than one pile of underbrush with twigs a-plenty snapped in two. A heavy creature had tread upon them. Or a man. Or several men.

She motioned her intentions to Amonsoquath that she planned to take a short detour. She wished to examine the patch of broken ground cover more closely. He twittered like a robin to signal for Wanchese and the others to halt.

She squatted to examine the first disturbed area. It looked deliberate, because there was ample room on either side to skirt the pile of twigs without stepping on them. Not more than ten paces away rested another set of broken twigs. Someone had left a deliberate trail. It led to an oak tree that was too thick to encircle with her arms.

A chill shot through her. Carved in the bark was the outline of a Maltese Cross. Inscribed in its center was a pair of initials. C.P.

Cecil Prat? Her heartbeat quickened. It was like her dream from the night before, except the letters were different. The most significant part of the carving was the cross, however. It was proof that an English colonist has passed through here, one in distress.

At the faint rustling of leaves beside her, Jane whirled. Wanchese's gaze clashed with hers. Fierce and searching.

He raised a hand, palm facing inward. It was a signal for her to come with him.

She rose from her crouch and gave a half-shake of her head.

He signed again that they should return to the others.

"We cannot just leave," she protested in a fierce whisper. "One of our missing colonists passed through here."

"He is long gone," Wanchese retorted.

How do you know that? "We must search for him, then, for he *was* here at some point. He left this message for us to find."

She pointed at the Maltese Cross. "'Tis our agreed upon sign of distress."

His nostrils flared in raw fury. "Why then does George carve them throughout the forests of Dasamonquepeuc?"

She wanted to strike her forehead against the tree. *Blast my foolish tongue, and blast George for persisting in pretending he is in distress!* Her mind scrambled to concoct a reasonable explanation.

"Do not lie to me, Jane."

"'Tis not that he considers us in distress so much as he hopes to communicate with those who are missing." The excuse sounded lame even to her. Her eyes flickered in dismay to George who examined another tree nearby. *Were there more letters?* She could not tell, for his shoulders shielded the trunk from view.

"Edward Powell was here." George announced, not bothering to lower his voice. His dark eyes glittered with accusation, when he turned to face them.

Wanchese addressed the lad in flawless English. "There is naught you can do for them now. They dwell beneath the earth."

Beneath the earth? As in dead and buried? The better question was how Wanchese knew of their fate. Jane scowled, wanting to demand answers but she preferred not to further incite George.

His jaw dropped at Wanchese's startling announcement. "By all that is holy," he exclaimed. "You are as well-spoken as an English lord." Suspicion trembled in his stance. "The signing with your hands, the pretense of misunderstanding us. 'Twas all a sham, wasn't it? Aye, you served in our Queen's court and learned our language well."

Wanchese's expression was stony. "The Englishmen you seek are no longer here. Let us return to the hunting games."

As if Jane and George would be able to focus on a game when there was a real hunt demanding their attention.

With Wanchese and George in close pursuit, she dashed between the trees in the vicinity, but there were no more carved initials. Only those of Cecil Prat and Edward Powell. Their trail of carved crosses and broken sticks stopped at the bank of a narrow creek.

She raised and lowered her hands in frustration.

"We must extend our search," George muttered in her ear, but she knew such efforts would be futile. They'd lost their trail at the waterway, and that was that.

"Not now," she whispered. There was nothing more they could do for Master Prat and Master Powell unless, by some miracle, they picked up their trail again farther downstream. "We will come back and search for them another time. You must trust me on this, George."

"Trust you?" His mouth twisted bitterly. "You knew Wanchese understood our language, yet you hid such knowledge from me. What else are you hiding, Mistress Jane?"

"Everything I do is to protect you and the rest of our countrymen."

"We do not need protecting from the truth," he snarled. "I was right when I claimed you are among those who need rescuing."

"Nay, I am quite safe. I have Riapoke and Cutto to guard me."

"Cutto is but a dog. *Half* a dog."

"Remove your moccasins," Wanchese ordered. He motioned them to follow him as he stepped into the creek. Amonsoquath wedged himself between George and Jane, cutting off their conversation. Silence resumed as they returned to the hunting games. Jane continued to scan both sides of the creek for any sign of the missing colonists but sighted nothing worth pursuing.

She waded behind Wanchese in water up to her knees. Amonsoquath followed behind her and George behind him. Riapoke brought up the rear of their party, walking backwards much of the time to scan the area behind them. The water crept to their thighs. Eels and salmon brushed past their ankles and butted against their calves.

Marching through the stream masked their trail from their competitors, but it chilled them to the bone. George and Jane fought to keep their teeth from chattering, but Wanchese, Amonsoquath, and Riapoke showed no reaction to the frigid temperature of the water.

After about a mile, Wanchese halted them with an upraised hand. He pointed to a cord traversing the stream and brushed aside two piles of underbrush to reveal its construction. It was a trip wire strung between two sticks pounded into the river bank.

Jane pointed out the noose of the hemp cord, pondering again how anyone could classify this as a game. A person could die in such a trap.

"This is where our assigned trail ends," Wanchese announced. Or where it began for them, since they were traversing it in reverse order.

And so the hunted became the hunters.

They exited the stream, one at a time with painstaking care. Jane was more than ready to leave the cool water and wanted to shout with relief when they slicked the dampness from their legs, dried for a few minutes, and donned their moccasins.

Amonsoquath dropped a stone atop the trip wire to dismantle the obstacle, thereby proving their team's success to the judges in circumventing it. Jane shivered as the noose yanked upward, empty of its mark. It swung eerily in the breeze overhead.

A quarter mile later, they encountered their second

obstacle. This one was a simple deadfall trap, hardly enough to catch a squirrel. A pair of sticks propped up the triggering mechanism. They only needed to give it a few feet of clearance before springing the trap with a long stick. *Way too easy. Or was it?* Alarm tickled Jane's senses.

Wanchese must have shared her alarm. Instead of immediately dismantling and skirting the trap, he paused and scanned the terrain.

A wise move, because it turned out to be a trap within a trap. If they had simply strode past the small deadfall, they would have walked straight into a much larger version of it. Jane gazed in awe at what she had initially mistaken for a dead hemlock lying against a cluster of pines. It was set to spring and crush a man — or a small group of men, in their case, and one woman.

Under the guise of brushing aside the leafy covering over the trigger, George hastily carved another Maltese Cross into the tree.

She cleared her throat and nudged the foolish lad's foot, but he refused to look at her. She was sorely fed up with his antics. They were going to have a serious talk before nightfall.

There was no need for Wanchese to point out the next trap. Located a mile from the first, it was plain to see. Too many branches lay in haphazard array across their path to be natural. One corner was askew, exposing a manmade cavern. It was careless work.

More than likely, it was big enough to contain a man and too deep for him to easily climb out. Jane and her pa had constructed a few of these for larger, lumbering animals. Once they'd even snagged a bear who'd been stealing the game from their smaller traps.

As with the deadfall traps, they searched the perimeter of the obstacle before venturing closer. Wanchese signaled for them to fan out with two of them passing on one side and three on the other.

A faint keening sound arrested them. Wanchese and Amonsoquath froze before and aft of Jane. They remained motionless for several moments, but the sound did not repeat itself. George and Riapoke stood back to back in front of the obstacle, observing their surroundings and waiting for the other three to join them.

Wanchese signed for them to move on, but Jane shook her head. She closed her eyes to absorb every nuance of scent and sound from the earth below and the air above. As sure as she lived, someone or something lurked nearby.

She felt and dismissed the faint slither of a snake through the ground cover. Something more vibrant caught her attention. Traits that only a warm-blooded creature could exude like heaving breaths and quiet sobbing.

She pointed to the exposed opening of the hole. Wanchese nodded and signaled to Amonsoquath. He tossed a pebble into the murky recess. They were rewarded with a sharp gasp that was distinctly human.

Wanchese nodded again to Amonsoquath. He cupped his hands over his mouth and proceeded to growl like a grizzly bear.

A sobbing intake of breath greeted their ears. "Wanchese!" a woman gasped.

He kicked aside the covering of branches and crouched next to the hole. Kanti gazed up at them, her face twisted in pain. The stripes on her face were smudged on one side as if she had scraped herself on the way down. A strip of animal skin was tied around her calf and seeped red.

Their team exchanged gleeful glances. Taking a prisoner would add points to their score. Wanchese motioned for George to toss him the roll of cord. Kanti's gaze never left his, and Jane's never left hers. The young native woman arched her back as if in agony, which only served to thrust her chest out farther. Instantly suspicious, Jane scowled down at her. Something was off about the whole scene.

The covering over the hole. That's it. The exposed hole had been too small to fit her willowy frame. If she'd gone crashing through the trap, she would have disturbed more of the branches.

"Wait, George!" she called, but the cord in his hand was already sailing towards her. Jane caught the faintest trace of triumph in Kanti's eyes. Then it was gone.

"Tah!" Jane snapped to Wanchese. "She is unhurt. 'Tis a trap."

"Uh?" he muttered and continued to unfurl the rescue cord.

Burn every man for their inability to resist a woman in distress.

As soon as the cord was within reaching distance, Kanti sprang for it. She yanked viciously — not to grasp it and be drawn to safety but to pull her would-be rescuer down into the pit with her.

Wanchese jolted forward, but Jane was there to grasp his arm and hold him back. To his credit, he must have registered the change in Kanti's movements when she leaped towards him on her bandaged leg. He let go of the rope the moment she switched from victim to aggressor.

At her scream of thwarted rage, her teammates came whooping down on them from the trees.

Jane didn't have time to leap from the path of the warrior who tackled her, but she sprang like a jackrabbit in the same direction upon impact. Employing a trick her pa had taught her, she used the man's weight to propel her across the opening of the trap. As she tumbled to her backside, she kicked upward with all her strength, plowing the chest of her opponent.

Astonished, he plummeted into the pit. This time Kanti's

gasp of pain was genuine. Jane made no attempt to suppress her grin of exultation.

Two down. Three to go. Invigorated to her fingertips, Jane leaped to her feet to rejoin the fray.

Riapoke and George had already overpowered the third man and were hog-tying his arms and legs. A quick glance at her other two teammates revealed them wrestling on the ground. Amonsoquath's opponent outweighed him. Despite his best efforts, the man edged him toward the opening of the pit.

She flew to his side to offer her aid, but she was too late. Amonsoquath was already tumbling over the edge. She skidded to a halt in the dirt, arms outstretched.

But he continued to fight mid-tumble. Using the momentum of his roll, he tipped the heavier man into the pit. He landed atop the opening of the pit with his hands on one side and his feet on the other. His body remained arched over the opening for a moment longer. Then he sprang free of the trap like a circus performer and landed in a crouch, panting.

Amonsoquath and Jane hastened to Wanchese's side as he yanked Askook's shoulders upright against a tree. Riapoke joined them moments later. The sneer on his scarred face was truly fearsome, but Askook appeared unperturbed. Only when Amonsoquath helped bind his wrists did Askook speak. His words made his brother's jaw tighten.

From their exchange, she deduced the brothers were at odds with each other. *Interesting.*

Apparently, her team was taking Askook as prisoner. She sliced another piece of cord and held it out. Amonsoquath took it and bound Askook's feet so he could only take short, skipping steps.

Glancing around them, she noted George's absence. *Burn*

you, lad, for taking off without telling me! She scanned the trees, wondering if he was attending the call of nature.

Dread coursed through her limbs when several minutes passed, and he did not reappear. She pressed a hand to her chest to quell the pounding there. The lad had truly abandoned them. She fastened beseeching eyes on Wanchese. They could not continue the hunting games. They needed to go after George.

He stalked her way, features black with rage. She took a startled step away, but he propelled her back against the nearest tree.

"Where is he?" he snarled low in her ear.

"I would that I knew," she exclaimed feverishly. "You cannot possibly think I had anything to do with his disappearance." Aye, but it was exactly what he thought. She felt the color drain from her cheeks, because she'd never seen such bleak anger in him before, such mindless intent bordering on madness.

His hands tightened like a vise on her upper arms.

"You must help me find him," she begged. "He is more foolish that I gave him credit for. Motivated by fear and grief. 'Tis not safe for him to be out there alone."

"*Weroance.*" Riapoke laid a hand on his chief's shoulder.

Wanchese shoved away from Jane and barked out a swift set of orders. Gone was the exhilaration on Amonsoquath's youthful face from besting his opponent in the earlier wrestling match. In its place was sad resignation. She knew without asking that he and Riapoke were being sent to overtake George.

She wondered what the consequences would be when they found him. Just yesterday, Wanchese had said they must perform each task assigned by their adopted families. The foolish lad would surely be punished.

Riapoke and Amonsoquath rolled two enormous logs

over the opening of the pit where Kanti and her comrades remained and balanced a boulder atop them. There would be no escaping without bringing the deadly anchors crashing down on themselves. Then the two men loped off in opposite directions.

She leaned against the hardy trunk of the fir, rubbing her hands up and down her arms. "What will you do with George when you find him?" Her voice was barely above a whisper. She harbored no doubts that Wanchese's most trusted warriors would find him before the day's end.

Wanchese nudged Askook into motion and ignored the calls of those in the pit. "Ireh!" he flung over his shoulder at her.

"Please. I beg your compassion on his behalf." Her voice broke. "The lad has no true understanding of these things."

"Aye, Jane. He does."

"Nay," she protested. "He is young and confused. Do not forget how his father was slain." *At the hands of the man we now hold prisoner in a game.*

Askook leered at her words. *Burn him!* He understood too much. Blinded by rage, she unsheathed her knife and leaped in front of him.

His dark eyes turned wary as she pressed the point to his neck.

"He is the one who gave the order to murder George Howe. Unless you pledge not to harm George, I will take my vengeance on this man here and now. Then you will have to punish me, too."

Wanchese made a sound of derision.

He valued not the life of this snake any more than she did. Gleeful at the knowledge, she increased the pressure of her blade.

Genuine alarm registered on Askook's face.

"A newborn member of my tribe who inflicts harm on

any man or woman of Dasamonquepeuc will be put death. Put down your blade, Jane. I've no interest in losing you in such a manner."

Why not? Do you care about me? She turned startled eyes to her chief.

He was much closer than she realized and reached over to pluck the knife from her hand. "George's problem is that he thinks he is still in England." The accusation hung between them and sank home.

"Aye, he is English to the bone," she admitted. "Given more time, I hoped and prayed he would accept our new life here." Dampness stung her eyes at the steely resolve in his.

She threw herself at his feet and pressed her face to the ground. "Whatever punishment you deem fit for the lad, I will pay it on his behalf. Even unto death." Her chest thudded with apprehension as she awaited her chief's answer.

Wanchese hauled her into his arms. "There is only one thing I ever asked of you, Jane, and it is not your death."

She drew a shuddering breath. *So those were his terms? Her virtue in exchange for the lad's life?*

"What is your answer?" he demanded harshly.

She turned her face aside. "Do what you will with me. It matters not, so long as you let George live." *I will already be dead inside.*

Wanchese grasped her chin and forced her gaze back to his. He studied her a moment. "Come." He dropped his hand, his expression inscrutable. "Let us finish the hunt."

"What about the rest of our team?" she inquired dully.

"We will finish with or without them. Ireh!"

Even with their opponents out of the race, other dangers lurked. If Jane's heart had not been so heavy, she would have been fascinated by the variety of obstacles they faced. There were two more versions of the deadfall. An avalanche of stones concealed one of them.

They exited the trees, at last, to face their final test. With a squeal, a boar charged the two of them. Still squinting from the dim interior of the forest, she pivoted a trifle late. One of the tusks grazed her calf as he shot past. She dove from the path and rolled to her feet, knife in hand, but Wanchese was faster. He pushed Askook aside and leaped atop the creature, slitting its throat.

In the end, they lost points for their missing teammates but gained them back when Riapoke and Amonsoquath reappeared, marching four more captured opponents between them. George was not among them.

From the grim set to their faces, she guessed they had found him. She pressed a hand to her chest. Had they executed him already?

I didn't get to say goodbye.

Her knees threatened to buckle as they paraded up the main village path. Jane blocked out the cheers of the Roanokes, no longer caring who won the contest. Her brain fought to make sense of what had happened. Of where she had gone wrong. Of all the things she could have done to prevent this latest tragedy.

How would she inform James, William and Blade? The death of George was a crushing blow to them all. Perhaps she would keep the discovery of the carved letters to herself altogether. Blade needed time to deal with the loss of his friend. She would not add to his misery by informing him they'd discovered and lost his father's trail in the same afternoon.

"The lad still lives, Jane."

She stumbled at Wanchese' words. "What?" she gasped. Straightening her back, she willed him to tell her more. Was George unharmed? Where were they holding him? When could she see him again?

Alas, his stoic features gave nothing away before the throng of villagers separated them.

Nadie awaited them in the council chamber. She stirred a steaming concoction in a wooden vat next to the fire. It smelled heavenly. Though Jane had no appetite, she picked out the scents of venison, fish, and wild onions.

She hurried to my side. "Are you injured?"

"Nay." Jane brushed aside her hands.

"You are troubled."

"Aye, *kicke*." It was the Roanoke word for mother, a new term she'd recently added to her vocabulary. She'd been waiting for the perfect moment to try it out.

In response, Nadie stretched out her arms. Though several inches shorter than Jane, there was strength in her frame. Jane rested her cheek against the top of her head. They stood in silence with no further display of emotion on either of their parts.

A firm clasp on her shoulders made her eyelids fly open. Jane knew without turning around it was Wanchese. Nadie's lashes were damp when they drew apart.

"*Kicke*," Jane cried softly and touched her hand.

"*Amosens*," she murmured and bowed low to their chief.

"You may go, Nadie," he said.

Jane jolted at the authority in his tone.

Nadie ducked from the lodge without protest. The skin slid into place behind her.

Jane shrugged away his hands and spun around. "What a way to speak to your own mother!"

His mahogany eyes flared. "Nadie the Wise is not my mother."

"Why, then, did you claim Amitola is your sister?"

"Amitola was given to Nadie to raise."

"Given? Did something happen to your parents?"

"Nay. 'Tis the way of the Roanokes." He drew her roughly against him. "But I did not come to discuss our people."

Her hands shook as they rested on his forearms. He had

come to collect his payment for sparing George's life. She tensed and waited for his next move.

"I care not for the way you look at me, Jane."

"What do you mean?" She bit out the words.

"You are afraid of me."

"I am not!"

"You have no reason to be." He scowled and tightened his arms around her waist, leaning in to nip light kisses along the side of her neck. "You know I will let none hurt you."

"You reserve that right for yourself alone, eh?" she retorted. His touch was making it difficult to think.

Wanchese cupped her chin in one hand. "How so?" he demanded.

"I thought, that is…did you not come to collect your payment?" she cried, desperately close to tears.

His scowl deepened. "I gave the order to spare George's life *before* you threw yourself at my feet."

Her jaw dropped. "Then why ask me to lie with you to spare him?"

"I wanted to know how far you would go to save him. 'Tis the same question I ask you every day. Will you lie with me, Jane?"

"N-now?"

"Aye, now. I want you more than I have ever wanted another."

She blushed at his admission and scanned his features, shivering beneath the intensity of his perusal. He was telling the truth. He desired her, and she desired him. Never had she been so utterly and wildly attracted to a man before. It took no more than a simple look from him to have her heartbeat quicken. Burn him if her breathing didn't hitch even now as he lowered his head.

"Do not deny that you want me, as well," he said hoarsely against her mouth.

"I cannot." She closed the small distance between them and pressed trembling lips to his.

He came undone at her touch. His hands and lips roved her face like a man dying of thirst. She dug a hand in his hair to pull him closer. He groaned and crushed his mouth to hers. Head spinning with the wonder of it all, she returned caress for caress and kiss for kiss until his heartbeat thundered beneath her hands.

He shuddered when she rested a hand over his heart.

"You are mine, Jane. Soon your belly will swell with my babe, and the whole world will know you are mine." His mouth roved lower.

His words chilled me. *His babe? Egad!* They had much to discuss before they ventured into the fearsome realm of childbearing. Jane could not imagine her frame swollen with child, like Dyoni's. How was a body supposed to hunt and trap in such a state?

"Wanchese, please."

"Please, what?" He arched her beneath him. "Say the word, and I will take you now." He trailed kisses along her throat.

She drew a heaving breath. "Nay, not in this manner."

His arms tightened around her waist. "Blast it, Jane! In what manner will you have me, then?"

Cringing inside, she whispered, "When we are married." Only then, would he be hers. All hers.

He straightened but kept his hold on her.

Her knees trembled. Had she actually just proposed to her chief? He seemed to be handling her proposition rather well, all things considered.

"We cannot marry while you serve as a new member of my tribe." He beheld her gravely. "Roanoke law prevents us. We must wait the required twelve moons."

Does this mean you wish to marry me, as well? "So let us wait." She ran a shaky hand down the side of his face. "If at the end of twelve moons, you still want me, I will give myself to you as your wife. I will be yours, and you will be mine." The thought made her dizzy.

"If I still want you?" He muttered something that sounded like a curse. "What if I do not last the twelve moons? What if I expire with the wanting of you, Jane?"

She brushed her lips against his jaw. Miracle of miracles, the blasted man was jesting with her. "Perhaps, I am equally at risk, my love, of expiring from the want of you."

He made a sound suspiciously like one of Cutto's growls. "I see you mean to torture me every day of these twelve moons, troublesome wench."

She grinned. "Why, I have hardly commenced my torture, and already you wail like one of the pitiful creatures caught in my traps."

His eyes smoldered dangerously as he yanked her flush against him. "Caught I may be, wench, but I warn you. You've built a powerful fire in me that only you can quench."

She blushed again as the meaning of his words sank in, but she hardly had time to process them before a horrific scream rent its way through the village. Bumps rose on her arms. The voice pulsed with pure terror.

Wanchese broke away from her and swept up his quiver and bow.

"Wait!" she cried. "You do not know what awaits you out there, my love." But the door flap was already falling into place behind him.

Longing for a good English rifle, Jane thrust an extra pair of daggers into her waistband and hurried after him with her bow in hand.

She could not have been less prepared for the sight that greeted her. At first, she thought Amonsoquath wrestled with a mangy wolf due to all the matted black hair flying. He had the creature pinned on the main village path. Riapoke and James hovered over the pair with bows notched and ready.

"What in heaven's name?" She crouched beside them. The mangy mass was a woman. An English woman, no less. She did not look at all the same as when they'd last met, but something about her wild, unkempt hair struck a chord in Jane's memory.

"It's Lizzie Glane." She waved away the crowd of Roanokes. "Lizzie, pray cease your struggles. You are among friends."

She nodded at Amonsoquath. "You may let her go." To her surprise, he did. Out of the corner of her eye, she caught sight of Wanchese signaling him to rise. *Ah*, he followed his chief's orders, not hers.

She knelt beside the whimpering woman and reached for her hand. "Lizzie, can you hear me? 'Tis Jane Mannering. I once served as school mistress for the City of Raleigh."

She raised up on an elbow and swiped a handful of dark matted hair from her eyes to peer at her.

Jane resisted the urge to recoil from her ravaged face. Her eyes were bloodshot and sunken. Faith, the woman was starving. Fragile and gaunt, the skin barely stretched across her bones. "When was the last time you had something to eat, my friend?"

"It matters not," she quavered. "We are as good as dead. All of us."

"Nay, Lizzie. We shall live." *Poor mite.* She hadn't changed. During their last encounter, she was raving about the Spanish coming to slaughter everyone. Her mind was addled.

Jane's gaze drifted over her head, past the braves who crowded around them, and settled on Wanchese. "A very brave man rescued us. He is chief of this tribe and will protect us from any who wish us harm."

He beheld her with a look of pure male pride, arms

crossed over his bare chest. He appeared unperturbed at the prospect of having one more would-be colonist to shelter, one more mouth to feed. Was there no burden too heavy for his broad shoulders?

Lizzie thrashed as if in pain. Another tortured scream escaped her. "Too late!" she gasped between shuddering sobs. "They are already here."

"Who is here, Lizzie?"

"The Spanish. I tried to warn you." She reared up and grabbed her arm. "They anchored their ships this morn on Roanoke Island. May the good Lord punish my Darby for eternity for leading our enemies to us."

CHAPTER 10: THE FEVER

*N*adie pushed through the crowd to kneel on the other side of Lizzie. She pressed her hand to the woman's forehead.

"Hot. She is ill." Nadie shouted. Bly and Dyoni sprang into action.

Startled at Nadie's announcement, Jane bent for a closer look at Lizzie. The poor woman was so filthy she had altogether missed the signs. Indeed, she looked as if she suffered from a fever. More so, her streaming tears cleared just enough grime from her cheeks to reveal mottled spots. She had the measles.

"Father, have mercy on us all!" Tugging Nadie to her feet, Jane cried, "Call them off, Chief Wanchese, I beg you! This woman is diseased."

Nadie attempted to return to Lizzie's side, but Jane stepped between the two women. "Nay. Pray go wash yourself in the spring." She mimed the act of bathing. "You have already been exposed, but anything is worth a try."

A harsh bout of coughing made her jump. Lizzie was

curled in a ball, teeth chattering. Her body was so wracked with chills, it fairly set her bones to rattling.

"Ireh! Get as far from her as possible." Jane waved the onlookers back. "James, you know what to do. Start by burning Amonsoquath's garments." She snatched up the shivering woman and ran for the palisade exit.

Wanchese jogged to catch up.

"Stay away from me!" she called to him, a note of desperation in her voice. "You have the rest of our people to consider. Pray do not expose yourself to this disease. Send someone else if you must, but order them to keep their distance. I will stay with her."

"Where?" He ground out the word.

Far away. Her mind raced over the possibilities and settled on one. "I will go to the trail of crosses." It wasn't as safe as staying within the city's palisade, but it would keep her within the outer reaches of their patrols. "I will return when I am certain I am not infected." If she was still alive.

A strange emotion flickered across his features. "What do you call this disease?"

"The measles. It is very dangerous. My friend, Agnes, taught me all that I know about treating it. The symptoms are coughing, red itchy spots, and a fever that lasts three days."

"Will Nadie become ill?"

Jane's heart pounded with dread. She shared his fear. "Hard to say. Let us pray she does not. The disease is far worse for adults than children."

"How bad is it?"

She understood the reassurance he sought but was reluctant to give him false hope.

"One in three who fall ill with it die. Isolate Nadie and Amonsoquath from the others. 'Tis the best we can do for them now. Bathe them in cold water if they turn feverish, and have them drink as much as they can tolerate to restore the body's humours."

Wanchese slowed to a halt just outside the palisade exit. Jane continued on another ten yards or so before she stopped and turned to face him.

"This is goodbye for now." She swallowed hard and met his gaze without wavering.

"Riapoke and I will ensure you have food and blankets." His features were set in stoic lines. "If you become ill, Jane..." A muscle in his jaw ticked.

"I will not come back and infect anyone else. It is too dangerous."

The burning woman in her arms whimpered.

Wanchese clenched his fists at his sides. His eyes raked over her entire person, hot and possessive, before returning to her face.

She wanted to run to him. Instead, she turned away with her burden. She would never forgive herself if he became infected.

"Jane!" he called after her. "You will not die."

She did not turn around again. She could not bear to meet his gaze.

"That's a command." His voice was hoarse.

She drew a sobbing breath and broke into a run. Though Lizzie probably weighed no more than seventy or eighty pounds in her sickly state, it felt like she was toting a pile of stones.

She pressed deeper into the dim forests. Sprawling roots and knobby underbrush threatened to trip her with each step. It took nearly an hour to locate the first Maltese Cross. If not for the freshly carved letters leaping whitely up at her, she might have passed right by them. She wrinkled her brow and set Lizzie Glane down on a bed of thick, decaying leaves. The poor woman had fallen unconscious during the run.

A shiver of foreboding crept down Jane's back at the new letters winking up at her from the base of the tree. *G.H. George Howe? Young George? How could he—*

"Jane? Is that you?"

She jerked at the voice.

With the snap of a twig, George emerged from the trees.

"George! I thought, that is, I feared..." Her words died as she took in his bruised and swollen eye, scratched arms, and torn buckskins.

His mouth twisted bitterly. "Have they banished you, as well?"

Banished me! "So that was your punishment?" The rush of relief made her weak all the way to her toes.

"More or less." He brightened. "It means I get to spend my days studying the trail of crosses."

"Is that so?" So great was her relief at seeing him that she could only stare for several moments.

"Aye, and this is what I discovered. After they were sold on the Great Trading Path, Master Prat and Master Powell were marched nearly all the way back to Dasamonquepeuc."

"But why? Have you discovered where the crosses lead?"

"Nay, and not for lack of trying. I've searched for miles in every direction. 'Tis like they disappear into thin air."

Wanchese knew something about their fate and, given the proper opportunity, might prove helpful in locating them. George would be much better off at Dasamonquepeuc working his way back into their chief's good graces instead of gallivanting off on his own.

"Maybe you will lend me your assistance, Mistress Jane?"

A few days hence, she might be confined to a sick bed and of no use to anyone. She squared her shoulders. "Of course I will, but first tell me something. Why are your garments in such ill repair?"

He shrugged, his expression rueful. "I suffered a fun-in

with a wild boar. I tried to leap atop him like I witnessed Amonsoquath do once. Guess I am handier with a rifle than a blade, for it was harder than he made it appear. You have to give these savages credit for their pluck."

She closed her eyes for a few seconds to summon her last reserve of patience. "You do realize, George, that winter is coming and this," she waved her arms, "this whole adventure of yours draws to an end. How will you feed yourself, and where will you live? Nay, do not rush to answer me. I asked for your trust. Your abandonment of us during the hunting game was a sore breach of my trust and a foolish move, at best."

"*Me* foolish! Did you note how quickly Chief Wanchese hustled us away from the trail of crosses? He does not intend to search for our people, Mistress Jane. The sooner you accept that, the better. Methinks your feelings for the brawny savage have quite clouded your judgment, as of late."

"My feelings are beside the point," she snapped, growing more incensed by the moment. "Our chief is a man of honor, even if you cannot see past his failure to be born English. You, on the other hand, persist on displaying the manners of an oaf. Riapoke took you into his household and treated you like a son, and this is how you repay his generosity? By running away!"

George ducked his head. "I did not mean to offend."

"Well, you did," she chided. "You dishonored him to the extreme. 'Tis high time you accept we are no longer in England, and we are not going back. Our plans to colonize the New World may never turn out the way we expected."

His head shot up. "I will not give up my father's dream of settling this land. Neither will I forget about building the City of Raleigh, nor abandon the search for our missing colonists."

"Give up? Nay," she retorted. "All I ever asked of you was

to adapt. You continue to envision lords and ladies strolling around with their parasols upraised, do you not? Cathedrals and manor homes popping up in the wilderness. Cobblestone streets bustling with horse-drawn carriages."

He stared. "Well, what do you envision, Mistress Jane?"

"Change, George. If we do not align ourselves with the Roanokes and survive the coming winter, nothing else will matter. What use are we to our missing comrades if we are dead?"

He shifted from one foot to the other as her words pelted down around his ears. "A month ago, you would never have taken such a tone with me, Mistress Jane."

"Lord Howe," she said coldly. "Pray forgive the oversight. I was not aware you still found comfort in such meaningless pomp and circumstance."

"Meaningless!" George attempted to glare down his nose at her, a difficult feat, for she bested him by a good two inches. "I earned the right to call myself by my father's title the day he was so hideously murdered by the beasts you now call family."

"Nay, you did not earn your title, Lord Howe. You were born into it. It was a matter of happenstance and nothing more."

"How dare you mock my noble lineage!"

"Noble, eh?" she pressed. "Let us reflect upon your most recent accomplishments. Hmm. Lord Howe holds quite the record, does he not? I recall how his waywardness earned him a flogging on the ship ride from England. It has kept him from enjoying the roof over his head his new father has so generously provided, the food on his table, the clothes on his back, and the endless lessons on how to survive in the wilderness. It has caused him to forsake his friend Amonsoquath. And, oh! Pray do not forget this same wayward lad most recently secured his banishment from all vestige of civilization here in the New World. Did I leave out any of your most noble feats, sir?"

"Nay, Mistress Jane. I believe that covers things well enough." George was visibly deflated. "You know better than to bait me like that. It has a way of bringing out my worst. There now." He crooked an arm at her. "Allow me to escort you—"

"Halt!" she snapped.

He raised a brow, but a weak moan from behind her had him reaching for his knife.

"Behold." She stepped aside to give him a better view. "Lizzie Glane is returned to us. Pray come no farther, because she bears bad tidings and suffers of the measles."

At the mention of the fearsome disease, George closed the distance between them. "Away from her, Mistress Jane, lest you become infected."

"You cannot follow even the simplest of requests, can you?" she fumed.

"There is no need. I contracted the measles as a wee lad and am unlikely to catch them again."

"I hope you are right." She shook her head regretfully. "Alas, I am already exposed. I carried Lizzie all the way from Dasamonquepeuc."

"And the others?" he asked in a hushed tone as he knelt beside her crumpled form.

"Nadie tried to minister to her before I realized the extent of her illness." Jane's voice broke. She squatted next to Lizzie and stroked her hand. "We should make her more comfortable."

"Wait here." George jogged away.

In his absence, the fading woman waffled in and out of consciousness. She sat up suddenly, eyes wild. "We must warn the colonists."

"Aye, Mistress Lizzie."

"Mayhap they will listen this time." She curled on her side, shivering convulsively in the dropping temperatures. Jane debated whether to cover her with more leaves or allow the nip in the air to work its magic on her fever.

"Here we are." George bustled towards them with arms full of sticks, hemp cord, and deerskin. "We will have our friend under shelter in no time."

Jane wondered if Wanchese had provided these supplies or if George had pilfered them from Riapoke's lodge before his defection. Either way, he was wholly dependent on the Roanokes for his sustenance, whether he admitted the fact or not. She squinted into the glowing rays of sunset. "The night is going to be a clear one."

"Aye. Not the least hint of rain."

"Pity." She grimaced. "'Tis been a desperately dry summer. If not for the irrigation ditches the Roanokes dug from the river, their crops would have shriveled to nothing."

"I say, Mistress Jane." George pounded the first tent stake into the ground. "For a group of savages, that is…" He paused at her glare. "For a group of rather primitive people, the Roanokes come up with some clever ideas."

"Clever and advanced." She snatched up the second tent stake and set it into position for him. "Our own colonists debated the topic of irrigation channels to no end on the ship ride here. Correction. The gentlemen discussed it, whereas the ladies moaned over the tiresome nature of the subject and excused themselves time and time again for another round of charades."

George stuck his tongue in his cheek. "You never did rub along too well with the ladies, did you, Mistress Jane?"

She sniffed. "I rub along well enough with anyone who carries an ounce of sense in their head."

He snickered. "You always did prefer a rifle over a parasol."

"Always." She set the last two stakes. "Blame my father. He wanted a son but worked with what he had."

A breeze whipped at the deerskin tent as they settled it over the stakes and tied down the ends.

A tingling sensation at the base of Jane's neck gave her pause. They were not alone. She pivoted, praying it was the next round of Roanokes on patrol. Other than her knives, she was unarmed. She had hoped they would be safe this close to Dasamonquepeuc. Only one man knew their exact whereabouts.

"Wanchese?" I whispered.

"Did you say something, Mistress Jane?" George slid a rolled up blanket beneath Lizzie's neck and produced a skin of water.

"Chief Wanchese has arrived."

He strode towards them, a bundle in hand.

"Pray, come no farther, chief." She bowed low, hands clasped like a proper maiden.

He halted and deposited the bundle on the ground. "I will send more on the morrow."

"I thank you," she murmured, drinking in the welcome sight of him, "but I beg you and the others to stay away from us. George will help hunt and fish and care for Lizzie. Though I did not seek him out, he stumbled on us by accident."

Wanchese appeared unsurprised at George's presence. He flicked a cursory glance over the lad. "What if he falls ill?"

"He claims it is unlikely since he had the measles as a child. Thus, I welcome his assistance."

"Our braves will patrol without ceasing so long as you remain here." His voice was grimly resolute. "Do not mistake them for another." The last warning he directed at George. "If threatened, they will shoot."

Beneath his barking was a genuine concern that made Jane's heart race. She bowed again. "We are much obliged."

"One thing more. A fishing party will pass by here in the morning and share their catch with you."

She wanted to kiss Wanchese right in front of George. The only thing that kept her was her fear of infecting him. That he cared so much for their welfare dazzled her.

He held her gaze several moments longer before taking his leave.

She bent to retrieve the supplies he left behind but stopped short at George's stunned expression.

"Why you...he..." he spluttered.

Brows raised, she interrupted sharply. "How does Lizzie fare?"

"I, er..." He rubbed a hand across his face and shook himself.

Jane carried the bundle to Lizzie, troubled by her labored breathing. George hunkered down next to Lizzie and tipped a skin of water against her lips. She shuddered and refused to drink.

Wanchese had supplied them with blankets, food, and a handful of tools and utensils. Tucking one of the blankets around the shivering woman, Jane rocked back on her heels. Poor Lizzy! She'd been claiming the Spanish were coming for months. Then she'd wandered off and not returned in time for their immigration to the mainland — perhaps not a bad thing, considering the ambush. It was truly amazing she was still alive after all her time alone in the wilderness. Well, barely alive.

Was there any truth to her claim the Spanish had arrived on Roanoke Island? If so, how had she managed to get herself to the mainland to warn them?

The questions brought Jane to her feet. If the Spanish discovered the remains of their abandoned Fort Raleigh on

Roanoke Island, they might send a search party farther inland, putting Dasamonquepeuc and all of its inhabitants at risk.

What to do? She paced the forest. The Roanoke braves were setting out on their deep sea fishing expedition tomorrow. They must be stopped, before they ran into the Spanish fleet. Assuming Lizzie's claims were real and not imagined, of course. Jane tapped a fist against her mouth, thinking hard, and came up with an answer.

Wanchese kept canoes hidden all along the coastline. If she could get her hands on one, she could paddle to Roanoke Island tonight to determine if Lizzie's claims were real.

She rounded on George. "If what Lizzie says is true, there is no time to waste. I must get to the island tonight, before the fishing expedition departs. Otherwise, they may sail straight into the crosshairs of a warship." She held up a hand when he started to rise. "Stay with Lizzie, please. If I do not return by morning, you will send word to Wanchese that we are in grave danger here. All of us."

He shot to his feet. "Pray let me go. He will skin me alive if anything happens to you."

"Trust me. I stand the best chance at getting to and from Fort Raleigh without being seen."

He scowled. "Chief Wanchese would not want you venturing out alone." But he did not attempt to stop her as she sped for the trees.

A pair of warriors on patrol followed her. She did not see them, but she heard the occasional snap of dry twigs as they stuck fast to her trail. She stooped behind a patch of tall, dead grass and pretended to tend the call of nature. They retreated a discreet distance, and she made a run for it, hoping Wanchese would not be too hard on them when they reported her absence.

The canoes were not difficult to find, since she had traveled with Wanchese before. A trio lay secreted in one of the thickets overlooking the water. Enough twilight remained for their outlines to be discernible in the deepening shadows.

She dragged the shortest canoe to the water, thrilled to see it was already stocked for the fishing trip. It contained nets, spears, and several skins of water. At the water's edge, she discovered how Lizzie had arrived to the mainland.

A lone raft rested in the sand. It was one the City of Raleigh colonists had constructed to transport themselves to the mainland. Rising seawaters lapped over one corner, tugging and lifting it. Jane pulled it farther up the beach so as not to lose it to the tide. With no desire to linger lest the guards catch up with her, she shoved her borrowed canoe into the waves and hopped in.

Only when the mainland was out of sight did she pause her rowing to splash saltwater on her face, arms, and legs. It would mask her scent. Soon, Roanoke Island jutted from the peaceful sound waters.

She scanned the jagged cliffs but detected no movement or fires. *God be with me.* She braced herself for a barrage of muskets that would require her hasty retreat. To her relief, no shots sounded as she approached.

Pulling smoothly into a narrow inlet, she camouflaged the canoe beneath the fishing nets by sticking branches through their holes. She sipped at a skin of water. A mere three-mile trek separated her from the Atlantic side of the island where Fort Raleigh stood.

Only a few weeks ago, the earthen fort with its palisade walls had marked the temporary settlement of one hundred and fifteen English passengers who'd arrived from Portsmouth. Their visit to Roanoke Island was intended to be a brief rendezvous between three lads in their party and their fathers who served as soldiers there.

Alas, their navigator, Simon Fernandez, had escorted all

the colonists from their three ships at gunpoint. The swine had claimed the summer too far spent to travel farther up the coast. Jane and her comrades knew he merely wished to shed the burden of passengers. An ex-pirate, he preferred to spend the final weeks of summer privateering before winter weather forced him back to England.

Pressing through the dim forests, Jane reached the fort in well under an hour. It was like stepping into a strange dream. She slid to her knees and crept forward to peer down the beach. Two grandiose galleons graced the waters about a quarter mile out, lit by what seemed like thousands of lanterns. Smaller vessels dotted the water's edge. Too many fires to count crackled across the white sands.

Ah, Lizzie Glane was right this time! Dark-skinned Spaniards in colorful doublets and shirts traipsed in and out of the remains of Fort Raleigh and its collection of weather-beaten cottages. Doors lay strewn about the small village, torn straight from their hinges. Several of the thatch roofs were engulfed in flames. Why, if these marauders were not careful, the entire dry and dusty island might very well go up in a few puffs of smoke!

Jane dropped to her belly and slithered closer. Squinting so that the whites of her eyes would not alert any onlookers to her presence, she watched in horrified silence. A group of seven men, laughing and swinging wine bottles, sidled over to the two graves at the edge of the clearing. They kicked and poked at the earth with sticks.

Swallowing a gasp of anger, she gritted her teeth in outrage as they dug up the remains of Sergeant Robert Chapman and Assistant George Howe. The bodies were given a cursory examination, then torched.

She understood only a small bit of Spanish but enough to learn that these evil drunkards presumed the English colonists had fled an ambush. They intended to search the entire island for them on the morrow.

She edged away from the clearing, sickened to the core. Wanchese needed to be warned with haste. She fled to the opposite side of the island and slid her canoe back into the water.

It was midnight when she scraped onto the mainland, a good half mile down the beach from where she'd discovered the canoe. Again, she employed the nets for camouflage, because returning the boat to its original location posed a different sort of risk. She did not wish to infect a group of innocent fishermen with the measles in the morning.

A tiny fire glowed in front of Lizzie's makeshift tent. Her condition had not improved. She rattled around her bedroll with the most awful cough.

George sat with his head tipped back against an oak, wearing an expression far too old for a lad of fifteen years. A Maltese Cross peeked above his tousled dark hair. He rolled to his feet at the sight of her. "She started coughing up blood an hour ago."

Jane winced, knowing Lizzie was not long for this world.

"Well?" he inquired with a frown.

Her report caused his frown to deepen. She withheld the part about his father's desecrated grave.

"You." He pointed to his empty bedroll beside the fire. "Get some sleep. I will hasten to Dasamonquepeuc at once to warn Chief Wanchese."

"No need," a cold voice intoned. "I overheard it all."

Wanchese stepped into the clearing.

"Halt," Jane pleaded, taking a protective step in front of George. "Lizzie is most grievously ill."

"My men feared the worst when you turned up missing tonight," he snarled. "As did I."

"My only thought was to protect Dasamonquepeuc."

The air crackled with the intensity of his fury. Wanchese glared at her for several long moments. Then he pounded a fist to his chest, the greeting of warriors.

Too exhausted to smile, she saluted him in the same manner.

"Once the danger is past, we will discuss the risks you took."

Not the least of which was incurring the wrath of her chief. "It was a small sacrifice to ensure the safety of our people."

Pride flashed in his eyes, but his voice brooked no argument. "Do not think to leave the island again without my permission, Jane. Ever. 'Tis far too dangerous. My scouts will handle the rest."

"Aye, chief." She gave him the bow of a loyal subject. When she straightened, he was gone.

She did not expect to sleep due to all the dangers pressing them, but George rustled up a second bedroll and insisted she lie down. As she stretched out with her back to the fire, her eyes fell on his latest carving. The letters etched on the newest Maltese Cross were L.G. for Lizzie Glane. This time George had the right of it, for Lizzie was truly in distress tonight.

Mumbling a plea for a miracle, Jane closed her eyes and drifted away.

---

*W*anchese sent several teams of scouts to Roanoke over the course of the next two nights. They reported how the Spaniards traipsed around the island like conquerors, dismantling the remaining palisade walls of the fort and torching the wooden cottages. On the third morning, the intruders declared the island free of the

English and departed in their glorious ships. It was their unbelievably good fortune the marauders did not venture to the mainland to continue their search for the English. They were probably too anxious to return to privateering.

It was the only miracle they would receive.

Alas, Lizzie's fever did not abate. It burned into the fourth day. On the fifth day, she rattled out her last cough and fell silent, no longer able to muster up the energy to purge her insides of its evil humours. Her spirit lingered for another day, but her final mission on earth was complete. She had lasted long enough to warn her countrymen of the Spanish invaders. On the seventh day, Lizzie slipped away and joined the everlasting congregation of the saints.

George pressed her eyelids closed and folded her hands across her chest. He and Jane attempted to smooth her tangled hair but to no avail. Giving up the fight, they constructed a narrow platform of deadwood and placed her body on it. They tucked the blood and phlegm-spattered tent and bedroll over her legs and set the tomb ablaze.

George and Jane tended the cremation in silence. They exchanged guilty looks when they rubbed their chilled hands together and held them out to Lizzie's flames for warmth. Jane's only comfort was knowing Lizzie would not have minded. Her concern had been for their collective safety, right down to her final breath.

The embers continued to glow for hours after she was gone.

Jane spent the next three days helping George hunt and gather food stuffs. They didn't gather near enough to last him the winter, but it was the best way to employ their energies while they waited to determine if Jane carried the infection. Perhaps Wanchese would reconsider George's banishment when his food ran out.

On the third morning after Lizzie's death, Jane discovered

a narrow cleft in a nearby ridge. She wound several handfuls of dry leaves and twigs around the top of a stick with a strip of greased hemp cord and lit it for a makeshift torch. She and George wedged their bodies through the opening and found themselves in a sumptuous cavern on the other side.

It was as large as a ballroom with a maze of corridors branching off in the distance. Its most significant feature made her want to weep with relief. Through the center of the room ran a natural stream.

She bent to thrust her hand in the water. George did the same. They grinned at each other in the flickering torchlight. It was lukewarm to the touch.

"Are you thinking what I am thinking?" His voice shook with excitement.

"You could survive the winter here, George."

"We," he corrected. "We could survive the winter here."

She shook her head. "I will check on you as often as I can, but I am needed more at Dasamonquepeuc."

His handsome face twisted bitterly. "You have no wish to leave *him*."

She knew without asking he spoke of Wanchese. His claim was true, but that was beside the point. "Our best hope of survival is to ally ourselves with the Roanokes," she returned evenly. "You know 'tis true no matter how much you try to deny it."

He skipped a pebble across the surface of the stream. "Even so, I would that you keep the whereabouts of my newest abode to yourself."

She shrugged. "As you will." Her gut told her Wanchese already knew of the place. Quite possibly, he had ordered his men to deposit George in this exact spot where he would discover it for himself.

"Jane!" George exclaimed. "Bring the torch hither." He pointed to the cavern wall. Scratched into the rock were the letters C.P. "The slavers brought our countrymen through here." He cast a glance at the myriad of passageways leading away from the main chamber, deeper into the earth. "I am going to search every inch of this cave."

She inclined her head towards the entrance. "Not now. Someone approaches."

"How do you know this?" George asked in exasperation. "I hear nothing."

They exited the cavern just before Wanchese emerged from the mists and halted at the tree line.

Jane's heartbeat sped. He was bare chested despite the cool morning air. Clad only in buckskins and moccasins, he carried a bow in one hand and a quiver of arrows strapped to the opposite shoulder. His long black mane was unbound and whipped in the morning breeze. A pale cloth covered his nose and the lower half of his face.

His mahogany eyes burned into hers. "Nadie is sick." His voice sounded muffled beneath the cloth.

A hand flew to her chest. She drew several tortured breaths. "How bad is she?"

"She calls for you."

Jane tasted fear. "I must go to her."

"Is that wise when you have escaped the illness thus far?" George demanded.

She raised hands that shook to her throbbing temples. The heat of her own skin surprised her. She pressed the back of her hand to her forehead to be certain.

Wanchese's face paled a few shades as he observed her movements. He took a step towards her and halted.

"Pray lead the way," she choked. "It appears I already have the fever."

CHAPTER 11: DELIRIUM

"James and William tend the sick without ceasing," Wanchese explained as they jogged to Dasamonquepeuc. "Like George, they endured the measles as lads and claim they will not fall ill with it again."

Chills shook her. "I pray it is so." She pictured James' scar-ridden face. He was a smallpox survivor, as well. Frowning, she recalled no such scars on William's smooth, round features and hoped his constitution was as hardy as his comrade's.

"How many are ill?" She coughed into her arm as they ran. She trailed behind Wanchese a good twenty feet or so, not wanting him anywhere near the sickness.

"Four. Nadie, Chitsa, Amonsoquath, and you."

Chitsa, too? Tarnation! She had hoped to contain the illness to Nadie, Amonsoquath, and herself.

"A few blame the English for bringing their disease to our village. A lad named Rowtag tried to provoke a fight with Blade this morning."

"Blade has the patience of a saint," she sighed. "No doubt he refused to trade fisticuffs."

"Rowtag demanded to know why only the Roanokes fall ill and not the English."

"Lizzie is dead," she protested, "and I am far from well."

"True," he said grimly. "However, the ones who mutter only observe James and William moving in and out of the sick bay."

The Roanokes possessed a sick bay? Indeed they must, because Wanchese led her past the palisade entrance to Dasamonquepeuc. Instead of entering the city, they continued west into the thick of the forest. A trio of tents were wedged end to end in a tiny clearing. Tendrils of smoke wafted through their vents, and a mournful chant met their ears.

"Achak seeks to conjure aid from the gods." Wanchese gave an exaggerated wave of his hand, which made her think he did not put much stock in his medicine man's conjuring.

Faith, the last thing their patients needed was a bunch of mystical mumbo jumbo. Hopefully, James and William had the sense to counter such nonsense by sending up a plea to the one true God for a real miracle.

"Achak allows no one but himself to tend Nadie."

Her heart sank. "Will he forbid me to visit her?"

"He cannot, for Nadie has summoned you and I hereby command you to obey her summons. To Achak, my word is like unto the gods."

The bitterness in his voice jolted her. "I will go to her at once."

"If only I had the powers of a true god," he muttered half to himself. "I would heal her myself." He raised the tent flap for her, careful to avert his face as she approached.

She wished he would not stand so close. For one thing, it was tempting to slide her arms around him and rest her burning head again his chest. Faith, she dared not even look up when she passed by him for fear of coughing on him.

"Do not be alarmed at Achak's appearance," Wanchese warned. "James bade him to cover himself in the manner of your English surgeons."

"I imagine James told you to do the same," she grumbled, flicking a dissatisfied glance over the wrapped lower-half of his face. It was not near enough, in her opinion, to protect him. She wished he were miles away from the sickness.

Inside the tent, she felt as if she had stepped back stage in a theater. Instead of his usual cape and blackbird cap, Achak's face was hidden behind a red and black ceremonial mask that grinned menacingly at her in the fire light. Draping his figure was a robe that dragged the hard-packed dirt floor.

Achak ceased his babbling and bobbing at her entrance. He retreated to his post at the corner of the tent to observe her. His dark eyes flashed from the eye holes of the mask, distrustful and accusing.

Egad! Another Roanoke who blames me for bringing the measles to his people.

Nadie's bedroll lay next to the fire. Draped beneath a pile of furs, she curled on her left side, shivering and staring into the flames. Red spots mottled her beautiful copper features.

"Nadie!" Jane fell to her knees. "*Kicke*."

She jolted at the sound of her voice and raised her head. "*Amosens*," she wheezed. The effort elicited a bout of coughing. She buried her face in the blankets while she struggled to regain control.

It was painful to hear the fluids crackling deep inside her chest. Alarm shuddered through Jane at how long it took her to catch her breath.

"So much to learn yet," she declared in a hoarse whisper. "Your training is not complete."

"Surely you jest," Jane said dryly. "You have worked my fingers to the bone since the day we met."

There was no answering humor in the older woman's bloodshot eyes. "We must train," she insisted and hauled herself with painstaking effort to a sitting position.

"You should rest, *kicke*."

In response, Nadie gave a sharp command that had Achak scurrying from the tent.

Well, then.

"You are ill," she accused after he left.

"I will live."

"Aye, you will. I have seen it," Nadie agreed matter-of-factly. She pulled the furs tighter around her shoulders.

Did she foresee her own recovery as well? Jane waited, hoping for an assurance that never came.

Nadie's dark eyes were edged with pain and the skin below them sunken, but she observed Jane as sharply as ever. She hunched forward to suppress another cough. "Tell me, *amosens*, about the English queen, her big boats, and fire sticks. Tell me how she gazes at the heavens and views the stars as if they were close enough to touch."

Startled, Jane sat back. Her own fever forgotten, she pondered the enormity of such questions. It was apparent Chief Wanchese had recounted his travels to her in detail. He had served an entire year, after all, as a diplomat to the English Crown along with Rose's husband, Chief Manteo.

"Instead of chief or *weroance*, we call Elizabeth our queen," she began. "I never had the honor of making her acquaintance, but 'tis said she surrounds herself with the finest talent the world has to offer. Poets, playwrights, mathematicians, astrologers, metallurgists..." Her voice dwindled at Nadie's brisk motion for her to halt.

"Poets?" she said with a curious lilt.

"Aye, they compose verses and sometimes even set them to music. I am happy to recite one if you wish."

At Nadie's emphatic nod, she continued. "Well, certainly. How about this one?"

Shall I compare thee to a summer's day?
Thou art more lovely and more temperate:
Rough winds do shake the darling buds of May;
And summer's lease hath all too short a date.
Sometime too hot the eye of heaven shines,
And often is his gold complexion dimmed;
And every fair from fair sometime declines,
By chance, or Nature's changing course, untrimmed:
But thy eternal summer shall not fade,
Nor lose possession of that fair thou ownest,
Nor shall Death brag thou wander'st in his shade,
When in eternal lines to Time thou growest.
So long as men can breathe or eyes can see,
So long lives this, and this gives life to thee.

"Ah." Nadie pursed her lips in concentration. "You speak of a man in love."

She chuckled. "Aye. Some say a man thinks nothing but nonsense when he is in love."

"Only fools laugh," she chided and dissolved into a fit of coughing.

So Wanchese had claimed. I raised my brows. No wonder the expressions of the Roanokes were set in such rigid lines. "Call me a fool then, *kicke*, for I cannot imagine a life without laughter."

She ignored Jane's attempt at gaiety. "Have you ever loved a man, Jane?"

Love. She blinked. She preferred direct speaking, but the topic baffled her. "In truth, I am not entirely certain I understand the emotion."

A ghost of a smile lifted Nadie's lips. "It is a burning

inside that never goes away, *amosens*. A light in your eyes and a knowing in your heart."

"You speak from experience?" she asked in wonder.

"Indeed I do. Noshi is my mate, a good and worthy man."

Noshi? He was the ageless one who served as priest to the Roanokes. *How intriguing!* The long looks they traded when she and Nadie passed by the temple suddenly made more sense. She wondered if taking a mate meant the same thing as getting married.

Before she could ask, Nadie fired her next question. "Does any man make you burn, Jane?"

Shaking herself from her musings, she gave careful consideration to her next words. "There is a certain connection, if you will, with one man."

"And the burning?" she probed.

Blushing, Jane lowered her eyes. "Aye."

"Does he burn for you?"

"I, well... Good gracious, Nadie! What does this have to do with my training?"

"We no longer speak of nonsense, do we, *amosens*?"

Her breath caught. Nay, her feelings for Wanchese were far from nonsensical. She sought to divert the conversation. "William Shakespeare is both a poet and a playwright. We just discussed poetry. When a playwright pens a story, men and women don costumes to act out the script."

"Script?"

"Yes." Springing to her feet in delight, she whisked a deerskin from Achak's pile of medicinal belongings. Too far from civilization to attend any parish services, she and her father had acted out plays in the meadow in order to round out her biblical education.

She threw the skin over her head like a veil and thrust out a hand towards one of the tent posts. "Why dost thou nail my Lord to a cross? Why settest thou Him amidst this company of thieves? Know thee not thou crucifieth the King of Kings and Lord of Lords?"

Nadie bent forward to stir the fire between them. Fresh smoke puffed towards the ceiling. "You speak of the gods."

"Not just any god. In England, we call Him the one true God."

"Uh? The Roanokes call our most powerful god Ahone, whereas the English call theirs the Christ. Are they the same?"

Jane cast a wary glance at the doorway. "Our chief bade me not to speak of Him."

"Then you will only speak of him to me. I have long desired to understand why your god insisted on slaying our king, Pemisapan."

"Hogwash!" Jane slid the deerskin covering from her hair and plopped back down before the fire. "Men have been slaughtering each other since the beginning of time and blaming all manner of deities for their actions. I very much doubt Christ had anything to do with the matter." She gave the deerskin a vicious shake to knock out the wrinkles before she folded it with meticulous care.

Nadie nodded, her forehead wrinkled in consideration. "I like your answer well, *amosens*. Some men simply act out of the blackness of their own hearts."

"Wise you are, Nadie." She rubbed her hands together briskly and held them to the fire.

"You called your Christ the one true God. By what authority does he place himself above the other gods?"

A surge of emotion made Jane's eyes burn. She leaned towards Nadie. "According to my pa, 'tis the greatest love story of all time." She proceeded to tell of the virgin lass named Mary and how shocked and disappointed her affianced, Joseph, had been to learn of her pregnancy before they were wed. She described the blindingly beautiful archangel, Gabriel, who had warned the grieving man in a dream not to discard the woman of his heart, because she would soon give birth to the King of the World.

Nadie was silent for a long time. Even her coughing ceased. She stirred the fire again. The flames popped and crackled. The only other sound was the faint murmur of voices outside the tent.

She set down her stick and turned to Jane at last. "It is the stuff of magic, yet you believe it."

"Indeed I do. 'Tis far more powerful than magic."

"Does Wanchese know you disapprove of the killing of Pemisapan?"

She sighed. "Aye, he knows, Nadie, but he feels the loss of his king no less. He prefers the life of a warrior, yet is forced to bear the burdens of a king."

Nadie pursed her lips. "Long have I sought a mate for him who understands these things. The other maidens," she grunted in derision, "merely seek pleasure beneath his blankets. Then again, how can I blame them? He is comely to look on, is he not?" She shot a sly glance at her adopted daughter.

Heat that had nothing to do with the fever crept up her neck. Comely was an understatement. The man was a legend of speed and agility, height and strength, stealth and cunning. It took but a simple look from those mahogany eyes to either pique her anger or stir her passion. It was utterly dangerous for any person to have such control over another.

Jane waved a hand. "He is comely, I suppose."

"You suppose?" She snorted. "I see how you look at each other. Aye, mates you are destined to be."

Does that mean she sees through our current sham? Jane ducked her head in embarrassment.

She continued, "No man acquires a concubine for the mere sake of protecting her. I begin to think you have succeeded where all the others have failed. Indeed, you have captured the heart of our chief."

"Nay, it cannot be!" Jane cried. "I am barely more than a slave, while he is a chief."

Her brows rose. "New tribal member or not, the deed is done, *amosens*. Matters of the heart do not always follow the rules."

Jane shivered at the finality in Nadie's tone. "Oh, but they must, for your laws prohibit us from marrying until twelve moons have passed."

Her fevered eyes lit. She leaned closer to peer into Jane's face. "You speak the truth," she said in wonder. "I am overjoyed to learn our chief will take a princess, at last."

"Not for another twelve moons."

"Bah! Nothing will keep him from you in the meantime."

Her words both thrilled and terrified Jane. "It pleases not my God for me to live as any man's concubine."

Perplexed creases deepened around Nadie's eyes. "He means to have you, Jane."

"In twelve moons, he may have me."

"And if he refuses to wait?"

"Then he will destroy everything worth having between us," she said firmly.

"To refuse a summons from the chief could cost your life, *amosens*."

"I did not refuse him, *kicke*. At his command, I went to live with him in his lodge."

"Where you choose to slumber next to a dog instead of a man."

"Cutto guards me at Wanchese's bidding. Wait." She frowned. "How did you know of our sleeping arrangements?"

"I know all there is to know about my people." Her ageless eyes raked over her in admonition. "By refusing to lie with your chief, you put him at great risk, *amosens*."

"How so?"

"Only while you serve as his concubine can he protect you from the likes of Askook. Otherwise, any man can challenge his claim on you."

"I do not see how this puts Wanchese at risk, Nadie, only myself."

"Then you do not see well at all, *amosens*."

She shook her head. "Pray explain yourself."

"Wanchese already claims you in his heart. He will not stand by while another takes you."

She blushed again. Wanchese *had* tossed Askook away from her as if he weighed no more than a rag doll.

"If Askook discovers the true state of things in the chief's bedchambers, he may challenge Wanchese's claim on you."

"Nay, he will not." She fiddled with one of the braids slung across her shoulder. "Askook fears Wanchese."

"Perhaps he will not make a direct challenge, but he will plant his poisonous seeds with the council. He will declare you bring shame to your chief."

She tossed her head. "His opinion matters not to me."

"It should. Any councilman may call for your execution should you bring harm or shame to our chief."

"Another one of your laws, I presume?"

"Aye."

"You are a member of the council," Jane pointed out.

"Aye."

Meaning you have the authority to call for my death, as well.

Jane crossed her arms. "Do you think I bring either harm or shame to him, Nadie the Wise?"

Nadie clasped her arms over her thin chest and considered the question.

How Jane wished she would lie down and rest. A wave of heat rocked her. To combat a dizzying need to lie down herself, she reached for a skin of berry-flavored water while she awaited the elder woman's answer.

"Nay," she said at last. "You bring him love."

"Love?" Jane drew back, aghast. The half-raised skin remained suspended before her. "We only met a few weeks ago. Doesn't love take time?"

"The deed is done." Worry wrinkled her brow. "You are not one to love easily, *amosens*. There will be no going back for you."

A rustling sounded outside their tent. "Jane, you must come. Now, please," James called.

She stood and bowed unsteadily to Nadie. "You should rest, *kicke*. I shall return soon."

Nadie inclined her head. *"Amosens."* Her face tightened with the effort of suppressing a cough.

Such a proud and dignified woman. Jane's heart swelled with affection as she took her leave and squinted into the mid-day sun. Its rays went a long way to warming up the crisp air. Trees rose like giants around the three tents. Their interlocking branches formed a near perfect circle.

"It is Amonsoquath," James explained as the tent flap fell into place behind her. He ran an agitated hand through his hair. "William continues to bathe his face and arms as you instructed. Nevertheless, he appears to be taking a turn for the worse."

"How so?"

"He grows hotter and does not recognize us anymore. Come. Examine him for yourself."

A shiver of premonition ran down her spine as she followed James inside the next tent. These were dangerous signs, according to her apothecary friend, Agnes, who was safely ensconced with Chief Manteo's friendly tribe of Croatoans. If she were here, she would insist on taking measures to reduce Amonsoquath's fever for fear of losing him.

Wanchese's nephew thrashed on a bedroll in the dim interior. William heaved a gust of relief at the sight of Jane, his round face glistening with sweat. "I, er, doused the flames a while ago in here," he said ruefully. "Both the patient and myself were nigh on burning to pieces."

"You did well," she assured and knelt beside Amonsoquath. His face and arms were mottled with the measles rash. He gazed up at her through listless eyes and muttered something to himself.

She bent closer.

"George," he rasped.

She drew back, startled.

"George is dead."

"Nay, he lives."

"Left to die."

"George is well. I spoke with him just this morning."

"George," Amonsoquath cried again, his face agonized.

"We must move him," she sighed. "It is time."

"Where to?" inquired James.

"We shall submerge him in the river."

"He will catch his death out there," William protested.

"Aye, or he might retrieve his life." She positioned her hands beneath his shoulders.

"Nay, Mistress Jane. Let me carry him." James nudged her aside and lifted the lad with a huff of exertion. "He weighs a ton."

"Nary an ounce of fat on 'em is why." There was pride in William's voice.

"Start the fire back up, William. He will need it upon his return. Go on with you, James." She nudged him towards the door. "I will catch up after I fetch more blankets." She prayed her plan would work.

"Aye, Mistress Jane." William tipped his cap at her and

went to work digging at the coals and blowing on them. "Shall I join you at the river?"

"Nay, I would rather not leave Nadie and Chitsa alone with, ah—" She caught herself in time before voicing Achak's name. How she longed to trade his remedies for Agnes's more practical ministrations.

Agnes had the build of a china doll and the tinkling laugh of a mindless socialite with naught on her mind but what gown to wear next. Beneath her head of cascading gold ringlets, however, was a mind comparable to any of the best trained doctors in all of England. Faith, she had managed to keep their three shiploads of passengers in excellent health during their treacherous trans-Atlantic crossing.

Her knowledge was endless. She knew every herb and growing thing and each of their powers to balance and restore the body's humours. There was something almost other-worldly about her administration of medicine, as well. She possessed the outward calm and inner strength that naturally soothed the soul. Jane had watched her employ her low, quiet tones on many an injured sailor, calming them in an instant.

---

*H*er voice still rang in her head. *"Faith, Jane! For a moment there, I thought you were one of the midshipmen. Are you ever going to shed those dreadful trousers?"* They'd *been pressed into sailing due to a shortage of sailors fit for duty.*

"Not if I can help it," she chuckled. "I find the extra freedom to move well worth the sacrifice of fashion."

"Sacrifice?" She gave a delicate shudder. "Nay, 'tis an outright butchering of fashion. I declare, you are the only woman on either side of the Atlantic who could pull it off, too. The trousers suit you somehow, with your endless height and impossibly slender frame."

She chuckled again, feeling awkward in the face of such praise. She was no good at small talk.

"*E*r, miss?" William interrupted her reverie. He held out a stack of furs. "I believe you were searching for these."

She swayed on her feet a moment. "On the contrary, I believe I was wool-gathering. Bless you a thousand times for fetching these blankets." Tarnation, but James had quite the leap on her by now. She would have to run to catch up. She stumbled from the tent.

"I say! Are you well there, Mistress Jane?" William called after her.

"The fire, William," she snapped. "All you need to worry your head about is the fire."

"Yes'm," he rejoined doubtfully.

She broke into a sprint. The cooler temperature of the forest provided instant relief from the fever threatening to swirl its way to a full boil. She hoped to buy enough time to show James what she needed him to do before it spiked out of control, rendering her useless.

Something was terribly wrong with the trees. They swayed at an alarming rate despite the lack of breeze. Their gnarled trunks twisted themselves into all manner of expressions and seemed to mock her. Burn them, if their dry, wooden laughter did not echo in her ears as she swept past them.

The greenish light of the forest splintered into a myriad of colors and danced across her vision. She rubbed her eyes.

Suddenly, one of the trees stepped directly in her path. They collided in a spray of sparkling colors. She threw one of her arms up for protection, which prevented her from planting her face flat into its trunk. Alas, the blankets went flying from her grasp. It was such a luxury to sink to the ground as she knelt to gather them.

She roused herself with a vicious shake when she started to nod off. It was too early to sleep. There was work yet to be done. She blinked several times to clear her vision.

Amonsoquath needed her. She shoved to her feet, vowing to come back for the blankets later. *Just a little bit farther, and I can rest.* Her steps fell into a rhythm. One foot in front of the other. One foot at a time was all it took. Just a little bit farther.

"Jane? Over here," James called.

She blinked again and spun in a slow circle.

"Over here," he shouted, louder this time.

His concerned features wavered into view. She tottered towards him, wondering what was wrong with her blasted feet.

"Mistress Jane?" He sounded taken aback. "Are you—"

"Aye," she snapped. "'Tis obvious I am sick, which is all the more reason..." She struggled to remain standing. "'Tis particu-lar-ly important that you dip our patient into the river. H-hold him th-there." Her teeth began to chatter. "M-mercy, 'tis c-cold." She folded her arms to contain more of her body's heat. "H-hold him 'til the r-redness in his face b-begins to fade. We m-must reduce the fever, else..."

She slid to her knees, because her feet refused to hold her any longer. "When you f-finish with him, p-pray do the s-same for m-me." With that, she slumped to the ground and rolled to her side.

"Jane!" A man's voice called her name, but she was past worrying. James was there, as capable as any man she'd ever known. He would care for her until she awoke. She was going to live. Nadie had foreseen it.

CHAPTER 12: WISE WOMAN

*J*ane dreamt she was lying on a bed of ice in a room so cold she could not muster up a shiver. The myriad of colors swirling behind her eyelids ground to a frigid halt.

Afterwards, she dreamt of nymphs flitting around her bed in a smoke-filled chamber. Dark-eyed nymphs toted warm, furry blankets into the room while their fair-skinned minions toted bowls with long-handled spoons out of the room. Every so often, a monstrous bird with black-gloved hands hopped over to her and bent to observe her through beady eyes. He did little besides squawk and wave his arms. Minutes passed. Hours. A day perhaps?

At last, one of the dark-eyed nymphs clapped her hands and stated in a matter-of-fact tone, "You have slumbered long enough. Rise, *amosens*. It is time for your training." It was the frenzy of coughing following her words that startled Jane into full wakefulness.

What training? She opened her eyes.

"*Amosens*! Jane!" Nadie cried, her voice cracking with

emotion. She pressed the backs of her fingers to her temples, cheeks, and neck. "You are back."

Jane frowned. "Where have I been?"

"Ill."

She raised her hands and turned them over. The faint outline of red spots remained. *Ah, right. The measles.* Memories flooded back of Lizzie Glane and her horrific warnings about the arrival of the Spanish, but she had delivered more than bad tidings. She had also brought sickness to their village.

She jolted into an upright position. "How does Amonsoquath fare and Chitsa?"

"Much better." The blanket around Nadie rested on shoulders thinner than she remembered. "Both of them beg to return to Dasamonquepeuc."

Homesickness tugged at Jane's chest, too. She had been away for too many days. Her heart ached for a glimpse of Wanchese. "Did anyone else fall ill?" She wriggled on her bedroll in search of her moccasins.

"Nay. Only the four of us."

Jane's throat swelled with emotion. It was a miracle. Back in London, such pandemics were known to sweep entire towns and take a third of the population with them before running their course.

Nadie's spine was straight as a board as she inclined her body towards her. "How did you know to immerse us in the river?"

"A dear friend named Agnes taught me the technique. She served as our, ah," Jane searched for a term her adoptive mother would recognize, "our medicine woman on the ship ride here."

She'd been bored senseless on the days when there was hardly a wind to blow them forward in the water more than a few inches per hour. While their ship lay idle, she had often drifted to the sick bay to lend Agnes a hand with her patients. When business was slow, she'd demonstrated procedures, mixed remedies, and explained the complexities of creating her healing poultices.

"James placed you in the river to break your fever."

That explains my dream about the bed of ice. Jane grinned. Fortunately, James was a quick learner, because she'd blurted out the instructions and had fallen senseless at his feet. "He will make Chitsa a good husband at the end of twelve moons."

"Nay. He will make her a good husband as soon as she returns to her lodge."

"What? I thought new tribe members could not marry for at least—"

"Normally, yes, but not so with James and William. They were born into the tribe to replace husbands who were slain in combat. The widow may claim her new mate whenever she is ready."

"Do you think she is ready?"

"Aye. 'Tis the first thing she stated when she woke this morning."

Jane grinned. To her knowledge, James had never been married. He was a man given to outrageous jesting and flirtation but not a man she'd ever pictured settling down. Watching Chitsa ensnare James in the bonds of matrimony was going to be a real treat.

It fascinated her to no end that the Roanoke women did the choosing when it came to courtship and marriage. It was the exact opposite of how things worked back in England where marriages were often arranged, and men generally took the upper hand in the selection process. To have so much control over one's destiny was very much to her liking. Given half a chance, she would choose a man of strength, courage, honor, and compassion. She would choose...

The door flap opened, and Wanchese ducked his head to enter. He sought Jane out in the shadowy tent, his gaze raking her entire person before settling on her face. For a moment, the passage of time shivered to a halt.

She resisted the urge to smooth a hand over her braids and straighten her tunic. It was good to lay eyes on him again, but what was he thinking to breeze his way into their sick chamber without a care? Where was his mask?

"You should go," she blurted.

His lip curled. "Is this how Nadie trained you to greet your chief?"

She wanted to slap him for his insolent tone. At the same time, she wanted to bury her hands in his black locks and pull him closer for a kiss. "I do not wish you to become ill," she explained stiffly.

"James says your *English* disease has run its course and abandoned our camp."

She made a sound of disbelief in the back of her throat and dug her fingers into the fringe of her leggings. How dare he throw her heritage in her face at a time like this? She had risked her life to isolate Lizzie from the others and then wasted away for days here in these blasted tents. Away from home. Away from him.

He gave a curt nod to his council woman. "You may leave us, Nadie. Methinks our Jane can stand to repeat a lesson or two of her training with me."

"As you will, chief." Nadie pulled herself with effort to her feet and shuffled toward the tent flap.

"How dare you speak to her so!" Jane spat, rising to her knees. "My *kicke* is welcome to stay."

"On the contrary, it pleases me more to send her off to rest," he retorted. As soon as she disappeared from view, he crossed the short distance between them. "You have worried her senseless with your lazing about, wench. I'll have no more such sloth. Get up."

She gaped in amazement.

"That was a command," he snarled.

With a shriek of rage, she reached for her dagger and sprang to her feet. Alas, a wave of lightheadedness sent her crashing back to her knees, except she never hit the hard-packed earth.

Wanchese snatched her mid-tumble and swept her against him. "If you ever frighten me again in such a manner, Jane, I swear to you, I will—"

The rest of his words were muffled as his lips blazed a warm trail from her earlobe to her chin.

She struggled to disengage herself. "Eew! I've lain here for heaven only knows how long. I must smell like the lowliest tramp from Cheapside."

"I'm a savage, remember?" His voice roughened. "What do I care about such things? Nonetheless, you've been bathed every day in the effort to lower your fever."

"How many days?" she asked as his embrace tightened.

"The worst three days of my life." His face was ravaged with worry. Lines of exhaustion creased the corners of his eyes, and the skin below them was sunken.

She trailed her fingers down his cheek "Are you sure it is safe for us to, er…" *Be together like this? To kiss?*

"James assures me you are well now that the spots are gone." He spoke agains the edge of her mouth. "You will return to your duties in my lodge."

"When?"

"Soon." He splayed one hand against the small of her back and drew away an inch to scowl at her.

"You miss my cooking that much?" she teased.

"Huh? Fishing for compliments, are we?"

"Bah. I state the facts and nothing more," she scoffed. "You whimper like a scrap hound for my stews. Aye, that is why you missed me so much, chief." She slid her arms around his neck, fisted both hands in the glorious silk of his black mane, and tugged.

He grunted in pleasure and yanked her closer. "There are ways to curb such an unruly tongue."

"Indeed?" she taunted. "All I hear are threats. So little action."

With that, he palmed her cheek and tipped her face up to his. He feasted like a starving man on her lips. When he drew his head up at last, he surveyed her with satisfaction. "Indeed, I am not the only one who needs you back in my lodge. I weary of consoling that blasted mongrel of mine from your prolonged absence."

She grinned. "Cutto misses me? 'Tis hard to believe the beast has any feelings at all for the blood dripping from his fangs." It filled her with guilt to realize the poor animal had gone without her attentions for nigh on ten days. With his ferocious growl and menacing stare, most of the other villagers gave him a wide berth. A creature like him needed a soft word now and again, a bowl of well-seasoned scraps, and a rub down of his ragged coat to keep him from crossing over the line into the realm of pure evil.

"He has been running wild, because you are not there to tend his needs." The last word came out on a groan. Wanchese touched his forehead to hers. "How much longer will you make me wait, wench?"

"Already a moon has passed," she whispered. "Eleven more and I shall be yours."

"Nay, you are already mine." He ran a thumb across her chin. "It has been so since you first stepped on my island. 'Tis only a matter of time before we mate."

She trembled at the fierce possession in his dark gaze. It was beyond besotted, bordering on maniacal. Her eyes fluttered closed. He never intended to let her go, *had* never intended to let her go from the beginning. Perhaps, Chief Manteo truly believed he had called in a favor when he sent Wanchese to fetch her from the Great Trading Path, but Wanchese had traveled with an agenda of his own. It was both thrilling and humbling for a spinster like her to be so ruthlessly pursued.

If only he would extend a bit of his single-mindedness to the retrieval of her missing countrymen, her happiness would be complete. There had to be a way to convince him. According to Nadie, she and Wanchese were in love. That had to count for something.

When she opened her eyelids, Wanchese's gaze still burned into hers, narrowed, probing and calculating. "What schemes do you hatch behind those ripe almond eyes?" The rich baritone of his voice sent delightful little chills running across her skin.

Her lips twitched. *Blast the man! He knows me too well.* But she was in no mood to wheedle at the moment. Looping her arms around his neck, she grazed his jaw with a kiss. "Take me home, Wanchese."

"Now?" He stepped back and ran his hands up and down her arms. "You think you can walk the entire way?"

She batted away his hands. "Can a fish swim? Can a bird fly?"

Anger flashed across his features. "Indeed? Then you may carry these." He bent to retrieve a stack of blankets from the ground and thrust them in her arms. "And these." He added Achak's medicinal pouches to the pile.

Her hands began to shake. She returned to her bedroll and sat with a huff of frustration. "Give me a minute," she snapped and was rewarded with a mocking glance. "I just need to catch my breath. How soon do we leave?"

"Whenever I deem you are well enough to make the trip,"

he retorted. "In the meantime, you may continue your training with Nadie. I will bid her return to you." He spun on his heel and ducked from the tent.

"Of all the insufferable—" she breathed as he disappeared from view.

The door flap flew open again. "Do you address your master or someone else?" Nadie asked sternly.

"I, well, yes." She ducked her head, flustered by the stoic set to her adoptive mother's face. With how quickly she had appeared, there had been no need for Wanchese to fetch her. *Drat her!* She'd been eavesdropping. "How long were you standing outside the tent?"

"Long enough." She advanced on Jane with purpose, leaning on her walking stick. "If you employ that tone with our chief in front of our people or ever again challenge his commands as you did earlier when he sent me away, I will gut you myself, *amosens*." She pounded the pole into the ground for emphasis.

Jane's mouth dropped at her ferocity.

"He is your master, above all else." She pounded the hard-packed earth a second time. "It matters not that he will soon be your mate."

Egad! Whatever had she done to raise Nadie's ire to such an extent? Jane shrugged off a sense of foreboding and beckoned her adoptive mother to come sit beside her, but she only glared and held her stance at the entrance of the tent.

"You wish to know what I heard? I heard you rouse our chief's passions in a way no other maiden has done before. I never dreamt how thoroughly he would fall. 'Tis a dangerous game you play, *amosens*, in a land seething with change, only a spark away from the upheaval of entire civilizations."

Nay, I play no games. Why would Nadie claim such nonsense? Earlier she seemed happy at the thought of her and Wanchese making a match of it. What had changed her mind?

Red-faced, she started to rise, but Nadie stopped her by shuffling closer and pressing her stick atop the fringe of her leggings, pinning her to her bedroll. "You will not use your womanly powers to manipulate him."

How dare you accuse me of such base intentions! Angry, Jane started to scramble to her knees, but again Nadie stopped her from rising.

This time, Nadie tapped the staff against her chest. "You will not raise your voice, strike, dishonor, or speak ill of him. You will revere him before our people whether he is absent or present. You will show him more deference than any other member of our tribe. This is how the mate of a king should carry herself."

The heat seeped from Jane's cheeks at the wild light in Nadie's eyes. She was not all that incensed with her, after all. Nay, she was afraid. Very much so. Of what and whom Jane was not certain. She wished the woman would cease spinning riddles and speak her mind. Alas, she was nowhere near finished with her tirade.

Sighing, Jane settled back on her bedroll and waited.

"As lovers, you will no doubt share and exchange ideas, but you will never seek to influence his decisions or the decisions of his counsel for personal gain. Every action you take will be for the good of the people. Our people, *amosens*. You no longer act for the City of Raleigh but for the Roanokes. Do you understand?"

"Nay, *kicke*, I do not understand at all." She and Wanchese would butt heads to the end of their days. She didn't see how it was Nadie's concern.

Her adoptive mother pulled the end of her staff from Jane's chest, but it remained suspended in the air between them. For a moment, Jane feared the woman intended to strike her with it. The only sound in the tent was the crackling of the fire.

She held her breath. Her eyes never left Nadie's face. To her relief the elder woman lowered the stick.

She had no wish to fight with Nadie and hoped she would share whatever had her so riled. Still weak, she was leaning heavily on the staff now. Her breath came in short gasps. "I thought to mold and nurture a daughter. Instead I mentor and train a woman who will give birth to a new nation."

"Please, Nadie," Jane whispered. She was truly starting to scare her. "Come sit with me. I will listen to all you have to say and learn what you have to teach."

"Ah, *amosens*, I sorely misjudged you from the beginning." She took a seat at last and rested her head against the stick, beholding Jane with soulful eyes.

"There is nothing to judge or misjudge," she hastened to assure the woman. "I am exactly whom I appear to be, a simple trapper's daughter from the mountains of England."

"Ah, then you know not what I see, *amosens*."

"Indeed, I do not." Jane sent her a curious glance and leaned forward to stir their fire. New flames shot up from the hot coals. She stood and pulled another two sticks of firewood from the stack along the tent wall and added them to the pit.

Settling herself on the blankets, she fondly surveyed her adoptive mother. "Tell me what you see when you gaze at me, *kicke*."

The corners of her eyes wrinkled in concentration. "These eyes do not work as well as they did when I was a maiden. Even so, they can still pick out the good and the bad in a person and everything in between. They see things that are now and things that will come to pass."

Jane was astonished. "You can predict the future?"

"Not clearly, but oft times I catch a glimpse of it. 'Tis easy enough to read a person by their deeds."

Nodding, Jane glanced away. Aye, most men and women of her acquaintance were as transparent as glass.

"You have the sight as well." Nadie's stick poked the ground between them. "It sets you apart from the others."

What sight? "What do you mean?"

She shrugged. "Perhaps you learned it from the man who taught you to hunt and trap, but you see more than others intend for you to see. Most men simply hear what is said by the lips and observe what is done in the light, but not you. You also hear what is left unsaid and discern many things that are hidden in the dark. Indeed, you understand the will of men."

Jane pressed two fingers to her temple. It was making her head ache, trying to keep up with Nadie's strange ramblings. Perhaps she was not as well as Wanchese claimed.

A faint footfall sounded outside the tent. Her gaze narrowed on the door flap, expecting a visitor.

"There," Nadie stated in a triumphant tone, pointing at the doorway. "You heard what I did not hear."

"With all due respect," Jane started to say and paused. There was no tactful way to state that her superior hearing could simply be explained by her younger age.

"You know who stands outside the tent even before he makes his appearance."

Aye, it was Wanchese, but Jane could not precisely say how she knew.

Good heavens! Is he eavesdropping on me as you did earlier? Her mind raced over her exchange with Nadie. She relaxed when she was unable to recall anything incriminating against herself.

"Fear not, *amosens*. He only listens to our training."

She gave a start at how easy it was for Nadie to read her thoughts.

"You must cultivate the voice inside you," the older woman continued. "What did it say to you when you arrived to Roanoke Island on three big ships?"

Jane's heart thudded. It was not a voice, per se. It had been more of a feeling, a powerful one she had all but ignored.

"We were in danger," she whispered. "From the moment we stepped foot from our ships. There was such a strong sense of evil in the fort, I entertained the cowardly notion of fleeing it and leaving the others behind."

"But you did not abandon your friends. Cowardice is not in your nature. You prefer to stand your ground and protect those you love."

"I failed, *kicke*. My pitiful efforts did nothing to save my friends from the slave trading block."

"Perhaps, *amosens*, and perhaps not. Perchance what happened on the Great Trading Path was meant to be. What if you were supposed to endure the shame of being sold, all for the sake of arriving here?"

To what purpose? Jane held the status of a new member within the ranks of the Roanoke tribe. She was little more than a slave. Surely, Nadie would get around to making her point, eventually.

"What is it that you want from me, *kicke*?"

A hint of a smile lit her face. "Again, you hear what is left unsaid. What I want is simple. I want you to stay."

"I am here." Jane spread her hands. "Where else can I go?" *Wanchese would stop me if I ever tried to leave.*

"I wish for you to stay," she repeated. "Not out of fear or duty but rather because you belong to our land now and to our people."

Jane snorted. She could not deny her heart belonged to the man who ruled this land and its people. Ah, well, and perhaps to the woman who had taken her into her bosom as her adopted daughter. And perhaps to her new friends — Riapoke and Amonsoquath, Chitsa and Alawa, Dyoni and Bly, Mukki and Cutto, and all the others. So many others.

Her eyes flew to Nadie's knowing gaze. *Tarnation! I no longer wish to leave. That is what she wants me to see.*

She wished it were so simple for her other countrymen. Burn George and his foolish desire to launch some vainglorious rescue mission farther inland. She had no interest in heroics and no real hope of gathering together their scattered colonists. Faith, they might be spread along hundreds of miles by now. Perhaps Nadie was right. Perhaps things had turned out as they were meant to be.

Meanwhile, she, James, William, and Blade were settling into Dasamonquepeuc rather nicely. Every one of them, except for George, would loathe to bid their new home adieu at this juncture.

"You are right, *kicke*," she agreed in a hushed voice. She pressed a hand to her chest. "My heart belongs here, to our people and our land, just as you said."

Nadie gave Jane's knee a light tap with her staff. "Your training is closer to completion than I imagined."

"For what?" she burst out, frustrated to no end with the aura of mystery surrounding the woman today.

She laid down her staff at last and folded her arms. "Patience, *amosens*. You will know all you need to know when it is time." She jerked forward in a fit of heavy coughing.

Time for what? Jane could not dispel the heaviness in her chest. Serious matters were afoot, not the least of which was facing her chief again soon. Alone. In his lodge.

Burn it but today's training session had her all agitated, disjointed, and raring for a fight. *Where is Wanchese?* He was one of the few people she'd run across in all her years on this earth that she did not have to tread lightly around.

He could hold his own in a fight.

CHAPTER 13: MALTESSE CROSSES

*J*ane felt much more like herself the next morning. Though still irked by Wanchese's high-handedness the day before, she arose strength-ened from the additional night of sleep, much better prepared for the trek back to Dasamonquepeuc.

Alas, Wanchese remained in a foul mood.

He stalked into her tent. "Hurry, wench. I have not all day to dally with your morning toilette."

She hurried to finish braiding her hair and reached for her pack. "As you will, chief." Sarcasm infused her voice. Recalling Nadie's words, however, she made an effort to shake off her frustration. She clasped her hands and bowed. "How else may I assist in our journey home?"

For an answer, Wanchese snatched her against him and caught her lips in a slow, searing kiss that curled her toes inside her moccasins. "Burn Nadie, for teaching you the ways of a coquette."

She stiffened and tried to pull away. *Egad! He is right.* What had Nadie been thinking? Wanchese was unaccustomed to her tripping all over herself to pay homage like his more zealous subjects.

"'Tis no attempt at flirtation," she assured coolly. "Nadie insists I pay you the deepest respect, more so than any other brave or maiden. She says it is befitting my role."

His arms banded her waist as he nipped at the edge of her mouth. "I have no objections to this newer, more pliant side of you. Indeed, I like it very much."

A delicious warmth crept across her cheeks. *Oh, dear!* Again she tried to disengage herself from his embrace. She needed to think of something quick to tamp down on his growing ardor before the flames leaping between them waxed out of control.

"Jane."

Her heart pounded at the tortured tenure of his voice.

"Cease your struggles."

What? Oh-h-h... She blushed. Her mind scrambled for something to say, anything to dull the razor sharp edge of his passion.

"If it is any comfort," she said in a dry voice, "I would just as soon be tending my traps this fine morn instead of fawning over you."

"Uh?" His mahogany eyes glinted dangerously down at her.

"Come winter, we'll have mouths aplenty to feed. I imagine our people did not slow the harvest on account of the measles. While you detain me here, precious time is slipping away. Time better spent in—"

His hand twisted in her hair. "I have killed men for less impudence."

That she did not doubt. *Ah, well, at least he no longer appears set on ravishing me.* She allowed her voice to turn rueful. "I fear this is neither the first nor the last time I will arouse your ire, should you let me live."

A hint of humor darkened his gaze. He released his hold on her. "Have a care when you bait me, Jane. I am not one of your pampered noblemen."

Nay, he was a Roanoke warrior, and there was a world of difference between the two. She bent to retrieve her bundle. *Tarnation!* Her impulsive tongue kept getting her into hot water. Would she never learn how to say the right thing? How to carry herself like a true Roanoke maiden? Or was she doomed to play the part of a sharp-tongued English school-marm forever?

"Oh, give way," she muttered. "I merely strive to follow Nadie's instruction. Alas, subservience is no strength of mine. I reckon this is the part where I vow to strive harder to master the virtue."

"Tread with care, lest you injure yourself in the process. Neither of us is particularly given to virtue."

She snorted, trying not to laugh.

"You are too stubborn." His voice slid smooth as silk over her. "And too independent. You would rather lead than follow. We are not so different, you and I, in that regard."

She straightened in disbelief and met his gaze. Was he attempting to make light of the enormous disparity between their stations in life? He was a native chief, whereas she was but a working-class maid from the lowest echelons of London society. With a little luck, their mutual attraction would hold. Someday they might even become mates, but she wasn't ready to swallow the idea that he or anyone else would ever view them as equals.

Her independent spirit had been her curse for years, because a woman of such humble lineage would never have the opportunity to lead, only to follow. Best not to snatch at any fleeting hope inspired by Wanchese's words.

Depressed, she swung her bundle over her shoulder and walked stooped beneath its weight to the doorway. She faced him. "I am ready to depart." But the thought of returning to Dasamonquepeuc did not inspire the same joy it had yesterday. This morning, she felt uprooted and adrift, restless and dissatisfied.

Wanchese stood between her and the tent flap, arms folded across the rigid contours of his chest. "Well, I am not. I want more than your token scraping and bowing before me at Nadie's instruction. Give me your loyalty, Jane."

She scowled at the nerve he hit. "You have it." *Mostly.*

"And your trust."

Her scowl deepened. Life had taught her it was wise to reserve a dose of healthy skepticism.

"I am aware you persist in withholding these things from me," he growled. "Take George, for instance. You knew he planned to run away."

"I only knew he did not wish to remain in Dasamonquepeuc," she protested. "He acted on a foolish impulse and nothing more."

"You could have shared your concerns with me."

"Not without sounding ungracious. James, William, Blade, George, and I deeply appreciate how you rescued us from Copper Mountain, but what are we now? Servants? Slaves? We are still not free to come and go as we please. George did not understand his role here any more than I do, and that is why he ran away." She ignored the flash of fury on Wanchese's face. He'd encouraged her to speak her mind. "I immigrated to the New World to liberate myself from the dictates of London society and the Church of England, but I am not free to worship, trap, hunt, or explore at will. In Dasamonquepeuc, I am not even allowed to mention the name of my God for fear of a deadly reprisal, yet this is the foundation on which you demand I build my trust."

With every word, Wanchese's features grew harder. She bit her lip. *What in heaven above am I thinking to air my thoughts with such abandon before a man with the authority to call for my death?*

He pointed to the bundle on her shoulder. "Set it down."

"Pray, pardon the outburst," she sighed. "Nadie warned me to guard my tongue."

A vein ticked in his cheek. "Others have reason to fear me. You do not. As I've stated before, you may speak freely when we are alone. Now set down the blasted bag."

Did he indeed wish to hear her opinions? Most men of rank sought only their own will.

His expression gave nothing away. "How can I earn your trust?" he demanded.

Shaken by the question, she swung her heavy bundle to the ground. She hardly knew what to say.

"I have always coveted what is rare and valuable. You do not give your loyalty to many, Jane. Thus, your regard is worth much to me."

Her chest ached. *He asks for so much, yet he does not ask for the one thing I wish to give him. My love.*

"I would know what you are thinking right now," he persisted.

Her breath came out in a slow whoosh. *Not in a million years.*

He waited a moment. "Trust between warriors is essential, Jane. How else can you face an enemy if you are busy watching your own back?"

She shrugged. "'Tis a challenge, to be sure."

"An unnecessary one between the two of us, Jane. Let us remove it, shall we?"

She raised a brow. "How?"

"Ask anything of me within reason, and I will grant it."

"Anything?" she repeated.

"Within reason," he reminded.

Her pulse leaped at his words. *Your heart. I want your heart, burn it!* But she could not demand his love any more than he could demand her trust. Best to start with something smaller.

"The missing English colonists," she said. "Let us search for the men whose names are etched on the trail of crosses."

He circled her, arms crossed. "Most maidens would ask for trinkets of copper and gold."

She glared. "Do not think to distract me with baubles. One of the men I seek is Blade's father."

"What else?" he demanded. "There must be something more."

"Amitola. Pray, let us search for her as well. 'Tis my fondest wish to restore her to Nadie."

"What if I inform you my scouts have already searched for her? What if I claim they have discovered where the trail of crosses leads? Would you ask for something different?"

"Aye. So long as there is any chance they still live, I would beg you to launch a rescue mission."

"I know not the status of Amitola or your missing colonists, only that the trail of crosses leads to Copper Mountain."

Dasan's lair. Her chest thudded as the news sank home. "We must go after them," she said quietly.

"Very well." Wanchese bit out the words. "Be warned, however, tampering with fate is not without its consequences. Perhaps your countrymen already travel the path meant for them."

She shook her head, incredulous at how much he sounded like Nadie. *Nay, they need rescuing.* But doubt flooded her mind. She certainly did not wish anyone to storm their way into Dasamonquepeuc and snatch her away from Wanchese. *Burn you for shaking my resolve!* Though not the least bit religious, he was all but accusing her of playing

God. She dropped her gaze, uncertain how to respond, since there was a good chance he was correct.

Perhaps he sensed her inner battle, for he tipped her chin up. "Hear me well, Jane. We will locate your colonists, but we will only rescue them if they suffer persecution. Any interference on our part could bring war to our people."

She nodded. There were so many things she had not considered.

"We may run across other colonists, as well, Jane. Women who may have mated and are with child."

"Mercy me!" she interjected.

"Regardless of your feelings on the matter," he answered in icy tones, "I will not separate an expectant mother from the father of the babe, savage or not."

"Savage?" she gasped. "You think I object to— Nay! I am only concerned at the prospect our women may have been taken against their will." *Egad! What if my own belly swelled with Dasan's babe?* She pressed a hand to her middle, blood running cold at the thought.

Wanchese threw up his hands. "Most men of this land are not the beasts you imagine them to be, Jane. They desire their women, woo them, and protect them. I will not come between a man and his mate, for such a thing rarely ends well."

She glared. "You begin to sound as if you fear for your own skin." Did he have no interest at all in the plight of her countrymen? They'd been sold as slaves, for pity's sakes! *Slaves!*

"I prefer to wear it across my bones, yes."

"What about Dasan?" she demanded. "You think he would have wooed me? Why, the man had me tied up like one of the hapless creatures in my traps."

"Hapless creature? You?" Wanchese raised a brow and managed to infuse as much haughty sarcasm into the word as any nobleman she'd ever run across. "He desired you greatly. That is all. I imagine he tied you for his own safety, not out of any wish to harm you. We both know his misconceived attempt at mating with you would not have ended well."

Pursing her lips, she fought an inexplicable urge to laugh. How right Wanchese was, but she had no intention of giving him the satisfaction of admitting it. Instead she changed the subject. "Will you inform Nadie we are going in search of Amitola?"

"Nay," he cautioned. "I would neither get her hopes up nor suffer her wrath for meddling in things best left alone."

"Things best left alone?" she snorted. "Your sister was led away bound and enslaved. How can you doubt she needs rescuing?"

"If you ask Nadie — and I am not advising it — you will discover that is far from how she views the matter. She is wise to believe all things happen for a reason. To her, Amitola's capture was meant to be as sure as the sun would rise in the morning. She is content to embrace you as her *amosens* now."

"Perhaps," she admitted. "Yet she hasn't stopped grieving for Amitola. She also talks about hearing the spirits of her forefathers calling her home." She glanced away from him and swallowed hard. "Sometimes I worry the only thing keeping her with us is our enormous and collective need for her guidance."

"Aye."

"There is none to take her place, you know."

A strange expression flickered across his face as he studied her. "Come," he said. "We must hurry if we are to follow the trail of crosses and return before winter sets in." He ducked from the tent at last.

"How soon will we leave?" She had to jog to catch up.

"Before nightfall." He issued orders to break camp and begin the long march home.

Nadie refused any aid and insisted on carrying her tent roll on her back. Her stoop seemed more pronounced than usual, and her breathing sounded tortured on the hills. Though the rest of the recovering patients were paler and thinner than normal, she was the only one who continued to cough.

Jane tried not to wince at the sound of fluids rattling in her chest. She knew her adoptive mother would not welcome her concern.

Hitching her own roll of supplies higher, she marched close enough to Nadie to come to her aid should she require any but far enough away to avoid being accused of coddling her. Wanchese was more transparent with his concerns. He ignored Nadie's vehement scolding and insisted on frequent stops, pressing a skin of water in her hands at every opportunity. The Roanokes were fond of sharing everything from spoons to bedrolls, but Jane noted he did not consume any of the water from Nadie's skin. Nor did he pass it around to the rest of them.

A celebratory whoop went up when they entered the gates of Dasamonquepeuc. Maidens rushed forward to relieve them of their burdens. James and Chitsa disappeared into her lodge. William ambled off to find Alawa, and Amonsoquath hurried over to the target range where Riapoke was administering a round of instruction.

At a nearly imperceptible nod from Wanchese, Bly and Dyoni whisked Nadie away. He ducked into his lodge and was followed by a long line of *cockarooses*. No doubt they had much to discuss. Jane held back, longing for a change of clothes but not wishing to intrude on their council meeting. She would have to settle for shaking the wrinkles out of her current tunic and leggings.

"Jane." The high-pitched feminine voice gave her a start for the amount of venom it contained.

Kanti held out her ceremonial garments, the ones Wanchese had given her the day he'd discovered her stranded at the spring.

Jane's brows shot up.

Kanti shoved the embroidered tunic and leggings into her hands and turned on her heel. Riapoke watched the two women from across the village path. She noted how Kanti stopped to bow to him. *Ah.* She had probably followed his orders to return the garments.

Apparently, the woman had either not expected Jane to live or not expected her to come back, for the hussy had claimed her possessions in her absence. *Or reclaimed them?* She suspected some of her new things had once belonged to the woman or at least had been at her disposal while she resided in Wanchese's lodge.

She bit back a sigh and nodded her thanks to Riapoke. Arms folded, he scrutinized her for a moment then returned to watching the archers. He marched behind their ranks and stopped every so often to correct the angle of a bow or adjust the trajectory of an arrow.

She glanced down at the soft deerskin garments in her arms. They were brushed clean and, according to her tentative sniff, rubbed with scented oils. Despite her heartless thievery, Kanti had cared well for the clothing in her absence. The thought of her parading in them before Wanchese irked Jane to no end, though. *Ugh!* She'd not even waited until Jane's body was cold in the grave before pilfering through her things.

She set her course for the spring, vowing to scrub off the last vestiges of her sick bed. She was anxious to smooth the tangles out of her hair, too. *How I must look!*

She frowned. *What is wrong with me? I've never been so*

missish about my appearance before. She tossed her ceremonial garments on a flat-faced boulder. There was no point in donning them. Her current crumpled leggings and cloak would be far better suited to their upcoming overland trek.

Steam curled up from the spring as she approached. *Ah.* The temperature of the water held even as the autumn air turned cooler. She snatched a handful of yucca leaves from the stash their maidens kept in a rocky alcove and peeled out of her clothing. It was sheer heaven to step into the warm water.

Riapoke might be lurking, but his presence in her life no longer bothered her. She was growing accustomed to his protective eye and was grateful for it. Thanks to him, she could bathe in peace. She trusted him implicitly, though she could not say why exactly. She just did.

She dove beneath the waters and kicked to propel herself through their depths. The warmth seeped through her bones, soothing every stiff and aching joint from days of being confined to her bedroll. The weakness ebbed from her limbs as she swam.

Smoke jolted her back to the present. It was not the faint sultry smoke of a distant fire, but the acute blast of a near one. It crackled with life beside the stream, though a quick glance around her revealed its maker was nowhere in sight. Grateful for the licking heat of the flames, she stepped from the water and knelt before them to comb her hair until it dried.

"Ah the sweet scent of a clean woman." Wanchese emerged from the trees the moment she finished dressing and plaiting her hair.

Alackaday. He almost made it sound as if any woman would do. She met his lazy searching gaze with a scowl. Let all his concubines past and present bask in his royal presence, grateful for a mere glance in their direction. She was a woman of dignity and virtue and required no such attentions. Gritting her teeth, she slung the spare garments over her shoulder and began to kick dirt on the fire. Burn him for making her feel so insignificant with his careless greeting.

"You intend to travel in style," he said with a curious look at the ceremonial outfit.

She snorted. "Nay, I was just returning them to my bunk. One of the maidens cleansed them for me while I was away."

"Huh." His gaze sharpened and turned calculating.

"It was most kind of her," she said, ending the subject. Her mouth tightened. She would deal with Kanti in her own way when the time was right.

Wanchese rested his hands on his hips. "My men are assembled and prepared to depart."

"I am ready," she assured breathlessly as he stalked her way to lower his head over hers.

"First, you must fortify me against the days ahead. Kiss me, Jane."

She had no will to refuse. She hooked an arm around his neck and pressed her lips to his. Perhaps she was driven in part by enormous gratitude for his willingness to send out a search party at last, because she had never kissed him with such abandon.

This time, he pulled back first.

"Ah, Jane," he said regretfully, kneading the back of her neck. "Our scouts are assembled. We must go."

Dazed, she willed her breathing to return to normal. "Aye, my love." She gave him a final peck on the cheek. "*Ireh.*"

Two of his strongest warriors, Kimi and Kitchi, as well as Amonsoquath awaited them in front of his lodge. Their copper faces showed no emotion as they stood shoulder to shoulder, arms crossed, quivers bristling against their backs. Their gazes rested on Wanchese, awaiting his next command.

Though the youngest among them, Amonsoquath stood in the center and towered a good inch or more over his companions. His cheeks were sunken and the corners of his eyes lined with exhaustion, lending an ominous cast to the black slashes of paint across his cheekbones.

"Amonsoquath should not accompany us," she declared in undertones to Wanchese. "He is not yet at his full strength."

"Neither are you," he returned mildly.

She straightened her shoulders and fisted her hands on her hips. "Launching a rescue of this magnitude bears many risks. Let us take your best scouts."

"Amonsoquath is the best," he retorted. "And we've yet to determine if any of your colonists require rescuing."

She tossed her braids, utterly out of patience with this game of words. *Blast him, but I intend to rescue every colonist we succeed in tracking down.* "As you will." She bit out the words. "Let us depart, then."

"We will. Soon." Wanchese raised his arm and signaled. Bly appeared, bearing a round sack tied atop her head. Her thin frame swayed while her head remained regal and steady. Jane sniffed and caught a whiff of dried meat. *Bless her.* She had packed provisions for their trip.

Bly held out the sack to her, inclining her frame with far more respect than Jane thought was befitting a new tribal member. In return, she took the ceremonial garments from Jane and tossed a deerskin cloak around her shoulders. Securing it with a bone clip at her throat, she stepped back to survey her work. Satisfaction gleamed in her eyes.

"I thank you," Jane muttered and stuck out a hand, intending to shake hers.

"*Tah!*" She declared. "*Kenah*, Jane." With that, she inclined her tall frame in a deep bow, her hands clasped with utmost reverence below her chin.

Jane glanced in askance at Wanchese.

He cocked his head. "This is the first time the diseases of the pale faces have touched our people without riddling our streets with corpses. We have you to thank."

"And James and William," she said quickly. Aghast at the reverence in Bly's gaze, she lost no time in beckoning her to rise. "Do not bow to me, my friend." She clasped her hand and shook it. After a startled moment, Bly's gaze lit, and she gave Jane's hand a quick pump in return.

Dyoni's blooming figure caught her eye next. Relief washed over her to see the young mother looking so well.

She shrieked at the sight of Jane and ran her way. Skidding to a halt several steps away, however, she dropped into a bow. Her belly kept her from stooping quite as low as Bly.

"Oh, stop!" Jane reached forward, intending to yank her upright, but Wanchese stopped her with a shake of his head.

"Let them pay tribute. They think you are something akin to a goddess, possessing magic that flowed through your fingers to infuse the waters with healing powers."

"Stuff and nonsense." She snorted. "You may set them straight at once."

"Never. I am enjoying your blushes too much."

"You take excessive pleasure in my discomfort, is all."

"Aye, there is that." It was as close as she'd ever come to seeing him smile.

There was no lust in Wanchese's eyes this time, yet she'd never shared a more intimate moment with a man before. The sights and sounds of Dasamonquepeuc faded and stilled until no one stood on the main village path but the two of them. In his gaze was a deep-seated contentedness.

She cleared her throat. *We've no time for wool gathering.* "How did you convince the council to send out a search party?"

He shrugged. "I might have suggested that the trail of crosses running in such close proximity to Dasamonquepeuc was a threat to our security. I also might have mentioned how the enslaved were destined for the copper mines."

Of course. "So that was what you meant about our men going beneath the ground."

"Aye."

Extracting them would be no simple matter. "The mines are well-guarded, I presume?"

"Aye."

"Why now?" she demanded. "You have been following the trail of crosses for weeks. Why didn't you launch a rescue sooner?"

"My council was only recently convinced that the gods are on our side in this matter."

"Pray assure me," she said, rubbing her thumb and forefinger across her eyes, "this has nothing to do with my recent elevation to goddess."

"On the contrary." Passion flared in his voice. "It was my most compelling argument during our brief war council."

The ground seemed to shake beneath her. She threw out her hands for balance. It was neither an earthquake nor a sudden bout of weakness brought on by her recent illness, yet she perceived she was falling.

In that precise moment, she tumbled most thoroughly and irrevocably in love with her master.

When she raised her astonished gaze, exhilaration smoldered in his eyes. He understood. There would be no more questions about trust or loyalty between them.

She would follow Wanchese to the farthest edges of the world with knife, bow, and spear. She would follow him all the way to the grave, if he asked, and he knew it.

CHAPTER 14: A MATTER OF TRUST

*W*anchese motioned Jane to join him when he stood before the other three warriors who comprised their rescue team.

Not yet trusting her voice, she wordlessly complied. She was grateful not to be alone with her chief at the moment. It would take time to sort through the enormity of her discovery that she was in love with him.

Love! It is like free-falling over a cliff. She and her father had done exactly that one summer after he taught her how to swim. To celebrate her mastery of the skill, he'd taken her cliff diving into the river at the base of the mountain where they lived.

Except this time she did not know what awaited her at the end of the fall. *Will Wanchese return my love? Sure, he is attracted to me as man to woman.* He felt something when they kissed. Faith, they both did. However, love was another thing altogether. As a school mistress, she'd read the glorious lines of poets and playwrights alike on the subject. Alas, none of her book learning had prepared her for such a helpless tangle of emotions.

She willed the heat in her cheeks to subside as she faced Wanchese's men, hoping they would attribute her heightened color to either her recent illness or the long hike back to Dasamonquepeuc. There was no place for such sentiments in their upcoming mission. She was not a simpering debutante but a huntress and a warrior.

As if undergoing a military inspection, the men stood straight as arrows before her and Wanchese. Heads held high and shoulders rolled back, they gazed past her straight ahead with their bows resting at their sides.

A sense of unaccountable pride flooded Jane. These were Wanchese's men. Her men, too, and they were about to put their strength and cunning into helping them track down Blade's father, Edward Powell, and Amitola.

Kimi and Kitchi resembled each other so closely, they could pass for twins. Only at close range did she detect any differences in their features. Kimi's face was a bit rounder than Kitchi's, and Kitchi bore a thin scar across the base of his neck. *Egad!* The man had endured a rather close shave with a blade. More than likely, someone had tried to kill him.

Kitchi returned her curious gaze with a cool, level stare.

Respect. Odd how natural some sentiments manifested themselves and required no conversation. He had cheated death at least once.

All her instincts screamed he was a force to be reckoned with. Grateful that Wanchese had chosen him to accompany the search party, she tapped her right fist across her heart and inclined her head to him.

Surprise flashed over Kitchi's features. He pounded an answering salute on his chest.

She and Wanchese moved to stand before Amonsoquath next. Her heart ached to note the exhaustion edging his face, making the strong lines of his cheeks and jaw more pronounced, yet… She squinted at him in the evening sun.

Ironclad determination compressed his lips and filled him with impatience to start the mission. He was like a glorious, dark stallion pawing at the ground. He might not yet feel up to full strength, but his resolve was as solid as any warrior who had ever gone into battle. More so than many, she suspected. Aye, they were correct to bring him along.

She saluted him and stepped in front of the last man, Kimi. Like so many of the Roanoke warriors, he was tall, broad of chest, and wore his hair shaved on his shooting side. A single black plait hung over the shoulder that boasted his quiver. Unlike his brother, his dark eyes glittered with humor. *Perhaps the Roanokes found smiling a foolish practice, but this man smiled with his eyes.*

She closed one eyelid in a long slow wink, fisted her heart, and tossed him a merry grin for no reason at all. To her delight, he winked back and pounded his chest in return.

The ladies back in London would have deemed him a real charmer.

Satisfied with their preparations, Wanchese raised an arm. "Ireh," he said simply, and their small group departed.

Dead leaves crackled and rolled across the ground as they jogged down the main village path, through the palisade, and out the front exit of Dasamonquepeuc.

It felt good to run again. Strength oozed back into Jane's limbs as she lengthened her stride to keep pace with her taller comrades. She drew in deep, cleansing breaths but had to muffle a cough at the dry, dusty air clogging her throat.

Deadened branches of drought-scorched trees rattled against each other in the crisp autumn breeze. It was the perfect temperature for running, but she knew it would dip several degrees cooler by nightfall. By her best estimate, they had no more than two hours before the blackness of night settled around them.

They stopped at the spring to fill their skins with water.

A thought struck her. "How do you suppose Cecil Prat and Edward Powell ended up in the copper mines?" It was a question that had burned in her mind for days. "I thought Chief Dasan only purchased James, William, Blade, George, and me."

"He sent several envoys to the Great Trading Path. They intimidated and discouraged the other bidders and purchased the majority of the English colonists."

They had not succeeded in discouraging Wanchese. He alone had dared to bid for her. She shivered. "Dasan must have known of our pending arrival. He was expecting us."

"Informants," Wanchese supplied.

"I didn't see any other colonists on Copper Mountain. Not the whole time we resided there. What makes you think they were taken there?"

"The increased number of guards outside the mines."

"How did you explore the mountain without being detected?"

He shrugged. "As a guest. Chief Dasan invited me."

"A guest!" she exclaimed. Premonition slithered its way down her spine. It was all starting to make a horrible sort of sense. "What, pray, made him extend such an invitation?"

Wanchese's face hardened. He was silent so long she feared he did not intend to answer. A muscle throbbed in his cheek. "He is Askook's father. My uncle."

Her jaw dropped. *By all that is holy!* No wonder Wanchese had kept so many things close to his chest. He had a bloody civil war brewing beneath his nose.

Weakness slid through her bones. She stamped her feet, willing the trembling in her knees to subside. She'd sought answers, but Wanchese's words only stirred more questions.

Through numb ears she heard him give the order to move out.

"Wait!" she cried. "How do you know Askook has not already reported to his father the presence of me and my comrades at Dasamonquepeuc?"

"My scouts watch him too closely. He's had no opportunity, but it's only a matter of time before he reports my duplicity in the matter to his father."

And when Askook did, Dasan would know Chief Wanchese was the one who had engineered Jane's rescue. "So what is our plan? Will you confront Dasan?"

"Nay. It is unlikely he will welcome me again into his city. We did not end our last visit on good terms. Instead, we will have to breach his mines uninvited. Ireh, Jane."

She jogged beside Wanchese as they re-entered the forests, their skins now full of fresh water. The shadows deepened around them, but night did not fall as rapidly as usual. The trees were so naked of vegetation that the setting sun continued to glow through their midst.

She mulled on the rift between Wanchese and Dasan. Men generally fought over power, land, money, and women. *Women!* Not unlike England and Spain, marriages often served as the means to form powerful alliances in the New World. In this case, Amitola, the sister of Chief Wanchese, had been taken by force.

"Has any man ever petitioned you for Amitola's hand in marriage?" she inquired suddenly.

Wanchese emitted a sound of resignation. "Dasan."

"You refused his offer, Askook arrived for a visit in Dasamonquepeuc, and Amitola disappeared soon afterward."

"Along with you, Jane, and most of the City of Raleigh's inhabitants."

The pieces slid into place to form an alarming picture. A thwarted suitor, Dasan had struck at the very heart of the man he held responsible for his humiliation. He had stolen the woman whose hand had been refused to him and used Askook to stir a hornet's nest of hostilities with Wanchese's nearest neighbors.

Even if they proved Askook helped coordinate the ensuing Mandoag attack on her countrymen, Wanchese ruled the tribe that resided in the nearest city. Therefore, Wanchese would be blamed for the entire ordeal when Governor White returned to Roanoke with their supply ships.

Jane felt sick. Her future husband and his people stood on the brink of war with both the English and the natives.

In the meantime, it was up to their small rescue party to retrieve her fellow City of Raleigh colonists. No doubt, they served as exotic additions to Dasan's growing legion of slaves, with their fair skin and varying hues of hair and eyes. It also pained her to think how the colonists had provided a treasure trove to Dasan's coffers. The supply rafts he confiscated from her countrymen had been laden with guns and cannons, farm plows and furniture, silver bowls and spoons, gems, and fine linens.

Their biggest value of all, however, lay in their abilities. The colonists were highly skilled. Their numbers boasted carpenters, brick masons, ship builders, coopers, cutlers, tailors, weavers, a lawyer, a college professor, a sheriff, and even a doctor. Add in their ability to hunt, fight, and plant new cities, and the English colonists could change the fortune of a village, a region, or even a nation.

About five miles past the bathing spring, they reached the outer perimeter of the Dasamonquepeuc hunting grounds. This placed them less than a minute's brisk walk from George's subterranean hideout and the trail of crosses. Both rested on the outermost perimeter of the Roanoke's daily patrols.

They traveled in complete silence now. Their soft leather

moccasins molded to their feet and carried them over the thin forest ground cover. The earth was parched and hard-packed from lack of rain, so their footsteps left no prints. They avoided stepping on and snapping small twigs and sticks, so as not to leave a trail for anyone who might follow.

The trees thinned as they reached George's lair. Rattling in the breeze overhead, the branches cast long, shivering shadows across the base of the foothills. A lone deer froze in his tracks at the sight of them, then launched himself down the hillside in the opposite direction. A spray of small rocks trickled in his wake.

An eerie quiet descended when the clattering of hooves faded. Jane strained to detect any sight or sound to indicate George's presence, but no prickle of awareness rose along her skin. *Where is the lad?*

The breeze swirled lower down the base of the trees, kicking up dry leaves and dirt. She drew to a halt and sniffed the air. A coppery scent wafted down the hillside. *Blood.*

She sprinted to the entrance of George's cave, but Wanchese easily outpaced her. *Blast this lingering weakness in my limbs!*

He positioned himself in front of the entrance, forcing her to halt, and signaled that they should proceed with caution. He was right, of course, which made her angry with herself. Apparently, her current weakness extended to her brain, for she had almost leaped into the cave without checking for traps.

Kimi and Kitchi took up guard on either side of the entrance while Amonsoquath crept like a dark spider up the hill overlooking the entrance to the cavern. Only when he signaled from above that the surrounding area was clear of marauders did Wanchese draw aside the covering of vines to expose the narrow fissure in the rocks.

Dark, hand-print-sized stains splattered the rocky

entrance. Wanchese drew his finger across one of the stains and held it beneath his nose. Jane did the same. It smelled like blood.

She motioned that she was going inside the cave. Wanchese nodded and unsheathed a pair of knives. He wedged a shoulder between the rocks and entered ahead of her. Drawing out her own blades, she followed, pausing a few strides inside the cave to give her eyes a moment to adjust to the darkness.

It was black as pitch inside. Wanchese struck his flint and ignited a torch. He held it up, and they surveyed the interior. It was George's abode alright, but his belongings lay in utter shambles. Ashes from a tiny fire pit were scattered as if someone had stamped clean through them. The spit had been kicked over, and a small bowl lay shattered on the ground. More copper-scented stains marked the floor.

Unable to muffle a cry of concern, she knelt beside the shattered bowl and sniffed. More blood. *Oh, George! What happened here?*

The faint brushing of leather against stone caught her ears. Wanchese notched an arrow in his bow, aiming in the direction of the scuffing.

They crept deeper inside the cavern until a figure took shape in the darkness. Animal or human, she was unsure, but he lay crumpled across a boulder just inside the largest tunnel leading from the main chamber.

Wanchese bounced a small pebble off of the creature who responded by scrubbing his foot against the ground.

"George?" she cried, running forward.

The figure raised his head. She gasped at the bloody face swiveling in their direction. One thing for sure, he was not George.

Wanchese's knife flew so quickly, Jane could only wince

as the native jerked away. It nicked his ear. Fresh blood dripped from his lobe. He drew a ragged breath and stared back at them through black eyes glazed with pain. Knife wounds punctured his coppery chest and belly.

Jane and Wanchese crept closer.

Wanchese shoved his torch in her hands and fired off a series of questions.

Her grasp of the language was improving, but she could not keep up with such a rapid exchange.

The man shook his head and muttered something.

Wanchese slung his bow over one shoulder and ripped the man's deerskin cape open to reveal a series of skeletal tattoos on his arms and chest.

Nostrils flaring, he fisted a hand in the man's hair and laid the blade of his knife across the man's exposed neck. This time he spoke quietly in the man's ear.

The captive gasped out another few words. Wanchese responded in tones too low for her to understand and promptly slit his throat.

As his body slumped to the ground, Jane raised aghast eyes to her chief. "You killed an unarmed man."

"Aye."

"You could have taken him prisoner."

"He suffered from a mortal wound and would have died anyway."

"I suppose he begged you to put him out of his misery," she said sarcastically, still reeling from what she had witnessed.

"He did."

Mercy! Wanchese saw nothing wrong with such callousness. She studied him in the dim torch light as he rummaged in the back of the cave and returned with a blanket of fur slashed to ribbons.

He laid it out flat and rolled the corpse in it. Lifting his burden, Wanchese headed for the entrance of the cave.

She hurried after him. "Where are you taking him?"

"To his grave."

"Well? Did he possess any news of George?"

"Aye. He was sent to kill the lad."

Her knees threatened to give out. "Go on."

"George was more skilled with the sword than he anticipated."

Ha! Most young lords learned the art of fencing at the hands of masters. It gave her no small amount of pride to realize George had mortally wounded his own would-be assassin. "You sound surprised." She resented that.

"He acts more like a spoiled child than a man of sound judgment."

Sad but true. "Willful he may be, but he grew up with a rifle in one hand and a sword in the other. He can wrestle and box, as well."

"The lad also had the advantage of a friend hidden in the shadows. The assassin was outnumbered and overpowered."

George had been entertaining company during the attack? "Perhaps he made contact with Chief Manteo and the Croatoans."

"Nay, it was a pale face, according to our witness."

An English colonist, then! Hope tingled in her chest.

The final gold and red rays of sunset streaked the horizon. Wanchese's team of warriors converged on them as they exited the cave.

Wanchese spoke to them in a hushed, guttural voice as he laid the body between two stately pines. Despite the gravity of the burial scene, his deep baritone washed over her, steadying and reassuring.

Kimi and Kitchi gathered stones and piled them atop the

deceased. She presumed they neither wanted to risk drawing attention with a crematory fire nor wished to take the time to dig a grave.

Wanchese and Amonsoquath watched the men, arms folded and faces grim.

At first, Jane attempted to help gather stones, but the men grunted in protest and shooed her away. Taken aback by the apparent hierarchy of labor within their group, she took her place beside Wanchese, feeling idle and twitchy.

"Did the assassin identify himself?" she hissed. "Or reveal who sent him?"

"He was Dasan's man."

Heavens! How did Dasan find George, and where is George now?

Kimi and Kitchi completed their task and stood before Wanchese, heads bowed with respect.

At a terse command from him, they sprang upright to secure their quivers and packs on their shoulders. The deep obeisance and reverence the Roanokes gave their chief amazed Jane. It was given without fear or hesitation, which spoke well of Wanchese. In her experience, loyalty and respect of that magnitude were not demanded. They were earned.

Living with the Roanokes had given her a different perspective of their leader. The English had spoken his name in fear. He was an utter failure as a diplomat, they'd said. Too stubborn and ruthless. Unwilling to negotiate and compromise. A dangerous man to cross. She'd since learned he was every one of those things and more. He was also unafraid of being outnumbered, relying on sheer cunning to best his enemies. In addition, he desired the trust of every warrior who fought beside him, including the sole woman in his party. A pale face, at that. *Aye, but I love the man!*

"Ireh," Wanchese commanded, and they resumed their jog inland.

To Jane's intense irritation, she quickly began to tire. She employed an old trick of breathing in her nose and out her mouth to control her panting. Just as she became certain she would have to slow to a walk, they exited the woods and arrived at the delta where the sound waters converged into the Roanoke and Chowan Rivers.

Jane halted in wonder, turning slowly to take in the miracle of nature rising before them.

Streaming rivulets splintered off to form a vast watershed inland. It was a gush of life surrounded by endless miles of dry, cracked earth in every direction. A lush and fertile V-shaped area lay in its midst, big enough to contain a village with a fort.

This was the location where her fellow colonists had hoped to build the first permanent English settlement in the New World. They had planned to call it the City of Raleigh. Within its gates, they had planned to construct a cathedral for worship, a schoolhouse for learning, and a row of shops containing every vocation necessary for the success of their colony — a mercer, tailor, cutler, saddler, blacksmith, apothecary, and lawyer.

It stretched before her, an uninhabited oasis from the drought, silent from the hustle and bustle of commerce, empty of all the colonists it should have contained. Alas, they'd been ambushed on the first leg of their journey here, some of her comrades killed, others sold into slavery, and all of them disbursed to the four winds. Fifty miles inland from the cursed Roanoke Island where they first landed, the delta taunted her now like a shattered dream, an unkept promise, an unanswered prayer.

Exhaustion settled over her. She needed a moment to rest

before they continued their trek to Copper Mountain, but something propelled her to walk a bit farther. While her fellow warriors paused to refresh themselves with skins of water, she followed the edge of the river until it veered off to the left. A fat robin squawked a warning as she neared the tree where he perched. Its branches stretched over the stream below. He retreated in a flutter of protest, and a single feather drifted down in his wake.

Bemused, she brushed away the feather and stopped short. Straight ahead, no more than ten paces from her, a Maltese Cross was emblazoned into the trunk of a fir. On a burst of excitement, she ran to the tree and knelt, tracing the flared outer edges of the cross. It was identical to the ones in the trail of crosses near Dasamonquepeuc. The imprisoned colonists had been here!

She squinted through the dusk at the winding river. It was the same waterway on which they'd escaped from Copper Mountain several weeks earlier. Strange how life could take a person full circle sometimes. She was far from thrilled at the prospect of returning to Dasan's lair, yet she harbored no fear about returning with her beloved chief at her side.

"*Cumear-ah*, Jane." The quiet baritone brought an instant calm to the inner storm brewing in her chest.

She stood and walked straight into Wanchese's arms. Breathing deeply of his woodsy scent, she buried her face in his neck. With untold dangers lying ahead, she needed to draw from his strength, to breathe him in. His fierce desire for her reaffirmed life itself.

"The colonists passed by here," she whispered.

"Aye." He rested his cheek against her and ran his hands up and down her back. Then he set her away from him. "Drink," he ordered and thrust a skin of water at her.

Amonsoquath swung down the river bank to the water's edge and kicked the covering from a long, narrow canoe. The engineering behind these sturdy, log-hewn crafts continued to impress her to no end. Swift and silent in the water, they could carry a far greater number of passengers than their humble construction indicated at first glance.

Apparently Wanchese intended for them to travel throughout the night. Her heart sank. She was nearly spent and would be worthless by the time they reached Copper Mountain. She stepped into the canoe, relieved when Kimi and Kitchi took the oars first. Amonsoquath took up his position in the rear of the canoe, bow notched while he scanned their surroundings.

"*Cumear.*" Wanchese commanded. When she raised an askance brow, he scooted closer to tug the load from her back. He shrugged off his quiver, stretched out his tall frame in the long belly of the boat, and beckoned her to join him.

"Lie with you?" she exclaimed. Her voice rose to an embarrassing squeak.

"'Tis the best position for sleep."

She eyed him doubtfully and swiveled in her seat to observe their comrades who sat fore and aft of them. None seemed to be paying them any mind. *Are they accustomed to their chief traveling thus with a concubine?* She blushed at the direction of her thoughts.

"*Cumear,*" Wanchese said again. "Fear not. I've no room to ravish you here."

She blushed harder and crept along the floor of the canoe to kneel before him. The boat swayed from side to side at her movements. Recalling her previous tumble overboard, she stretched out beside Wanchese with her back to him. However, the steep, hollowed-out interior walls of the boat rocked them against each other.

Faith, what a scandalous position to find herself in! She

hardly knew where to begin stating her objections. The moral high ground lay in retreating to one of the seats in the back of the canoe. Instead, she squeezed her eyes shut and tried to pretend she was not lying next to the handsomest, most desirable man on earth.

The dratted warrior actually patted her hip with a sound of pure male satisfaction and hooked an arm around her waist to pull her closer.

Oh glory, he feels good. Too good. Every inch of her vibrated with awareness. He smelled of pine needles and campfires. His smooth jaw rested against her shoulder, and his steady breathing caressed the back of her neck. *How in the blazes is a girl supposed to slumber like this?*

He, on the other hand, seemed to be having no trouble relaxing.

How unfair! Breathe, she reminded myself. *In and out. In and out.* But her breathing continued to hitch on account of his nearness.

After several minutes of heart-pounding agony, Wanchese uncurled his arm from around her waist to lace his fingers through hers. He propped himself up on one elbow and peered down at her in the darkness. "Look at me, Jane."

She sucked in a shuddering breath and glanced over her shoulder. In the moonlight, his eyes flamed with under-standing and passion. Slowly he lowered his head. Hot and possessive, his lips sought and claimed hers. Somehow, he turned her to face him without upsetting the boat.

All reasonable thoughts fled.

It no longer mattered what his braves thought of them. They might all die tomorrow. She held nothing in check, and returned kiss for kiss and caress for caress as if their lives depended on it. Tonight, he would revel in the depths of her feelings for him, and tomorrow they would face the battle together.

Seconds passed, minutes, perhaps hours as they reaffirmed their devotion to each other in breathless whispers and the brush of fingertips over heated skin.

"Wanchese," she sighed as sleep threatened to overtake her at last. Her fingers relaxed their grip on his hair. She stroked the loosened silk strands and buried her face in his neck, doubting she would ever get her fill of him. "I adore you."

"I know," he whispered into her hair.

"This was not supposed to happen," she murmured sleepily. "This whole thing between you and me, I fear I am falling in love."

He splayed a large hand across the small of her back and rubbed lazy circles. "By the gods, you better be. You are mine."

His.

She smiled against his throat and gave in to the luxurious lethargy spreading through her limbs. Aided in part by the gentle rocking of the boat, sleep claimed her in swirling waves of sweet oblivion.

---

*J*ane awoke and sat up in the darkness, rubbing her eyes. Wanchese and Kimi now rowed the canoe, and Kitchi pulled guard. Next to her, Amonsoquath rested an arm on a bent knee and tipped up a skin of water. He looked much more rested than earlier.

Good heavens! How much longer than Wanchese did I sleep? Twice as long? Embarrassed, she scrambled to her knees, remembering at the last second to balance her movements so as not to upset the craft.

When she reached for Kimi's oar, however, Amonsoquath thrust his water skin at her.

She accepted it gratefully. "*Kenah.* You should not have let me sleep so long."

His dark eyes twinkling with understanding, he tapped a fist to his chest and inclined his head with respect.

She marveled at the ageless quality to Amonsoquath's features. Such depth of wisdom and maturity would never come from a token stint at Cambridge. It took years of intense training to instill these traits in a person. Comparing him to the impetuous natures of the English lads who had sailed with us to the New World, he seemed at least a decade older.

"Take Kimi's oar." Wanchese sounded none too pleasant, interrupting her reverie. The moonlight only accentuated his glare.

Puzzled, she traded places with Kimi, who appeared grateful to turn over his burden. He stretched out in the belly of the canoe and was instantly asleep. Amonsoquath maneuvered past her to trade positions with Kitchi in the rear of the boat. He promptly joined his brother and closed his eyes.

Regretting how long she had wasted sleeping, Jane dug her oar deep. She was thrilled to be allowed to help at long last. "You should have awakened me," she hissed to Wanchese who sat in front of her.

"You seemed comfortable enough next to Amonsoquath."

"You are jealous." Stunned, she raised her oar for a moment, forgetting to paddle.

With a whispered oath, Wanchese switched his to the other side of the canoe so as not to break the momentum of their progress.

"Burn it," she muttered and plunged her oar back in the water, mirroring his efforts. "You could have wakened me and saved yourself the trouble."

"The illness took its toll. You needed your sleep."

"Then why are you angry with me?" she burst out.

"I did not enjoy the sight of you lying next to another man."

Oh, for pity's sake! Wanchese was the only man she'd ever kissed. If anything, she should be jealous of *him* because of the many concubines he'd taken in the past. She'd learned it was a common practice of native chiefs to maintain multiple relationships, not unlike the wealthy lords of London.

The natives took it a step further, however, and some-times married more than one wife, particularly those in posi-tions of power. Men of council, warriors, chiefs — men like Wanchese. It was a depressing thought. She tried to push it from her mind as she rowed.

The moonlight splayed across the water in a dappled mix of whites and grays as the current churned past them. The trees along the banks reached out their gnarled branches, threatening to snatch them from the canoe as they rowed. She scanned the trees for any sign of camp fires, torches, or movement, any glow of eyes from animals or men.

If she accurately recalled the time it took to traverse this route, they had another three hours, maybe four, until they reached their destination. This time, they traveled against the current, but it was too weak in the shallow waters to slow them down much. Due to the drought, the waters had receded so far down the river banks as to expose thousands upon thousands of tree roots.

A night owl hooted, and a flock of bats nickered as they passed overhead with a rustling of wings. Bows and quivers rested beside the rowers on their seats. It would only take a second or two to lay down their oars and take up their weapons, if necessary.

After an hour, Amonsoquath took Jane's oar, and she moved to guard. Another hour passed, at the end of which

Wanchese moved to guard, and she returned to rowing. They continued this rotation until the first streaks of sun glowed on the horizon, indicating the cover of night would soon disappear.

"Halt, Jane." Wanchese pulled up his oar. She did likewise, and the canoe slowed. He maneuvered them into a shadowy inlet, where they roused Kimi and Kitchi and pulled the canoe ashore.

Amonsoquath concealed the craft beneath a screen of branches and underbrush while Kimi and Kitchi covered their footprints by brushing a pine branch across the dusty river bank.

Wanchese signed to them to spread out for the final leg of their trek to Copper Mountain. Amonsoquath took his position at the point, while Kimi and Kitchi covered their side flanks. Wanchese took the rear, leaving Jane in the center. *Drat him!* She was trained as a scout and could easily cover one of the flanks. Alas, any protests might alert their enemies to their presence, so she fumed in silence.

They pressed through the deadened forest with acorns and pine cones plopping to the ground around them. A light breeze stirred the brown leaves on the forest floor and sent them clattering across their moccasins. The faint glow in the skies gave away to the full blast of dawn.

Every step took them closer to Copper Mountain. Jane pictured the missing colonists working deep within the mountainside, scurrying along a maze of mining passages and throwing their backs into the endless task of harvesting copper. She raised an arm to shield her eyes from the sun and pondered what it would be like to live in subterranean darkness, never to bask in the warm light of day again.

The familiar prickling started at the base of her neck and skittered up the back of her skull. Someone was watching them. She signed to the men that they should halt while she closed her eyes to concentrate. Without her sight, the sounds and scents of the forests grew more prominent. It was not so much the sound as it was the scent of sweat that gave him away.

Her eyelids flow open. She tilted her head up at the nearest ridge and stared into the face of a man she hardly dared hope to ever see again.

CHAPTER 15: UNEXPECTED VISITOR

*I*t had been weeks since she laid eyes on the barrel of a good English pistol. This one was pointed at her head.

"Jane?" Sounding shocked, the man lowered his weapon.

Mud smeared his face and hair, concealing his once fair skin and white-blonde locks.

"Christopher!" she cried, infused with joy at the sight of him. It was good to behold a familiar face, especially one so dear as his.

A man with a boyish smile and firm handshake, Lord Christopher Cooper had served as their vicar on the ship ride across the Atlantic to the New World. Though not given much to piety, herself, she respected him. Unlike so many of their shipmates who were steeped in religiosity, he had always been more approachable, easier to converse with.

"I presume the men with you come in peace?" he inquired, pinning her with his stunning ice-blue eyes.

"Aye, but allow me to identify you first."

Wanchese was already striding towards them, his three

braves fanning out before him in a protective shield. Their arrows were notched and ready.

"Are you quite certain they come in peace?" Christopher muttered, skidding down the ridge and landing on his booted feet.

"Chief Wanchese." She bowed low, hands clasped. "Meet Lord Christopher Cooper from the City of Raleigh. He is a man of the cloth like Noshi."

"Call me Christopher." He stretched out a hand.

"His nephew, Amonsoquath." She gestured to the teen. "And two of his finest warriors, Kimi and Kitchi."

Admiration flickered in Christopher's gaze. The Roanokes stared back, expressionless. Ever the perfect English gentleman, he bowed. "My pleasure, gentlemen. Pray forgive my people for their intrusion on your island." His features were wry. "By now, Jane has surely relayed the unfortunate circumstances which led to the necessity of burdening you with our presence."

Wanchese inclined his head. Tension thickened the air as the memory of the slaying of George Howe, Sr., shivered its way into their midst.

Jane pushed away the vision of his battered head and torso full of arrows. There was no bringing him back. What was done was done. Her countrymen needed to quit blaming every Roanoke they met for the misdeeds of a few.

Amonsoquath, Kimi, and Kitchi watched Christopher with black suspicion in their gazes.

Egad! This will never do.

"What brings you here, my friend?" she asked quickly. Strange that the morning did not find him on the Island of Croatoa holding devotions for the English colonists.

"The same as you." His voice was grave. "I seek the where-abouts of our missing brethren and sisters. All too many are still unaccounted for."

She frowned. "Aye. It is terrible for the families who were torn apart. I imagine the Dares are frantic to recover their daughter, Virginia, though we are fairly certain she is—"

"Save your breath, Jane." Christopher held up a hand. "George reported to me all that you discovered."

"You spoke with George? When?" she demanded. The lad was missing. *Faith, how am I going to explain George's banishment and now his absence?*

"Fear not. We were together during the attempt on his life." Christopher's lips curled in a half grin. "He lives."

"I was you!" she exclaimed. "You were the pale face we heard about."

He bowed. "It had to have been divine direction that led me to him, for I was able to shout a warning before his attacker struck. The savage, er, pray pardon my poor choice of words." He shot a rueful glance at Wanchese. "His assassin made the classic error of presuming the lad was alone." His smile did not meet his eyes. "I set him straight during the interrogation, and he sang like a choir girl about the number of pale faces imprisoned at Copper Mountain."

"You can speak the tongue of the natives?" She took a closer look at him. Our vicar was ever full of surprises.

"Enough to get by, my friend." He did not elaborate on where he had learned such skills. She would quiz him about it later. There were more important concerns at the moment.

"Where is George now?" She raised a hand to shade her eyes against the sun.

"Nearby," he answered cryptically with a sideways glance at Wanchese.

Wanchese's mahogany eyes sparked with anger. "Then our mission is aborted. Ireh." He gestured to his warriors and me. "We are leaving."

"What?" she gasped. "But we have only just begun."

"Nay." His jaw hardened. "We are quite finished."

Disappointment flashed across Amonsoquath's tired features. Kimi and Kitchi maintained their stoic expressions, as they watched their leader intently.

"We will find a way to work together," she protested. "All George ever wanted was to locate our missing colonists. I swear it. It was the sole reason for his discontent."

"He is impulsive and unable to follow orders," Wanchese retorted. "His presence jeopardizes us all. Come, Jane."

"I am willing to take the risk," she cried, "and you are afraid of nothing."

"On the contrary, I fear a good many things. One of them is your safety." He towered over her and stroked a finger beneath her chin. "Dasan will stop at nothing to dispose of me. Even your role as my concubine will not protect you from him."

Christopher's mouth dropped in astonishment. "Pray pardon my aging ears. Did you say concubine?"

"'Tis not what it sounds," she hastened to explain. "Wanchese claimed me as his property in order to protect me from an imminent threat. According to Roanoke law, anyone who tries to harm the chief's concubine will pay with his life. Ah, never you mind," she sighed at the vicar's deepening alarm. "Suffice to say, I am safe with Wanchese. In *every* respect," she stressed with a painful blush.

"I see." Christopher's voice was bland. Sharp blue eyes assessed them, weighed her words, and turned calculating.

Wanchese's hand closed around her upper arm. He drew her protectively against his side. "We go, Jane. Bid your priest good day." He rubbed his thumb in circles on the soft underside of her arm.

"'Tis a good day, indeed. We can agree to that all day long."

They turned to catch Christopher's blinding smile. Perfect teeth flashed white in the sun, a strong contrast to the muddy rest of him. "Let us negotiate, Chief Wanchese.

Methinks, I can offer you a reason to continue with your search and rescue mission that you will find impossible to resist."

"Nothing comes to mind." Wanchese's tone was brusque. His hand dropped from Jane's arm to her waist. His display of possession could not have been missed by a deaf and dumb man, and Christopher had all his wits about him.

"My credentials as a man of the cloth are still valid."

Jane frowned, unsure of any point in such ramblings. Much as she was opposed to the notion, she would be departing with Wanchese if Christopher did not come up with a convincing reason for them to continue their mission.

"The power and authority vested in me by virtue of my office are blissfully intact. I can write and deliver sermons, minister to the sick, and preside over all manner of ceremonies from birth to death." He paused and cocked his head at us. "I can also join men and women in holy matrimony."

Wanchese's fingers tightened on her waist. "You would join me to Jane in the manner of the pale faces?"

"Aye, chief. In exchange for your continued assistance in the search for our lost colonists." Christopher bowed, his eyes glowing with triumph.

"Your vicar is cunning." Wanchese spoke in her ear. "He offers you a chance to claim me as your mate here and now. Will you do it?"

She nodded, hardly believing the conversation was happening at all. Their Roanoke wedding ceremony would still not be able to take place for another eleven months.

Her voice trembled as she sought to recover it. "A marriage performed by an ordained English minister would be valid in the eyes of my God. I pray the union would be valid in your eyes as well, my love."

"Indeed, it would be." His tone was fervent. "It is decided, then. We will marry now; and in eleven moons, we will stand before Noshi in the tradition of the Roanokes and marry again."

She drew a tremulous breath, unable to think of any objections.

"Pray assure me this means you will become mine at last, Jane. All mine."

The breath strangled in her throat, as Wanchese lifted her hand and pressed it to his chest. His heart pounded beneath their joined fingers.

"Aye," she whispered.

"Then it is settled." Wanchese cradled her against him. He spoke over her head to Christopher. "You may proceed."

"Now?" she squeaked.

"You must agree to the whole proposition," Christopher prodded, his sharp gaze fixed on Wanchese's face. "I will marry you, and afterwards you will escort us to Copper Mountain to seek the whereabouts of our enslaved colonists."

Wanchese scowled down his nose at the vicar. "Nay, I do not escort. I *lead*. You and George will follow my orders every step of the way."

Jane's blood chilled. She hoped Christopher understood the Roanoke code of a warrior. Wanchese would shoot any man who defied him in combat.

Christopher stepped closer, blue eyes boring into Wanchese. He gave a satisfied nod.

"You will not endanger Jane." Wanchese's voice was as cold and flat as metal.

"Agreed." Christopher stuck out a hand.

"If I have to choose, I will save her at your peril."

"I will do the same," Christopher returned evenly. "At your peril, chief."

The men shook hands.

With unbelievable smoothness, Christopher slid a small

leather-bound Bible from his doublet and began to speak before he opened its covers. "Therefore shall a man leave his Father and his Mother and shall cleave unto his wife, and they shall be one flesh." He spoke the age-old verses without glancing down at the pages.

Jane spared her crumpled tunic and leggings a rapid glance. As a confirmed spinster back in London, she had not counted on finding herself in this position. Ever. However, young women will dream during unguarded moments of whimsy, and in none of those whimsical moments had she imagined her wedding day to look like this — a hasty ceremony in the wilderness without music or adornments.

"She will be bone of your bone, and flesh of your flesh," Christopher continued.

They stood before him armed for battle, laced to the hilt with weapons, and smeared in war paint.

"What therefore God hath joined together, let not man put asunder." He closed his Bible.

It was the briefest wedding ceremony Jane had ever attended. In light of the dangers surrounding them, Christopher skipped all the formalities.

She suppressed the laughter gurgling in her throat, not wishing to begin her marriage on a fit of unholy guffaws. Nonetheless, she could not have designed a more fitting ceremony for her and Wanchese. Neither of them would have preferred to stuff themselves in stifling suits and gowns and travel to a dusty cathedral to stand for hours. She surely did not wish for a bevy of women to primp over her hair and accessories. The mere thought gave her the shudders.

Though lightning quick and beautiful, the ceremony was undeniably real and irrevocably binding. Jane was about to become a married woman. *Me!* A confirmed spinster. She leaned into Wanchese's grasp lest her knees buckle beneath her. *Drat this foolish weakness.* Had she not been ill recently, she would not be trembling so.

Christopher raised a hand. "With the powers vested in me by our Creator and the Queen of England, I pronounce you man and wife. You may seal this sacred union with a holy kiss."

There was nothing holy about their kiss. Wanchese drew her to her tiptoes and crushed his lips to hers. She buried her hands in his silken mane and clung.

Christopher cleared his throat once and then a second time before her new husband bothered to raise his head.

Wanchese held her for several moments longer, eyes blazing exultantly into hers before releasing her and stepping back. Then his expression returned to its normal stoic lines. He signaled his scouts to disburse into a round of patrols.

Jane was left facing Christopher alone.

"Congratulations, my friend." His eyes twinkled with humor and interest.

"I thank you." Not wanting to answer any of the questions she imagined were bubbling on the tip of his tongue, she sought to change the subject. "Where is George?"

"He is indisposed at the moment."

Wanchese returned to her side and stabbed a finger in the direction of Copper Mountain. "If that foolish lad has gone ahead of us alone, our agreement ends here."

"Then I'd say our agreement is very much intact." Christopher smirked as if enjoying a private joke. "Sadly, our dear George was unable to take the journey with us."

"Why? What happened to him?" Jane blurted in alarm.

"There, there, Jane. You were always so excitable. He took a knife in the shoulder during the assassin's attack, is all. Not much more than a scratch."

"I will determine his state for myself. Take me to him at once," she demanded.

"I will but not today."

She unsheathed her blade and advanced on him.

"Hold your fire, Mistress Jane, and hear me out," he chuckled, raising his hands. "I may have bungled the job of bandaging his injury which made it appear worse than it was. Alas, he perceived himself to be mortally wounded and insisted I deliver him to Agnes's care."

Bungled my buttons! She waved her knife for emphasis. "You did it a-purpose to get rid of him, didn't you?"

Christopher's grin spread. "On our way to Croatoa, George shared all he knew about the trail of crosses and Copper Mountain. I studied a map, borrowed a canoe, and hightailed it out of there before he grew wise to my deception."

She lowered her knife. "You sure know how to dance all around a topic before getting to the point." She frowned, trying to choose her words with care. "I thank you for ensuring George's safety on Croatoa. He has a good heart, but he isn't suited to life in the New World one whit. I wish he and his pa had never left London." She shook her head, deeply regretting her many failures to acclimate George to their new life here.

A sound caught her attention. The three of them froze and swiveled their heads in unison. It was faint at first, but she could make out the cadence of running feet. They were not the careful, stealthy steps of the Roanoke warriors, either.

"On guard," she hissed and dove behind a tree.

Wanchese and Christopher did likewise just as a man pounded into sight, eyes wild with fright. He threw an agonized look over his shoulder at his pursuers. Amonsoquath was only a few strides behind him. Kimi and Kitchi converged on either side, trapping him. Christopher stuck out a booted foot as he flew past, and the man went crashing to the ground. Wanchese leaped atop him, blade drawn.

He was from the Copper Mountain tribe. Jane recognized the beaten earrings and pendants all too well, though she did not recognize his face. He was not Hassun or any of the men who had guarded her at Chief Dasan's behest. For one thing, his complexion was paler than the others, and his deerskin garments were streaked with dirt.

This one must spend his days in the mines. Was he some sort of overseer? Prison guard? And how in the blazes had Amonsoquath, Kimi, and Kitchi managed to separate him from the rest of his comrades?

She did not understand the furious battery of questions Wanchese fired off in the stranger's native dialect nor the gasping answers he gave. Nor did she care for the hard look in Wanchese's eyes when the man was done talking and lay there panting, his expression terrifyingly expectant.

"Mercy!" she pleaded, perceiving they were about to execute him. "Perchance he has more information to share."

"They work your English colonists as slaves in the mines," Wanchese's voice was noncommittal. "He described their precise location. Three men and one small lad. They harbor a pale-faced babe, as well, in the mountain village."

The babe had to be Virginia Dare. She suspected Cecil Prat and Edward Powell were two of the men but dared not venture a guess as to the identity of the third one or the lad.

Christopher tucked her arm in his. "You know they cannot send him back up the mountain. This is war, Jane. Sacrifices must be made."

She tried to shrug out of his grasp. "You are at peace with killing a man in cold blood? You? A vicar?"

The fair-skinned reverend turned out to be stronger than he appeared. Much stronger. "Walk with me." He employed his gentle preacher's voice that belied the fact he was holding her in a vise-like grip. A good several inches shorter than her husband he might be, but she had no choice but to accompany him away from the interrogation. He led her, fuming, about a quarter mile into the woods.

"Unhand me, you knave!" She shook his long, slender hands away from her arm at last. "How dare you pull such a high-handed stunt in front of my people. You will be lucky if my husband does not slice off your hands for putting them on me in such a manner."

Christopher smiled in superiority and dusted off a sleeve. "Methinks Chief Wanchese would have sailed a knife into my back had he not precisely wished me to escort you away from the, er…"

"Oh, quit dancing around the topic! I know our prisoner is dead by now," she mourned, rubbing her hands up and down chilled arms. "I may never get used to this." Her voice shook. "So much senseless violence."

"If we did not dispose of him, Jane, he would have alerted the entire mountain to our presence. All six of us would be dead by nightfall, and you know it."

"Aye, but mercy, Christopher! The man I just married has killed two men in the past twenty-four hours." How much blood could a man have on his hands before it tainted his very soul?

"Jane. Jane. Jane." Christopher tried to lay an arm across her shoulders, but she shrugged him away. "I know you hunt, lass, and are quite handy with a rifle and blade. But you've never been to war; and, please God, you never will have to go."

"On the contrary," she said tartly, "I've been in the middle of a war ever since we stepped foot on this wretched land. I have been shot at, beaten, sold, and nearly ravished. Twice."

"True, however—"

"Oh give way!" she snapped. "I understand this is war,

Christopher, but I don't have to like it." She clutched her head in her hands.

"It's because you love him, is it not?"

Her head shot up. "How is that relevant?"

"You fear he will lose his humanity. You fear for his soul."

Such remarkable intuition undid me. "When he kills," she whispered, turning her face away, "he turns into a different creature. A peculiar hardness sets in, and I no longer recognize him as the man I have embraced. Kissed. Loved." She whirled to face Christopher. "What sort of person have I married?"

This time she did not resist when he slung a careless arm across her shoulders. Her limbs were exhausted, her emotions frayed.

He chuckled. "I've a tale to share with you, lass. Once upon a time, there were two young princes, both heirs to their respective kingdoms. They met, became friends, and grew closer than brothers. Before either of them could be crowned, however, a foreign army attacked, killed one of their kings, and took both princes as prisoners. They traveled across the ocean on a large ship to an ancient country where they were paraded before the foreign queen as trophies of war. Behind the scenes, they were interrogated often and forced to share information about their kingdoms. Information that would eventually help the foreign army conquer their people and lands."

She stiffened, knowing he spoke of Chief Wanchese and his cousin, Chief Manteo.

"One of the princes was entranced by the glorious art, literature, science, and military prowess of his captors. A true diplomat at heart, he negotiated long and hard for peace between their two countries in the hopes of avoiding an outright war. The other prince, however, hated his captors and escaped at first opportunity. His king was the one slain, you see. Hatred festered in his heart until the desire for revenge eclipsed all other desires. He vowed to be ready when the assassins returned. Alas, they never did. Instead, a new ship arrived bearing innocent families and one spirited young woman in particular who captured his interest and his heart. After years of warmongering, he at last found someone who matched his fighting spirit. Maybe this lass will breach the hard outer layer encasing his heart, remind him of his humanity, and turn the beast into the man he was meant to be."

"What a silly story," she muttered, not caring to hear Wanchese compared to a beast. At any rate, she was no charmer of men or beasts. Anyone pinning their hopes on her abilities in that direction was destined for disappointment.

"Unhand my wife." The words were spoken in a quiet but deadly tone.

Jane's head snapped in the direction of her new husband's voice. "No worries. Christopher was simply— Faith! You are hurt!"

Blood spattered his tunic. She leaped to his side, running her hands over his chest and arms to assess his injuries. But he was unharmed. Then the truth dawned. It was not his blood. She drew back, deflated. It was the blood of the man he'd slain. Horrified, she stiffened when his hands settled on her upper arms. Only moments before, those same hands had taken a life.

"Pray pardon me," she said hoarsely, turning away. "I-I need a moment."

Wanchese dropped his arms. She fisted her hands to keep them from shaking. *This is war,* Christopher had said. She needed to focus on scaling the mountain and rescuing their English comrades. Once their mission was complete, then she would take the time to ponder the exact sort of man she had married.

She turned back to Wanchese, dry-eyed and void of all emotion. "I am ready now. What is next?"

His tortured eyes rested on her face. "Come, wife." His voice was bitter. "You may assist me in washing off the traces of battle."

She gaped. He wanted her to help him bathe? Where? They should be helping with the patrols and planning their attack on Copper Mountain. And how dare he talk to her in such an intimate manner before Christopher! *Egad!*

She spun around, but Christopher was gone. With a huff of frustration, she sprinted to catch up with Wanchese as he stormed in the opposite direction of Copper Mountain.

"Are you certain 'tis safe for us to traipse around the forests in this manner? More of the mountain people could arrive at any moment."

"You saw what happened to the last visitor. So long as we stay within the perimeter of our patrols, we have nothing to fear."

"You should not bathe. You will catch your death of cold if you undress in these temperatures."

"Not if you keep me warm." He leered over his shoulder at her.

There was nothing at all caressing or lover-like about his tone. Disgusted, she slapped the air. Her irritation was replaced with amazement, however, when he led her through a cleft in the rocks to an underground spring. The chamber was lit by a pair of torches.

The chill in the air lessened the moment they stepped inside. She bent down and trailed her finger in the gurgling water. It was unseasonably warm, which explained the temperature of the room.

Wanchese stripped off his tunic and loosened the ties of his leggings.

"Wait!" she exclaimed, whirling around. "I, er—"

She heard a splash of water as he stepped into the stream. The water lapped at his chest as he bent to scrub the telltale red stains from his hands and torso. The scars on his upper back stretched with his movements. He pivoted slowly to face her. "Come, Jane."

"Your scars," she whispered, walking slowly forward. "What happened?"

He shrugged. "Rites of passage."

"To what?"

"According to my uncle? Manhood."

At her elevated brows, he made a sound of resignation. "It is called the Sun Dance. When I turned twelve moons, Dasan took me to the forked tree on Copper Mountain. He hung me and another lad by the skin of our backs until we broke free."

How cruel to torture a child of twelve in such a barbaric manner! "Why would he do such a thing?"

"'Tis something he learned on the Great Trading Path. He heard how many tribes farther inland celebrate the Sun Dance in this manner. The participants fast for several days, then dance while staring at the sun until they pull free of their hooks. A medicine man tends their wounds and helps them interpret the spiritual vision gained from their experience."

What a brutal tradition! "And thus you became a man," she said softly.

"Nay. I became a lad of twelve moons with a pair of scars to boast about to my friends. The best part was getting to hunt and fish with the men afterwards. I no longer had to farm and chop wood and help with the women's work."

"Indeed," she snorted. *That sounds more like the Wanchese I know.* He didn't appear any more impressed or enamored with the tradition than she did. She hoped he never intended the lads in their tribe to dance the Sun Dance.

"Did Dasan raise you like Nadie raised Amitola?"

"Aye. My parents disappeared shortly after giving me to him to raise. As an adult, I sought their whereabouts here in the coastal region where they were last seen, but I never found them. Instead I met Pemisapan. He let me fight for him and gave me a seat on his council. You know the rest of the story."

She did now. Her husband was an orphan who had escaped the clutches of a madman and risen to become chief of his tribe. Other than the fact that her impoverished Aunt Constance Warde had not been quite as cruel and barbaric as Dasan, their childhoods bore a startling resemblance. It was yet another connection they shared.

Wanchese is my perfect mate. Shaking off her earlier bout of reservations and bridal nerves, Jane indulged him in a lazy smile and took a few more swaying steps to the edge of the spring. She could not restore the years he'd endured without the love of a mother and father, but she could offer him the love of a wife. Starting now.

He held out a hand. "Jane." The word held a world of longing. His gaze glinted as she kicked off her moccasins and dipped a toe in the stream.

"You wish to torture me all afternoon, lass?"

She grinned and kicked an arc of water in his direction to distract him while she disrobed. It didn't work. He caught her ankle from behind and pulled her in. With a yelp of surprise, she tumbled against his chest, clinging to right herself.

His face registered dazed pleasure, as his arms closed around her.

She stared back, equally awed, wondering how she could

have ever thought him callous and unfeeling when the water fairly steamed with his fierce adoration for her.

He traced damp fingers across her collarbone. "I have wanted to do this ever since I first saw you."

"When was that?" she murmured, recalling the day in the wood he had shot her father's top hat from her head.

"The day you stepped on my island." He splayed a hand across her back and pulled her closer.

"I love you, Wanchese." She melted into his embrace and gave herself fully to her fellow warrior, chief, and husband at long last.

They stole a full hour away from their preparations to storm Copper Mountain. It was the briefest honeymoon in the world, snatched straight from the yawning jaws of danger, but it suited Jane just fine. She would not have cared to spend a week in some fancy inn ordering room service. Or a month in Paris strolling the cityscapes in stifling gowns beneath fussy parasols. Nay, a cave and a spring were far more to her liking. So was the glorious man in her arms who was as ruthless as a demon with his enemies but as tender as an angel when they were alone.

It was like waking from a perfect dream when she and Wanchese donned their clothing and weapons once more. His tunic still bore the spatter of blood. Each rusty stain leaped from his chest at her like a slap, shattering the cocoon of bliss he'd spent the last hour wrapping her in. She berated herself as she finger combed her damp hair before the fire he'd built. *Why does it bother me so much?* She had hunted all her life, gutted and dressed her own meat, and was no stranger to blood — both animal and human.

Aye, but it troubled her. Deeply. In the blackest, most hidden recesses of her mind, there was blood. Hideous amounts of it. Pouring off the ends of her fingers, running down her apron, and dripping on her worn leather boots.

According to her Aunt Constance, whom she'd been sent to live with soon after the incident, she had been the one to find her parents after they'd been mauled by the bear. From the state of things afterward, it was said her father had perished trying to defend her mother. An entire decade had passed since she'd run screaming for help to their nearest neighbor. Ten whole years, and she had not been able to remember a single detail of those final moments of their passing.

Until now.

With a moan of agony, Jane pushed away the memories of her parents' outstretched hands, their pleading eyes, the last damp expulsion of air as her mother's frame grew limp and her lashes closed. Lord help her, she finally understood why her mind had chosen to bury the memories, because she had arrived on the scene too late to save them.

It was not, however, too late to help the colonists who awaited rescue in the copper mines. This time she would not fail.

"Jane." Wanchese squatted next to her and cupped her chin in his hand. "Are you ready?" His dark eyes scanned her face with concern, as if sensing something was wrong.

She stared back, her heart in her throat, and nodded. *Lord God, give us strength for what is coming!* She wasn't normally a praying woman, but this was worth praying for. Wanchese was worth it, and their marriage was worth it.

"Good. Because it is time," he whispered.

She reached out and traced the largest red stain on his chest, too close to his heart for her comfort. These blood drops would never be his if she had anything to do with it. Never!

"I am ready," she said simply.

CHAPTER 16: COPPER MOUNTAIN

*J*ane's face heated as she brushed away the droplets on her tunic caused by the overspray of the spring during her all-too-brief romantic tryst with her new husband. The Roanoke braves would easily guess what they had been engaged in for the past hour, but there was no helping it.

"Dasan employs guard dogs. We must mask our scent to confuse them." Wanchese drew out a vial from one of the pouches at his side and dug two fingers in a black paste. He painted a pair of lines across each of her cheeks.

Her nose wrinkled in disgust. *Egad, it smells foul.* She followed his example and dipped her fingers in the vial to rub more paste on her face and hands.

Wanchese spread some on the back of her neck beneath her hair, and she did the same for him. Then they smeared the substance across their tunics and down their leggings. *Faugh! It will take years to remove the stench from our clothing. If ever. Maybe these garments will have to serve as my new hunting outfit.*

They exited the cave. Wanchese leaped atop the ledge

above the entrance and pulled guard while she poked small sticks and branches into her hair and clothing. Then with their quivers slung over their shoulders and knives sheathed at their hips, they fanned out and circled until they encountered the first member of their patrol, Amonsoquath.

He averted his eyes from them as he gave his report to Wanchese. It was a sign of respect, according to Nadie, for subjects to lower their gazes before their leaders. She was taken aback to be given such deference from the chief's own nephew. Though one of the few witnesses to their English wedding ceremony, he was well aware she would be regarded as nothing more than Wanchese's concubine on their return to Dasamonquepeuc.

Gone was the fiery passion of her perfect mate. Wanchese was all calculating and cunning again. His features were stoic, eyes hard and flat. She thought wistfully of their stolen moments at the spring, then pushed them from her mind. She'd married a hardened warrior with the ability to focus solely on the mission at hand. As the wife of a hardened warrior and a huntress in her own right, she would do the same.

She tightened the strap of her quiver and downed a swig of water, wondering what role Wanchese would assign her. Though not experienced in battle, her hunting and scouting abilities were superior. Once on the trail of any creature, she possessed what her father had claimed was an uncanny ability to sense the intent of her target.

She peered into the surrounding forests, allowing her eyelids to drift closed. She blocked out the conversation of the men and drew in every scent and sound. Beyond the soured muddy concoction on her clothing, there was the dusty scent of earth falling dormant for the winter, the deterioration of twigs and leaves, the curious nip in the air that marked the autumn season. Some lone critter rustled in the underbrush a few yards to her left. In the distance, a dog barked faintly. *A dog!*

Both men swiveled their heads in her direction at her sharp hissing warning. She mimed the ears of a dog loping towards them. Wanchese nodded and signaled for them to spread out and converge on the creature.

She chose a short ridge overlooking the clearing where a patch of tall, dead grasses swayed in the breeze. Slipping to her knees, she crouched as low as possible while notching her bow. Through a tiny gap in the grasses, she watched and waited.

Wanchese chose the entrance to the cavern, fifteen to twenty yards away. It was well concealed by dead branches and scraggly vines. If she had not observed him hide, she would have been unable to pick him out from the landscape.

Amonsoquath scaled one of the trees in the center of the clearing. Her heartbeat quickened in anticipation as the barking grew nearer. She wondered if Kimi, Kitchi, and Christopher drove the dogs in their direction as they had their last visitor.

A pair of dogs dashed into view. Some of the tension left her shoulders. Dealing with two hounds was far better than facing an entire pack of them. They circled the small clearing where she, Wanchese, and Amonsoquath had most recently stood. They sniffed around their footsteps but gave no warning barks of alarm. Instead they snuffled off in opposite directions, noses against the ground. It was too soon to sink an arrow in them, for they needed to determine the location of the dogs' handler first.

The lavish bird plumage atop his head and the wide copper loops in his ears materialized first. As the man stepped into the clearing, the sun glinted from an array of trinkets suspended from his neck. He was foolish to wear such brightly hued adornments while sauntering alone in the woods. Jane had expected greater stealth and cunning from Dasan's men.

Two things were immediately clear to her. He was running a routine patrol, and he did not expect company. That meant Dasan and his advisors had not yet noticed their missing guard from earlier.

She parted the grasses further, hoping to catch Wanchese's eye. A stone flew into the clearing and popped one of the dogs on the nose. He slumped to the ground, pawing at his snout and howling in pain. The second dog paused in his tracks and looked over his shoulder at the pitiful creature, while the handler ran to the wounded hound. He skidded to a stop at the sign of the stone and fumbled for an arrow, swaying in a drunken circle. He never got the opportunity to notch it.

Wanchese and Amonsoquath let their arrows fly, and the handler and his second dog went down. Jane drew a silent breath of resignation and put the first dog out of his misery. He ceased his painful lolling back and forth and shuddered into stillness.

As with the first captive, Wanchese leaped on the man and cupped a hand over his mouth before he cried out. An arrow protruded from his midsection, a mortal blow. He put up little fight when Wanchese spoke low in his ear and waited. The interrogation was over in seconds.

Wanchese bent his head to address them in hushed tones, pausing on occasion to translate for Jane's benefit. "We will access the mines at the base of the mountain, through one of two side entrances. Here and mostly likely here." He sketched a quick layout in the dirt. "Kimi guards this one, and Kitchi is still searching for the other. The first man we interrogated verified there were two entrances, and the dog handler confirmed they are only guarded from within."

She nodded in reluctant admiration. It was clever on

Dasan's part, because the presence of external guards would only draw attention to the mine.

"Chief Dasan has archers embedded to prevent intruders from entering though the main gates. Most of the inhabitants simply move inside their city through a labyrinth of passageways built into the side of the mountain."

Copper Mountain was beginning to sound like an impregnable fortress. "Can you describe his defenses?" Jane inquired. "How many warriors we can expect to encounter?"

"He maintains a sizable team of guards," Wanchese supplied, "mostly slavers working beneath the ground. That is all. The copper trade has made him vastly wealthy and overconfident. He hires spies and scouts and pays well for his patrol dogs, and their respective handlers. He mostly employs mercenaries when it comes to clashing with other tribes. With so much of his business taking place under-ground, he sees little need for an organized band of his own warriors."

A fortress without an army to properly secure it? Maybe it was not as impregnable as it appeared.

Jane pointed with a stick to his drawing in the dirt. "What sort of resistance may we expect when we breach the lower entrances?"

"Other than a handful of guards, only slaves and their handlers inhabit the mine shafts."

It was difficult to believe Dasan had survived this long without a major attack. Then again, he had loyal men like his son gathering intelligence against their enemies and securing powerful alliances across the region.

"Askook," she whispered. "He will know we've breached Copper Mountain the moment we enter Dasamonquepeuc escorting Blade's father and any others we rescue."

"Aye, and his reaction will prove his guilt." Wanchese's

voice was cold. "My council will not be so quick to pardon him this time."

"Have you learned anything of your sister's whereabouts?"

"Nay," was his grim reply. "Our first captive denied knowledge of any woman who fit her description. The dog handler refused to answer the question."

Then again, the first man could have been lying. He knew he was dying. He had no reason to cooperate with them. Jane frowned. Dasan had to be holding Amitola captive. For political reasons, alone, she was too valuable to give up. If she was ever allowed to return to her own tribe, she would be a living, breathing witness to his treachery against the Roanokes. That meant he would keep her close and well guarded. Surely they would find someone in the mines tonight who could verify her presence on the mountain. Better yet, her location.

"And the babe. What have you learned about Virginia Dare? Anything?" Jane inquired hopefully.

Wanchese shook his head. "She resides with a wet-nurse in the mountain village. That is all we know."

Her heart sank. They did not have enough warriors in their rescue party to breach the village atop the mountain. Once they entered the mines, they would have only a handful of minutes to extricate the colonists before more guards converged on them through the labyrinth.

"Here are the sleeping quarters of the enslaved Englishmen." Wanchese drew a circle in the dirt with his stick to indicate the center of the mines.

It was far enough from both entrances to make it difficult for the slaves to escape and just as treacherous for outsiders to force their way in. She was amazed at Wanchese's continued confidence in their mission. Most men would have lost heart by now.

"We must be prepared for anything," he continued. "Dasan

maintains a diverse and continuous supply of slaves. Not too many from any one tribe or language for fear of a coordinated uprising. Once assigned to a mine shaft, many of the slave handlers themselves are not allowed to leave."

It was no wonder so little information about Dasan's darker deeds ever made it to the light of day.

Wanchese's voice hardened. "One of the buyers at the Great Trading Path verified my suspicions that Dasan likes to take an occasional high-born captive for himself."

Like your sister. "He's created a powder keg just waiting to explode," she murmured.

"If you light the right fuse," Wanchese agreed.

Ah. You are going to set another fire. Well, it had worked well enough with her own rescue.

Her thoughts returned to Amitola. "What does he do with his high-born captives?"

"He mostly collects concubines to use and discard at will. Some of them he delivers over to his guards as a reward for their loyalty. Others he sends to the mines when he tires of them or if they displease him."

"Amitola cannot be more than fifteen years old," Jane protested. "Why, he is at least thrice her age or more." Likely more.

"She is sixteen, plenty old enough to be married. She was fourteen when he first requested her hand for Askook."

"You were right to refuse him." She beamed at her husband with immense pride. "How humiliating for Dasan to have his offer rebuffed by a nephew he must have considered hardly seasoned enough to serve as a chief." She had no idea his age.

He looked amused. "I am twenty and six, Jane. You only had to ask."

She was greatly relieved to learn her husband was two years older than her. After nearly six years of enduring the title of spinster, marrying a younger man would have made her feel, well, old all over again.

She forced her thoughts back to the mission at hand. "What about the other captives? Once they realize we have arrived to liberate the English..." She shot him a hopeful look, hoping he would find a way to let them all go free.

"Nay." Wanchese shot her a warning look. "No matter what sympathies they may inspire in you, their battle is not ours to fight. At least not tonight."

She opened and closed her mouth, biting off a protest. Well, she would see about that. It made no sense to refuse assistance to the other displaced miners if the opportunity arose. She would be delighted to flood the surrounding forests with refugees.

Wanchese held her gaze without wavering. "Christopher volunteered to create a diversion on the mountain. It should give us just enough time to force our way through the lower two entrances, incapacitate the guards, and extricate those we seek. Ten minutes is all we need."

She bounced on the balls of her feet, ready for action. "Well, let us locate that second entrance at once. Time's a-wasting."

Wanchese stood and said something in the Roanoke tongue to his nephew. Amonsoquath bowed and backed away, breaking into a run.

He explained. "Amonsoquath will try to divert the dog patrols while we search. We can expect another round each hour before nightfall."

"As a point of reference, how did Kimi discover the first entrance?" she asked.

"A worn trail leading straight to the side of the mountain."

She sniffed. *Our enemies are as overconfident and careless as you claim.* In that case, she would focus on picking out other features in the terrain that did not make sense — a plant where it should not be or a boulder that may have been moved recently..

They spread out and crept to the base of Copper Mountain, stopping where the trees thinned. They hunkered in the dry scrub of dead grasses to scan the area and get their bearings. Wanchese signaled that they should circle in opposite directions and meet on the other side.

The mountain towered over them as far as she could see, spearing straight through a swirl of clouds. Thick groves of pine, fir, and hemlock hid Dasan's village from view. She recalled the lavish rock dwellings he claimed for his personal chambers and council rooms and wondered how many more rooms and passageways were tunneled through the heart of the mountain.

The high altitude of the village was enough to muffle the hubbub of day-to-day activities. Such sounds were further masked by the breezes whistling down the steep incline. Any smoke from their cooking fires merged with the low-hanging cloud cover. It was an ideal fortress for a wealthy copper mine owner, the perfect place to hide a legion of slaves.

Jane conjured up the faces of Cecil Prat and Edward Powell. Cecil was a taller, older version of the weedy, sandy-haired Blade. A short, stocky man, Edward bore traces of Italian ancestry in his face and mannerisms. Both should be easy to recognize among the other slaves, given their European roots.

She squinted at the position of the sun. In a few short hours, they would commence with the rescue of her countrymen from this horrid place. Heaven only knew how the colonists had suffered since she last visited with them. She was not particularly a fan of the pompous Edward Powell any more than she had been of his vain and social climbing wife, Winifred. *God rest her soul*. However, none of the City of

Raleigh colonists deserved to be worked to death at the hands of these copper-plundering heathens.

She squatted behind a boulder and squinted at a rather curious pile of stones at the base of the mountain. The sunlight glinted off their jagged, crystalline edges. Her eyes followed the line of damage leading up the mountainside. It was the result of a landslide. Nothing unusual about that. She edged away from the boulder and moved on.

The next feature that caught her attention was a trickle of water shimmering down the rocks. It seeped from a crevice overhead. Steam rose from its source, making the mountain appear to be a living, breathing beast. *Not large enough for an entrance.* She inwardly shook her head.

The first hour sped into the second. Another handler with a pair of dogs traipsed from the main mountain path. Jane froze, but their heads did not so much as turn in her direction. The knots in her shoulders uncoiled when they moved out of sight. Thinking it best to eat before their return, she withdrew a strip of dried meat from her pack. She ate with haste and tipped up her water skin to wash it down.

Evening shadows fell as she scouted farther along the base of the mountain. A grove of fir and hemlock appeared, an extension of the surrounding woodlands. Their size was another matter altogether. Twenty or more had been planted far more recently than the others. While new trees might not shield the missing entrance to the mine, they did signal the presence of men.

What was their purpose? The foothills were so full of hardwoods, there was no need to replenish them through re-planting. Disappointment stabbed her as she studied the rocky terrain. Despite the presence of new trees, an entrance here was unlikely. Sheer walls of stone rose before her with no outcroppings, openings, or crevices.

She frowned again at the short, new grove. Regardless of its purpose or lack thereof, it was out of place.

Perhaps a closer look was in order. She inched forward on her hands and knees. Only when she pressed into the grove itself could she see they shielded an unnatural mound of deadfall — the kind that tended to cover traps. In the past, she'd built quite of few of them to ensnare unsuspecting animals. It was an odd spot for a trap, though. She would have built it deeper in the forests where more creatures grazed, not against a barren mountainside.

Other than the cover of trees, the trap was not well hidden. Anyone with hunting experience would recognize it for what it was. If she had constructed it, no creature would have been allowed to venture this close without springing a secondary trap.

She halted, glancing to one side then the other. Every instinct in her screamed she should not move another inch until she was sure of proceeding safely. She mentally retraced her steps and verified she had employed her usual diligence in watching for danger. It was a habit as natural as breathing. There had been no trip cords stretched across her path, no yawning trap doors, yet she sensed she was missing something. She glanced into the canopy of treetops above her head. *There it is.*

A thick sapling drooped over the pathway leading to the pit. Nay, it did not droop. The tension was too strong. It was masterfully secured by a means invisible to her from her current vantage point by a second pile of deadfall branches. Somewhere nearby was a noose strong enough to snap a man's neck...or the neck of one overly tall female. She scanned the area again both above and below her. That was when she felt its tug on her pack.

Burn it all. How could I have been so foolish? She had crawled inside the blasted noose itself. Her mind raced through the possibilities. No bottom length of cord rested on the ground beneath her, so it must be buried to a shallow depth. With the hook snagging her pack, only a few inches more of crawling would have sprung the trap.

She gritted her teeth. Unless Wanchese appeared soon, she would have to get herself out of the mess unaided. On the brighter side of things, she was willing to bet her life on the odds she had located the second entrance to the mines.

The position of the hook tugging on her pack put the lower segment of the noose roughly beneath her shoulders. *Or neck.* She inched her fingers toward the blade at her waist and ever-so-gently lifted her hips to unsheathe it. Holding the rest of her body immobile, she scored the hard-packed earth beneath her neck and shoulders.

It was a painfully slow process, since it was growing darker. Plus, any sudden movements might spring the trap. She alternated between scraping with her knife and brushing the loosened earth with her fingers, until she uncovered the cord. Grasping it with a thumb and forefinger, she gauged it to be a quarter inch thick. *Mercy!* Once sprung, it would hold.

She slid her blade across the cord in a seesawing motion. One by one, the individual strands gave way and snapped apart. Sweat dampened her hair line as she worked. A final popping of threads severed the cord, at last. Now to extricate her pack. Despite having dismantled the noose, she still did not wish to spring the trap for fear the sound and reverberations would carry beneath the ground and give away her presence.

She reached behind her and walked her fingers over the pack until she located the hook with its multiple barbs. One of them pricked her. A sharp burning sensation followed.

"Poison," she breathed, watching the first drop of blood well on the tip of her finger. Treating it like a snake bite, she stuffed the wounded appendage in her mouth and sucked.

She spit out the contaminated blood and sucked again. She sucked and spit for several minutes until the burning subsided. It looked like she was down to two remaining options, spring the trap or wait for help.

The distant barking of dogs turned her insides to jelly. *Dear heavens! My blood.* The hounds would have no trouble picking up her scent this time around.

She brushed furiously at the rocky ground, but there was very little loose dirt to cover the blood other than the fistful or two she'd dislodged with her knife. She tensed as the barking grew nearer. If the blasted creatures picked up her scent, it would compromise their entire mission. Blade's father and the others depended on her to remain hidden.

Hands shaking, she sliced a square of deerskin from the neckline of her tunic. She twisted it around her fingers and reached across her back again. Protected by the leather, she was able to ease the barb from her pack and scoot backwards. She retied the severed ends of the noose, just as one of the dogs burst through the trees. He snarled at the sight of her, gold eyes snapping with blood lust. Only the rounded opening of the snare stood between them.

Teeth bared, he leaped at her in a blur of shaggy brown and white fur.

He never saw the noose. His barking turned frantic when the cord jerked, and the trap sprung. The sapling whipped upward with so much power that the dog catapulted over the treetop, squealing and writhing with terror. Alas, the cord held when the tree sprang upright. Suspended far above the ground, the hapless creature pedaled the air as he swayed in a deadly pendulum.

Jane slithered on her belly through the remaining trees and pressed herself against the side of the cliff, praying the deepening shadows would conceal her. Then she narrowed her eyelids to slits to hide the whites of them.

Peering between a fork in the nearest tree trunk, she observed the dog handler burst on the scene and throw his hands up in frustration. The second dog circled beneath the swaying corpse, whining and pawing at the base of the tree.

The enormous pile of deadfall shivered into movement, no more than ten feet from where she crouched. The branches were drawn aside and a short, broad-chested man appeared. His profile was enough to send a cold spike of fear through her gut. It was Skull Face, the same slaver who had rounded her and her comrades up like cattle and driven them without remorse to the Great Trading Path.

What is he doing here? Does he serve in Dasan's employ?

The skeletal paintings on every inch of bare skin were a hideous reminder of his cruelty. He had not hesitated to employ cudgels and fists, nor had he bothered to slow their pace despite the bonds that scraped the skin from their wrists and ankles. Each time one of them had stumbled or fallen, his wrath had flowed over the lot of them like a crazed volcano.

Fear leaped into the eyes of the dog handler, who waved his hands, speaking rapidly. Was he apologizing? Offering excuses?

Skull Face spared no time listening. His fist swung in a cruel arc, and the dog handler crumpled to the ground.

Skull Face shouted a command, and two braves emerged from the pit. Four pale, waif-like creatures trailed them. *The slaves.* Dirty tunics hugged pitifully thin legs, exposing their blackened knees and bare feet.

Jane bit back a cry of surprise when one of the captives jerked aside to avoid stepping in the pool of blood forming beneath the dog. His face was much thinner than she remembered, but that was Cecil Prat standing before her as sure as she was born. Edward Powell shuffled next to him, his ankles bound. He could only slide his feet forward a few inches at a time.

The four slaves paused beneath the sapling. Cecil and Edward strained to hoist up their shorter companions. Robert Ellis — there he was, the wee little mite — scooted along the branch where the noose was tied and worked his fingers over the knot. Bless him, but the lad's dark wavy hair had grown past his shoulders. In his baggy tunic, he could easily pass for a thin lass. The older lad crawled after him. Was that actually Will Withers?

Jane bit her lip with the effort to resist calling out to them. *Four of the missing colonists standing nearly close enough to reach out and touch. Oh, where is Wanchese?* She scanned the surrounding trees, looking for something, anything to create a diversion. How marvelous it would be to seize the English colonists before they returned underground!

Skull Face signed to the prisoners to hurry their removal of the dog. *Blast him!* They had no means with which to cut down the beast, and Robert appeared to be making little headway in loosening the knot. Will reached around the smaller lad and added his fumbling efforts to the stubborn cord.

Beneath the boys, the braves circled Cecil and Edward, snapping out orders and administering an occasional cuff or kick. The men dropped to their knees and clawed at the ground with their bare hands. Anger clouded her vision. It would take half the night to dig a grave in such a manner through the hard-packed earth.

Jane lifted her bow and notched an arrow, waiting for the perfect moment. It would be her against three armed men and a dog, but she had the advantage of surprise.

She wanted to groan aloud when the pit opened and a third guard emerged. Though she was certain she made no sound, he turned suddenly and stared straight at her. She yanked back the string of her bow, but another arrow sank between his shoulders before she could let hers loose. He slumped forward, unmoving. Darkness pooled around the protruding shaft.

Startled, she followed the direction of the arrow. Wanchese sprinted forward, while Amonsoquath, Kimi, and Kitchi closed in from the sides. Arrows flew in rapid succession, punctuated by gasps and grunts of pain.

Skull Face and the two remaining prison guards were disposed of in a matter of seconds. The dog snapped and growled at the newcomers, but she quickly silenced him with an arrow.

As a precaution, she notched another arrow as they approached the bodies. Kimi and Kitchi straddled the first two men and rolled them over to ensure they were dead. Amonsoquath did the same with Skull Face. Nodding in satisfaction, he started to step over the corpse. However, Skull Face's arms shot up as if pulled by marionette strings. He grabbed the teen's neck and squeezed.

There was no time to think. Only act. Jane let her second arrow fly. Skull Face slumped to the ground for the last time, relinquishing his hold on Amonsoquath.

Her hands shook so badly she nearly dropped her bow.

Amonsoquath's head jerked in her direction, and his eyes widened in surprise. He straightened and faced her, pounding a fist to his chest.

She pounded her fist in return. No words were necessary.

While Kimi and Kitchi bent to retrieve their collection of arrows, Jane ran to assist the colonists.

"Mistress Jane, is that you?" Cecil Prat quavered. "I barely recognized you. Thank God, you found us at last!" He stood with his shoulders hunched while she slashed the bonds from his hands and feet.

She yanked the trapdoor wide open and peered into the

darkened passage leading underground. "How many more Englishmen serve in the mines?" she demanded. Shadowy figures shifted and cringed away from the light.

His paper-thin brow wrinkled. "Why none, Mistress Jane. Just us."

She shot an agonized look at Wanchese. *Burn it, where are the others?*

Her husband shook his head. "Four is better than none. Come, Jane." He prodded the colonists into action. They were thin as ghosts from lack of nourishment. She feared they did not possess the strength to make it all the way to the river.

"What about Amitola?" she sputtered, glancing once more through the darkened entrance of the mines.

"We must leave, Jane. Now. Ireh!" His voice hardened as he broke into a moderate jog, setting their pace.

Where in tarnation is Christopher? As Jane ran, the scent of ash and burning things curled around her nostrils. She sniffed and glanced over her shoulder. The mountain behind them billowed with flames. *Mercy! This was no trick of smoke like last time.*

Edward Powell stumbled beside her and went down. She halted and lifted him to his feet. "Just a little farther," she muttered in his ear. She wrapped one arm around his waist and braced her other hand against his shoulder to hold him upright. "Steady does it."

He nodded, gasping for air, but his knees buckled a few steps later.

She bit back a curse and threw her other arm around him, huffing with the effort to propel him forward.

In front of her, Kimi and Kitchi ran with a hand under each of Will's elbows. Amonsoquath swept Robert into his arms without breaking stride. Only Blade's father continued to run unassisted, though his breathing grew labored.

Wanchese fell back to assist her. Panting her thanks, Jane was able to increase her pace with Edward wedged between them.

It could not have taken more than half an hour to reach the river, but it felt like a fortnight.

Kimi and Kitchi kicked away the covering of their canoe. Amonsoquath helped them carry the heavy, hollowed-out log to the water's edge. Instead of shoving off, however, the braves ministered to the comfort of the English colonists.

Slices of meat were passed around which they ate ravenously, and skins of water were offered. Robert drank so much he vomited over the side of the boat. Afterwards, Amonsoquath held on to the skins and forced their refugees to slow their intake.

Jane scooted over to Robert and helped wash his face. "There, lad," she soothed. "Take deep breaths and give your belly a moment to settle. Aye, you've got the hang of it." She rubbed his back.

He fixed her with a blank stare. Gone was the wicked twinkle she remembered. Gone was his dimpled cherubic face. In its place was a much older, more gaunt spirit.

He jumped in alarm when she drew his head against her shoulder. "Oh, poppet," she sighed. "You are safe now." *Right?* She raised her brows at Wanchese. *What in heaven's name are we waiting for?*

He kept his gaze trained in the direction of the mountain. A flock of startled birds took wing as two figures broke through the tree line and flew in their direction.

Christopher! Praise be to God, he is safe. She recognized his young companion as the exotic woman who had been sold ahead of the City of Raleigh colonists on the slave trading block. *Amitola!*

Jane beheld her in awe. She was family now. Her sister-in-law, to be exact. Faster than Christopher, she ran with the lithe grace of a deer. Her unbound black hair floated behind her.

Something in the sheer frenzy of their speed and movements made Jane peer at the darkened forest behind them. A cacophony of barking met her ears. *Dogs.* Far more in number than the pairs which ran patrol. They poured onto the beach in all shapes and sizes, snapping and snarling.

Amonsoquath caught Amitola in mid-air as she leaped in the canoe. Christopher shoved them off the bank, water splashing on either side of him as his legs plunged into the river. He lost his footing and clung to the stern, dragging himself over the side and causing their craft to rock wildly. Kimi and Kitchi righted them with the oars, and they were on their way.

They pressed the newly rescued colonists to the belly of the boat. Wanchese and Amonsoquath faced inland, their bows notched and ready. Jane disengaged Robert's clinging arms and followed suit. Christopher reached for Kimi's bow. They waited, breathless, with four arrows trained on their seething pursuers.

No war whoops sounded, however. Only dogs crowded the river's edge. Dozens more spilled from the forest, barking and clambering over the backs of one another to snatch a better view of the rescue party. Several splashed into the water and attempted to swim after the boat, but their rowers rapidly outpaced the creatures.

Amitola trained smoldering eyes on her brother's shoulders and snapped out a sentence in their native tongue. Jane had conversed with Nadie long enough to venture a translation. Unless she was mistaken, the young woman said, "You should not have come."

Jane frowned. *Why is she not grateful to be on her way home?*

As was characteristic, Wanchese kept his own council.

"*Chamah,*" Jane greeted warmly. "I am your *cursine.*" It was the word for sister, and she had been dying to try it out. She pointed to herself. "Nadie is my *kicke*."

Amitola's lovely eyes narrowed in suspicion at first. At the sound of Nadie's name, however, they softened and grew anxious. She fired off another question. At Amonsoquath's answer, her face emptied of all expression. "*Cursine*," she intoned to Jane and tapped a fist across her heart.

Her eyes widened. The last thing she expected was for the woman to acknowledge her as a warrior.

Puzzled, she tapped her fist in return and started to incline her head. Amitola was the sister of her chief. That made her a princess.

"*Tah*," she said sharply and stopped Jane with an upraised hand. She bowed low to her from the waist, hands clasped beneath her chin.

By all that is holy, something is wrong. Jane touched her shoulder, bidding to her to rise.

With a sound of animalistic fury, she brushed away her touch.

Jane frowned in Christopher's direction, willing him to provide some sort of explanation to this mystery.

He raised his eyes at last, with cold blue fire glinting from their depths. Instinctively, she knew he had witnessed something terrible on Copper Mountain, something involving her new sister.

CHAPTER 17: DAY OF THE DEAD

Wanchese struck his flint against a mound of sticks and brown leaves on a bed of sand in the center of the canoe. Soon a fire crackled. Christopher shivered and squatted before it to dry his dampened moccasins and leggings. Amonsoquath produced a net and unfurled it over the side. Within minutes, they had two fat fish baking in the embers.

Their newly rescued comrades remained silent. They kept their heads bowed. On occasion, they darted a glance at Jane but lowered their eyes when she nodded in return. Surveying the occupants of the boat, she imagined they appeared rather formidable in their war paint, mud, and camouflage. Though she had grown accustomed to the scent hours ago, she knew they also smelled awful, drenched as they were in black hunting paste.

She reached across to Cecil Prat and squeezed his clasped hands, alarmed at how much the bones of his knuckles protruded from skin stretched too thin. "We have Blade," she announced. "He is safe."

His lips parted and trembled behind his overgrown beard.

"M-my son?" he inquired in wonder. He cleared his throat and continued in a stronger voice. "You have my son?" Moisture dimmed his coffee-colored eyes.

"Aye, he resides at Dasamonquepeuc. James and William live there, too."

Fearful recognition of the village crept into the man's gaunt features. "How?" he said carefully, running a hand through the unkempt, brown locks that hung to his shoulders. He darted a glance around them and lowered his voice to a whisper. "As slaves?"

"Nay," she said. It would be hard for him to hear this, but she preferred plain speaking. "We were adopted into the Roanoke tribe. They held a special ceremony." A most horrific one through which they had not expected to live, but now was not the time to share such details. "During this ceremony, we were claimed to replace those who perished at the hands of the English."

As she spoke, the hopeful light in Master Prat's eyes died.

"'Tis the way things are done here," she said quietly, but he understood what she left unsaid — that Blade was not free to go with him. "William and James replaced husbands who were lost. I am the daughter of Nadie, their Wise Woman. You will like her, Master Prat. She has taught me the ways of the Roanokes, and I have grown to care for her very much. Blade lives with Wanchese's elder brother and chief advisor. His name is Riapoke."

"Will I be allowed to visit my son?" he choked.

"Of course." She twisted around to Wanchese for affirmation. His mahogany gaze smoldered into hers as he nodded.

Edward Powell pinned her with resentful dark eyes. "Are we the only survivors?"

"Oh, nay," she protested. "At least thirty more colonists reside with Chief Manteo's people on the Island of Croatoa. They still plan to travel into the mainland to build the City of

Raleigh. You will need to decide whether to stay with us at Dasamonquepeuc, or go with them." Again, she looked to Wanchese for any indication of his plans for these men.

Master Prat frowned. "I had hoped to open a shop of my own. Build a new life here for me and my son. However..." He shook his head, eyes downcast.

She understood what he was trying to say. Nothing had turned out as any of them had planned. Her heart wrenched with sympathy. So much had changed. Their circumstances had changed. They had changed. Gone, or at least postponed, were their plans for English exploration and colonization. Those fortunate enough to be alive were expending all their efforts on preparing for the coming winter.

She watched Cecil Prat from beneath her lashes. It was apparent he cared little for the prospect of being separated from Blade. She would give him a few days to settle in, then she would press him to stay when the time was right. They could use a man of his skills in Dasamonquepeuc. Her eyes widened at the thought.

Egad! Married for a day and already I am thinking like a Roanoke maiden, plotting without shame to strengthen our tribe.

"Aye, things did not turn out at all as we planned," she mused aloud, "but you and Master Powell, Will, and this young poppet are survivors." She hugged Robert close to her. "For that I am thankful."

"Thankful?" Edward Powell rasped. Bloodshot eyes accused her from a once-handsome face. Unkempt brown hair waved in utter chaos around his temples, and his olive skin stretched over protruding cheekbones. "You did not descend into the mines, did you, Mistress Jane? The only thing I am thankful for is that my Win died before we were taken. She could never have been able to bear what took place down there." He bent forward to hold his head in his hands. His tunic slid aside, revealing puckered red slash marks rising on one bony shoulder. He had been beaten.

"You are safe now, Master Powell," she soothed and made a mental note to repeat these words as often as it took to penetrate the horror the colonists had endured in the mines.

"Ah, here we go. Fresh baked fish." She beamed her appreciation at Amonsoquath who broke apart and passed around the steaming chunks. "And that is not all. Tonight you will bathe in a heated spring and sleep on beds covered in furs."

"Blade." Master Prat's voice was muffled by a mouthful of fish. "Tell me more about my son, please. How does he spend his days?"

"Like the hard worker you raised him to be." She grinned. "He labors to help prepare us for the coming winter. Fishing, hunting, and creating knives of stone. Aye, he has not ceased practicing his cutler skills."

A faint smile of pride quivered at the edges of his father's mouth.

"I expect he will be quite overcome at the sight of you. He hardly dared to hope…" Her voice trailed off.

Will listened attentively as she spoke, eyes flashing with boyish excitement. The poor lad had been orphaned long before their ships landed in the New World. Jane held high hopes he was young enough at fifteen to bounce back quicker than the adults from some of the losses they'd collectively suffered. He seemed to be lapping up every bit of news about Blade as if his friend was on a grand new lark. *Boys!*

"The Prat boy. You say he makes knives for *them*?" Edward Powell sounded aghast.

"Well, who else would he make them for?" She sniffed. "He is a Roanoke brave now."

"Who else, indeed," he echoed, his voice thick with disapproval.

No sooner had he eaten his fill did Blade's father's shoulders droop with exhaustion.

She pointed to the belly of the boat. "Make yourself comfortable. We've many more hours to travel."

The ex-miners needed no further convincing to curl up and doze. Even Robert closed his eyes and tipped his head against her side. When he started to slide, she caught him and laid him next to Master Prat. He threw an arm around the wee lad without opening his eyes.

She picked up her bow and fingered the string. There was much to do upon their return to Dasamonquepeuc. Much to discuss with Wanchese. For one thing, they were bringing home four more mouths to feed.

The canoe swayed as Wanchese scooted her forward in her seat. He slung a leg around each of side of her, with a grunt of satisfaction, and pulled her against his chest.

"*Noungasse*," he muttered and bent to nuzzle the skin at her nape.

She lowered her weapon to her lap, both thrilled and stunned. He had called her his wife in the language of the Roanokes, and he had done so within earshot of Amitola and his men. They were married. It was still hard for her to believe it.

I must resemble the lowliest of hags, burn it! Reaching up, she began to pick the twigs from her hair and toss them overboard.

"You are magnificent just as you are," Wanchese whispered huskily, but he helped her untangle the largest pieces. She leaned over the side of the boat and scrubbed the muddy paste from her face and arms but was not convinced the murky river water improved her scent. When she settled back in his arms, he bent to nibble her earlobe. "I promise to clean every inch of you during our bath tonight."

She twisted to sit sideways in his lap and twined her arms

around his neck. "I thank you," she whispered. "I thank you for fighting so valiantly to bring more of the missing colonists home."

He claimed her mouth in a thorough kiss.

"Huh!" Amitola's sound of disgust carried all the way from the end of the canoe where she sat near Christopher. "You bewitch my brother and his braves into bringing war upon our people."

Jane twisted her neck in surprise to stare at Amitola. "Why, you speak beautiful English!"

With a sound of resignation, Wanchese swiveled around with her in his lap to face his sister.

Her lovely oval face was twisted in a glower. Black eyes snapped at Jane. "Because of you, we will have to move our entire village, for Chief Dasan *will* pursue us."

"Not before spring," Wanchese retorted matter-of-factly.

"How can you be so sure?" she spat. "You stole his pale face concubine and his pride." She stared hard at Jane. "I trust you know what you are doing, brother?"

"Jane is my wife," he answered in a voice that brooked no questions. "The reverend over there," he cocked his head in Christopher's direction, "performed our English wedding ceremony today. In eleven moons, Jane will claim me again as her mate in the tradition of the Roanokes." His hands tightened on her waist.

Awed at the beauty of his words, Jane searched his face. *My husband. My mate. To claim you as such makes me dizzy with joy.* Although he'd never precisely stated so aloud, he acted like a man in love.

She pressed her lips to his.

"Ah, Wanchese," his sister mocked. "You swore marriage was sacred and that you would never come between a man and his wife."

Jane broke off their kiss, astonished at the ferocity in Amitola.

"What changed?" Her face crumbled at his blank expression. "You have no idea what I'm talking about, do you? Strange, but I figured by now your scouts would have reported the news. Our uncle forced me to wed him." Her voice faltered. "I carry his child."

"Tah!" Wanchese's head tossed in fury. He set Jane abruptly off his lap and uttered a series of commands to Kimi and Kitchi. They held their oars steady and swiftly turned the canoe to face Copper Mountain.

"That will not be necessary." Christopher's calm voice carried from the stern, cutting through the blanket of tension thickening the air. "I had hoped to be long gone from Dasamonquepeuc before you discovered what I did. Alas, it cannot be helped."

He spread his hands. "In all truth, I had no knowledge of your sister's marriage. Not that it would have stopped me." He paused for emphasis. "On the contrary, it would have strengthened my resolve." His admiring gaze rested on Amitola. "Do with me as you will, princess, for what I did to Chief Dasan made your child fatherless and yourself a widow." He bowed his head as if expecting a mortal blow.

Egad, the poor vicar is smitten. Again. Jane had seen that look on his face one other time. He'd been quite taken with her friend, Rose, back on the ship. However, she had eyes for no one but their native diplomat, Chief Manteo. According to Wanchese, Christopher had performed their wedding ceremony not too long ago. It must have been difficult for him.

Wanchese held up a hand, and the canoe drew to a halt a second time. For several long moments, they drifted in silence along the current toward the sound waters and Dasamonquepeuc. "You disposed of my uncle?" he said at last.

Christopher threw up his hands. "If that viper was truly a relation of yours, then yes."

"A distant one," he admitted stiffly, but humor quirked the corners of his eyes. "How did you do it?"

Christopher shrugged. "'Tis a long story."

"He spoke perfect Algonquin," Amitola declared in an accusing tone. "He was admitted into Dasan's presence as a mercenary for hire." She looked ready to spit.

Unbelievable! Jane could not suppress a grin of admiration. While she had been struggling to disengage herself from the poisonous barb and noose, he was entertaining a king. Then again, she was forgetting Christopher's past. Before he joined their colonial venture as a vicar, he had served as a double agent for the Crown.

"You put him to sleep with your negotiations." Amitola's lovely features twisted with scorn.

"Indeed I did, my lady. What else did you observe?"

"Nothing. Chief Dasan remained in his council chamber when you departed, resting on his mat as he is want to do of an afternoon..." Her voice dwindled, and her brow puckered.

"Aye. Still as death, my lady," Christopher said softly.

And as cold as death by now. "Poison?" Jane ventured to guess.

Christopher shot an imaginary pistol in the air by way of confirmation.

She grinned again. "Be assured I intend to make every effort to stay in your good graces, m'lord."

"Thus, another native perishes at the hands of the English." Amitola trailed two fingers in the water, watching the vicar from beneath sooty lashes.

Jane drew a sharp breath. *Why, the little minx!* She was taunting Christopher, on purpose. She bit back a chuckle.

"We are in grave danger." Amitola straightened her spine. "We must warn Chief Manteo. As our closest neighbor and ally, Croatoa is as much of a risk of a retaliatory attack as we are. Dasan's survivors will stop at nothing, because they are aware I carry the heir of Copper Mountain in my belly."

"We crippled their strength," Christopher assured. "In addition to torching their storehouses, I may have dismantled one of their dams and flooded the mines. What?" he asked at her horrified expression. "I was supremely confident in your ability to breach the entrances and set the captives free."

She rubbed her eyes tiredly, shaking her head. Indeed, they'd left both entrances wide open. She could only pray the slaves had escaped in time.

"It will require many moons for them to regroup and launch an attack," he finished, crossing his arms in defiance.

"Perhaps," Amitola mused, but doubt chased across her features. "We must not underestimate Askook. He has built powerful alliances throughout the region. As soon as he lays eyes on your English colonists and me, he will blame us for his father's death and the devastation of Copper Mountain."

"He is not the only one with allies," Wanchese said coolly. "Do not forget I served as Pemisapan's chief advisor."

Before the English had slain him.

"Aye, and you were out of the game for more than a year when the English took you prisoner," Amitola countered. "Plenty of time for such relations to grow cold."

"I have been back for a year," Wanchese reminded. "I will call for a peace talk. I will feast with my brethren and reveal my uncle's sore betrayal. These Englishmen will serve as my witnesses." He gestured at the sleeping figures on the floor of the canoe. "Together, we will disclose how many local braves and maidens served in the copper mines."

She grimaced as if tasting something rotten. "It may be too late for peace talks. Dasan once hinted to me that Askook has already commenced a campaign to turn our neighbors against us."

"If the alliance will not stand with us, we will move our people from Dasamonquepeuc," Wanchese declared, and the subject was closed.

It would not be the first time the Roanokes had been forced to leave their homes. Upon the arrival of the first English ships, their chief had moved them from Roanoke Island to Dasamonquepeuc. But it had not been far enough to avoid war. The English soldiers had pursued and attacked them.

This time was different. Vastly different. This time the English served as allies to the Roanokes, and it was Wanchese's own blood and kin threatening the peace. Meanwhile, Askook dwelt within the borders of the village and spied on their people every day. *To what end?* Jane wanted to howl in frustration.

The last few hours of their journey to Dasamonquepeuc passed in relative silence, each lost in their own thoughts. They rotated positions every hour. She took several turns at pulling guard and a few less turns at paddling the canoe. Just shy of daybreak, they pulled into view of Dasamonquepeuc.

Instead of the blackness of night, however, large bonfires dotted the beach. Grotesque silhouettes leaped around them to the rhythm of a deep, resounding bass drum.

"Wanchese." Jane gripped his forearm as nightmarish memories came flooding back. She could still hear the shrieks of the ambush party and see the ghostly darts raining their fire down before disappearing into the rippling sounds.

He pulled her against his chest. "Fear not, Jane. The dancers are our sisters and brethren. They celebrate the Day of the Dead."

She blinked. "You celebrate All Hallows' Eve?"

"Huh?" His puzzled expression faded into seriousness. "I

know nothing of All Hallows' Eve. Nadie the Wise calls for these celebrations when a person of tremendous import is about to pass into the spirit world to join our forefathers."

Someone is dying? Fear shook her as she ran through the names of the most prominent and oldest members of their tribe. There was Achak, the medicine man; Noshi, the priest; Riapoke, our war chief and Wanchese's chief advisor and man of council; and Nadie, the Wise. *Nadie!*

Oh, how she hated to list her adopted mother's name among the possible causes for this "celebration." She wanted to run to her the moment their canoe scraped on the beach, but the newly rescued colonists required their attentions.

Robert woke on a sobbing gasp and grabbed her hand to pull himself into a sitting position.

She hastened to set his mind at ease. "We have arrived to a village called Dasamonquepeuc. This is where Mistress Jane lives, my love. Blade lives here, too, with Master James and Master William. Do you remember them from the ship?"

He gave a jerky nod.

She patted his hand. "Your father is not here, Robert, but he is safe on the neighboring island of Croatoa."

He grew as still as a rock at the mention of his father. No words came, but some of the glassiness left his eyes.

"I will deliver you to him soon. Very soon, poppet." It was a promise she prayed she could keep, for Wanchese had not yet revealed his intentions for their refugees. "'Tis the middle of the night still. How about we clean you up, then find you a warm spot to sleep?"

A lone tear streaked its way down his dusty cheek.

Oh, child. Her heart ached to witness such a display of gratitude for things they used to take for granted. She drew him against her shoulder in a tight hug.

Their arrival created quite a stir. Several of the dancers ceased their leaping to stare as they roused and lifted their fair-skinned companions over the side of the boat. Each one was little more than skin and bones.

With Robert tightly gripping her hand, Jane churned her way up the beach through the cold sand.

Blade, bless his freckled face, was the first to separate himself from the revelers. His lanky legs ate up the beach as he ran to greet them. "Father! Oh, father!" he cried. He skidded to a halt in a spray of sand. Wide-eyed and unblinking, he hesitated, as if expecting Cecil Prat to disappear.

"Well, son, 'tis a mighty fine sight you are." His father lurched forward on unsteady feet and fell into Blade's embrace.

The fourteen-year-old lad picked up his pa as if he weighed no more than a child.

Jane blinked back tears as he carried him the rest of the way up the beach and deposited him with care in front of one of the fires. Riapoke stepped away from the circle of councilmen and greeted Wanchese with a fist to his heart. Wanchese pounded a fist to his own chest and commiserated in undertones with his chief advisor, no doubt informing him of all that had transpired at Copper Mountain.

Askook observed their approach, as well. He conversed with a cluster of braves, half hidden in the shadows of the trees. Kanti faced him, a possessive hand on his chest.

Riapoke took a menacing step in his direction. Askook backed slowly from the group, turned, and dashed for the woods.

A sharp command from Riapoke sent a team of five braves sprinting after him, hatchets drawn. Kanti watched in confusion and growing fear.

Good! Let her worry. She was weak-willed and foolish. Jane suspected her recent liaison with him stemmed from little more than the desire to make Wanchese jealous.

Bless her sorry hide, but that is an emotion she is going to have to live with. Wanchese belonged to her now — every inch of him — and she had no intention of sharing. May that particular tradition among the Roanokes be tossed into the deep, for all she cared. Her husband would *not* be taking a second wife or any more concubines, so long as she lived.

Once his warriors were dispatched, Riapoke strode to the fire and squatted before Master Prat and Blade. Abashed, Blade shot to his feet to bow to him and make the introduction.

Riapoke motioned for him to return to his seat.

What an awkward situation for the lad! Jane could see how torn he was in his devotion to both the men.

Keeping in mind she still served as Wanchese's concubine in the eyes of the Roanokes, Jane dropped Robert's hand and inclined her body forward from the waist in a low bow when her husband turned in her direction.

Wanchese signaled her to approach him.

Gently shoving Robert towards a grinning James and William, she approached and flattened her face to the ground before him.

"Jane." Wanchese lifted her to her feet, cupped her neck, and drew her into a heated kiss.

She blushed when he drew back his head, more than a little dazed with the depth of passion glinting in his eyes. Even with his war paint — nay, especially with his war paint — he was the most magnificent creature she had ever beheld. So handsome it made her heart ache.

She would never grow tired of running her hands over the strong lines of his jaw and cheekbones, nor would she tire of raking her fingers through the silk strands of his hair. Her cheeks heated at the thought.

He rubbed a calloused thumb against her lips, his expression grave. "You must go with Nadie's handmaidens now," he said huskily. "They will prepare you for what comes next."

"Nadie?" she whispered. "Is she well?"

"Go and prepare yourself," he repeated in a voice roughened with emotion. "Those are her wishes."

And then she knew. Nadie was the reason for the celebration of the Day of the Dead. Her husband's face blurred.

Strong arms pulled her from Wanchese and tugged her in the direction of the spring. No longer caring how foolish the Roanokes considered any show of emotion, Jane wept the entire way. She was grateful the maidens pulled her from the rest of the revelers, from the English colonists in particular, because she did not wish to dispel one whit of their happiness while they were being reunited with friends and loves ones. Her pending loss, however, poured over her like waters gushing from a broken dam.

"*Cursine!*" a woman shouted when she stepped blindly into the spring. A series of ringing slaps met her cheeks.

Jane cracked her eyes open through swollen lids. Amitola faced her, surrounded by torchlight and swirling spring waters.

"You will not shame Nadie during her crossing over," she snapped. "Cease your wailing, for we are warriors, you and I."

Jane's shoulders shuddered as she fought to compose herself. Hot, fat tears continued to roll. "I lost a mother once," she quavered. "I cannot bear to lose another. Maybe if we tell Nadie how much we need her, she will tarry a bit longer."

Amitola slapped her again, but this time it held little sting. "Do not be selfish. She is ill and weary. The spirits of our fathers call to her. Their voices are strong tonight."

Amitola's puffy lids and splotchy cheeks registered at last.

"You have seen her already? Spoken with her?"

"Aye, *cursine*. If she loved me any less, I might resent the bond that grew betwixt the two of you in my absence."

She reached out and placed an arm around Jane's shoulders. It was as close to an embrace as she was going to give.

She did the same, more to steady her shaking knees than for any other reason.

Amitola straightened her petite frame to its full height and raised her chin. "Make haste, *cursine*. Time grows short, and Nadie the Wise would have us attend her one last time."

They stood, arms locked, in the steaming waters while the maidens began their ministrations. The bevy of young women drew them apart and stripped them of their soiled garments. Jane would not miss the foul-smelling items any time soon and hoped someone saw fit to burn them. It was a relief to be scrubbed clean once more. She wanted to look her best for whatever ceremonies lay ahead tonight. She owed it to Nadie.

The maidens rubbed a myriad of creams and ointments over their arms, hands, chests, and faces. One of them clucked dismally over her puffy eyes and applied a second coat of cream to her face. She beckoned one of her comrades to bring one of the torches nearer. Raising a narrow stick of charcoal, she outlined Jane's eyes with it.

At first she stiffened in apprehension, not wanting to make her last appearance to Nadie hidden behind some hideous mask. When she watched them apply the same pencil to Amitola, however, she was astounded how the charcoal accented the beauty of her eyes. It made them seem larger and rounder. The effect was stunning.

They rejoined the Roanokes on the beach in full ceremonial garb with their hair freshly braided. Thick rows of necklaces graced their necks. Certain she looked her finest, Jane brushed a hand over her beaded and embroidered belt to ensure her knives were securely sheathed.

When she wanted to run to her adoptive mother, Amitola insisted she remain at her side. "Nadie requested us to approach her together as she crosses over." Her voice trembled over the last words.

Jane drew a shaky breath and nodded.

"No more tears," Amitola ordered. "Dawn breaks on the Day of the Dead. We shall celebrate one of the greatest spirits ever to enter a mortal body until the sun sets again on the horizon."

"How do you bear it, *cursine?*" Jane's voice broke. "To get her back and lose her in the same day?"

"Because we do not let her go entirely. She will continue to guide us from the other side."

Indeed, she would. If there was a way to do so, Nadie the Wise would find it. Jane tried to console herself with that thought.

In addition, Nadie's teachings would remain with her forever. Her stories. The legends of the Roanokes. Her wisdom in dealing with her people from the smallest child to the eldest member of the council. Her knowledge of the harvests and ability to manage the activities of the women, in overseeing the building and maintenance of the longhouses, in the tanning and curing of each hide brought to the women by the men from their hunts, in the dressing and storage of their precious meats, in the usage of every part of every creature so that nothing was wasted. Everything had its purpose. According to Nadie, this was the circle of life.

The fires billowed higher on the beach. Vats of savory stews steamed in preparation for the coming feast. Breads baked beneath red-hot coals in shallow pits. Dancers undulated to the rhythm of the drums. The music dimmed at the approach of Jane and Amitola.

Wanchese's council fanned out before a ceremonial tent constructed for tonight's sacred purpose. The door of the tent drew aside.

Jane caught her breath.

Wanchese and Riapoke emerged with a much frailer version of Nadie than she remembered. Her eyes held an otherworldly glow as if part of her had already departed, but her gaze regained its sharpness at the sight of her daughters.

"*Amosens!*" she cried, stretching out her arms to them. "You have returned to me at last." Her dark gaze glinted with joyous tears.

Jane slid to her knees, partly out of the desire to kiss her hand and partly because her legs refused to hold her any longer. Amitola knelt beside her.

"I have missed you, *kicke,*" she whispered brokenly. *I will miss you even more when you are gone.* She raised stinging eyes to meet her adoptive mother's steady gaze.

Understanding glinted in their depths. And love. A love like Jane had never known before. It settled deep in her heart and found a home there. It would remain after her second mother was gone, strengthening and molding her. It had become a part of the essence that defined her. More so, it would define the way she would lead the women in Nadie's absence, in the same spirit she had led them for so many years.

Jane's eyes widened in shock. Where had *that* thought come from?

"Aye, *amosens,*" Nadie touched the underside of her chin with a hand that trembled. "At last, you understand. You will serve our people as I have served. You will grow like a new shoot from an old tree. You will begin where I end. Such as it was meant, so shall it be."

Me? She intends me to serve as the next Wise Woman? Jane pressed a hand to her pounding chest and listened to her final words to Amitola.

"My daughter, you will venture into places unknown and give birth to a new nation."

Amitola placed a protective hand over her flat belly. Had she told Nadie about the babe, or had Nadie discerned it on her own?

"A whole new people will gather beneath your wings. Many different colors have I seen flowing together into one new and glorious strand. A long time ago I saw this, when you were but a wee babe."

Amitola kissed her hand. "Fear not, *kicke*. I accept the path I must take. As you have seen it, so shall it be."

Nadie's features relaxed, at peace with the world now that she'd spoken to both her daughters. "Rise, *amosens*. Lead me to the place where the spirits of our fathers await."

And so they stood. Grasping Nadie's hands and blinking back tears, they drew her to her feet in a circle of her closest family and friends until her eyelids fluttered down for the last time. Her fragile shoulders relaxed between the grasp of her daughters' hands in the peace that comes from crossing over.

Wanchese and Riapoke lifted her while Amitola and Jane walked on either side of her, holding her delicate hands. They placed her on a mighty pier erected on the beach. Noshi stood atop the pier, eyes as puffy as theirs. His lips trembled in a farewell chant over his beloved.

The rest of the ceremony passed in a blur. Jane was inducted into the council to take Nadie's place. They christened her *Damisac* the Wise. The councilmen then bade her join their ranks as they formed a semi-circle behind Chief Wanchese. She stood next to Noshi at one end, Achak stood at the other end, and Riapoke anchored their small group of seven. Jane did not yet know the names of the other elders. Their expressions could not have been more solemn, nor their hearts more devoted to honoring Nadie's last wishes.

They convened in Wanchese's longhouse for their first council meeting. Only seconds into the meeting, Amonso-quath interrupted them with an urgent request to address Riapoke.

Wanchese gravely interpreted his nephew's announcement for Jane's benefit. Kanti had just been discovered unconscious beside the tree to which the Roanoke braves had tied Askook. One guard suffered multiple stab wounds and was not expected to live. The other was dead.

The Council swiftly voted to send another team of scouts to recapture Askook, but Jane did not have high hopes of finding him. He had a sizable head start.

They also voted to send a runner to all the tribal leaders in the region. A date was set a week away for a hasty war council. Lastly, Riapoke introduced the topic of moving their villagers to a safer location.

Jane resisted the urge to rub her arms to dispel her chills as the debate took an ominous turn. Achak pounded his staff against the ground and shouted down his nose at Noshi. The councilmen were divided right down the center with Wanchese, Riapoke, and Noshi in favor of moving and Achak and the other two councilmen in favor of staying.

Egad! My vote will decide the issue.

Jane bent her head and breathed a prayer she would not disappoint Nadie's legacy. Her adoptive mother had warned her that fear was the battle that could a defeat a person from within before the first arrow flew. So much darkness filled their council tent. So much discontent. She needed to dig up her own fears first and eliminate them before she could dispel the trouble brewing at the heart of their council.

Maybe she would set up one of Nadie's famous sweat tents after the Day of the Dead and wrestle her fears before a pit of simmering coals. Sitting before a fire sounded vastly appealing as the chill of autumn spiraled towards the icy blast of winter. She would confer with Chitsa to determine if any other maidens wished to join her on her spiritual quest.

A sharp exclamation from Noshi the priest had all heads turning Jane's way.

"What do you see, Damisac the Wise?" Wanchese asked. "Should we move our people from Dasamonquepeuc?"

She leaned forward to stir the fire, not to conjure up phantom figures in the smoke as Achak enjoyed doing, but rather to stall for time. They should move. No question about it, but she wanted to cast her vote in a manner that would inspire respect just as Nadie had been respected.

The wind screamed outside the tent as she pondered the question, pulling loose one of the wall coverings. Through the damaged wall, she glimpsed seething storm clouds amassing overhead. Maidens scurried to cover the hole. Jane closed her eyes and listened to their anxious chatter on the other side of the wall as they performed the repair. The air smelled like rain, not the cloyingly sweet kind that ushers in the fresh growth of springtime but the dusty rotten scent of stale air being stirred for the first time in a very long time. The parched earth was crying out in agony for the first droplets to squeeze away from the stingy heavens.

Jane recognized the signs. This was hurricane weather if the ominous tension in her belly was any indication, and Nadie had encouraged her to listen to her inner voice. Best to follow her intuition as a huntress on this one.

Snapping her eyelids open, she faced the men. "Why cast a vote now? Let us first secure Dasamonquepeuc against the coming storm, meditate on the matter, and reconvene to cast our votes before the sun sets on the morrow."

A pregnant silence settled over the gathering. Wanchese's eyes bored into hers, hard and searching. Without relinquishing her gaze, he rapidly translated her words.

For a full minute, nothing but the sound of wind filled the tent. Then Noshi the Priest nodded. He puffed three times on the peace pipe and passed it to her. Approval glinted from his large, sad eyes.

"Ireh," Wanchese commanded. "Let us retreat to the caves. Go with haste and spread the word to our people."

The maidens and children were Jane's responsibility. She took a long, bracing drag on the pipe before she exited the tent, hoping the smoke would burn away the apprehension rising in her chest. Thunder rumbled overhead, much closer than she liked.

They did not have much time before the storm unleashed its demons on them.

CHAPTER 18: MIXED LOYALTIES

The wind increased its tempo throughout the night, battering the beach front without mercy. The Day of the Dead celebration was cut short. The weather was too foul for festivities. The blowing sand extinguished their fires and thickened their stews with so much grit as to render them inedible.

After a final tribute to his mate, Noshi and a team of braves hustled Nadie's remains to Dasamonquepeuc where they would begin an extensive preservation process. Soon she would be laid to rest in the temple with the other elders.

It did not set well in Jane's gut, the thought of walking past the shrine and seeing Nadie lying there cold and unmoving. She preferred to remember her dashing around their village in her usual spritely manner as she directed the day-to-day tasks of the maidens.

Dawn broke with an eerie, grayish glow. Jane stood at the tree line overlooking the beach and the frothing, churning sound waters beyond. Young braves and maidens scurried to clean up the remains of the festivities and tote the tents, wooden stewpots, bowls, and ladles back to the village. Sharp bursts of wind slapped stinging granules of sand against her exposed neck and face, forcing her to shield her eyes with an elbow.

Wanchese joined her but had to shout to be heard above the moaning wind. "Come, Damisac the Wise. Kanti awakens. It is time for questions."

At the mention of Kanti, Jane ventured a sidelong glance at his crossed arms and unsmiling face. Not so very long ago, the willowy Kanti had served as his concubine. She shifted from one foot to the other. The interrogation could easily turn awkward for all of them.

"As you will, chief." She bowed low, hands clasped beneath her chin.

They turned and headed into the forest together, but Wanchese did not lead her to the palisade entrance of Dasamonquepeuc as expected. Instead, he drew her toward the rocky cliffs that sheltered the spring. They continued past the spring and followed the ridge until it curved to form an alcove.

"*Cumear-ah.*" Hands on her shoulders, he steered her backward into the alcove. "We will be safe here from the wind and debris."

"What are you—"

He cut off her words with a searing kiss. Molding her against him, he tenderly worshiped her lips.

Tracing the strength of his jaw and caressing the line of his ear along the way, she plunged her fingers into his hair and tugged him closer.

He guided her against the cliff wall, drawing out the kiss as if his life depended on it.

"Wanchese," she murmured, breathless as he claimed her as his wife and perfect mate. Afterward, she rested her head against his shoulder, spent and deliriously happy. Despite the nip in the wind, she was as warm as a thousand candles.

"I love you." She pressed a kiss to his collarbone.

"Aye."

She frowned against his neck, wishing he would return the endearment. At his continued silence, she tipped her head back.

He met her gaze with an intensity that stole the air from her lungs. He pulled her in for another lingering kiss.

Still irritated at him for withholding the words she wanted so badly to hear, she nipped another kiss at the edge of his mouth. Then she bent directly in front of him to straighten her leggings.

"Cruel, cruel, wench."

She arched a brow at him over her shoulder.

"You have done naught but torment me from the first day I laid eyes on you."

"'Twas a dreary summer's eve. Overcast," she mused. "You should have known it was a bad omen and kept your distance."

"Nay, the sun was out. Enough to blind a man."

"Oh, come now," she scoffed. "I recall the cloud cover, for it ushered in the first hint of cooler weather."

"Nay, it was a stifling evening. Difficult to breathe."

"Indeed," she murmured. Her heart felt suddenly lighter. She could almost forgive him his earlier omission of the words she longed to hear. Almost. He was going to speak words of love to her. Eventually. A gal carrying knives had her methods for making a man talk.

Jane sheathed her pair of blades at her waist and marched beside her husband into the village. The wind continued to whip at the trees. They had to dodge more than one falling branch.

Just outside Dasamonquepeuc, Wanchese stopped her. "As a member of my council, you must step aside and allow me to enter in front of you. You will walk to my right and keep one stride behind."

Ah, so we would enter the village as chief and wise woman. For that she was grateful. It was far better than trailing at his heels as a concubine. She straightened, rolled back her shoulders, and walked solemnly at his right with her head held high.

It was a very different promenade down the main village path than any other time she'd walked it before. Villagers paused their activities and dipped into bows. Among them were Chitsa and James, Alawa and William, Blade and his father, Amonsoquath, Noshi, and Mukki. Some bent from the waist. Others knelt as they passed and pressed their faces to the ground.

Jane hated drawing attention to herself, but the transition to Wise Woman was not as difficult as she feared. She had earned the regard of her people, and Nadie had taught her to accept what was meant to be. She felt neither pompous pleasure at their show of deference nor fidgeting discomfort beneath their curious stares. Unadulterated pride flooded her as she nodded to the maidens, waved to the children, and tapped a fist to her chest to honor each warrior.

The sight of Wanchese's lodge brought a lump to her throat. It was so good to be home. Cutto bounded beneath the door covering and dashed up to her. He growled and wagged his tail, butting his enormous head against her hand.

"*Cumear*, you mangy beast." She scratched his ears and bent to press her face to his neck. How she had missed him! She could not wait to bask before a warm fire in their lodge tonight with him sprawled at her feet.

But first they had to deal with Kanti.

They made their way past their lodge to a much simpler structure erected near the cornfields. Normally, it was reserved for the storage of farm tools. Today, it served as an interrogation chamber. Kanti knelt in the center of the room between Riapoke and Amonsoquath, hands bound behind her back.

At the sight of Wanchese, relief leaped in her heart-shaped face. She trained soulful eyes on him, ignoring Jane altogether.

He strode in a complete circle around her without saying a word.

Jane wondered if the bruise rising on her temple tugged at his sympathies. She also wondered if he noted how his former concubine thrust out her bosom for his perusal. She was attractive in a wispy, delicate sort of way that tended to bring out the protective nature of men.

As much as Kanti seemed to be enjoying playing the role of weak and helpless damsel, however, Jane knew the woman was far stronger than she pretended. She recalled the wiles she had employed in her attempt to entice Wanchese into the pit during the hunting games. What Kanti might lack in physical strength, she made up for in guile.

Wanchese barked a series of questions in Algonquin, most of which Jane understood. "Why did you help Askook escape? Where has he gone? What are his plans?"

Her responses were to be expected. She had mistakenly thought Askook cared for her and had welcomed his attentions after Wanchese set her aside as his concubine. He had plied her with all sorts of questions about Wanchese and his council during their courtship, but she'd assumed he was just making conversation. Yes, she aided him in his escape, convinced he was being treated unfairly. She never dreamt he would kill his guards or knock her unconscious when he escaped. If she had it to do all over again, she would neither court nor aid the scoundrel. Nay, she had no idea where he was headed or what his plans were.

Kanti was clearly counting on her past relationship with

Wanchese to help soften her punishment. Jane resisted the urge to roll her eyes at the batted eyelashes and soft husky voice when Kanti claimed she had been deceived by the vicious Askook.

"May I?" She inquired calmly to Wanchese.

His lip curled in distaste, but he nodded after the smallest hesitation.

Convinced Kanti knew more than she was telling, Jane crouched before the woman, making it impossible for her to continue ignoring her.

The sensuous tilt of her lips turned sullen, and a wary look crept into her eyes.

With Wanchese translating, Jane began. "Do you have any idea what men like Askook and his father do to small children like Mukki?"

Uncertain, she glanced between Wanchese and Jane.

Jane adopted a conversational tone, "I just returned from a trip to Copper Mountain. Let me share what I witnessed." Instantly serious, she lowered her voice and spoke directly in the woman's ear. "Way down beneath the ground where there is neither sunlight nor witnesses, Dasan and Askook score the backs of their prisoners with leather straps until they bleed. They withhold food until the skin of their victims fights to stretch across their bones, much like the newcomers we carried up the beach last night. They remove the shoes of every miner so that their feet crack and redden on the cold, hard floor of their copper prison. The only relief these innocent lads and maids find from such dismal working conditions is death."

In less than a minute, Kanti broke. "I know not where he fled," she sobbed. "He despises Chief Wanchese for refusing him Amitola in marriage and you as his concubine. I thought to comfort him, not assist in harming the other villagers."

"You did not trust the council to issue a fair judgment for the deeds of the accused?" Riapoke inquired, his eyes hard.

"Nay, and I was wrong." She hung her head, defeated. "Do with me as you will."

Wanchese straightened his shoulders, his expression bleak.

"Please be merciful," Jane whispered, touching his arm. She finished the plea in her head. *She is but a foolish young woman.*

He frowned but placed a hand over hers. To Riapoke, he said, "Deliver Kanti back to her family. She may never return to Dasamonquepeuc." Then he repeated the order in Algonquian.

Jane caught the word 'Chesapeake,' and guessed her original tribe was located farther north in the Chesapeake Bay region. Alas, that was one tribe they would no longer be able to count as an ally.

Kanti was fortunate Wanchese did no more than banish her. If she had been a man, Jane feared his punishment might have been far more harsh.

The banishment made another thing apparent. Jane no longer needed to worry about Wanchese harboring any residual feelings for Kanti.

She must have recognized her complete loss of control over him, because her tears evaporated rather quickly. In the end, her expression reflected more outrage over her punishment than genuine regret for her actions.

When Wanchese's back was turned, she shot Jane a look of pure hatred.

Jane raised a brow and fingered the blade at her waist.

The native woman averted her gaze first, and Jane tried to take comfort in the knowledge she would soon be too far away to spill any more of her poison on their people.

*a*s Nadie would have done, Jane ordered their English guests to be de-loused and scoured within an inch of their lives. Bly, Dyoni, Chitsa, and Alawa joined her in herding them to the spring. Blade tagged along and alternated between chatting with his father and long-lost friend, Will. Though they shared a few chuckles over old times, Jane noted Will was quiet on the topic of serving in the mines.

Cecil Prat gazed in adoration at his son and hung on his every word, questioning him in detail about the building of native weirs to harvest large schools of fish. Edward Powell maintained a brooding silence but seemed to listen intently to the conversations flying around his ears.

Robert clutched Jane's hand the entire trek. She had to peel him away off her when the spring came into view. The maidens wasted no time in ridding them of their torn and filthy garments.

Jane muffled a chuckle at their varying levels of shock and mortification to find themselves completely disrobed. She turned away to lend them a bit of privacy.

She gathered an armload of sticks, tossed them in the fire pit next to the spring, and struck a flint to ignite them. She had to cup her hands over the tiny flame for several minutes so it would catch. The wind blustered without relenting overhead, but the stony ridge overlooking the spring provided a moderate shelter from the worst of its fury.

Bly muttered her thanks and tossed the entire pile of shredded tunics into the flames. The maidens proceeded to examine the colonists for lice and other ailments, then scrubbed away their countless layers of grime. They also trimmed their hair and beards.

Though weak and exhausted, Cecil, Edward, and Will appeared invigorated from their baths. Robert, however, ran to bury his face against Jane's leg and refused to submit to the ministrations of her maidens.

She sighed and took charge of the task of washing him, surmising he was unaccustomed to bathing and therefore fearful of it altogether. Back in England, all too many families subscribed to the superstition that bathing would bring on disease or even death.

She resorted to an old trick to gain his acquiescence. "I will bake you a bread cake if you sit still for your bath." She allowed her voice to drop to a conspiratorial low note.

He uncurled his fingers at last from her leggings and looked up. The vacant cast to his eyes dissipated into faint hope.

"Aye, you heard me," she coaxed and maneuvered him skillfully into the spring. He squirmed as she dunked him beneath the water and gasped for air when she brought him back to the surface. In the end, he was no match for her. She cleaned him from his matted hair to his dirt-encrusted, callused toes.

To her disappointment, he did not once speak or cry out in protest. He uttered no sounds at all. After a while, he ceased his struggles and adopted a faraway look.

Ah, poppet. You have become rather proficient in the art of disappearing inside your own head. She gave him a final rinse, squeezed the excess water from his hair, and deposited him on a clean reed mat before the fire to dry.

With her face carefully averted from the drying men, Jane sent Bly and Chitsa to solicit donations for enough clean tunics, leggings, and moccasins to go around.

"Promise each family we will sew new garments to replace their gifts. We will repay them with the current hides we are tanning."

Bly nodded, her stoic features softening in approval.

Within minutes, Master Prat, Master Powell, Will, and

Robert were shrugging into their new outfits. Grateful smiles played about their lips.

"Riapoke says you can come stay in our lodge," Blade offered excitedly, while the men puzzled over how to tie their leggings. "All of you. Me and Will can bunk up, and we've more sleeping platforms to spare in the back of our lodge." He cast an uncertain glance at Robert who was clinging to Jane's hand.

Dyoni squatted down in front of him. Though unsmiling in the manner of the Roanokes, her wide brown eyes were warm with understanding. She murmured to him in her musical Algonquin tongue and produced a tiny wooden figure from the pouch at her side.

She bounced the toy towards him to imitate a man running. Next, she whisked out a miniature carved horse from behind her back. She clicked her teeth to create the clatter of hooves as the horse galloped to catch up. Just as the animal was about to pass up his owner, the rider leaped upon the horse and drew him to a skidding halt. The horse neighed and tossed its head, but the rider held on with a cry of triumph.

Fascinated, Robert reached out to finger the horse's flying mane. It was a rather skilled likeness. Jane wondered at the identity of the master carver.

In response to the lad's touch, the horse whinnied again and leaped into his outstretched palm. Dazzled, Robert closed his fingers around the precious figures and clutched them to his chest.

Dyoni nodded in satisfaction and held out her hand. He handed the toys back with reluctance, eyes downcast, but she shook her head. "Tah." She closed his fingers around the toys, once more.

Again, she held out her hand. This time, Robert placed his hand in hers but remained tense and ready to bolt.

Jane patted his back. "All is well, Robert. This is my friend, Dyoni. See how her belly grows? She carries a small mite inside her."

He glanced wide-eyed at her swollen middle and relaxed. Then he ducked his head and trotted beside her as they returned to the village.

Relieved to have one dilemma solved, Jane strode ahead to join the men. "Gentlemen, if I may have a word with you. Our head of council is pleased to extend his hospitality for as long as you wish to reside in Dasamonquepeuc. Of course, it will delight Blade to no end to share their hearth and lodge. He has missed you tremendously and, I dare say, would hate to let you out of his sight tonight."

"I accept the offer and will thank Riapoke for his kindness." Cecil Prat's tired eyes glowed with happiness. "Maybe I can repay him with a bit of work."

Edward Powell was silent for a moment. He ran a hand through his freshly washed and shorn hair. "About the Roanokes, Mistress Jane." His face was haggard with grief, the sort that would take a long time to heal. "I would just as soon return to our kind. I..." He glanced around at the Roanoke maidens who accompanied them and lowered his voice. "They have been most diligent in attending to our comforts, but I could never build a life here."

Why not? James, William, Blade, and I have. His reference to 'our kind' rankled. *Wanchese is my kind, burn it!*

"I will send word to Chief Manteo about your arrival. More than likely, our chief has already done so. It would not surprise me to greet an envoy from Croatoa in the next few days. For one thing, Master Ellis will be anxious to reunite with his son."

Edward Powell looked relieved. "In that case, Mistress Jane, I'll be departing for Croatoa at first opportunity."

Moving closer to Cecil Prat so as not to be overheard by the chattering lads, he laid a hand on his shoulder and muttered, "Never you fear, Assistant Prat. We shall appeal to Manteo for the release of your boy. For the release of *all* our colonists."

Master Prat frowned and scratched his chin.

Jane wanted to roll her eyes at Master Powell's conceit. Here less than a day and already he was trying to exert his influence over matters that did not concern him. But she held her peace. He would learn soon enough, his pride and conceit would get him nowhere in the New World.

Oblivious to her growing resentment, he straightened and turned to her. "Pray enlighten us to the purpose of the ceremony you took part in last night after that savage's funeral."

She stiffened. "Nadie was her name, my lord. She served as Wise Woman to the Roanokes and taught me all that I know about this land and the ways of the people who call it home. Though humble in stature, she was one of the greatest women who ever lived." Her voice trembled with the effort to keep her hands from encircling the neck of the pompous creature. "She was a warrior, farmer, teacher, and mentor. A very wise woman, indeed."

He looked moderately contrite. "Pray forgive my poor choice of words, Mistress Jane. Clearly, this Nadie meant something to you. I fear my recent experiences have soured my regard for, er, a good number of things."

Well, of course, they had. Serving as a slave in the copper mines would leave a poor taste in anyone's mouth. *I am being too harsh.*

"About last night's ceremony," she said in a gentler tone. "The elders inducted me into the Roanoke council to serve as their next Wise Woman."

His jaw dropped. "You don't say?"

"It was Nadie's dying wish that I step into her shoes once she was gone."

He stopped in his tracks, astounded. "Mistress Jane, you cannot think to accept such a responsibility. Why that would mean—"

"Indeed." She increased her pace, anxious to leave the odious man behind, but he hurried to catch up with her. "This is my home now, Master Powell." Perhaps he did not mean to do so, but he was starting to unnerve her, to reduce her somehow into something less than she had become.

In her short walk from the spring to the village, she felt as if she was being thrust back into one of her many subservient roles from the past. Orphan. Companion to a distant aunt. Nanny. School mistress. Spinster. And eventually unemployed and penniless.

By all that is holy, I am not returning to any of those things. Why, she'd received more respect as a concubine among the Roanokes than any capacity she'd ever served among her own countrymen. No sooner did the thought strike, that remorse consumed her.

Edward Powell and the rest of the City of Raleigh colonists had been most kind to her, despite their nauseating notions of propriety and social status. They also possessed an immense supply of Puritan piety and fervor, which had inspired them to rescue her from an uncertain future on the streets of Cheapside. She might very well be starving by now if they had not offered her the position of school mistress on the ship ride over.

She swallowed the remainder of her indignation. Let Edward Powell bluster all he wished. Perhaps he needed to blow off a little steam, so to speak, after what he had suffered in the copper mines. His words could not diminish her unless she allowed them to.

She was Damisac the Wise, and Nadie had taught her a thing or two about holding her tongue.

***

*D*espite her efforts to remain calm, she entered the lodge she shared with Wanchese in high dudgeon. A quick glance around the council chamber proved it clear of occupants. She untied her cloak. Instead of hanging it on the hook next to the doorway, however, she succumbed to the boil of anger and hurled it to the ground. There was no longer any need to maintain pretenses now that she was out of sight of the English refugees.

She stormed to the fire, fists clenched at her sides, muttering oaths beneath her breath. The only thing that prevented her from shrieking was the knowledge of how well sound carried through the thin reed mat and deerskin walls. *Aargh, but Edward Powell is a pompous mule!* It would serve him right if they assigned him the basest tasks for the remainder of his stay in their village. One word from Wanchese, and he would be shoveling dung at the privies. If nothing else, it would do Jane a world of good to witness him hauling manure for 'their kind.'

Cutto reared up on his hind legs and tried to lick her face. Caught off guard, Jane yelped and pushed him off her person. He backed away and slunk against the wall.

"Oh, Cutto," she chuckled, chasing after him. "A sloppy kiss is precisely what I need right now." She bent to hug him, and he bounded to his feet. They bumped heads, and she tumbled sideways. He pounced. She laughed and wrestled with him on the floor.

A loud weeping outside the tent drew her to the doorway. Parting the flap, she observed Kanti being led from the village by two braves. Wanchese stood next to Noshi in the foyer of the temple, arms folded. *Good riddance!*

Kanti broke away from her escorts to fling herself at Wanchese's feet. Jane discerned she was pleading with him to allow her to stay. The wind whipped at her hair and garments. Thunder sounded in the distance.

Jane dropped the flap back into place, unable to endure her antics any longer. Wanchese would deny her request. In truth, she wished to gain an audience with him herself to discuss his intentions toward the refugees, but she felt it was best to keep her distance until Kanti left the village.

Minutes stretched into an hour, but Wanchese did not return to their lodge. Disappointed, Jane drifted outdoors to check on the maidens. The most energetic ones were tanning hides. Those with the best eyesight were sewing garments, and the eldest were stirring large vats of venison stew. With a critical glance skyward, Jane ordered all food preparations to be moved indoors on account of the poor weather.

She pulled together another team of maidens and set them to securing the loose items blowing around the village. Baskets, a cloak, children's toys. She rotated from group to group, offering suggestions and pitching in wherever she was needed the most. It was nigh on dinner time when she finally caught up with Wanchese.

He stalked into their lodge. "Where have you been?" he snarled.

Taken aback, she could only stare.

"You returned hours ago from the bathing session, and still I've no report on the state of our English visitors. What is the extent of their injuries? Where will they stay? In what manner shall they employ themselves?"

"I,ah..." Jane backed away from him, hardly recognizing the furious man standing before her. "Didn't Riapoke already provide some of the answers you seek?"

"Riapoke did not minister to the comfort of our guests."
He advanced on her. "He did not accompany them to the
spring or engage them in conversation. What are you hiding
from me? As a member of my council, there can be no more
secrets between us."

"You question my loyalty?" Her voice rose to a higher
pitch. "After everything we have endured together?" Raw
anger surged.

"It would not be the first time I was betrayed by a
concubine."

"Is that so?" Her temper neared the snapping point. "Well,
I've a fine bit of news for you. I am not just another one of
your concubines. I am your *wife*."

They circled each other, chests heaving. The wind outside
picked up its fervor. Something heavy clattered against the
exterior wall. The voices of two maidens called in fright to
one another.

"Chitsa fears one of your Englishmen is bent on leaving
and taking all of you with him. Naturally, when you avoided
me the remainder of the afternoon, I assumed the worst."
Wanchese's lips pinched in fury.

She must have overheard the exchange with Edward
Powell. Guilt stabbed Jane. The thought of losing James must
be distressing her to no end. She would go and set the poor
woman's mind at ease as soon as she finished with Wanchese.
*Burn him for allowing her to believe such a thing for even a
moment. Why, Chitsa must be frantic!*

"You think I would abandon you without a word?" She
bared her teeth. "Turn my back on our maidens and all that
Nadie entrusted to me?"

"As opposed to being tied to a savage for the rest of your
life? Aye, the thought crossed my mind."

Red flooded her vision. With a cry of anguish, she
launched herself at her husband. The wind shrieked and

369

moaned outside, matching the storm within their home. She pummeled nothing but air, because Wanchese neatly evaded the blows. He hooked a leg around hers and sent her sprawling. Instead of crashing to the hard-packed earthen floor, however, she somehow landed atop him.

She grabbed his shoulders for leverage and tensed to spring upright, but he rolled to pin her beneath him. He straddled her while holding her wrists in a manacle grasp on either side of her head.

"I will have your report now." His voice was deadly calm.

My report? She stared up at him, baffled to find herself restrained in such an inglorious manner. If Nadie were here, she would berate her to no end for her gross lapse in decorum. Jane doubted the woman had ever conferred with her mate, the priest, from such a position on the floor.

She fought to regain her composure. "Blade's loyalties are torn between Riapoke and his father." She panted from her struggles "But 'tis more likely Master Prat will stay than Blade will leave. In the past, Will followed Blade's lead, and I expect the same from him now, because the two lads always stick together. Master Powell cannot depart Dasamonquepeuc soon enough, and 'tis no great loss to us if he does. He's a pompous toad, if you ask me. However, my biggest concern is young Robert. He still has not uttered a word since his arrival. Maybe fetching his sire from Croatoa would be the best medicine. All are undernourished, but none possess any crippling injuries. Only a world of cuts and bruises both inside and out."

Wanchese digested the information for a moment. Then he loosened his hold on her and stood. "You will never again keep such things from me."

She sat up and crossed her arms protectively in front of her. His words stung, but he had the right of it. She should have reported to him. Instead, she'd spent all afternoon avoiding him, all for the jealousy wound as tight as a ball of yarn in her chest.

"Maybe Nadie chose the wrong one," she whispered. "Have you considered that, Wanchese?" Her voice grew stronger with regret. "What if I do not have what it takes to fill her shoes?"

She braced for his answer, but none came. A frantic call for help had them both leaping for the doorway. Several voices called for Wanchese. Others cried for Jane.

She remembered her place at the last moment and paused, allowing him to exit in front of her.

"There's a boat coming our way," Blade shouted. "We must help, else they'll never make it to shore."

"How many passengers?" Jane demanded as she ducked back into the lodge. She swiftly hefted a large roll of hemp cord to her shoulder.

"Two, Mistress Jane." His voice was muffled by the door covering.

She hitched the coil higher and grabbed a second roll from the wall. Who in all tarnation would be foolish enough to venture into the waters during such foul weather?

"'Tis Amonsoquath," Wanchese said when she stepped outside the lodge. He took the heavier of the two rolls from her. "I sent him last night to notify Chief Manteo of Askook's betrayal." Concern darkened his eyes.

Amonsoquath was a highly skilled warrior, neither careless nor impulsive. An urgent matter must have arisen, one necessitating the risk of delivering word back to his hometown in the midst of the gathering storm.

"To the sounds!" she cried.

CHAPTER 19: TWISTER

*W*anchese and Jane sprinted for the palisade exit of Dasamonquepeuc. Blade and Will joined them at a dead run. More shouts and footsteps pounded in their wake. She prayed Kimi and Kitchi were among them. It was too dangerous to swim or put another boat on the water. Thus, it would require a sizable team to haul in the stranded sailors with ropes.

Maidens, elder villagers, and youths swarmed the village, dismantling tents, lodges, and platforms. They lashed light-weight items to heavier items. Even the children took part, carrying smaller loads and leading the dogs toward the shelter of the cliffs where the caves awaited. Several of the poor creatures' coats of fur stood on end. Some trotted with their tails between their legs. Others howled their fear to the heavens as the wind rained twigs and other debris down on them.

Noshi and Achak directed a team of braves to evacuate the temple of its sacred occupants. They wrapped each body in layers of deerskin and placed them in a deep trench to be exhumed after the storm. These hallowed men and women would be laid to rest beneath the ground, if only for a short time.

The moment Jane and Wanchese exited the protected walls of the village, the dangers intensified. They pressed their way into high winds that bent the trees sideways. They looked as if they would snap in two. Some did. Severed limbs tumbled to the ground and continued to thrash and roll in the frenzy of the wind.

They shielded their eyes and fought their way forward. An enormous splintering filled the air. Wanchese threw himself against Jane and plastered the two of them to an aged oak, shielding her as a tall fir crashed to the ground beside them and shivered into place.

At his rapid expulsion of breath, she discerned her husband had been injured. They pushed away from the tree, and she reached for him, but he waved her on.

"Tah," he mouthed and propelled her in the direction of the sound waters.

They ran with their hands over their heads but took several more hits, albeit the falling branches grew smaller as the trees thinned.

At last, they burst onto the open strand of beach. They squinted and shaded their eyes from the flying sand that threatened to blister every inch of their exposed skin.

"Mercy!" Jane muttered. If only the rain would start, the dampness would weigh down the sand.

The waters surged and crashed on the beach in scourging intervals. Glancing out over the sounds, she pitied the occupants of the boat.

"'Tis going to capsize on Amonsoquath and George," Blade cried as they unfurled the first cord.

George! What was *he* doing in the boat? Why wasn't he at Croatoa?

The two teens rode the next mighty swell. The wave

crested and plunged. This time, the canoe careened to one side and belched its occupants into the seething waters.

Manteo pounded a wooden peg in the ground with the flat side of his hatchet. He lashed one end of the cord to the peg, while Jane dashed for the water with the other end.

"Tah!" He bellowed, chasing after her and wrestling the rope from her hands. He encircled his waist with it.

The wind shrieked like a wounded animal in its final death throes, and the roaring of the waves grew thunderous. May God have mercy on the capsized men, for it was going to take a miracle to save them now.

Do not go, Jane pleaded with her eyes.

"Tah." Riapoke stepped between them and knelt with a fist to his heart, reminding Wanchese of his role as chief and his duty to their people.

There was no time to argue, at any rate. Wanchese surrendered the rope to his war chief and helped secure the cord around his waist. The waves pummeled the figures in the water. Jane glimpsed only an occasional head or arm break the surface.

"God be with you!" she called into the wind and ran with Riapoke to the water's edge.

Wanchese caught up to her and yanked her shoulders against his chest as the cold, wet sand began to suck at her feet and ankles. "Not one step farther," he grated in her ear.

They took their positions next to Will and Blade, who grasped the middle of the rope, preparing to haul in Riapoke as soon as he surfaced with the first survivor.

Kimi and Kitchi pounded in a second stake. Kitchi looped the end around his waist and tied a thick knot. As he ran towards the water, the first rope grew taut and gave a vicious yank.

It was difficult to hold the smooth length of the cord steady. The flying sand only served to make it more slippery.

With each tug, the cord glided a bit farther from their grasps. While Wanchese fought to loop it around his wrist, Jane shot an anxious glance over her shoulder at the peg. It shifted but so far had held each time they lurched forward. She feared it would spring loose any moment.

"Tarnation!" She abandoned the rope and bent to loosen a rock that had become lodged in the sand at her feet. She ran to the peg and pounded the rock on its head to drive it deeper, but the bed of sand proved unstable. If anything, her efforts dislodged the peg more quickly. It popped from the ground and sailed towards her face. She dove from its path in time to avoid a direct hit, but the edge grazed her temple.

She tottered to regain her equilibrium. Then she scrambled after the peg as it bounced and scraped a jagged path to the water's edge. Wanchese, Kimi, and the lads helped her pursue the runaway cord, but inch by precious inch, the frothing surf swallowed it.

Wanchese, Kimi, and Jane outpaced the younger lads. The three of them dove in unison for the final snaking length of cord. Their momentum dragged them all the way into the slushing sand at the water's edge before they skidded to a halt.

Jane lay heaving in the sand and held on to the end of it with all her strength. Wanchese rolled atop the cord, and with the lads rejoining them, looped the end twice around his torso. With the four of them gripping the section in front of him, he stood and backed slowly from the water.

Without warning, the sky opened up. Rain sheeted down, drenching their clothing and rendering the cord as slippery as glass. All of them except for Wanchese slipped and slid along its length, their efforts sorely negated by the rain. Kitchi abandoned the second cord and raced to add his efforts to theirs.

They struggled to regain traction, but step by terrifying

step, they were forced into the thrashing water where they quickly lost more ground. They peddled their feet in the ankle-deep sludge, at first, but were sucked farther in. Jane was soon submerged to her knees, the lads to their waists, and Kimi and Kitchi stood in water up to their shoulders.

Thunder pounded in their ears, and lightning flashed across the ominous green and yellow sky. One of the zig-zagging bolts of light illuminated a dark black funnel rising from the waters about a quarter mile or so out at sea.

"God have mercy," Jane breathed, stunned. The storm resembled a tornado; but instead of trees and vegetation, massive amounts of water rose in its swirling vortex. She had overheard superstitious sailors speaking fearfully about waterspouts during their journey to the New World but had never before witnessed one with her own eyes.

The funnel whirled faster and faster over the rolling sound waters, growing wider and blacker by the second. A mountain of water rose up in its midst, until it seemed as if the ocean itself would upend. The roar of the funnel drowned out the screaming wind and crashing waves as it spun towards the men and women on the beach.

"Father God, have mercy!" Jane prayer.

The funnel lurched nearer. Then it made a sharp turn and headed back out to sea, spinning blackly against the sky and growing smaller until it disappeared on the horizon. The roaring stopped.

Jane let the breath out she had been holding and returned her attention to the cord, but her hands continued to slide as if it were made of freshly polished boot leather. She gave up her section and turned to face her husband, pushing against his chest with all her might to stop his advance into the sea. She reckoned that would do more good that her useless grip on the rope.

The cord suddenly went slack. Had Wanchese not

regained his footing, they might all have been swept into the deep. But he prevailed and jogged back a few steps to regain the tension on the cord only a second before the next mighty tug shook it.

Once more, they threw all their weight and strength into pulling. This time Jane faced the water, pressing her shoulder blades into her husband's chest. *Mercy!* The funnel cloud must have released its mountain of captive seawater at last, because a gigantic wall of it was hurtling their way. They watched its advance in horror.

Frantic, Jane turned and pushed Wanchese with all her might, desperate to remove him from harm's way. The veins on his neck and temples pulsed with the effort of holding his ground.

"Go," he gritted through his teeth.

"Nay."

"Go," he repeated. "As your chief, I command it." He reached up to cover the hands she had resting on his chest. For a moment he squeezed them, his mahogany eyes burning into hers. Then he peeled her fingers from his chest.

"Nay," she yelled, terrified. "I will not leave you."

His face hardened with resolve.

"Stop!" she gasped. "I love you."

"I know."

"I love you," she cried again, her teeth chattering from the cold. "We live or die together." She was fairly certain she'd promised to do such in their wedding vows.

With an agony in his eyes that seared her very soul, he shoved her behind him.

"Nay! Please! Nay!" She sobbed, pitching to her knees and flailing in the shallow surf. Frantic, she splashed her way back to him on all fours and lunged for his feet. Her hands closed around his ankles. Someone grabbed one of her legs and pulled.

A wave crashed over them, and her head went under water. She strained to maintain her grip. Seconds ticked away until her chest burned with the need to inhale. *Air. By all that is holy, I need air.* Still she refused to let go of her husband. She held her breath until she thought her lungs would explode. Bright lights splintered behind her eyelids, and her fingers grew weak.

Suddenly, an immense surge of water shattered her hold on Wanchese. She tumbled backwards from the force, rolling head over heels again and again. Spluttering and choking, she came to rest lying flat on her back in the cold sand. Then everything went black.

When she opened her eyes, rain splattered her face. *Air. I am breathing again, which must mean I am still alive.* With a hoarse cry, she sat up to search for Wanchese and groaned. Sharp pain shot through her arm from wrist to elbow. *Tarnation, I have no time to nurse a broken limb.*

She probed the area and clenched her teeth. *Egad, it hurts.* No rough edges of bone showed, but the skin swelled. If broken, at least it was a clean break. She would need to fashion a splint after she ensured the safety of—

"Jane!" George sprinted towards her. His pale brow was wrinkled with concern.

"George." She frowned up at him, wondering if she was dreaming. "How did you make it out of the sea?"

"Riapoke saved me." His words held no joy, however.

"What about Amonsoquath?" she asked quickly.

"He is still out there."

She cradled her arm and swiveled to take in the flurry of activity. The cord remained tied around Wanchese's waist. He double checked the knot. A few yards down from him, Kimi looped the same cord around his waist, as well. Will and Blade did likewise, and Riapoke secured himself to the cord in front of them. Kitchi picked up the far end. They were sending another man into the water. Apparently, this time Kitchi would lead.

Teeth chattering, Jane glimpsed another mighty wave build and crest. It spewed the canoe into the air. Her mouth dropped, for Amonsoquath was clinging haplessly to its side. His legs cycled as the boat plunged back into the water no more than fifteen yards from the water's edge. *So close and yet not close enough!*

It amazed her that the craft was still intact. Any one of their English clinker-built ships would have been lying in pieces on the ocean floor by now. If Amonsoquath could hang on just a bit longer. She shot George a glorious smile despite her pain. Their men actually stood a healthy chance at saving him.

George did not return her smile. He knelt beside her and grasped her good hand, bending one knee to kiss the top of it. "Just in case I don't make it back, this is farewell, Mistress Jane."

Farewell! "What?" Then she knew. He was the one going in. "Oh, George!" cried.

"Amonsoquath is my friend," he said simply.

She started to shake her head, but he stopped her. "I must. 'Greater love hath no man,'" he quoted.

Than a man who would lay down his life for a friend. She finished the age-old verse inside her head and nodded, emotion clogging her throat. *Burn it, George.* It was just like his impulsive nature to do something so foolhardy and yet so gallant. "I'll not say farewell but rather wish you Godspeed."

He kissed her hand one last time and stood. Lightning flashed across the sky, illuminating the cloud framing his head from her vantage point. It gave him an unearthly, almost angelic appearance. Snapping a salute, he turned on his heel.

Her tears mingled with the rain and rolled down her face.

With a huff of pain, she jerked to her feet and staggered towards Wanchese. *Faith, my whole body hurts.*

She took comfort from the fact the rope was secure this time. They would not be losing it again unless the water-spout returned and swept the entire lot of them to sea. The storm still raged overhead, but the funnel cloud was gone.

George dashed up to Kitchi who stood lashed within the rope at the water's edge. The loose coils lay at his feet. Just as George drew the first loop around his own waist, another wall of water started to form. It was still a good distance from Amonsoquath, but it was gaining momentum and would be atop him all too soon.

Not taking the time to knot the rope, George sprinted into the sea, bellowing, "God save the Queen!" He disappeared in the frothing depths.

All Jane could do was wait, pray, and add her dwindling strength to the line of men on the rope. She stepped in front of Wanchese and leaned her good shoulder into his chest, bracing herself for what was to come.

The cord remained slack as George battled his way through the waves. For several heart stopping moments, he disappeared then surfaced closer to Amonsoquath. *Bless him!* The lad was a powerful swimmer, to say the least.

Every few seconds, the waters surged and attempted to drive him back to the beach, but he persisted in diving beneath them to avoid the brunt of their force.

Not until George reached the vicinity where they last saw Amonsoquath did the ropes pull taut on their end. This time they were prepared. They held their ground in the cold, clammy sand.

Wanchese slid both arms around Jane's waist to anchor her against him. "You are hurt." The fury of the winds subsided somewhat, so she had no trouble hearing him now. If only the waves would calm their fury, as well.

"'Tis a c-clean break. It will heal j-just fine." She sounded ridiculous with her teeth chattering. The heat of his body slowly permeated her near-frozen frame. She shivered and burrowed closer, closing her eyes for a moment. She had come way too close to losing him today. Her heart. Her husband. Her life.

Wanchese kissed the top of her head as they watched George's slow but steady progress. She could only see one figure.

Where is Amonsoquath? Ah, there. Another head bobbed. The canoe was no longer in sight. She drew a bracing breath. They only needed to give George enough time to grab hold of Amonsoquath. Then they would pull them both to shore.

Maybe the cold was addling her brain, because she heard herself babbling, "You never speak to me of love."

"Huh?" Wanchese sounded truly astonished.

In for a penny... "Do you love me?" she persisted.

"Love," he said in disgust. "It is an English word. I have little use for it."

"Say it in Powhatan, then."

"*Nouwmais,*" he answered shortly. "But it is not the right word for us, either."

"Oh." The breath left her lungs in a rush. She had been so sure he loved her. Apparently, she was mistaken. How awkward of her to be making an issue of it here on the beach when much weightier matters were at stake.

Wanchese cradled her closer and nuzzled the side of her neck. "Every day, you are my sun. At night, you are my moon and my stars. During the dry summer, you were my rain. My heart rises with you in the morning and escapes with you into the world of dreams at night."

Her breath caught on a sob. His words shook her, humbled her. They raised her to a higher place than she had ever known.

"Wanchese," she whispered, overcome.

The rope went suddenly slack, and a lone figure was swept onto the beach.

Wanchese leaped aside with her, so Kimi and the others could tumble into the sand without landing on her injured arm.

The figure on the beach rolled once and laid still. One figure. There should have been two. Fear leaped into Jane's throat as they raced towards him. Riapoke reached him first and lifted the lad by his shoulders.

Amonsoquath's head lolled back.

The men bent him forward and pounded his chest and shoulders. In moments, he began to gag up sea water.

Praise be to God, he is alive! But where, oh where, is George?

Riapoke wrenched him to his feet, speaking rapid Algonquin. Amonsoquath raised an arm and pointed drunkenly while he responded to the questions. As a group, they followed the direction of his arm, gazing over the choppy surface of the sea. It was starting to calm, but neither George nor the boat were anywhere in sight.

Wanchese interpreted. "George must have spent himself reaching Amonsoquath, because he tied the rope around his friend and let go."

Stunned, Jane continued to scan the water, hoping by some miracle George would surface, even though she knew in her heart he was gone. In her mind's eye, the three ships they'd arrived on rose from the waves in all their grandeur. The Lion, the Roebuck, and the Swallow. The English flag waved in vivid color over the main deck while George and his friends cuffed each other on their shoulders and hung over the rail for a closer look at the grand New World. Then the vision shifted. George's friends disappeared, and he stood alone, gazing solemnly at her.

She pressed the fingertips of her good hand to her

eyelids. It was only a vision, but nay. When she opened her eyes, George was still there. He grinned his wicked grin, as if he was up to another one of his many larks, and raised a hand to his handsome brow in a final salute. The ships receded to a distant speck on the horizon. Then Jane understood. George's heart had always belonged to England. He was finally going home.

"Mistress Jane?" Blade's voice cracked.

Tears streamed down her cheeks. "He is with his father, now, and our Lord."

Blade nodded and ducked his head. "May he rest in peace," he muttered and took a knee.

She knelt beside him in the sand, cradling her arm. Will joined them, and the two lads offered up a final tribute for their departed friend.

Wanchese and his braves stood tall and unmoving while they knelt, giving George's ultimate sacrifice the reverent silence it was due.

Dashing a hand across his eyes, Blade arose first. "Shall we carry you home and attend to that arm, Mistress Jane?"

"Aye." She preferred to walk but saw no point in protesting when Wanchese scooped her up in his arms. It was an argument she would never win, at any rate.

---

*T*he trek back to Dasamonquepeuc was far from a simple task, though the wind abated and the rain dwindled to a light sprinkle. Fallen trees and limbs littered the forest floor. Boulders blocked their path along the base of the rocky ridge, and an avalanche of smaller debris sprawled half in and half out of their bathing spring.

As they walked, Amonsoquath explained the reason for his deadly attempt to return home during the storm.

Wanchese interpreted. "Chief Manteo's braves captured a scout last night from a river village about thirty-five miles north of here. With a little 'encouragement', the scout shared that Askook is amassing a war party."

George had insisted on accompanying Amonsoquath, claiming two rowers stood a better chance of outpacing the storm than one. In the end, the teen had sacrificed his life to ensure the warning was delivered in time for the Roanokes to prepare for the coming attack.

George had died a war hero.

Jane and her comrades rounded the final bend and stopped short at the sight of Dasamonquepeuc, or what was left of it.

Horror gripped her. Only a few posts remained of their palisade entrance. Most lay scattered on the ground. Some were missing altogether. Not one structure in the village was left standing. No lodges, temple, or tents. Even the targets from the firing range were gone. She could only pray their maidens had dismantled and stored the most important items in time.

The landscape was ravaged, as if an enormous beast had torn through its midst. Many of the trees remained bent to their sides from the force of the winds. Some of the top-heavy ones had snapped mid-way down and lay propped on the remaining trunks, forming tall Vs.

After a long summer drought, it was particularly odd to feel the pull of mud on their moccasins. Even the air was soggy, albeit it was warmer and balmier than before the storm. They were fortunate for the briefly warmer temperatures, else those gathered might be catching their death of cold right now in their wet clothing.

Wanchese led the way across the shattered poles of the village palisade. He and Jane stood in the empty village, numb with disbelief. She had expected damage but not complete devastation. It took very little time to search the wooded sections of Dasamonquepeuc. No people came running. Nothing. The breath left her chest. At least, no bodies lay broken and still on the ground.

Please God, let us find them safely in one of the many caves riddling the countryside. Thankfully, the temple graves as well as the pits containing their food stores appeared intact.

Wanchese gathered them in the center of the village. "Kitchi, go examine the cave entrance at the trail of crosses and report everything you see. The rest of us will begin clearing the landslide blocking the closest entrance."

Kitchi bowed, tightened the strap on his quiver, and dashed away.

The caves at Dasamonquepeuc were connected to the same one George had resided in? Egad! That meant the caverns stretched at least five miles from here to the outer reaches of the Roanoke hunting grounds. Jane had never gotten around to exploring them in their entirety. She had been too busy.

She gave Wanchese a pained look, wondering if Askook had taken it upon himself to explore the caves. If he had, the Roanokes may have fled the storm, only to encounter a greater danger.

It would explain how he had evaded their patrols so easily. Was it possible he had secreted himself in the caves and not attempted to outrun their warriors, after all?

CHAPTER 20: PROPOSALS

"*Nawpin!*" Wanchese ordered Amonsoquath who swayed on his feet. He gestured to an enormous felled pine. Then he crooked a finger at Jane. "You, too. Sit."

She resented the command but could come up with no good argument against resting a bit while the others gathered around. It was a relief to perch on the thick log, her arm immobilized at last.

Riapoke remained on vigil, facing outward with his arrow notched while he circled their small group.

Speaking first in the language of the Roanokes and then translating for the sake of his English listeners, Wanchese addressed them. "Since I ordered a retreat to the caves, we shall begin our search there. Riapoke will oversee the removal of the landslide sealing the nearest cave entrance, but first..." He paused and met their gazes one at a time. "Refill your skins with water at the spring and drink. Jane and I will join you there shortly."

She shivered and watched with envy as Riapoke, Amonsoquath, Kimi, Blade, and Will departed. Since the wood strewn about was much too wet for building a fire, the best antidote against the fast dropping temperatures was to keep moving until their garments dried.

She scowled at Wanchese. "You should have insisted Amonsoquath stay and rest a bit longer."

"Huh." He snorted. "He would have refused." She had never before seen his features so tense and haggard. He was feeling the weight of his chiefdom heavily on his shoulders.

"I foresaw the damage of the storm," she whispered. "I knew it would force the hands of our dissenting councilmen to support our upcoming move from Dasamonquepeuc. I did not, however," she added firmly, "foresee the destruction of our people. Not by any means. Not by war, famine, or storm. Nor did Nadie. On the contrary, she envisioned a great many wonderful things in store for us and wanted us to embrace what is to come."

"We've dealt with too much change already," he muttered. "It threatens us and our way of life." He selected one of the palisade poles from the ground and twirled it.

"Change does not discriminate. It pursues us all," she mused. "We must adapt, so it doesn't catch us unaware. Like it did George," she reminded sadly. "He was unable to adapt and settle. It was not simply the storm that swallowed him. He had no roots to hold him here."

"I should have never allowed the lad to go back into the sea." Wanchese balanced the pole on the log and brought his hatchet down in a vicious chop.

"It was his choice to make, his life to give. Nadie often instructed me not to interfere in things that were meant to be."

"You feel his loss no less because of it." Wanchese continued to chop until he held two narrow sticks in his hands. He measured one of them against her arm and set it against the log to chop it down and shorten it some more.

"Nay, of course not." Hot tears prickled behind her eyelids. She blinked hard. "However, I take great comfort in knowing he did not sacrifice his life in vain. Every time I see Amonsoquath, I will remember George's unselfish love for his friend."

Wanchese shrugged out of his damp tunic, baring his blade and slashing several inches from the bottom. Her mouth went dry at the breathtaking sight of her husband without a shirt on.

"I am still trying to decide if *your* actions were brave or foolish." His gaze burned into hers as he placed the wooden slats on either side of her arm to form a splint. "You risked life and limb to save me from the sea."

"Of course I did, you bull-headed warrior," she choked. She stopped speaking, so she didn't break down and weep again. She swallowed hard before she could continue. "I could not help myself. It's always difficult to keep my hands off your brawny self, you know." She bit down on a moan as he wound the end of his severed tunic around her arm to secure the splint.

"You disobeyed me, Jane."

"It was a command you had no right to give. I am your wife. You should have known I would never let you escape me so easily."

He grimaced. "You risked everything I hold dear."

"And all I did was snap a single bone in the process. A small price to pay for your life."

He grunted. "And you call *me* bull-headed." Emotion roughened his voice as he finished tying the splint into place.

She gave him a wry smile.

He bent his head and touched his lips to hers. His arms remained at his side. She tasted tenderness, adoration, and something akin to worship.

"Blast you, Jane!" he groaned, pulling back. "What am I to do with such a stubborn wife?"

"Ugh." She beheld her bandaged arm. She could think of dozens of wonderful things he could do with his stubborn wife. "This is inconvenient with so much work to be done."

"I do not expect it will slow you down overly much," he returned dryly. "This, however, might." He wound a second strip of leather around her neck to form a sling.

"Faith." The radiating pain nearly took away her breath.

"I will tighten the cloth once the swelling goes down."

"Heartless beast." She tapped a foot and willed the throbbing discomfort to subside. "I find no fault with the view, however." His damaged tunic hung open like a vest.

"You'd best not think such thoughts right now, wench. We have work to do." He bent and kissed her again. "Time to rejoin the others. They'll be needing my assistance at the landslide."

"And I will—"

"Nay, you will not." He flicked a finger against the tip of her nose. "You will settle yourself on the nearest boulder to swoon and sigh over the sight of your mate hard at work."

She snorted, though that wasn't the worst idea he'd ever come up with. "I was going to suggest that someone should oversee the operation."

"Oversee to your heart's content." He pressed a hand to the small of her back to nudge her in the direction of the spring. "But you will obey me this time."

"Of all the high-handed, over-bearing..." There was no reason to treat her like a brittle piece of pottery. She was made of sterner stuff.

"*F*ather!" Blade shouted in the distance. "James! William?"

"Mayhap they uncovered the cave entrance already," she breathed to Wanchese.

They arrived at the ridge overlooking the spring. She bit her lip and clutched her injured arm to reduce the jostling as they climbed over debris to reach the lads.

Blade and Will stood atop one side of the rocky pile, digging furiously to dislodge the small and mid-sized stones while Riapoke, Kimi, and Amonsoquath threw their collective strength into moving aside the larger boulders at the bottom.

"Father?" Blade cried again.

A babble of voices sounded from the other side of the pile.

The men paused and straightened, listening.

"'Tis James," Blade informed us in excitement. "They are all inside except...my pa." He whirled. "Get down, Will." The color drained from his face.

His expression waxing frantic, he leaped from the pile and tugged at the rocks below with new fervor. "He refused to enter the cave, though the others begged him incessantly to take shelter from the rain."

"Why?" Jane cried.

"He swore he would never step foot beneath the earth again, preferring instead to take his chances outside."

"Well, burn him for his stubbornness! Where did he go?" she wondered aloud, perplexed at Master Prat's foolhardiness in the face of such a deadly storm.

"Not far enough," Wanchese informed us grimly as a low groan from deep within the pile drew their attention.

"He's alive." Blade shuddered and drew back. "What should we do? If the rocks shift..." His voice trailed away.

Cecil Prat was buried alive, and every move they made risked crushing what was left of him.

She laid an arm on Blade's shoulder. "We will get him out," she assured. They would lose no one else today.

"Aye." Wanchese's voice brooked no arguments. He glared at Jane. "You may take a seat now to oversee our efforts."

"You will take every precaution," she commanded in fierce undertones to her husband. "After everything we have endured in the past twenty-four hours, I will *not* lose you to a rock slide."

"This was no act of nature," he noted in a grim voice. "See the hatchet marks on this boulder?"

He was right. Her heart pounded at the knowledge someone had deliberately caused the rockslide. Askook, most likely. "Someone approaches," she whispered, grabbing his forearm.

In an instant, Wanchese, Riapoke, and Kimi notched their weapons and moved to stand in front of the rest of them.

Kitchi burst into the clearing. He sprinted to Wanchese and bowed before giving his report.

Wanchese nodded and turned to Jane. "The other entrance is also blocked by a pile of boulders. I suspect Askook is behind this."

"By all that is holy!" she exclaimed. "Has he gone completely mad?"

"Aye," Wanchese agreed grimly. "And he will return with an army any moment to finish us off."

Meaning the Roanokes trapped in the cave were targets for a quick and brutal slaughter if they did not succeed in digging them out with haste.

Shaken, she sank to the boulder, frustrated at her inability to offer any material assistance. The men proceeded to unearth Master Prat from a most unlikely arrangement of stones. Two boulders flanked him and one wedged atop, providing a protective cavern, of sorts. Alas, his exposed legs were pinned beneath an oblong slab that canted to one side. One of his feet moved. The other, however...

She drew a sharp intake of breath at the odd angle of his ankle. The men lifted the slab.

"Father!" Blade fell to his knees and pressed his ear to Master Prat's chest. He glanced her way in relief. "He breaths, Mistress Jane. He's alive!"

Unable to remain seated, she rose and crouched next to the injured man.

He groaned and rocked his pasty face from side to side. He must be in agony over his mangled foot.

"It hurts so much, because you're alive," she assured gruffly as he gritted his way through the pain. "That's right. Fight it, sir. We've been through too much to give up now. Riapoke is here, your son is here, and we're going to set that foot to rights in no time."

With Blade's assistance, Riapoke formed a split. The most difficult part, however, was straightening the ankle.

She squeezed Cecil Prat's thin hand while Riapoke set a short stick between his teeth. The poor man reared up in agony and gnashed down when Riapoke twisted the bones back into proper position. Then he slumped in his son's arms, his face a ghastly pallor.

"The m-mines," he shuddered. "I recognized them the moment we fled here last night in the storm."

"Nay, you are mistaken, my good sir. The cave behind us is nothing but a regular ol' cave," Jane soothed. "We are many miles from Copper Mountain. We are safe." *At least until Askook returns.*

"Safe?" He groaned with the effort of sitting up. "Not so long as your village rests within a skip and a hop of Dasan's next mine. We spent days digging samples from mile after mile of those passageways until we finally struck copper."

George's cave. Cecil Prat's initials on the wall. The last pieces of the puzzle fell into place. That was when Cecil Prat and Edward Powell had created the trail of crosses. No wonder Askook had been sent to turn their neighbors against them. Their village and all its inhabitants stood in his way of him staking his claim to another big vein of copper.

He'd tried to create a position of strength within their tribe by marrying Amitola. At Wanchese's refusal of her hand, however, he'd been forced to seek a new way to claim the copper vein and expand his father's empire.

By force.

Wanchese and his braves quickly uncovered the rest of the cave entrance. The liberated villagers poured from the cave on both sides of Jane and Blade as the two of them continued to tend his father beside the spring.

Bly, Dyoni, Chitsa, and Alawa crowded around to exclaim over her splinted arm.

Too delighted at the sight of them to be put out by their fussing, she briefly and soberly recounted the horrific waterspout that claimed George's life.

"If by some magic you might conjure up a fire to dry our garments," she finished. "I will be grateful 'til the end of my days."

Chitsa bowed. "*Bocuttaw,*" she promised and sprang into action. It was the Roanoke word for fire.

Bly, Dyoni, and Alawa hastened to assist her. Bless them, if they did not uncover a few dry branches with which to coax a flame into existence. She signed for them to move Master Prat closer to the fire. Then she sidled over to Amonsoquath in the hopes of wheedling him nearer the fire, as well. To her relief, he complied without resistance when she beckoned.

Wanchese called a council meeting. They assembled themselves around a second fire. Jane shared Cecil Prat's revelation about the discovery of the copper vein. It was the final encouragement their dissenting councilmen needed in order to change their vote. This time, all were in favor of their immediate departure from Dasamonquepeuc.

They also voted to dispatch a canoe of armed scouts to notify Chief Manteo of the escalating danger, then hunkered closer to plan the details of their move. Jane was hopeful Manteo and his faithful Croatoans would consider joining them on their journey inland.

Christopher Cooper, who had been trapped with the Roanokes, filled two skins of water at the spring. "May I hop a ride to Croatoa, chief?" he called jovially.

Wanchese nodded his approval.

Christopher circled behind their group and squatted next to Jane. "We should join forces," he rasped in a voice barely above a whisper. "Both the Roanokes and the English have cities to build before winter sets in. Methinks, you might have the power to influence such a decision. Use that power wisely, my friend." His ice-blue eyes bored into hers, but he slipped away before she could respond. She stared thoughtfully after him. The idea held merit, though she did not expect it to be well received by her husband or the council.

Shaking her head, she returned her attention to the meeting. They decided to gather their people and belongings at Dasamonquepeuc to best oversee the packing and loading of their precious food stores. They also determined with a vote of six to one to leave their past leaders entombed in the ground for now. Understandably, Noshi was the sole dissident.

As much as Jane sympathized with his grieving, no other course made sense. They might be at war soon. Moving the dead would slow their migration and prevent them from carrying other items far more pertinent to their collective survival.

The biggest question was where to relocate their tribe. With winter fast approaching, they did not have time to travel far. Fortunately, their needs were simple. They needed a more defensible location, one located near a major waterway with room to farm and hunt.

The first suggestion came from Noshi. He favored moving to the Island of Croatoa to spend the winter with Manteo's people and find a more permanent home come spring. The council quickly voted him down, too fearful of bringing their war to the Croatoans' borders.

Riapoke introduced the possibility of taking a northerly route into the Chesapeake Bay area. His biggest concern were the indigenous tribes located along the way. Many were allies, but there was no sure way of determining which ones Askook and his cronies might have poisoned against them in recent weeks.

Jane pursed her lips. The longer their meeting ran, the more merit she found in Christopher's offer. Drat the man for putting her in this position, but it would be a dreadful disservice to them all if she failed to present his offer to the council. On the other hand, she could lose her scalp for suggesting something as scandalous as joining forces with the pale faces.

Wanchese sat beside her, legs crossed, both leading the meeting and interpreting what was said for her benefit. "Damisac the Wise, Achak the Medicine Man would hear your thoughts on the matter."

Achak fastened his cold, rat-like gaze on her.

Faith, the man was unnerving. She resisted the urge to fidget.

In for a penny. The time to present a new plan was now or never. "Just a few minutes ago, Reverend Cooper offered to combine forces with us and travel together to the mainland. The English and their Croatoan scouts are moving fifty miles inland where the Roanoke and Chowan Rivers converge."

Shock registered in the lined features of the elders. Chief Wanchese bent his head to confer with them.

Achak gave a sharp response, which Wanchese interpreted as, "the river delta lies along the direct path the Copper Mountain warriors will travel to attack Dasamonquepeuc."

"True," she rejoined. "However, we will not be able to avoid their attack unless we leave the region altogether. Yesterday, you were in favor of remaining at Dasamonquepeuc and preparing for battle. Why not prepare for it from a more defensible location?" She paused a moment for Wanchese to interpret.

"The river delta will place us where three major waterways converge. It increases our maneuvering options and makes it virtually impossible to trap us. It will also force our enemies to sail past an English fort with mounted canons."

A flurry of conversation ensued. Noshi requested Jane to explain the design and capabilities of the English canons in detail.

Interest in Christopher's plan lit and caught fire. In short order, the council cast a vote to set sail for the river delta. This time Achak was the only dissenting vote. A second team of scouts was sent to Croatoa to inform them of the Roanoke's newest decision, along with their desire to depart at once.

The councilmen bowed first to their chief and then to Jane before taking their leave to begin organizing their respective families. "*Werowansqua*," Noshi said with deep reverence. He inclined his head for several moments.

Awed, she bowed to him in return. When he ambled away, she leaned to Wanchese and whispered, "Please explain why Noshi just bowed and called me his queen."

"The council regards you as such, *Damisac* the Wise. Second only to your chief."

"How is that possible?" she sputtered. "We have not yet joined hands in marriage in the manner of the Roanokes."

"A mere formality. You have already secured their allegiance through wisdom, courage, and the occasional foolhardy risks you take to protect your chief and the rest of your people."

"Oh, Wanchese!" *From huntress to slave, slave to concubine, concubine to Wise Woman, and Wise Woman to queen.* Jane found her rapid ascension to a position of such enormous honor and responsibility unnerving. How could she ever hope to live up to so many expectations? Sooner or later, she was bound to disappoint. She rubbed the bridge of her nose and tried to pretend the ache in her arm was not so unbearable.

Wanchese leaned over to nuzzle her check. "Do not look so alarmed. Whenever your role as queen becomes too oppressive, I promise to toss you on my bedroll and use you as my concubine for the night."

She shouted out a laugh, muffled in part by the hand she clapped over her mouth. "I've no doubt you will stick as close as a cocklebur on my backside." Ah, how she loved the man! He knew just what to say to restore her spirits and distract her from her pain.

A sharp pinch on the aforementioned spot made her jump. She tried to come up with a scowling reprimand, but Wanchese was quicker. He bent his head and claimed her lips in a tender kiss. "Back to work, wench," he ordered huskily. "The maidens await your orders."

Suddenly invigorated, she found the strength to rise. Wanchese rejoined Riapoke who was directing a group to empty the cave of everything stashed there during the storm.

Seeking out Chitsa, Jane instructed the maidens to begin carting their belongings back to Dasamonquepeuc.

The women loaded their arms with rolls of reed mats, furs, coils of hemp cord, fishnets, and enormous baskets of bowls, spoons, and other accoutrements. The braves gathered quivers, bows, knives, and spears. Items such as the wooden targets from the shooting range would be left behind. They could be rebuilt.

The maidens protested with vigor when Jane attempted to help.

"Tah," Bly snapped in disgust and wrestled the basket from her that she'd slid over her good arm. Thus, she walked empty-handed beside them back to Dasamonquepeuc, surrounded by a team of armed braves.

She bade the maidens stack the supplies in neat rows. Then she set them to the arduous task of digging up and packing their precious food stores. The shadows of evening crept over them as they worked. But, again, her resourceful maidens managed to build a pair of bonfires large enough to finish drying their damp garments. How good it felt to be warm again. Alas, the heat made her injured arm throb and tingle more than the cold air had.

Basic tents were erected for the night and bedrolls laid out. Riapoke organized a perimeter of security. Wanchese called for another council meeting to convene at dawn to finalize the plans for their journey inland.

The tent Bly and Dyoni prepared for their chief and Wise Woman was luxurious compared to the others dotting the landscape. A coat of sand covered the damp earth and was nearly dry from the heat of an inviting fire in the center of it. A pair of reed mats rested on the sand and were piled with layers of furs. Ah, but there were benefits to the life of a nomad. How easy it was to set up camp and indulge in the comforts of home.

They sipped hot tea from stone bowls. Jane had to wonder what sly Chitsa had slipped into her bowl, when the pain in her arm lessened considerably as she drank.

Wanchese shrugged off his ravaged tunic, and the heat in the tent spiked dramatically.

Jane set her bowl down to revel in the sight of him. Powerfully built and radiating a reckless sort of energy, he was truly the most glorious creature she'd ever beheld. And he belonged to her.

He tossed the tunic to the edge of the tent and turned to her with purpose.

Though her sling posed a great inconvenience, all she could think of was how badly she wanted Wanchese to take her in his arms.

He stretched himself out on the mat next to hers. In one swift movement, he rolled in her direction. "You must be exhausted."

She arched a brow at him. "And if I am not?"

He traced lazy circles on her knee. "Then we will rest later." He lowered her to the furs, careful not to jostle her injured arm. "Maybe this will help with the pain."

He was right. She completely forgot the pain in her arm. In fact, she found she could not form a single, blessed thought past the silken glide of his lips. She gave up and let him spin a web of magic around her. Afterwards, she was too weak to open her eyes.

"Sleep," he commanded, and she did.

---

*I*t was not the glow of sunrise that awakened her, although their tent flap was pinned open. Rather it was the sound of many voices calling back and forth in excitement.

Jane propped herself up on her good elbow and squinted through the doorway.

"Come, Jane." Wanchese ducked inside the tent flap and held out a hand. "I have something to show you."

Children ran to the nearest ridge, tossing small sticks and handfuls of leaves. Maidens and braves clustered at the top, pointing and chattering. Mystified, she allowed Wanchese to lead her towards whatever it was that had so thoroughly captured the interest of their people.

The morning air was crisp but clear. The scent of seawater wafted over them as they ascended the hill. Waves lapped at the beach below.

Though the sand was littered with debris from the storm, the sound waters winked at them, gold-peaked and crystalline beneath the morning sun. They formed a stunning backdrop for the army of canoes paddling in their direction.

"Wanchese!" She grasped his hand. "Are we under attack?"

"Look again, my queen."

She did and was able to breathe again. It was no war party but the City of Raleigh colonists accompanied by the Croatoans. Thirty or more boats drifted their way. As they drew closer, she could pick out the figures of Anthony in his black top hat and Agnes with her white gold hair, Eleanor and Ananias Dare, the pinch-faced Margaret, Emme and her giant beau, Mark, and oh my! The Croatoan chief himself.

He was not alone. Manteo and his bride, Rose, rode in the furthermost canoe. Her glorious red tresses waved over her shoulders like swirls of fire.

Her dearest friends in the world had arrived.

They were accompanied by at least a hundred of Manteo's people. Nay, more. Jane counted nigh on a hundred and fifty figures. *Egad. Was his entire village present?* Behind their boats drifted dozens of supply rafts.

The first canoes scraped to shore. Their occupants disembarked and gathered on the beach to await the next arrivals.

"What are we waiting for?" Jane cried, tugging at her husband's hand.

Wanchese led her down the hill and around the ridge, just as their guests began moving up the beach path.

Chief Manteo and Rose were flanked by a stern group of councilmen. At the sight of Jane, though, Rose broke their ranks and ran to her.

"Jane!" she called joyfully. Her green eyes widened in concern when they rested on her sling. "You are hurt."

She waved a hand in dismissal. "'Tis little more than a scratch."

She sniffed. "I've seen much smaller scratches."

They beamed at each other.

She was spectacular in a soft deerskin dress richly adorned with beads. An eagle pendant of beaten copper glinted at her throat.

"Royalty agrees with you, princess." Jane nodded at her. Like herself, she'd originated from the dredges of working class London. On the ship ride to the New World, she had served as their clerk. Despite years of working a man's job, she remained the picture of soft-spoken femininity with a wee bit of Scotland clinging to her accent.

"Ah, so you've heard about my marriage." She gave a breathless titter. "Da would be so proud. He sent me off to London, if you recall, to change my stars."

"Maybe you will get the opportunity to tell him yet." *Someday.* Heaven only knew when the next English supply ships would arrive and if they would be able to locate the colonists after their move inland.

"'Tis so good to see you, my friend." She offered a misty smile. "I know you prefer a solid handshake, but pray indulge me this once." She stood on tiptoe to kiss Jane's cheeks. "I regret how long it took to pay you a visit. I begged Manteo for an entire month to bring me here, but he insisted we wait until the sickness passed."

"You have been ill?" Her voice grew sharp. Rose looked well enough to her, albeit a bit pale around the edges. Still too thin, though.

"Oh, not that kind of sick." She chuckled. "I am with child."

While Jane reeled beneath that piece of news, Agnes and Anthony's boat scraped ashore. She ran towards her friends, shrieking with delight. She noted Jane's arm just in time before flinging herself into their embrace.

"What happened to you?" she demanded, bending instead to examine the splint with care.

"'Tis a long story." One filled with both joy and tragedy. Right now Jane wanted to celebrate their arrival. She would recount the details leading up to her injury later.

Fortunately, Rose changed the subject.

"What is it like living with Chief Wanchese?" she inquired anxiously. "I questioned Manteo at length on the wisdom of sending him, of all people, to your rescue."

"If that beast has harmed you in any way…" Agnes' voice dwindled as Wanchese approached with Riapoke and Amonsoquath striding behind him.

Clearly Christopher has not yet shared the news of our English nuptials.

Jane's heart swelled with pride as Wanchese's gaze caught and held hers. It was still hard to believe this magnificent warrior belonged to her. "Rose and Agnes, meet my husband."

Agnes gasped. "Please tell me you jest," she begged in a whisper.

"Nay, she does not," Rose declared in wonder, gazing between the two of them. "Methinks our feisty Jane has at last found a man who inspires something other than her normal level of disdain."

Jane chuckled as she finished making the introductions. Wanchese stared a bit longer than was considered polite by English standards at her two friends, but she forgave the blunder. Both were ravishing beauties.

"*Kenah*, Sunfire. *Kenah*, Agnes," he greeted them.

Sunfire? How fitting for Rose! Jane grinned as Rose clasped her hands and bowed before her husband. *Ah, she is familiar with our protocol.* Agnes dipped in an English curtsy.

Jane stretched her uninjured arm to Riapoke and Amonsoquath." May I present Riapoke, my husband's head of council and elder brother, and Amonsoquath, his nephew." Her words elicited another rounds of bows and curtsies.

"Our joint council meeting commences soon," Wanchese informed her. He tipped up her chin and kissed her thoroughly in front of her friends.

"Faith, what a handsome trio!" Agnes sighed as the men departed. "What happened to his poor brother's face?"

"A fight with a bear."

"At least he won." Agnes stared after him, admiration shining in her eyes. "I've heard about him. He's something of a legend among the Croatoans."

"Speaking of romantic figures." Jane winked. "Has Lord Anthony Cage gotten around to declaring himself yet?"

Agnes's smile faded. "Nay," she said shortly but did not elaborate.

"More the fool he." Jane took the opportunity to glower in his direction, not caring what he thought. In return, he tipped his hat and bestowed a jovial smile on their trio. She wanted to ask more, but Wanchese turned and strode back to retrieve her with one large hand splayed between her shoulder blades.

"It is time." He nudged her to the clearing where their joint council meeting was forming.

Rose hurried to join her husband, a fiery splash of color in the midst of their stoic line of councilmen. Christopher Cooper, Anthony Cage, and the Dares represented the City of Raleigh colonists.

Their meeting began with a series of formal greetings. A few minutes later, their two tribes and one English colony voted to travel together fifty miles into the mainland and settle at the Chowan and Roanoke river delta.

Exhilaration filled Jane. The recent storm might have leveled their village, but they stood nigh on three hundred people strong now. There were few tribes in the region who could command such numbers.

The council dismissed, and the Roanokes wasted no time in disassembling tents and securing their supplies. They planned to travel by canoe with the supply rafts in tow. An advance party of scouts would press through the forests and alert the rest of them of any pending dangers. Teams of warriors would accompany and guard the sailing fleet. Other teams of warriors would follow on land in the wake of the scouts.

There would be no surprises this time. No ambushes they weren't capable of swiftly crushing.

They had a difficult journey ahead and three cities to build before the icy blanket of winter settled on them. But they would stand shoulder to shoulder, three powerful allies in a strategic river delta, and brace themselves for the hordes that would soon descend from Copper Mountain.

Wanchese and Jane returned to the ridge overlooking the beach, while the Roanoke maidens and braves loaded the last of the canoes in their convoy.

"Our enemies will pursue us," she mused.

"And we will be ready." He bent and touched his lips to hers, sealing the promise.

A cry of eagles sounded as the Croatoan braves launched their first boats into the sounds. Wanchese's mahogany eyes glinted with anticipation. "That is our signal."

Her heartbeat quickened. She offered him a tremulous smile. "Into the mainland we go."

<<< THE END >>>

KEEP TURNING FOR AN EXCERPT FROM
INTO THE MAINLAND,
BOOK THREE IN THE LOST COLONY SERIES.

SNEAK PREVIEW: INTO THE MAINLAND

EXCERPT FROM CHAPTER ONE

January 15, 1587 - Worcestershire

*A*gnes gazed out the window of her departing carriage, already homesick, and not at all convinced a season in London was the best way to celebrate her eighteenth name day. Having been raised in the country, she knew nothing about the ways of the ton — not the latest fashions or dance steps or gossip — but her mother refused to listen to her pleas to remain in Worcestershire. Where her life had purpose as Agnes Wood, apothecary-in-training to a fast growing parish congregation. Where she was needed.

Her mother's only sister was childless and begging for company, and she could think of no better solution than to deliver up a dose of Agnes's youthful companionship. *Her words. Not mine. Faith! Why can't Mother pay a visit to her own sister and be done with it?*

The esteemed Lady Hester Ravenspire, was fetching Agnes in a private carriage to save her the discomfort of public transportation. As much as she appreciated her aunt's kindness, the gesture didn't generate the least bit of excitement about being tossed into the frivolity of city living on such short notice.

Mother positioned her tiny self atop the knoll beside the parsonage, no doubt for the better view, as Agnes rolled away. She waved to her daughter, the glossy strands in her white-blonde hair gleaming in the morning sun. Neither age nor her somber navy morning gown could mute her porcelain beauty. Her stance was regal enough to grace the Court and her mannerisms a dead giveaway of her highborn heritage.

And now she was sending her only child back to everything she'd willingly left behind. To the parties and the balls she claimed were wearisome and the politics she hated. She'd not smiled once since she'd made the decision a week earlier. Agnes's insides prickled with foreboding, though she could come up with no tangible reason for her concerns.

Mother was desperately in love with Father, and they'd been a happy family of three as long as Agnes could remember. They'd endured their share of lean years, true, but this was not one of them. A new flood of church goers from around the countryside had begun flocking to Father's sermons. They adored the way Abbott Wood served the poor and nobility alike, trading in his priestly garments for more simple apparel when he visited the humbler sections of town. And they often lingered long enough to purchase the poultices and herbal potions she and Mother spent so many hours preparing during the week days.

Why send her away so abruptly when things were going so well? It made little sense.

She returned her mother's wave, never dreaming it would be the last time she would see her.

INTO THE MAINLAND
Book THREE in the Lost Colony Series
Available now in e-book and paperback

Early November, 1866

*E*lizabeth Byrd rubbed icy hands up and down her arms beneath her threadbare navy wool cloak as she gingerly hopped down from the stagecoach. It was so much colder in Montana than it had been in South Carolina. She gazed around her at the hard-packed earthen streets, scored by the ruts of many wagon wheels. They probably would have been soft and muddy if it weren't for the brisk winds swirling above them. Instead, they were stiff with cold and covered in a layer of frost that glinted like rosy crystals beneath the setting sun.

Plain, saltbox buildings of weathered gray planks hovered over the streets like watchful sentinels, as faded and tattered as the handful of citizens scurrying past — women in faded gingham dresses and bonnets along with a half-dozen or so men in work clothes and dusty top hats. More than likely, they were in a hurry to get home, since it was fast approaching the dinner hour. Her stomach rumbled out a contentious reminder at how long it had been since her own last meal.

So this was Angel Creek.

At least I'll fit in. She glanced ruefully down at her workaday brown dress and the scuffed toes of her boots. Perhaps, wearing the castoffs of her former maid, Lucy, wasn't the most brilliant idea she'd ever come up with. However, it was the only plan she'd been able to conjure up on such short notice. A young woman traveling alone couldn't be too careful these days. For her own safety, she'd wanted to attract as little attention as possible during her long journey west. It had worked. Few folks had given her more than a cursory glance the entire trip, leaving her plenty of time to silently berate herself for accepting the challenge of her dear friend, Caroline, to change her stars by becoming a mail-order bride like a few of their friends had done the year before.

"Thanks to the war, there's nothing left for us here in Charleston, love. You know it, and I know it," Caroline had chided gently. Then she'd leaned in to embrace her tenderly.

"I know you miss him. We all do." She was referring to Elizabeth's fiancé who'd perished in battle. "But he would want you to go on and keep living. That means dusting off your broken heart and finding a man to marry while you're still young enough to have a family of your own."

She and her friends were in their early twenties, practically rusticating on the shelf in the eyes of those who'd once comprised the social elite in Charleston. They were confirmed spinsters now, yesterday's news, has-beens...

"However, there are still scads of marriageable men lined up and waiting for us in Angel Creek." They'd discovered this marvelous fact by an ad placed in The Groom's Gazette. "Every one of our friends who traveled there last year are happily married and very anxious for us to join them. All you have to do is pack your things and get on the train with us."

And leave behind everyone and everything I've ever known. Elizabeth shivered, pulled her cloak more tightly around her, and attempted to duck her chin farther down inside the collar, wondering if she'd just made the biggest mistake of her life. She was in Angel Creek days later than most of her friends had agreed on, having wrestled like the dickens with her better judgment to make up her mind to join them.

There were six of them this year — Caroline, Melody, Emma, Viola, Ginger and herself. All were former debutantes from Charleston, just like the five brides who'd begun this outlandish venture the previous Christmas. All were from impoverished families whose properties and bank accounts had been devastated by the war. It was the only reason she'd been willing to even consider such a foolish idea. She was fast running out of options. Her widowed mother was barely keeping food on the table for her three younger sisters.

Even so, it had been a last-minute decision, one she'd made too late to begin any correspondence with her intended groom. She didn't even know the man's name, only that he would be waiting for her in Angel Creek when her stagecoach rolled into town. Or so Caroline had promised. Her friend had arrived days ago and was likely already married now.

With a sigh of resignation, Elizabeth reached down to grasp the handles of her two travel bags that the stage driver had unloaded for her. The rest of her belongings would arrive in the coming days. There'd been too many trunks to bring along by stage. In the meantime, she hoped and prayed she was doing the right thing for her loved ones. At worst, her reluctant decision to leave home meant one less mouth for her mama to feed. At best, she might claw her way back to some modicum of social significance and be in the position to help her family in some way. Some day...

Her hopes in that regard plummeted the second she laid eyes on the two men in the wagon rumbling in her direction. It was a rickety vehicle with no overhead covering. It creaked and groaned with each turn of its wheels, a problem that might have easily been solved with a squirt of oil. Then again, the heavily patched trousers of both men indicated they were as poor as church mice. More than likely, they didn't possess any extra coin for oil.

Of all the rotten luck! She bit her lower lip. *I'm about to marry a man as poor as myself.* So much for her hopes of improving her lot in life enough to send money home to Mama and the girls!

The driver slowed his team, a pair of red-brown geldings. They were much lovelier than the rattle-trap they were pulling. "Elizabeth Byrd, I presume?" he inquired in a rich baritone that was neither unpleasant nor overly warm and welcoming.

Her insides froze to a block of ice. This time, it wasn't because of the frigid northern temperatures. She recognized that face, that voice; and with them, came a flood of heart wrenching emotions.

"You!" she exclaimed. Her travel bags slid from her nerveless fingers to the ground once more. A hand flew to her heart, as she relived the sickening dread all over again that she'd experienced at the Battle of James Island. She was the unlucky nurse who'd delivered the message to Captain David Pemberton that his wife had passed during childbirth. The babe hadn't survived, either. But what, in heaven's name, was the tragic officer doing so far from home? Unless she was mistaken, his family was from the Ft. Sumpter area.

"Nurse Byrd." The captain handed his reins to the man sitting next to him, a grizzled older fellow who was dressed in a well-pressed brown suit, though both knees bore patches. "We meet again." He offered her a two-fingered salute and reached for her travel bags. He was even more handsome than she remembered, despite the well-worn Stetson shading his piercing bourbon eyes. During their last encounter, he'd been clean shaven. His light brown sideburns now traveled down to a shortly clipped beard. If the offbeat rhythm of her heart was any indication, he wore the more rugged look rather nicely.

Which was neither here nor there. Elizabeth gave herself a mental shake. She'd been searching for a sign, anything that would shed light on whether she was doing the right thing by coming to Angel Creek. Encountering this man, of all people, only a handful of minutes after her arrival, seemed a pretty clear indication of just how horrible a mistake she'd made.

She nudged the handles of her bags with the toe of her boot to put them out of reach. "Y-you don't have to go through with this, captain. I can only imagine how difficult it is for you to lay eyes on me again." If it was anything close to how difficult it was for her to lay eyes on him, it would behoove them both to take off running in opposite directions. "I am quite happy to board with one of my friends until I can secure passage back to South Carolina." The whole trip had been a horrible miscalculation of judgment. She could see that now as she stared stonily into the face of the officer who'd led the man to whom she was once affianced into the battle that had claimed his life. Captain Pemberton didn't know that wretched fact, of course. How could he? They were neither personally, nor closely, acquainted at the time.

The expression in his eyes softened a few degrees as he regarded her. "I gather you found the young man you were searching for during the war?" he noted quietly. "Otherwise, you would not be here."

Preparing to marry you, you mean! "I found him, yes." Her voice was tight with cold and misery. It was all she could do to keep her teeth from chattering. "I found him and buried him."

"Ah." He nodded sadly. "Words are never adequate in situations like these. Nevertheless, I am deeply sorry for your loss."

His regret appeared genuine. She sensed he was a kind man, a good man, despite the deplorable circumstances under which they'd made their first acquaintance. *More's the pity!* Though she couldn't exactly hold the captain responsible for the Union bullet that had taken her Charley's life, she couldn't just up and marry the man responsible for leading him into harm's way, either. Could she?

Perhaps it was the cold breeze numbing her brain, but suddenly she was no longer certain about a good number of things.

"Come, Elizabeth." The commanding note in David Pemberton's voice brooked no further arguments. "You must be famished after such a long journey, and you'll catch your death out here if we linger in the cold."

This time, Elizabeth's toes were too icy to function when he reached for her travel bags. She stood there shivering while he tossed them inside his wagon. She was both shocked and grateful when he proceeded to unbutton his overcoat and slide it around her shoulders.

It was toasty warm from his body heat and smelled woodsy and masculine. "I th-thank y-you." She was no longer able to hide how badly her teeth were chattering.

"Think nothing of it, Miss Byrd." He slid a protective arm around her shoulders and guided her on down the street. "A friendly fellow named Elijah owns a restaurant next door. Since our wedding isn't for another two hours, how about we head over there for a spell? We can grab a bite to eat and thaw out at the same time."

Our wedding? Her lips parted in protest, but she was shivering too hard to form any words.

As if sensing her confusion, he smiled and leaned closer to speak directly in her ear. His breath warmed her chilly lobe and sent a shot of...something...straight down to her toes. "Surely an angel of mercy like yourself can spare the time to swap a few war stories with an old soldier?"

She clamped her teeth together. *An angel of mercy, indeed!* She'd felt more like an angel of death back there on the battlefield. There were days she lost more soldiers than the ones she managed to save. It was something she preferred never to think of again, much less discuss.

"If I cannot make you smile at least once in the next two hours, I'll purchase your passage back to South Carolina, myself," he teased, tightening his arm around her shoulders.

Now *that* was an offer she couldn't afford to pass up. She didn't currently possess the coin for a return trip, though she had to wonder if the shabbily dressed captain was any better for the funds, himself.

She gave him a tight-lipped nod and allowed him to lead her inside The Eatery.

The tantalizing aromas of fresh-baked bread, hot cider, and some other delectable entrée assailed them, making her mouth water. A pine tree graced one corner of the dining area. Its bows were weighed down with festive gingerbread ornaments and countless strands of red ribbon. A man in a white apron, whom she could only presume was Captain Pemberton's friend, Elijah, cut between a line of tables and hurried in their direction, arms outstretched. "You rebel you! Someone might have at least warned me you were one of the lucky fellers gittin' himself a new wife."

"Oh-h!" Elizabeth's voice came out as a warble of alarm as, from the corner of her eye, she watched a young serving woman heading their way from the opposite direction. She was bearing a tray with a tall cake and holding it in such a manner that she couldn't see over the top of it. She was very much at risk of running in to someone or something.

David Pemberton glanced down at her concern, but all she could do was wave her hand in the direction of the calamity about to take place.

His gaze swiftly followed where she pointed, just in time to watch the unfortunate server and her cake collide with Elijah. White icing and peach preserves flew everywhere. His hair and one side of his face were plastered with a layer of sticky whiteness.

The woman gave a strangled shriek and slid to her knees. A puppy dashed out of nowhere and began to lick the remains of the gooey fluff from her fingers.

Afterwards, Elizabeth would blame it on the long journey for frazzling her nerves to such an extent; because, otherwise, there was no excuse on heaven or earth for what she did next.

She laughed — hysterically! It was ill-mannered of her,

unladylike to the extreme, and completely uncalled for, but she couldn't help it. She laughed until there were tears in her eyes.

Captain Pemberton grinned in unholy glee at her. There was such a delicious glint in his whiskey eyes that it made her knees tremble.

"A deal's a deal, nurse; and the way I see it, you did more than smile. You laughed, which means I'll not be needing to purchase that trip back to South Carolina for you, after all. Unless you've any further objections, we've a little less than two hours before we say our vows." He arched one dark brow at her in challenge.

Their gazes clashed, and the world beneath her shifted. As a woman of her word, she suddenly couldn't come up with any more reasons — not a blessed one — why they couldn't or shouldn't get married.

Tonight!

I hope you enjoyed this excerpt from
ANGEL CREEK CHRISTMAS BRIDES:
Elizabeth
This story is available in ebook, paperback, and Kindle Unlimited on Amazon!

Much love,
Jo

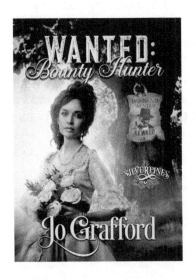

November, 1900 — Silverpines, Oregon

*R*achel West shivered as she stepped onto the train
platform. It wasn't the chill of the late autumn
breeze so much as the feeling of stepping on ghosts that
shook her up on the inside. For a moment, she fought the

urge to spin around in her designer boots, sprint back to her private cabin on the train, and keep on riding.

She'd been away for eight long years from the one town in the world that felt like home. Or should have…

Squinting against the glare of the morning sun, she turned in a full circle, trying to find one familiar structure or one familiar face from her treasure trove of memories.

And utterly failed.

A spurt of panic gurgled through her mid-section at the sight of the new-looking cafe facing her. A freshly painted butcher's storefront rested to the left of it, and a post office was located just across a side street from it. They had to be new, because the paint was so bright and un-peeling, and none of their roofs boasted the usual slight ripple of unevenness that so many buildings take on once they've had the chance to settle.

Her head swiveled. There was also a book store she didn't remember standing next to the post office. It was an inviting little building with a big, cheery picture window crowded with books. Normally, she would have tossed all her earthly cares to the winds and made a beeline for the cozy nook for book lovers, but she was too busy pondering the notion that she might have made a horrible mistake at disembarking.

Why, even the depot building squatting behind her looked new! Had she misunderstood the announcement and gotten off at the wrong stop altogether?

"Rachel? Is it really you?"

She jolted at the soft, lilting alto wafting across the train platform. Nothing around her looked familiar, but she'd recognize that voice anywhere.

"Penelope Wallace!" she cried joyfully, whirling to face her childhood friend. She was in the right town after all, even if it didn't look right.

"It's Cooper now. Penelope Cooper."

They threw themselves in each other's arms with squeals of sheer delight, and Rachel experienced a pang of remorse at the knowledge it had been more than two years since they'd last exchanged letters, maybe three. Good heavens, how the time had flown!

To avoid making any awkward excuses for her lack of correspondence, Rachel fell back on her good manners and well of natural charm. "Eight years hasn't changed you one bit. You don't look a day older than sixteen." The moment the words sailed from her mouth, she regretted them; because it was painfully clear that Penelope had indeed changed.

She still looked young and girlish, but the sparkle that had always lurked in her wide, innocent eyes — despite how hard her temperamental, overly controlling mama had tried to extinguish it — was entirely gone. In its place was bone-weariness and the bruising shadows born of hard times. A recent tragedy, if Rachel were to venture a guess. They were the same kind of shadows she witnessed in her own eyes every time she stood in front of a mirror.

"How is your mother?" she asked hastily, bracing herself for the worst kind of news.

Penelope made a snorting sound, and her pink petal lips quirked up at the corners. "Still as sour as vinegar and prickly as a cactus."

Rachel laughed and tasted the sweet tang of relief on her tongue. "Some people never change, I suppose." Though way too many people did, in fact, do exactly that.

Such as her own parents who'd died in a carriage accident the next town over, and her great-aunt who'd swept into Silverpines on her sixteen birthday and whisked her back to the East Coast to finish raising her…who was also now gone, and her husband who had cherished and adored her for two whole months before succumbing to a fever and left her widowed and childless at the age of twenty-four…

With an inward shake, Rachel forced her agonizing memories back to the darker recesses of her mind and tried to focus on what her friend was saying.

"Yes, indeed. Mama still carries a grudge against the world the size of California for all the things she's suffered." Her voice dropped to nearly a whisper. "Though the good Lord knows we've *all* suffered this past year." Her pallor turned a sickly gray to match the plain, wool gown she was wearing.

Rachel reached for her friend's hands and squeezed them. "I'm so sorry. I heard about the earthquakes. It's one of the reasons I came back." She'd daydreamed for months about returning to Silverpines to help with the rebuilding, imagining she could put to good use her inheritance, teaching credentials, and experience working at one of the poshest finishing schools in Boston.

Penelope's fingers tightened on hers. "Oh, dear! Is that all you heard? The quakes were merely the beginning of our troubles." She drew a shaky breath before plunging on. "The mines collapsed, and the mud slides claimed most of our menfolk, my husband included. Then there was the big fire last April that wiped out a sizable section of town. We're rebuilding as fast as we can, but those things take time and money and lots of hard work." She sighed and nodded across the street to take in the new cafe, post office, and book store.

So they *were* all new buildings. "I'm so sorry about your husband," she said quickly, feeling guilty all over again about their lack of recent correspondence. It looked as if she'd missed her friend's engagement, wedding, and the funeral that had followed.

Penelope nodded and ducked her head, blinking rapidly. "I married Cliff Cooper, God rest his soul."

"I'm so sorry," Rachel said again, amazed to discover any woman had wanted to marry the heartless, uncouth prankster she remembered Cliff to be from their school days. "I, ah…" It was painful to speak of it, but Penelope deserved no less than her utmost honesty now that she was moving back to town. "I lost my husband, too. Matthew West." She swallowed hard. It would be so easy to lean forward a few more inches to sob her heartache against her friend's shoulder, but Penelope had suffered enough. They both had. Tears wouldn't bring either of their husbands back. "It was a fever that took him from this world."

Her friend blinked hard as if trying to keep the moisture in her eyes at bay. "Both of us married since the last time we wrote, and now we're widows," she mused softly. A sad smile tugged at her lips as if she found comfort in sharing her pain with a fellow sufferer. "Dare I ask what brings you to Silverpines, of all places?"

"Memories, I suppose." Rachel wasn't quite sure how to put her feelings into words. "When my great aunt passed, there was suddenly no reason whatsoever for me to remain in Boston. So I decided to come home."

Home. The word came out on a bittersweet note. The truth was Rachel didn't really belong anywhere anymore. She'd been uprooted from Silverpines at the age of sixteen and transplanted into a much bigger city back East, but she'd never fully fit in. As her Great Aunt Gertie liked to say with great asperity, *you can take the girl out of the country, but you can't take the country out of the girl.* Alas, no amount of dancing lessons and social graces had been able to transform her niece into a true society girl.

"Home?" Penelope's voice rose in excitement. "Do you mean you're here to stay?" She glanced around Rachel's shoulder, and her eyes widened at the growing pile of luggage on the platform. "Dear me! It appears you've brought half of Boston with you."

Rachel shrugged and admitted sheepishly, "That is only

my autumn wardrobe. My furniture and other belongings will arrive in a few more days."

"Other belongings!" Penelope looked astounded. "Where in tarnation do you expect to put all that? It'll never fit at the hotel, and I can't think of a boarding house big enough to hold it, either." She withdrew her hands from her friend's and fisted them on her hips. A frown wrinkled her brow. "I could maybe talk to a few friends about finding you a place to store some of it until you can come up with a more permanent solution."

Wondering if this was the part where she should confide the news about her vast inheritance to her friend, Rachel opened her black silk reticule and withdrew a few bills. "Here." She handed the money to the two workmen waiting patiently by her mound of luggage. "Pray deliver my things to the Silverpines Inn. I have a reservation." She also had an appointment this morning with the town banker, Joel Richards, to discuss the purchase of a vacant old mansion on the northern edge of town. If things went the way she hoped, she'd be holding the keys to the future Silverpines Finishing School for Young Ladies before nightfall.

Noting the generous denominations on the bills Rachel handed the workmen, Penelope turned suspicious eyes on her. "Exactly how much furniture are we talking about?"

For a split second, Rachel glimpsed a sliver of Widow Wallace's busybody ways in her daughter. She sighed, forcing the horrible thought away. No. Penelope was nothing like her gossipy mother. She was simply curious; and if they were going to be friends again, they needed to be completely honest with each other.

"Aunt Gertie's things were too lovely to part with, so I had them shipped here." To be precise, they were being transported by train beneath the watchful care of her great-aunt's gardener, cook, and housekeeper — all of whom she'd also been unable to part with. In the past eight years, they'd become like family to her.

Penelope's eyes widened further. "*All* of them?"

"Yes, and she was quite the collector of antiques." Rachel smiled fondly at the memory of her crotchety old aunt and her hodge-podge of rare and ornate souvenirs from all over the world. "I can't wait to show you her pair of velvet fainting couches from France. She always swore they were from the castle ballroom of Napoleon Bonaparte himself." In addition to the fainting couches, there were train cars headed their way full of four-poster beds drenched in real German lace, two grand pianos, three china cabinets, five full sets of china, an entire gallery of paintings and ancient family portraits, Oriental rugs, busts, vases, tapestries, and more. Mercy! She could only hope the mansion she would be touring today with Joel Richards was big enough to hold it all.

"Fainting couches, eh?" Penelope sniffed. "Whatever do you intend to do with a pair of royal fainting couches here in Silverpines, Oregon?"

It was a question Rachel was all too happy to answer. "I'm certified to teach now, Pen." She grinned widely at her friend. "I'm going to open my own finishing school for young ladies."

"A finishing school?" the young woman asked doubtfully. "I'm not entirely certain I know what that means other than it sounds rather la-de-da for a town this size."

Rachel chuckled. "It will be a school focused on social graces. Yes, I'll still teach math, grammar, and geography; but there will also be lessons on deportment and etiquette, French and Italian, dancing and singing, painting and sculpting, and my favorite — playing musical instruments. I will start off giving piano and violin lessons; but, in time, I hope to hire other instructors to teach more instruments." Her mind was awash with ideas for lessons she couldn't wait to try out on her new pupils.

Penelope had gone silent during her gushing tirade about the new school. "Can you really do all that?" she finally asked in a hushed voice. "Play the violin and speak Italian and the like?"

Rachel rolled her eyes. "Believe me, if you'd spent the past eight years with my Great Aunt Gertrude as your guardian, you'd be speaking French and Italian as well." And a wee bit of Spanish, German, and Dutch. Her aunt had been all about turning her only niece into a cultured and refined high society girl.

Her friend sniffed. "All I can speak is down-home Oregon, and that's true of everyone else around here." The train platform was swiftly emptying of Rachel's luggage, which the workmen were fast loading into a wagon. "I wish you well with your school, my sweet friend. I truly do, but…" She shook her head with a bemused smile.

It was clear she thought Rachel was way out of her element bringing her big city notions to a small town like Silverpines. "I, ah…it's so good to see you again, but I must be going. I serve part-time as a nanny to Collin McGregor, and his mum will be expecting me soon. I only came this way to pick up the book she ordered as a birthday gift for him. I just happened to look up and see you across the way."

"I'm so glad you did." Rachel reached out impulsively, and they embraced again. "I cannot tell you how good it is to see a familiar face. I've missed you, Pen." She'd missed everything there was to miss about Silverpines. The small town atmosphere, the crowd of chattering mothers who took their young ones to the park for play dates, the noisy and some-what chaotic schoolhouse where she'd spent so many happy hours, the small cottage across town where she'd lived her first sixteen years with her semi-invalid mother and miner father…. She'd work up the courage to pay a visit to that part of town soon but not today.

Penelope's shoulders relaxed. "I've missed you, too. Welcome home, my dear." She pressed their cheeks together then stepped back to flutter a hand in goodbye.

Rachel watched until she made her way down the street and disappeared inside the bookstore. Sighing, she smoothed her gloved hands down her black silk mourning gown, straightened her saucy travel hat, and set her nose in the direction of Main. According to the telegram she'd received from Mrs. Ella Grace Karson, proprietress and co-owner of the Silverpines Inn, the room she'd reserved was just a hop, skip, and a jump down Main Street past the bank and law firm.

Though it was a bit on the chilly side, the sun was out and it was a fine morning for a walk. She pulled the ends of her black travel cloak a little tighter against the breeze and moved down the platform stairs. A few pedestrians on Main Street eyed her curiously, and a dusty cowpoke on a horse tipped his hat to her as he clopped past.

A gentleman in a dark leisure suit and walking cane stepped from the cafe to her left and paused at the sight of her. "Well, if it isn't the belle of Boston herself." He tucked his cane under his arm to give a muffled clap with his gloved hands. "Welcome home, darling."

Rachel frowned at the faintly familiar cocky arch of blonde brows and scrambled to place a name to the handsome face smiling at her. "Mr. Banfield?" *Unbelievable!* He was one of her former co-dance instructors and dance partners at the Boston Young Ladies Finishing School where she'd worked until she'd married a year ago. What was he doing in Silverpines?

"Finneas to you, darling, or Finn, if you prefer." He removed his hat and bowed low before her, making two young women who were standing outside the cafe titter behind their hands.

Darling! Rachel drew back in surprise. She was nobody's darling, at least not any longer. She was still officially in mourning for her late husband and hadn't a single romantic prospect in sight.

Without waiting for her to respond, Finneas Banfield returned his hat to his head, reached for her hand, and drew it through his arm. "Where to? I am most happy to escort you wherever you are going." He tugged her gently on down the sidewalk.

The first tendrils of alarm curled in her bosom as she was assailed by the heavy-handed scents of too much aftershave and cologne. Though it was nice to see another friendly face, his show of over-familiarity struck her as odd. They'd never been close friends and certainly never courted. Quite the contrary! He'd always struck her as snobbish and aloof, a cut or two or three above her humble background due to his distant connection to some duke back in London.

Her feet ground to a halt, forcing them to pause their promenade. She removed her hand from his arm and pivoted to face him. "What a surprise to see you! If you don't mind me asking, what brings you to Silverpines?"

"You," he replied simply.

"Me!" She took a half-step back. "I don't understand." She peered anxiously into his aristocratic features, wondering if he'd become a tad "touched" in the head since their last encounter.

But his piercing blue eyes stared back at her without the slightest tinge of madness in them as he slowly expelled his breath. "I've been waiting for the right time to approach you about this, but then you upped and left Boston before your mourning period was over."

Rachel's sense of alarm grew to prickles that danced

across the tops of her arms beneath the sleeves of her gown and cloak. "Approach me about what?"

He returned his gaze to hers and spread his hands. "I made a deathbed promise to Matthew that I would look after you."

She folded her arms. "You knew my husband?" It was difficult to picture Professor Matthew West socializing with an independently wealthy gentleman of leisure like Finneas Banfield. They'd not moved in the same circles.

He gave an offhand shrug. "We attended school together. Our families go way back."

It didn't sound like a close friendship to her. "I wasn't aware of your acquaintance with my late husband. And though I greatly appreciate whatever comfort you may have offered him in the hospital, I don't need looking after." She couldn't recall him once visiting Matthew during his final days, and she should know. She'd hardly left her beloved's side. She crossed her arms to mask a shiver.

He bestowed a disparaging glance on their surroundings. "I'll admit this isn't the place where I pictured myself settling down, but a promise is a promise."

Now that sounded more like the snobbish man she remembered. "Settling down?" she inquired incredulously. "You plan to stay?"

"I may not be perfect, Rachel, but one thing I am is a man of my word. I've secured a townhome over on 8th Avenue and Ash."

To look after me? Shaking her head at his casual use of her given name without her permission, she took yet another step back. "I hardly know what to say." It was true. For once, all her training and decorum failed her. Her mind was utterly empty of casual niceties. Her encounter with Finneas Banfield was too sudden, too unexpected. She needed more time to process it.

"Say you'll have breakfast with me." His cultured baritone with its faint British accent waxed a tad husky with pleading. "I hear the Silverpines Inn serves a hash brown casserole worth sampling."

"Thank you for asking, but I cannot spare the time. I have a prior engagement." *Thankfully!* She wasn't in the mood to break bread with a tiresome man from her past who had himself convinced she needed looking after.

"Oh?" he inquired. His ocean blue eyes sharpened with interest.

"Good day, Mr. Banfield," she said firmly, strolling across the street to the entrance of the bank. She didn't like it one bit that he would witness where she was heading next.

"Finneas!" he called after her.

I hope you enjoyed this excerpt from
SILVERPINES SERIES
Wanted: Bounty Hunter
This story and its sequel
The Bounty Hunter's Sister
are available in ebook, paperback, and Kindle Unlimited on Amazon!

Much love,
Jo

READ MORE JO

Jo is an Amazon bestselling author of sweet and inspirational romance stories with humor, heart, and happily-ever-afters.

Free Book!

Visit www.JoGrafford.com to sign up for Jo's New Release Newsletter and receive a FREE copy of one of her sweet romance stories!

1.) Follow on Amazon!
amazon.com/author/jografford

2.) Join Cuppa Jo Readers!
https://www.facebook.com/groups/CuppaJoReaders

3.) Join Heroes and Hunks Readers!
https://www.facebook.com/groups/HeroesandHunks/

4.) Follow on Bookbub!

https://www.bookbub.com/authors/jo-grafford

5.) Follow on Instagram!

https://www.instagram.com/jografford/

amazon.com/authors/jo-grafford

bookbub.com/authors/jo-grafford

facebook.com/jografford

twitter.com/jografford

instagram.com/jografford

pinterest.com/jografford

ALSO BY JO GRAFFORD

Visit www.JoGrafford.com to sign up for Jo's New Release Newsletter and to receive your FREE copy of one of her sweet romance stories!

—————

Heart Lake

written exclusively by Jo Grafford

Winds of Change

Song of Nightingales

—————

Disaster City Search and Rescue

a multi-author series

The Rebound Rescue

The Plus One Rescue

The Blind Date Rescue

The Fake Bride Rescue

The Secret Baby Rescue

The Bridesmaid Rescue

The Girl Next Door Rescue

The Secret Crush Rescue

The Bachelorette Rescue

—————

Born In Texas: Hometown Heroes A-Z

written exclusively by Jo Grafford

A = Accidental Hero

B = Best Friend Hero

―――――

Black Tie Billionaires
written exclusively by Jo Grafford
Her Billionaire Champion — a Prequel
Her Billionaire Boss
Her Billionaire Bodyguard
Her Billionaire Secret Admirer
Her Billionaire Best Friend
Her Billionaire Geek
Her Billionaire Double Date

―――――

Billionaire's Birthday Club
a multi-author series
The Billionaire's Birthday Date
The Billionaire's Birthday Blind Date
The Billionaire's Birthday Secret

―――――

Mail Order Brides Rescue Series
written exclusively by Jo Grafford
Hot-Tempered Hannah
Cold-Feet Callie
Fiery Felicity
Misunderstood Meg
Dare-Devil Daisy
Outrageous Olivia
Jinglebell Jane

Absentminded Amelia

Bookish Belinda

Tenacious Trudy

Meddlesome Madge

Mismatched MaryAnne

———

Mail Order Brides of Christmas Mountain

written exclusively by Jo Grafford

Bride for the Innkeeper

Bride for the Deputy

———

Angel Creek Christmas Brides

a multi-author series

Elizabeth

Grace

———

Once Upon a Church House Series

written exclusively by Jo Grafford

Abigail

Rachel

Naomi

Esther

———

The Lawkeepers

a multi-author series

Lawfully Ours

Lawfully Loyal

Lawfully Witnessed

Lawfully Brave

Lawfully Courageous

―――――

Widows, Brides, and Secret Babies

a multi-author series

Mail Order Mallory

Mail Order Isabella

Mail Order Melissande

―――――

Christmas Rescue Series

a multi-author series

Rescuing the Blacksmith

―――――

Border Brides

a multi-author Series

Wild Rose Summer

Going All In

Herd the Heavens

―――――

The Pinkerton Matchmaker

a multi-author series

An Agent for Bernadette

An Agent for Lorelai

An Agent for Jolene

An Agent for Madeleine

Lost Colony Series

written exclusively by Jo Grafford

Breaking Ties

Trail of Crosses

Into the Mainland

Higher Tides

Ornamental Match Maker Series

a multi-author series

Angel Cookie Christmas

Star-Studded Christmas

Stolen Heart Valentine

Miracle for Christmas in July

Home for Christmas

Whispers In Wyoming

a multi-author series

His Wish, Her Command

His Heart, Her Love

Silverpines

a multi-author series

Wanted: Bounty Hunter

The Bounty Hunter's Sister

―――――

Brides of Pelican Rapids

a multi-author series

Rebecca's Dream

―――――

Sailors and Saints

a multi-author series

The Sailor and the Surgeon

Made in the USA
Monee, IL
07 August 2021

75132840R00270